VAMPIRO

VOLUME I: THE NIGHT CRAWLER PROTOCOL

DON W. HILL, M.D. AND TOM CAVARETTA

ARCHWAY
PUBLISHING

Archway Publishing books may be ordered through booksellers or by contacting:

Archway Publishing
1663 Liberty Drive
Bloomington, IN 47403
www.archwaypublishing.com
1 (888) 242-5904

ISBN: 978-1-4808-7021-5 (sc)
ISBN: 978-1-4808-7020-8 (hc)
ISBN: 978-1-4808-7019-2 (e)

Library of Congress Control Number: 2018911208

Print information available on the last page.

Archway Publishing rev. date: 10/25/2018

To the Vampire Bat

Desmodus rotundus – You are truly one ugly and repulsive excuse for a mammal, and for that reason, I would like to dedicate this work of fiction to you.

—D.W.H.

CONTENTS

INTRODUCTION

Could human vampirism actually exist? Well, maybe that is indeed the case. Perhaps the annals of human depravity should be scrutinized to find historical examples which are well beyond what has already been recounted ad nauseam concerning a certain individual known as Vlad "Dracul" Tepes who died a mere fifteen years before Christopher Columbus "discovered" the New World on behalf of Queen Isabella of Spain.

Before we take a look at two historical vignettes that arguably fall into the realm of human vampirism, the coauthor of this tome issues a disclaimer that the following material may not be particularly suitable for some readers who have made it thus far into this formal introduction. The following recounted vignettes are as disturbing as they are bona fide historical facts. As it has oft been touted, the truth is indeed stranger (and likely more terrifying) than fiction. Well, here it goes, you fellow aficionados of the genre of horror and science fiction; you have been sufficiently warned. What follows is a bookend presentation of two specific cases separated by four centuries of human history.

Historical event #1: Between 1585 and 1609, the "Blood Countess" of Csejte tortured, murdered, and consumed the blood of up to 650 young women who were her Hungarian subjects. Depending on how one might analyze the historical data, the Blood Countess either truly loved or truly hated young virgins. Arrested for her heinous crimes on December 30, 1610, the Blood Countess was sentenced to a life of incarceration without any chance for parole. She died four years later in solitary confinement in a tiny, bricked-up, unfurnished cell room that only had a small slot in the wall for the passage of trays of food, and that offered the rare opportunity for the countess to catch a brief sniff of putrefied prison air. Nice.

There are indications that once the countess was imprisoned, she had no further contact with any other human beings. If that was indeed the case, what could have possibly made her prison guards so wary of this individual while she was still alive? One might very well presume that the Blood Countess was considered to be an extraordinarily dangerous animal up until the time that she had finally died from an unspecified acute illness at the age of fifty-four.

The Blood Countess (Countess Elizabeth Báthory de Ecsed), b. August 7, 1560, d. August 21, 1614.

Historical event #2: There is an old saying that has been heard among the senior and wizened members of the Hispanic community: "*El Diablo sabe mucho porque es viejo, no porque él es el Diablo.*" In the English language, this translates as, "The devil knows a lot because he is old, not because he is the devil."

Maybe if somebody was fearless and truly wanted to determine the veracity of that pearl of wisdom, such person would go to the Prisión Federal de Mexico in Nuevo Laredo, located in Estado de Tamaulipas, and pay a visit to a prisoner named Z-40, a man who appears to be the devil incarnate. If indeed he is the devil, this evil entity would surely know if the aforementioned old saying is true or not. Maybe the old saying is wrong. *Tal, el Diablo sabe mucho porque él es el Diablo.*

Z-40 is the former head of the Zeta drug cartel in Mexico. During his reign of murder, up until the time of his capture in 2013, he was a sadistic killer who was apparently very much at home among the gruesome drug war product distribution battles in Latin America. Z-40 delighted in his reputation for escalating the cartel's violence with unspeakable acts of brutality and torture. His signature was a Z deeply carved into his victims' mutilated remains. Sadly, the bodies of many victims were never fully recovered. As an act of terror, he loved to employ a form of torture that he referred to as "El Guiso." This translates as "the Stew." The authors of this tome would like the readers to reflect on this fact for just one moment and conger up in their own minds what terrifying vignette might be coming next.

Inspired by the very popular so-called El Guiso culinary canned good that one might find south of the border, Z-40 would enjoy watching his live victims "stew" in an empty fifty-five-gallon oil drum (stew can) that was filled with flammable liquids and then subsequently set on fire. Nice.

His other favorite coup de grâce was the decapitation of his victim, but only after he mutilated the unfortunate individual's reproductive genitalia, likely while such person was still very much alive. Many of his victims were found on display hanging upside down from bridge railings. Some of the murdered individuals were found with their hearts removed and their entire blood volume drained. What would Z-40 possibly do with the heart and blood of his victims? It should give a reader pause to wonder.

Mass graves of his victims litter Mexico, from Cancun all the way to the outskirts of the deserts surrounding Juárez. How many people had Z-40 murdered? When he wasn't dumping thirty-five bodies in the tourist town of Veracruz, he was personally torturing and murdering the likes of seventy-two South American immigrants who unfortunately ran into the Zeta cartel while crossing through Mexico on their way to what they erroneously thought would be a better life. Because these migrants could not pay their "ransom," they were heinously slaughtered to the last man, woman, and child. The earthly remains of these tortured souls were casually disposed of as if they were nothing more than roadside refuse. Z-40 remains in a Juárez prison across the border from El Paso, Texas. If he's not the devil incarnate, he's at least a very dark angel. *El Diablo sabe mucho, ¿sí?*

Z-40 (Miguel Angel Trevino Morales), b. November 18, 1970, d. —not soon enough!

The authors of this work of fiction wanted to include many other true and terrifying examples of human vampirism, however the editor pummeled us until we relinquished and only reported two examples as recorded in the above introduction. As the "beta" test subjects who sampled our original manuscript believed that the historical vignettes concerning bona fide cases of vampirism were too disturbing, many potential readers turned away in abject disgust and horror without even being able to complete the introduction!

As the VAMPIRO series is hopefully a successful commercial enterprise, the authors concluded that the better part of valor would warrant a more genteel approach to the intro. Be that as it may, if the reader needs anymore examples of barbarism suggesting that human vampirism may indeed be real, he or she should carefully peruse the biographies of the following evil and depraved subjects from around the world:

1. *The Vampire of Hanover (Friedrich "Fritz" Haarmann), b. October 25, 1879, d. April 15, 1925.*
2. *The Vampire of Dusseldorf (Peter Kürten), b. May 26, 1883, d. July 2, 1931.*
3. *The Sacramento Vampire (Richard Chase), b. May 23, 1950, d. December 26, 1980.*
4. *The Rostov Ripper (Andrei Chikatilo), b. October 16, 1936, d. February 14, 1994.*
5. *The Milwaukee Cannibal (Jeffrey Lionel Dahmer), b. May 21, 1960, d. November 29, 1994.*
6. *The Otaku Vampire (Tsutomu Miyaza), b. April 21, 1962, d. April 14, 1997.*

Perhaps human vampirism may be the etiology of the above-mentioned horror stories. If vampirism cannot account for these terrifying reported scenarios however, then the only other plausible explanation is that the grisly historical vignettes cited above reflect the actual capacity for evil behavior that may be found within the spectrum of human existence, nothing more and nothing less.

Even more troubling if that's indeed the case, it's crystal clear that the authors and the readers of this work of fiction have much more to worry about regarding the behavior of our fellow *Homo sapiens* who walk among us than any mythical, pathetic, lonely, and miserable creature that may be out there lurking in the shadows.

It is hoped that the readers of this work of fiction will find this endeavor as thought-provoking and disturbing as the coauthors found it to be while we were writing it. Could human vampirism actually exist? Well, maybe that's indeed the case...

—D.W.H.

1

THE LOTUS POSITION

As soon as one of the emergency medical technicians was able to procure a toasty-warm spatula from the back kitchen area of an adjacent local restaurant, the frozen scrotum of the dead hippie Jody was successfully liberated from its icy incarceration. Jody's hypothermic ball sack and its delicate intrascrotal contents had become adhered to the slick red brick sidewalk pavers by a thick sheet of ice as a consequence of the sub-zero temperatures that hammered northern New Mexico in the wee hours of the morning.

Once this unpleasant task had been successfully executed, the site underneath the portico of the Woolworth store, located at the southwest corner of the Santa Fe Plaza, instantaneously became a religious shrine for New Age cosmic crusaders who were in search of an astral projection levitation portal. With a third eye wide open, visitors would come to see for themselves the precise spot where Jody had mysteriously died on a cold January night in 1982, when he assumed the lotus position outside of the bargain-bin retail establishment sans jacket or even a pair of trousers.

Wearing only a greasy wifebeater tank top that was peppered with countless tiny burn holes, Jody no doubt had rendered his minimalistic wardrobe in such a shabby condition as a consequence of his chronic use of "medicinal" cannabinoids. Nevertheless, his sparse antemortem accouterments would present a bit of a conundrum to the local constabulary officials who eventually presided over the dead man's inquest.

Clearly, the how and the why of Jody's death must *mean* something, and the new wave of hippies who would eventually flood the site would be bound and determined to discover the gnostic secrets that Brother Jody possessed while he was still breathing.

His postmortem evaluation revealed a deep incision in the palm of his left hand that appeared to be a self-inflicted wound. When Jody's corpse thawed out, the authorities found out that the dead man was clutching a razor-sharp obsidian knife in his right hand.

It became apparent during the postmortem inquest that the doomed individual purposefully cut the palm of his left hand and artfully left a small pool of blood on the ground in front of him before old Jack Frost diligently lowered his body core to a temperature that was no longer compatible with mammalian life.

What did it all mean? Who could say? In any event, after the famous Loretto Chapel in Santa Fe, this new spiritual focal point adjacent to a tall, vertical support column portico corbel (where Brother Jody had transitioned into a different plane of existence) oddly enough became the most popular holy spot in the entire territory.

Although the spiral staircase in the Loretto Chapel was allegedly built by a roaming carpenter without the use of nails or any visable means of structural support, this spiritually significant legendary site became sadly obscured by the deluge of long-haired, unkempt pagans who invaded and subsequently conquered the City Different.

Amidst the chaos, it was the unenviable responsibility of the local Woolworth store manager, Mr. Blake Barker, to maintain the sidewalk area underneath the portico in a pristine and hygienic state, free of any of the noxious fumes that might emanate from human waste, curry powder, patchouli, marijuana, and sometimes *blood*.

Even four years after the misguided hippie Jody died at the Santa Fe Plaza, copycat miscreants would still occasionally show up on the anniversary date of his death to either hold a séance or attempt to accurately restage his dreadful demise. Members of the JODY IS ALIVE! religious cult, on special ceremonial occasions, would attempt to emulate their prophet by exposing themselves to the elements while assuming the lotus position on dark nights when the thermometer would plunge deep into the subzero temperature range. Cult members would then, following the precise historical details of how Jody died, don what their beloved guru was wearing (or not wearing) at the time he was found frozen to death. Why not? To any rational human being, it would make sense, would it not?

After four years of putting up with this type of incessant harassment, Blake Barker had had enough. It was time for the store manager and his family to bail out of Santa Fe once and for all. The cost of housing in New Mexico's capital city was ridiculous, and the city had become a veritable magnet for a league of lumbering lunatics. A managerial position had opened up in a hardware shop in Las Cruces, and Blake decided to submit his resignation at the Woolworth store and move his family south. Unbeknownst to Blake Barker, he would be unable to escape the weird vibrations of Santa Fe. Trouble would soon follow him down the I-25 corridor to the warmer climate of the southern New Mexico desert.

A particular disciple of the late prophet Jody was a young woman named Ruby. She was from the small town of Big Spring, Texas, but for anybody who speaks in the sophisticated, high-tone, "ed-ja-macated" West Texas Trans-Pecos dialect, her hometown and beloved state was properly pronounced "Baig Sprang, Tetzis." If Ruby could only have the opportunity to facilitate her own demise by freezing to death like her prophet Jody, she was absolutely certain she would become spiritually fused to him when Halley's Comet took another spin through the solar system.

The young woman had specifically come to Santa Fe to meet the Woolworth store manager Blake Barker, as he was reportedly the very last human being to have spoken to Jody before he died. Surely Jody must have imparted to Blake Barker the secrets of the universe before the misguided hippie froze to death. Ruby was crestfallen to learn that Blake and his family had already left Santa Fe and were now living in the small community of Mesilla, New Mexico, just on the outskirts of Las Cruces.

One of the Woolworth employees in Santa Fe unwittingly informed Ruby that Blake was now the new manager of a franchised Nuts and Bolts hardware shop in Las Cruces, not far from New Mexico State University. That was all she needed to know.

When Ruby arrived at Las Cruces courtesy of a Greyhound bus, she easily found the Nuts and Bolts hardware shop and then went straightaway to talk to the store manager. At that time, Blake Barker happened to be busy with a broom and dustpan, sweeping up the earthly remains of one of the shop's overhead fluorescent light bulbs that had apparently committed suicide, spontaneously exploding and showering small shards of glass all over aisle number six, right between the display of various outdoor insecticides and the hefty fifty-pound bags of garden fertilizer.

"Excuse me, sir, are you the famous Blake Barker?"

"Well, that's me," Blake replied, "but I'm not certain that anybody would ever consider me to be famous for any particular reason. How can I help you?"

"Oh, you're quite mistaken, Mr. Barker, as you've already achieved considerable notoriety!" The religious pilgrim proudly proclaimed, "You're the last human being to have spoken to Prophet Jody before he entered the astral portal of Tezcatlipoca. By the way, my name is Ruby. It certainly is a pleasure to meet you."

"The astral portal of Tez-cat-porker'?" Blake asked. "Is he some kind of sick and twisted individual involved in sexual acts of bestiality? Tell me now before we go any further with this conversation."

"No, silly!" Ruby replied. "He happens to be a Mesoamerican god!"

"Oh," Blake said, "*that* Tez-cat-porker. As I'm now on the threshold of middle age, I must confess that I'm a bit hard of hearing, so please accept my humble apologies in advance if I happen to misconstrue what you're saying to me to me," Blake Barker noted as he furrowed his brow and eyed the young woman with considerable suspicion.

Tall, slender, and dressed in a paisley-print halter top that covered a dirty white sleeveless T-shirt, Ruby's long black hair had been pulled back and fashioned into a long French braid. If it were not for her fair skin, Blake Barker would have assumed that his unexpected visitor was of Hispanic descent.

"Tell me something," Ruby said. "As a cosmic wayfarer, do you think that Prophet Jody is now among the Aztec and Maya gods of old?"

Blake Barker could only shrug his shoulders in bewilderment. Given that Jody's malnourished and drug-ravaged earthly remains had been cremated after he died, perhaps what Ruby meant was that her late beloved religious prophet was not a "cosmic wayfarer" but simply a "cosmic wafer"; after all, Jody was ultimately launched off into the wild blue yonder after his corpse had been ignominiously reduced to cylinder of simple carbon ash.

"What was your last conversation with Jody?" the hippie asked. "It must have been very meaningful!"

Blake Barker was stunned, but he managed to stammer an editorial assessment regarding the peculiar circumstances in which he now found himself. "Oh, for shit's sake! I thought I escaped you crazy-ass people in Santa Fe when my family and I moved down here to Mesilla."

"I didn't come here to bother you," Ruby said, "but I really need to know."

"Okay, I'll tell you exactly what happened." In disgust, Blake finally dropped the broom and dustpan and moved within just a few inches of Ruby face. "My last words to Jody were, 'Get the hell off my storefront property, you stoned, stinky, hippie dirtbag!'"

Although Ruby was reverently mesmerized, she had needed to know much more. "Oh, that was righteously beautiful, what you told Jody. Please, tell me the last words the prophet said back to you. I'm just dying to know."

Blake scratched his chin for moment and then replied, "Well, it was a long time ago, but I clearly remember that there was a specific spiritual task that Jody consigned to me. I'll confess to you, it was indeed a very complex assignment. Layered with the subtle nuance of a deep and mystical wisdom the likes of which is rarely seen by mere mortals such as me, what he instructed me to do proved to result in a true religious epiphany. Yes, indeed. His prophetic edict forever changed my life, and it made me the deeply spiritual man who humbly stands before you on this very day."

"I'm splitting at the seams in anticipation!" Ruby exclaimed. "Tell me, tell me, tell me!"

"What he requested of me confirmed beyond any shadow of a doubt that Brother Jody was indeed a divine prophet who was an enlightened transcosmic being," Blake Barker thoughtfully mused. "As best I can recall, he said, 'Fuck off!' Yeah, that was it."

"May praise and honor be extolled upon Tezcatlipoca!" Ruby exclaimed.

"Yes indeed, and may his holy radiance forever blow up your lower colonic tract," Blake added. "I know what I just told you has a lot of moving parts, so why don't you get a pen and paper and write it all down so you won't forget it. I'm serious. Afterward, you'll be able incorporate his last words into your stinky hippie stoner loser cosmic scripture."

"How can I ever thank you?" Ruby wondered.

"Easy," Blake replied. "When you write the Gospel According to Saint Ruby, Just remember that you'll need to site-source the exact quotations that I mentioned. Once this is done, I'll likely become immortal."

"You're my hero!"

"Swell," Blake said as he took Ruby by the elbow and guided her past the cash register aisle. "I certainly hope one day that I'll also be able to travel across the astral portal of 'Tez-cat-feces,' or whatever in hell the name is of your pagan god."

"Is there anything else that you remember?"

"No, that's about all that I can tell you," Blake answered. "I hope it was helpful. Have a nice day. It's time for you to get the heck out of here. Go away. In fact, you should go far away. Let me be a gentleman and escort you to the exit."

Upon Blake's revelations, Ruby was overwhelmed with great joy. She buried her face in her hands and began to weep passionately, in utter spiritual ecstasy.

"Now, now, enough of that," Blake pleaded. "You need a breath of fresh air. I think it would really be better for you to take a hike."

"I'll do whatever you say."

"Good!" Blake replied. "Look, Ruby, perhaps you should walk back down to the bus station. That might be the ideal place for you to hang out until you leave town. I'm certain the cosmic wayfarers over there would be quite interested in listening to all your mumbo-jumbo holy horse manure."

"Thank you, gracious sir," Ruby replied. "You've been most kind. In honor of the Aztec god Tezcatlipoca, I would like to wash your right foot in extra-virgin olive oil and delicious, spicy cilantro chutney."

"Now wait a minute, just my right foot?" Blake asked. "What's wrong with my left foot? Is my left foot not worthy enough to warrant a similar hetero-erotic hygienic intervention? If you are going to wash my right foot, I'm going to insist that you wash my left foot at the same time. Afterward, I would like you to dry off both my dogs with your long, black braided hippie hair while you whistle 'The Yellow Rose of Texas.'"

"Don't be silly, Mr. Barker," Ruby said. "The god Tezcatlipoca lost his right foot in battle. It was hacked off with a dark and dangerous Sangre de Indio obsidian blade. There are only two confirmed types of obsidian blade that can injure a god, and Sangre de Indio happens to be one of them."

"Is that so?" Blake asked. "Tell me more. I'm sure this is going to be a good story."

"I'll bet you didn't know that the other type of obsidian that can injure or kill a god is called vampire glass," Ruby explained. "It's true! I couldn't make that up. Well, in any event, although Tezcatlipoca was indeed a god, he would never recover from this particular injury. You should worship Tezcatlipoca and pay homage to him. After all, you were the very last person ever to speak to Brother Jody."

"Why, of course!" Blake Barker exclaimed. "How could I be so ignorant of Mesoamerican folklore?"

"Would you like me to service you with physical pleasure before I leave?"

"No, thank you," Blake answered. "That's quite all right. At this time, I must respectfully decline your most generous offer. I'm concerned that either one of us, or perhaps both, could get seriously injured by engaging in high-impact aerobic activity. Plus, I'm a bit busy at the moment."

"Well, how does tomorrow's schedule look for you? I could work you over then," Ruby suggested.

"How about never? Does never work for you? It certainly works for me," Blake cheerfully answered. "If you'll excuse me for a moment, I'm going back to my office to pencil your name on my calendar for never."

"I have dentures that I can easily pop out of my mouth if you like, and then I could gum on you like a wild vampira mexicana!" Ruby exclaimed. "Afterward, I'll share with you the secret ceremony of the blind sarnak."

"The sarnak went blind?" Blake asked in feigned astonishment as he wondered if the blind sarnak was an animal, a vegetable, or a mineral. "I had no idea! Is his particular affliction a recent complication?"

"No, silly! His injuries occurred long ago."

"Perhaps he was foolishly running about in a willy-nilly fashion while clutching a sharp object, and he unwittingly managed to poke his own eyes out." Blake sneered. "I'll be so bold as to postulate that's the real reason for the sarnak's current unfortunate medical condition."

"Well, if the truth be told, he's only blind in his left eye," Ruby explained.

Blake, having had enough, extended his palms as if he attempting to push the woman off the store's portico. As he returned to the hardware shop, he scratched his head in utter bewilderment.

On the following morning when the Nuts and Bolts hardware shop opened its doors for business, Blake Barker found that Ruby was in the lotus position on the store's front portico. The manager walked back to his office and pulled out a twenty-dollar bill to give to Ruby so she could purchase a bus ticket to Sedona, Arizona.

"Wake up, Ruby. What's the matter with you? Did you drink too much bong water last night? You need to get your carcass to Sedona, Arizona, and do it pronto. That's the new place to be. There's going to be a love-in there, so be sure to wear some flowers in your hair."

Déjà vu. Oddly enough, this was the same conversation that Blake Barker had with the dead hippie known only as Jody four years earlier to the very day. Blake had the very strange sensation that he was a witness to some kind of cosmic convergence. As he brushed her long hair aside, he noticed that she had a large wound on the lateral aspect of the contralateral side of her neck, opposite where he had just placed his index and middle finger in an attempt to find out if she had a pulse.

Blake also noted that there was a deep laceration on the palm of Ruby's left hand, and a small pool of blood adjacent to her body had congealed into the consistency of red currant jelly.

Blake discovered a peculiar hand-crafted obsidian knife in the dead woman's right hand. The shopkeeper smiled because he had just stumbled upon a long lost treasure. Surprisingly, the blade he found clutched in Ruby's right fist was actually a memento that had mysteriously vanished from Blake's possession years before.

"I never thought I'd see this thing again!" Blake said as he carefully extracted the sharp obsidian blade from the dead woman's hand. "So, Ruby, you must have been the crazy bitch who originally pilfered my knife. Thanks for bringing it back! Sorry you kicked the bucket, but that's what you get for being an idiot..." Blake softly exclaimed to no one in particular.

Blake previously kept the sharp tool on public display in a glass case at the Woolworth store in the Santa Fe, but immediately after Prophet Jody froze to death back in the winter of 1982, some miscreant had broken into the display case and scurried away with the artifact.

Blake had no idea if the pre-Columbian tool had any real monetary value. However, he certainly had a sentimental affection for the peculiar bladed weapon. How could the obsidian knife suddenly appear again in such a bizarre fashion? What were the odds of such an astonishing event ever occurring to begin with? The likelihood was astronomically remote. Blake felt uneasy now that a second dead person appeared on his store's front portico in the course of just four years. It appeared to him as if everything in the universe was connected somehow.

After wrapping the obsidian blade with a handkerchief and slipping it into the pocket of his trousers, Blake called 9-1-1 and asked for both an ambulance and some much-needed assistance from the Las Cruces Police Department. When the authorities arrived, the crime scene investigators presumed that the deep laceration on Ruby's palm was a self-inflicted antemortem ceremonial wound, although no weapon was found on or about the premises.

Ruby's earthly remains were stretched out into a recumbent position by the emergency medical technicians and then heaved onto the top of a wheeled gurney to be taken to the county morgue. The local police extensively documented the scene with photographs and a dusting for fingerprints. "I gave the stiff a pat-down, and I sure as hell didn't find any kind of knife or blade that could account for the cut on her left palm," a detective explained to his lieutenant. "What you think?"

"Not sure," the supervisor replied. "Maybe she was assaulted."

Blake stood by quietly and watched the police proceedings, but he had no qualms about the fact that he had pilfered an item from a potential crime scene. Without the recovery of an obvious evidentiary tool or weapon, Blake was well aware that the authorities would never be able to fully explain the wound that Ruby sustained on the palm of her left hand, but he simply didn't care. After all, he'd recovered his long-missing historical artifact, and at that moment, that's all that really mattered to him.

Unlike the late Prophet Jody, Ruby's dead body had neck wounds over the carotid artery and adjacent jugular vein. As various other superficial injuries had been previously noted among other members of the JODY IS ALIVE! New Age cult, it was natural for the authorities to assume that all of these wounds were self-imposed religious scarifications. As it would turn out, the assumptions that all the wounds found on Ruby's corpse were somehow self-inflicted would be found to be erroneous.

After being interviewed extensively by the police, Blake Barker decided to close the hardware store for the day and send everybody home early. In the manager's office at the hardware shop, he carefully pulled the knife out of his pocket to perform a better inspection of the incredibly sharp artifact. He never had a clear idea of what purpose the glass-like weapon may have served. He originally found the blade years ago while he was on a quail hunting trip in southern New Mexico near Kilbourne's Hole.

Blake tried to justify his spontaneous, yet ill-advised, act of snatching the knife away from Ruby's grasp before the authorities arrived on the scene to conduct their investigation. He managed to rationalize that after all, the blade had belonged to him to begin with, so it was rightfully his for the taking ...

Although his actions were fraught with moral ambiguity, Blake believed that if he had turned the weapon over to the authorities when Ruby's dead body was hauled away to the morgue, he would likely never have seen it again. To Blake, that prospect was totally unacceptable, especially since he had just been reunited with the obsidian relic after four years.

Morally ambiguous individuals tend to engage in morally ambiguous behavior, or so it would seem. In any event, Blake thought he *deserved* to be reacquainted with his long-lost souvenir after all the tribulations that the old-fashioned hippies and New Age pilgrims had put him through since the prophet Jody died under the Woolworth portico in Santa Fe.

"God almighty," Barker told the police detective at the scene, "I really need to start thinking about getting out of New Mexico altogether. Maybe I should move to the Lone Star State. I know damn well that the good people from Texas would not put up with this type of bullshit. If this keeps up, someday I'm going to find dead bodies on the doorstep of my own home!" Sadly, Blake Barker had no idea how prescient his offhanded comments were.

Blake Barker called his wife, Lynne, who was a medical assistant working at the office of a local family practitioner. Barker implored her to take off from work early on that horrific day, saying that he anxiously needed her company and her counsel. If his wife was able to ditch work, then Barker would be able to dismiss the family caretaker, Lorena Pastore, as soon as he and Lynne returned home.

Lorena was the live-in domestic who was watching over the Barkers' only child, Nathan. The five-year-old boy was ill with a serious case of chickenpox, a common childhood viral infection. Unbeknownst to the Barkers at the time, Lorena was a respected Mexican folk healer, known in the Hispanic community as a *curandera*. Lorena had her own peculiar, albeit well-intentioned, ideas of medical intervention when it came to the matter of the health and wellness of young Nathan.

—◁◁◁◁▷▷▷▷—

The forensic pathologist Dr. Evelyn Stern changed into a set of green surgical scrubs. It was now time for her to go to work. The lifeless body of Ruby finally arrived at the county coroner's office, and a postmortem examination was mandated. When Señor Miguel Pastore arrived at the morgue, he pulled his wallet and car keys out of the pockets of his green scrubs and placed the items safely in the top drawer of the coroner's desk.

"I already gowned up in a set of scrubs that I had at home. Time to rock and roll," Miguel said to Dr. Stern. "I'm at the plate and up to bat. ¿Estás listo?"

"Ready as we'll ever be, I suppose." The forensic pathologist relied upon Miguel to provide much-needed help in completing the autopsy. The invaluable services rendered would be forthcoming from the individual who was designated not only as the morgue diener but also as the pathologist's long-standing primary assistant. Señor Miguel Pastore, by coincidence, happened to be the older brother of the Barker family's domestic caretaker, Lorena. In his midthirties, Miguel stood at an average height of 5'8" and was graced with a trim physique. Others who knew Miguel would readily acknowledge that he was a man who had an "honest face."

"Miguel, your skills with the knife and attention to detail are commendable," Dr. Stern observed. "I think your talents are likely squandered in your current role. Have you considered further education at the 'zoo'? After all, you're still in your prime."

"You're very kind, Dr. Stern," Miguel replied, "but the six years I spent at NMSU were quite enough. I can't imagine going back for further formal education at this time in my life. After completing my master's degrees in biology and anatomy, I briefly thought about medical school, but I decided upon this career path instead."

"Would you care to elaborate?"

"Frankly," Miguel answered, "I really like the working parameters and exceptional employment benefits offered through this job at the morgue."

"Is that so?"

"More than you'll ever know," Miguel answered with a grin.

"Are you on the level with me?"

"Scout's honor, Doc!" Miguel answered. "It's quiet and the hours are flexible. There's no stress in working as a diener. After all, my patients are not usually in a big hurry to be seen for their scheduled office appointments and I'm rarely if ever subjected any verbal complaints from my clientele regarding the postmortem services that I've rendered upon their behalf! Thus far, I've not been subjected to any malpractice lawsuits, either. Not one, as a matter of fact!"

"Is that enough to keep you happy?"

"All joking aside," Miguel elaborated, "when I was a youngster I read a story about a great medieval knight who began his journey as a diener. The job of a diener back then was to haul off the dead and dying from the battlefields once the smoke and dust cleared and the combatants parlayed a temporary truce in the hostilities to interrupt the carnage and the overt shedding of blood."

"Wow!" Dr. Stern responded sarcastically. "Sign me up!"

"Did you know that the word diener comes from the German word leichendiener?"

"What does that mean?" Dr. Stern asked.

"It translates into our language as corpse servant!" Miguel explained.

"You, good sir, are a font of trivia!"

"Sorry to ramble, Doc," Miguel said. "The point I was trying to make was that the first step towards knighthood for an aspiring peasant began as a diener. If a young man survived in the capacity as serving as a diener while confronting the pestilence and filth encountered as a consequence to savage warfare, he could subsequently become a page boy and then finally a squire before knighthood eligibility."

"I imagine the road to knighthood was less arduous if one had been born into nobility to begin with."

"Perhaps not," Miguel countered. "Nonetheless, not many recruits made it past the stage of being a diener. It was a ghastly occupation filled with infectious and parasitic diseases, stench, and death. As historical accounts confirm, the dieners were the lowest caste in the knighthood hierarchy."

"How so?"

"Reportedly, the dieners survived by scavenging and cannibalism!"

"'Oh, my God!' Dr. Stern exclaimed. "They were what—*ghouls*?"

"Or worse," Miguel speculated. "I suppose the macabre specter of the medieval diener appeals to my dark side, yet the nobility of knighthood remains a siren call to the better angels of my innate constitution!"

"Well," Dr. Stern noted, "if it comes down to good and evil, or perhaps the yang and yin of what comprises the human condition, I pray that the better angels of your innate constitution will always prevail during your own life's trials and tribulations. Perhaps from time to time we must all reflect upon the culpa of our own moral ambiguity that defines the very essence of what it means for us to be Homo sapiens."

"Can I get an 'Amen' from the congregation?" Miguel asked. "However, as often said, if white is good and black is bad, then all my friends are grey and plaid."

"That's exactly what I'm talking about!" Dr. Stern exclaimed. "The culpa of moral ambiguity. We're all *good* and *bad*, are we not?"

"Nonetheless, I'll be the first to admit that I always root for the cowboy who wears the white hat," Miguel professed, "especially if he's the underdog."

"As well you should!"

"Be that as it may," Miguel added, "you don't have to worry about me for even one minute, Doc. My life has always been a blessing."

"Gum drops, a pot of gold, and a unicorn with rainbows shooting out of its ass-end?"

"Now you get the picture," Miguel said. "I'm going to skate through my time here on this planet without any trials, tribulations, or anything bad ever happening to me as a matter of fact."

"Is that so?

"Guaranteed!" Miguel beamed.

"Even if you've already achieved Nirvana," Dr. Stern mused, "it doesn't mean that you still couldn't pursue a doctorate in the near future."

"No dice, Doc," Miguel explained. "As I mentioned before, my mother was a curandera, just as my younger sister is now. As it turned out, my mother had a strong influence over me."

"What do you mean?"

"She was a Latina faith healer," Miguel explained. "If the truth be told, she was the ultimate arbiter who orchestrated my current station in life. Because of that, I must stand fast in the ranks and maintain discipline. Discipline and order, I tell you. You see, Dr. Stern, in many ways the Hispanic family is best described as a matriarchal unit."

"Spare my life!" Dr. Stern harshly protested. "By your own account, your parents died long ago. Do you still feel you must honor remote parental directives at this juncture? Maybe you're walking around with one hand tied behind your back. If that's the case, this maternal edict of which you speak, and what you now perceive to be an imposed familial obligation without any contractual expiration date, sounds nothing more than an unreasonable burden to bear."

"An obligation? Yes. A burden? No. Mom was wise. She was the one who always insisted that my sister was to be the family member who should go into a medical field that attended to those dwelling in the land of the living. For some reason, my mother always felt I would be best suited to a consignment amongst the dead..."

The first order of business was to obtain blood samples for routine blood counts and chemistries. It was necessary to see if Ruby had been under the influence of any intoxicants prior to her demise. Dr. Stern instructed the diener to draw out several tubes of blood to be submitted to the chemistry and blood analyzers, and this had to be done quickly before the blood in the corpse completely congealed. If this untoward event were to occur, it would make this particular component of the postmortem examination that much more difficult to complete. As the body was found nearly frozen, Dr. Stern requested these serum and hematological analytics be processed even before a gross external examination of the dead woman was initiated.

Miguel Pastore attempted to comply with the pathologist's request, but he was hitting a stone wall. "I'm just getting a dry tap on every poke, Dr. Stern," Miguel said. "Try your hand at this, Doc, and see if you can drill down and strike oil."

"It looks like it is time for the big dog to step up to the plate." Dr. Stern laughed. "Let me take a proverbial stab at it." Unfortunately, Dr. Stern also encountered a series of dry taps. The pathologist then decided to do a vascular cutdown, but she and the diener were both stunned to see that the lifeless corpse had no evidence of any residual blood at all!

Miguel pulled the sheet away from the patient's face. Upon closer inspection, Miguel found several puncture wounds in the anterolateral aspect of her neck buried deep within in the larger irregular neck wounds.

To the diener and the forensic pathologist, the etiology of the perfectly round puncture marks was self-evident. Contrary to the initial erroneous assessments of these wounds that were rendered at the scene of the crime, it was obvious that these peculiar puncture marks could not have been made by the tip of a bladed weapon. No, this was sadly something much more sinister. For but a brief moment, the pathologist and the diener looked at each other in stunned silence. They had both seen this type of injury before. Although it had been many years since Miguel and Dr. Stern had witnessed similar traumatic wounds, they were both well aware of what kind of trouble they were now dealing with.

"Shit. Oh dear!" Dr. Stern exclaimed. "This autopsy ends right now! Strip off your scrubs. Everything you're wearing must be burned with this corpse. Miguel, you'd better call the nearest funerary service and have them fire up their furnace. We need to get this corpse incinerated right now before there's an infectious outbreak that gets out of control."

"I'm on it, Doc! What are you going to do?" Miguel asked.

"I'm going to call the governor's office and tell him to initiate the emergency Night Crawler Public Safety Protocol. Keep this on the q.t.!"

Long ago, Dr. Stern and Miguel Pastore had taken an oath of secrecy about these types of cases, as it was the intent of the state government that the public should never find out about such matters to prevent general panic.

"We're not the only ones who encountered this dead body," Miguel said. "Everybody who had contact with this dead body, including you, me, the police who arrived at the scene, the emergency medical technicians, and the hardware store manager, will need to have blood tests done within the next twenty-four hours."

"That will have to be handled by the CDC according to the guidelines written up in the established protocol," Dr. Stern explained. "They'll need to send down Dr. Blanks and their in-house epidemiology team from Atlanta, and they need to do it ASAP! Damn it to hell, this sure throws a monkey wrench into our lives."

"Simmer down, Dr. Stern," Miguel said. "We'll be fine and dandy."

"Are you certain about that?" Dr. Stern asked.

"From what we learned during the last outbreak in 1979, the disease is transmitted by contaminated blood and serum when patients are bitten by others who're infected," Miguel said. "This lady's dead. She didn't bite us. We should be good here."

"Hold your horses," Dr. Stern said. "We just don't know at this time if this disease process can be readily transmitted by incidental cutaneous contact. Can't take any chances, Miguel!"

As soon as the emergency phone calls had been made, Dr. Stern and Miguel Pastore showered up with antigermicidal soap and then regowned into full hazmat garb. Ruby's corpse, along with the contaminated medical gowns, were placed in a giant biohazard plastic bag and then stuffed into a simple wooden casket. The lid was then nailed shut. Once the dead body and the other contents of the casket had been reduced to ash at a nearby funeral home, the diener and the pathologist finally had an opportunity to breathe a sigh of relief, although it was only a brief respite.

They both knew that something dark and evil was now in the community. And it had to be eradicated before the disease could spread to others. Miguel secretly placed a phone call to his sister, Lorena, to let her know what was going on. Of all the people in southern New Mexico who had ever encountered this kind of emergency, Lorena probably had the most experience with this type of potential calamity.

Lorena and her brother both realized that a serious disease had just reappeared that could quickly become a widespread epidemic. Although Lorena was not licensed yet, she was attending nursing school at New Mexico State University in Las Cruces. Until she graduated and was granted a license, she was honored simply to help out the members of her community as a competent curandera.

Lorena and Miguel could trace their bloodline in España Nueva back to the late 1500s. Just as there were rare outbreaks of the bubonic plague in New Mexico from time to time, there were also occasional peculiar outbreaks of this rare and dangerous night crawler plague. It was just something that had to be dealt with—and dealt with expeditiously.

When the Barker family lived in Santa Fe, they dwelled in a small 1,100-square-foot pueblo-style bungalow that was only about a mile from the plaza. This house, the first property they had ever owned, was in an old neighborhood previously declared to be a historical district. Simply put, all of the small homes in the area had flat roofs and had the same drab uniform color of either sandy dirt or baby poop.

When a toxic black mold appeared on the ceiling between the viga beams from a roof that chronically leaked (despite numerous attempts at remedial repair work), it was simply another reason for the Barkers to move out of the City Different.

The home that they were moving away from was actually the second house the Barkers had lived in during the time they were residents of Santa Fe. Sadly, their first home had burned down to the ground. As a consequence to the crimson flames of the raging house fire, the Barkers had lost their most precious possession in the entire universe.

For the rest of their lives, Blake and Lynne would alternatively awake in terror, as they could still hear the high-pitched screams of anguish that emanated from the inferno. It was something that they would *never* get over. After all, how could they? The experience was so painful that Blake and his spouse could never bring themselves even to speak about the dreadful ordeal, much less find solace in each other over their perpetual and unrelenting mutual grief.

The couple tried to compartmentalize and sequester the horrid nightmare deep within their souls. Sometimes they were able to briefly delude themselves into a self-inflicted transient state of amnesia just to carry on in what would be for most a dreadfully mundane and unfulfilling existence. At times, at least for brief moments, it was as if the life-changing catastrophe had never happened.

Although the fire marshal would eventually confirm that the accident was a consequence of faulty, cheap, substandard aluminum wires that had been jury-rigged into the fuse box by the previous tenants, Lynne nonetheless had to *blame* somebody. God in heaven and her husband Blake sadly became the target of her relentless subconscious ire ever since the house fire occurred.

Alas, it was not a surprise to Lynne and Blake's relatives that this was indeed a tragedy that could never be reconciled. The accident would painfully haunt the couple, bringing with it an eternity of self-doubts, self-incriminations, and nonproductive countercondemnations.

It was a wonder to the family and friends of Blake and Lynne Barker how their fractured state of matrimony could ever survive such an ordeal. Unbeknownst to everybody else, however, Blake and Lynne at that juncture were simply going through the motions of still being alive. Frankly, at that painful time, nothing could have been further from the truth.

2

La Curandera

Blake and his wife, Lynne, decided to buy a small four-acre farm directly east of the city of Las Cruces in the small township of Mesilla. What appealed to the couple was that their new house was not encumbered by the onerous and stifling progressive zoning restrictions found in Santa Fe proper.

Blake and his wife acquired a moderate-sized, stucco-covered, concrete block home with a steep-pitched metal-seam roof built in what in architectural circles was known as the northern New Mexico style. This style of architecture was decidedly different from the territorial-style homes and pueblo-style architecture that dominated the homes within the confines of the Santa Fe city limits. In Santa Fe, the mere sight of a pitched roof on a home was visually offensive, and it was considered to be just too different for a place that proudly relished being known as the City Different.

As with everything in life, there was a give-and-take in this situation. There can never be a perfect domestic situation. Although water was plentiful through a shared *acquecia*, the site of the Barkers' new home was designated as a zoned agricultural area. This would reduce the burden of property tax, but the Barkers would have to *produce* something on the farm according to their zoning designation.

Lynne had a great idea to acquire a mated pair of alpacas to put on the farm. These creatures would cheerfully trim the four-acre spread on their own accord. The happy herbivores could actually be heard humming to themselves as they clipped and ate the scrub grass throughout the day! Needless to say, these fuzzy, two-toed, affectionate ungulates were merely large family pets.

Blake also went through the trouble to plant twenty-four young pecan trees on the four-acre spread, but it would obviously be years before they would become productive.

The Barkers' next-door neighbors who lived just north of their spread were a gregarious, if not mildly overbearing, late middle-aged couple named Cappy and Jo Lopes who had a mixed farm of onions and green chilies. Specifically, the Lopes's farm produced the famous medium-hot NuMex #6-4 chili pod variety.

According to the boastful claims of Cappy Lopes, the *Capsicum annuum* species that he and his wife cultivated could be traced all the way back to the Antonio Espejo expedition of 1582 when the Spanish conquistadores marched up the Rio Grande Valley through what is now the heart of New Mexico. The grow time for the chili pods was about three months, and each plant would yield about a dozen or so delicious pods. As there was a constant demand for New Mexico Hatch chilies, Cappy and Jo could count on a steady, albeit modest, yearly income from their small farm.

Cappy and Jo also had a small herd of sheep and goats that they attended. Cappy was quite insistent that the Barkers become "real farmers" one day and eventually learn how to grow onions and green chilies also. However, Cappy's well-intentioned suggestion actually seemed to be too much like real work for Lynne and Blake.

To augment the façade of being real farmers, the Barkers also added a chicken coop. However, because the noisy domesticated fowl were foul, the Barkers entirely relegated the task of avian husbandry to the woman who was the family caretaker, Lorena Pastore. Unlike the alpacas, the chickens were never considered to be pets per se. After all, the chickens and the eggs that they produced were grub, nothing more and nothing less. In any event, the elaborate rural ruse turned out to be quite successful, at least initially.

Lynne and Blake even attempted to raise turkeys, but this particular endeavor turned out to be an unmitigated failure. They acquired a breeding pair of the big birds, but apparently the creatures were not particularly bright. On one occasion, the big tom escaped the coop and wandered out onto the road that passed by the front entryway to the family farm. Unfortunately, the dim-witted turkey decided to physically challenge a passing pickup truck. Sadly, he ended up losing that particular "WrestleMania" extravaganza.

Just before the mysterious death of Ruby, which occurred in front of the Nuts and Bolts hardware store, somebody had broken into the Barker family coop and had actually stolen the remaining turkey hen, in addition to three chickens and a clutch of eggs.

The Barkers did not get particularly worked up about the whole matter, but the same could not be said for their caretaker, Lorena. It seemed that the young curandera perceived the theft of the domesticated fowl and eggs to be some kind of an unspeakable catastrophe. The Barkers could not understand Lorena's lamentations about the petty theft. For a whole week after the event, Lorena continued to howl and openly weep in anguish about some great calamity that would likely befall the miscreant who had absconded with the turkey, chickens, and eggs.

For reasons unclear to the Barkers, Lorena expressed the bizarre opinion that a serious illness would strike down the thief if he or she were to consume the ill-gotten items. What could possibly be her concern? Did not Lorena Pastore and the Barker family ingest the same biological products that were harvested from the avian coop?

Despite these ruffled feathers, the future looked bright for the Barkers. Their sham farm enterprise lowered their property taxes significantly, and this provided a modest boost to the family's financial bottom line. In the same spirit of the song lyrics belted out by Clifford, Cook, and the Fogarty brothers in the recorded song

"Fortunate Son," the Barkers were assured, by careful planning, that "when the taxman comes to the door, Lord, the house looks like a rummage sale, y'all!"

———

Blake arrived at the homestead first, but his wife was only moments behind him. When Lynne entered the front door, she called out to her husband. "Blake, what happened today?" With dishwater blonde hair and gray eyes, Lynne was starting to develop a slightly protuberant abdomen now that she was in her late thirties. Nonetheless, her long legs and enormous bosom ensured that she could still draw the attention of any man she met, irrespective of his age or place in life's hierarchy.

"Something creepy is going on," Blake said. "Do you remember that hippie who froze to death underneath the Woolworth portico?"

"How could I ever forget that crazy bastard?"

"Well, you're not going to believe this, but it's happened again!" Blake professed. "This time, it was a young woman. I discovered her in the lotus position just like the other guy, but this time it looks like she may have been murdered."

"Why would you think that?" Lynne asked.

"I know this is going to sound insane," her husband replied, "but she had wounds on her neck that were located about an inch and a half away from each other. The holes looked like the bites on a victim that one might see in an old, stupid 1950s vampire movie. I can't make this shit up."

"Well, what do you think this all means for us?" Lynne asked.

"There might be a psycho killer out there who thinks of himself as a vampire. If he's out there clipping people in the dark, why wouldn't this guy come back to the store someday and attack me or my employees?" Blake asked.

"You worry too much."

"No, Lynne, because things are even stranger than that," Blake warned. "What I'm about to tell you is going to rock your socks. Four years ago, after that hippie named Jody died on the portico outside my Woolworth in Santa Fe, somebody broke into the store's glass display case and stole the obsidian artifact that I had found years earlier at Kilbourne's Hole."

"I remember," Lynne said. "What was peculiar was that the thief left behind other valuable display items that were in that glass case."

"Now, you might not believe this," Blake added, "but the woman who died outside my hardware shop last night was clutching that very knife that had been previously stolen from me. It was in her right hand. The only thing I can figure is that she was the person who pilfered the item four years ago."

"Now, don't you think that you are being just a bit melodramatic?" Lynne asked. "Random acts of violence are actually fairly rare events. If the poor woman was actually murdered, she probably got whacked by her husband, her boyfriend, or some acquaintance. Really, sweetie, I don't think you have anything to worry about in this situation."

No sooner were those reassuring words generated by Lynne's vocal cords than Lorena entered the living room. She had been attending to young Nathan, who was fast asleep in the back bedroom in the midst of an acute case of chickenpox. In her early thirties and just under 5'2" tall, the domestic had a slight frame, jet-black hair, and soft brown eyes. Although strikingly attractive, she maintained a perpetually stern countenance.

Lorena noted what Lynne had professed, but she countered, "*Disculpe me,* Señora Barker, but you're wrong. *Mi hermano,* Miguel, is the diener at the county coroner's office, and he says the young woman was likely murdered. It was indeed, as you said, a random act of violence. The forensic pathologist and my brother, Miguel, found that the victim had no blood in her body. No blood was found whatsoever! Think about that fact for a moment. It had all been sucked out of her. Can't you see? She was killed by *el vampiro.*" Pausing a moment, Lorena added, "Mr. Barker, would you be so kind as to show me this obsidian knife you mentioned?"

With that request, Blake Barker carefully unwrapped the handkerchief that protected the artifact and then passed the blade to his caretaker. "Here, Lorena, knock yourself out."

"*Dios mío,*" Lorena said. "I don't know much about how obsidian can affect los vampiros, but this weapon must be very powerful indeed. The very fact that you recovered this blade after it was previously stolen from you is an omen. I fear you are about to become deeply entangled with los vampiros. You see, this was no coincidence. Everything in the universe is connected somehow."

"So, do you think that this woman was murdered by members of the Calle Vampiro drug cartel?" Blake asked. "Those gangsters have been all over the television news lately."

"I heard that these criminals are entrenched in Juárez, Nuevo Laredo, and even Matamoros," Lynne chimed in, "but you don't think these guys would be stupid enough to actually make an attack on our side of the border, do you?"

"If that's the case," Blake added, "we should build a wall along the border with Mexico to keep these bad hombres out! Maybe this lady was just a drug mule who got caught skimming from a shipment."

"That has to be it," Lynne said. "I read an article in the newspaper saying that if anybody gets caught stealing from this particular cartel, these self-ordained vampiros will decapitate the thief with a ritualistic obsidian knife, but only after the doomed victim has been offered one last gourmet meal. Is that sick or what? I'll bet that it all went down something like that."

While Blake and Lynne meandered off course on an irrelevant tangent, Lorena Pastore stared at the ceiling and shook her head in obvious frustration. "No, señor, *no entiende lo que estoy diciendo.*" Lorena raised her voice for emphasis and said, "Listen to me! I'm not talking about the Calle Vampiro cartel; those bad boys are just amateurs as far as I'm concerned. I'm talking about a real living and breathing vampire. I'll have you know that I've encountered them in the past, and I know how to protect you and your family from this potential harm."

Lynne was stunned. "Is that so?"

"*Mira*; I have just now performed the huevo limpia ceremony on your behalf, and I left one of the eggs that I used for the spiritual cleansing underneath your bed. I also put one of the eggs underneath Nathan's bed. If this were a usual huevo limpia ceremony, it would last for a full twenty-four hours," Lorena explained. "Under normal circumstances, I would be planning to complete the ritual tomorrow."

"What in the world are you talking about?" Blake asked.

"Look, Mr. and Mrs. Barker, if I were merely trying to protect your family from some type of a normal illness, I would just recover the eggs from beneath your beds, take them out into the backyard, break them open, and bury the contents deep into the earth," the young curandera tried to clarify. "Vampirism, however, is not a normal illness. The eggs that I placed underneath your bed and the bed of your son must remain in place until the outbreak of this illness has run its course."

The Barkers should have taken heed of what Lorena said. Instead, the married couple looked at each other with their mouths agape for what must have seemed to be an eternity to Lorena before they turned back to face the domestic.

"Holy smokes!" Blake exclaimed. "Bloodsucking vampires? You've got to be joking. Look, Lorena, I didn't know that you believed in this kind of superstitious nonsense, but Lynne and I won't tolerate it in our household. I want you to go to all the bedrooms and bring out any of these magic chicken eggs, or whatever in hell you placed under my family's beds. Go get them before they rot and start stinking up the house like brimstone. Do it now!"

Crestfallen, Lorena recovered the two huevos limpias that she had placed under the beds and brought them for Mr. and Mrs. Barker to examine. Except for their bright yellow color, each of the magic chicken eggs, as Blake had derisively described them, appeared to be completely normal.

"These look like they've been colored like Easter eggs. Did you paint these things?" Lynne asked.

"No, *amarillo* is their natural color," Lorena answered. "This is how a curandera can tell if a chicken egg is endowed with special powers. Any regular, healthy chicken egg can be used in a normal limpia ceremony to assist in a patient's recovery from any other type of common illness, such as the chickenpox, which your son is now afflicted with. However, only the huevos that naturally appear to have a bright yellow color seem to be effective in offering protection against the evil vampiros."

"So, you're a curandera, are you?" Blake asked. "Well, I don't believe in voodoo or vicious vampires. What in hell is a huevo limpia ceremony, and what do chicken eggs have to do with it, anyhow?"

"I will tell you all about the ceremony and how it is performed," Lorena offered, "but first you must know that the infection that causes a person to become a vampire can also live inside of chickens, ducks, turkeys, and other types of birds such as geese and swans."

"I don't understand," Lynne said.

"That's the reason why I became so upset when somebody stole several birds and a clutch of eggs from our coop," Lorena clarified. "I'm certain that the thief absconded with one or more contaminated chicken eggs. At least two of the chickens in the coop started to occasionally lay bright yellow eggs, and I immediately knew that these birds were carrying the night stalker disease."

"Why on earth did you not consider destroying every bird in the entire coop if that was indeed the case?" Lynne asked. "My husband and I don't believe in Mexican voodoo, but if you do, as you now profess, why didn't you do something?"

"The infected eggs and any chicken that produces them are

actually quite valuable to me, as you will see," Lorena replied. "Chickens and other birds do not get sick from the infection. They just carry the illness, but sometimes these birds may pass on the infection through the eggs they lay. Well, if a vampiro is out looking for a blood meal, he will not likely feed upon another vampiro. It would appear that these beings have an extraordinary sense of smell."

"How could that make any difference?" Lynne asked.

"If he smells an egg from a chicken or some other bird that is carrying the infection, and if that particular infected egg is near a healthy human being, the vampiro will likely refrain from initiating an attack. The vampiro might mistakenly believe that his pending victim is already infected. It's a very simple concept, but it works! That is why a well-trained curandera understands the value of finding a bright yellow chicken egg, but it is imperative that she educate her clientele to avoid eating such an egg at all costs. You may have noticed that I have never, nor will I ever, harvest a bright yellow egg for consumption."

"If this is true, how does the disease spread?" Lynne asked.

"To my knowledge, there are two ways to acquire *la infección de vampiro*. One way is to get bitten by a vampiro and survive the attack," Lorena explained. "The other way is to eat a bird or egg that is a carrier of the infection. I know a lot about the disease, but there are just some things that I don't understand. For example I have no explanation for why cooking a bird or an egg that carries the disease does not eradicate the infectious material."

"That doesn't make sense to me at all," Blake said.

"Well, it doesn't make sense to me either," Lorena confessed. "In addition, I don't understand why the disease may lie dormant for decades and then suddenly reappear to cause trouble. My brother, Miguel, and I were here during the last outbreak in New Mexico back in 1979."

Blake dismissed Lorena's explanation as gross superstition, but maybe he should have taken her more seriously. After all, there are at least sixty infectious entities to which birds may serve as the host. Various birds are actually de facto biological disease reservoirs, if you will. These pathogens can potentially pass on to unwitting human beings, and such trans-species infection may result in serious illnesses or death. The scientific and medical term for a disease state that can be passed from lower species to human beings is *zoonosis*.

The entities that birds can pass on to human beings are legion and include a wide variety of microbes: bacteria, fungi, protozoans, viruses, and chlamydia. Just a few of the diseases on the zoonosis list are influenza, Newcastle's disease, erysipeloid infections, pasteurellosis, trypanosomiasis, toxoplasmosis, cryptosporidiosis, cryptococcus infections, histoplasmosis, tuberculosis, eastern equine encephalitis, and salmonella infections, including the troublesome *Salmonella arizonosis*.

Part of what may make birds potentially dangerous to human beings is that the anatomy of birds allows for a simplified genitourinary/reproductive tract that is shared directly with the lower excretory digestive tract through a cloacal aperture. Nasty! Nobody has ever claimed that birds are particularly tidy creatures.

Lorena's assertion that pathogens may disappear and become dormant for prolonged periods of time, only to eventually reemerge and cause possible illness and death down the road, is quite an accurate empiric historical observation. As a case in point, one disease that has been noted to behave in this exact fashion in the state of New Mexico is the bubonic plague. Although the bacterium (scientifically recognized as *Yersinia pestis*) that causes this illness may utilize the rodent population as a biological reservoir, the disease may remain quiescent for years.

Nonetheless, for unclear reasons, occasional human outbreaks will occur.

As Mr. Barker only studied business in college, he was totally unaware of the aforementioned nuances of zoonosis, biological pathogen reservoirs, transmissible infectious disease, and other such weighty matters. He was therefore not buying any of the storyline that he had just heard from his live-in domestic.

━━◦○◦━━

"Lorena, take Lynne and me to the coop and show me which chicken you believe is producing these bright yellow huevos limpias that you claim may be infected with some type of vampire virus, or some such nonsense."

Lorena complied with Mr. Barker's request. She guided Blake and his wife out to the coop to investigate the matter at hand. The chicken that Lorena identified as being the culprit appeared to be a completely normal, healthy, docile domesticated bird. The chicken, for its part, softly clucked away in a rather benign and unalarmed manner upon the arrival of the three upright bipedal mammals.

Once the domesticated fowl recognized Lorena, it hopped over toward her, expecting the usual dispensation of a treat of grain or corn to be thrown down upon the floor of the coop. Blake and Lynne looked upon the hen with curiosity as it mindlessly pecked away at the coop's dirt floor. Lorena pleaded her case to Mr. and Mrs. Barker. "Don't you see? This creature appears to be completely healthy."

"Enough of this Mexican voodoo!" Blake Barker countered as he nudged the hen away with the tip of his shoe. "Lynne and I don't care if you are a curandera. I'm going to give you a warning, and I'm only going to tell it to you this one time: if you bring any more of these huevos limpias into the house and continue to spew these superstitious vampiro myths, my wife and I will consider such actions as potential grounds for termination of your employment!"

"Wait, Mr. Barker," Lorena pleaded. "You must believe me."

"Don't forget your contractual agreement with us," Blake cautioned. "We promised that we would help you complete your nursing training at New Mexico State."

Lynne circled behind Lorena and whispered in her left ear, "You'd be well advised to be very careful about what you do and say from here on out."

As part of her compensation package as a live-in domestic, Lorena relied upon the tuition support provided by the Barkers. She only had two more years to go before she would earn a nursing degree, and she didn't want to jeopardize the opportunity to complete her college education. The ball was now in her court as to what would happen next.

"*Un momento,*" Lorena said. "Perhaps it would be best if you and your husband pray over this matter and ask for spiritual guidance before you make any unwise decisions."

"For our own painful reasons," Lynne said, "Blake and I became atheists a few years ago. Please don't ask us why; it's something that we just can't talk—" Lynne momentarily became very quiet, and then she started to weep.

Sensing that his spouse was yet again clawing at a nasty emotional scab that would invariably start to hemorrhage profusely, Blake reached out to offer her comfort. It was to no avail. Lynne sharply pulled away from Blake in anger. She personally blamed him for the great unspeakable loss that occurred in the house fire that happened in Santa Fe years ago.

When she was finally able to compose herself, she wiped the tears from her eyes. "We detest spirituality, whether it's found within the context of a formal religion or within the nonsensical voodoo vampirism that you apparently believe in. We'll do everything in our power to keep Nathan from being exposed to any, and all dangerous religious beliefs."

Lorena, stunned by this rebuke, countered, "Un momento, *por favor.* Frankly, it saddens me that you're both atheists, but what

I tried to explain to you has nothing to do with religion, voodoo, superstitions, cloves of garlic, silver bullets, driving a wooden stake through somebody's heart, or even Transylvania."

"Sounds like it to me," Blake said.

"What I told you is the truth!" Lorena said in protest. "Vampiros do exist, and vampirism is an actual disease. From time to time, there have been outbreaks of this disease in New Mexico and in the Sonoran and Chihuahuan Deserts in old Mexico for centuries. As far as I know, it may have even existed in the jungles of the Yucatán in pre-Columbian times."

"Now see here," Blake Barker interrupted, "I'm stunned that you are continuing to talk about this matter as if it were based in fact. You're just our domestic caretaker."

Lorena was debased by Blake's comment. "Mira, I know that you think I'm only your *ninera*. I know that you think I'm only your live-in maid. I know that you think I'm only *la esclava* who shovels the shit out of the chicken coop. You people clearly think very little of who and what I truly am, and frankly, that saddens me. As I stand before you, I certainly think that your family is my own family, and I'm only trying to look out for you."

"Lorena," Lynne said with embarrassment, "I don't think that Blake meant to hurt your feelings—"

"*¡Silencio!* An evil illness is now afoot. It's going on right now. As a curandera, I have seen the yellow eggs. You have too. This has been going on now for about ten days. I didn't tell you about this before because I knew that you would never believe me. I needed to talk to you about it right now because already one person in this community has died from an attack by a vampiro just down the road in Las Cruces."

"Suppose I believe you. Let's burn down this chicken coop and be done with this ridiculous superstition this very minute," Lynne suggested.

"You can't stop the process by killing the chickens or destroying the eggs," Lorena noted. "Such prophylactic attempts have been tried many times in the past, but it just doesn't work that way."

"How could that be?" Blake asked. "If there's such a disease as vampirism, as you say, why can't we prevent a pending an outbreak by destroying the disease at the source? Killing all the birds that are carriers for this illness would be the winning ticket, would it not?"

"I don't profess to understand the phenomenon," Lorena replied, "but if you kill one bird that's carrying the infection, then two more birds will appear that carry the disease. If you kill those two birds, then certainly four more creatures will appear that are carriers of the infection. Tell me; just what should a curandera like me do under these circumstances? Should I try to kill all the birds in the entire territory?"

"No," Lynne said, "I guess that just wouldn't be practical."

"Historically, these outbreaks occur every two decades. Judging by oral tradition, it would appear that these outbreaks were even less frequent in the remote past. When the illness mysteriously reoccurs, the outbreak will generally only last six months or so, and then it suddenly disappears again. The entire objective in the management of this disease is to try to prevent human beings from becoming infected and turning into vampiros. Over the centuries, we have learned a lot about this illness, but we just cannot explain it all."

"You can't explain it all," Blake scoffed, "because it's all hogwash."

"Go ahead and laugh if you must," Lorena said. "The only thing that really can be done as far as I know is for a person to try to protect themselves at night when the vampiro will most likely attempt to initiate an attack. If a person keeps one of the infected huevos limpias in close proximity, this will generally deter a vampiro from attacking."

"We live out in the middle of nowhere," Blake Barker said. "Even if vampires do exist, they won't find us out here."

"Yes, they most certainly will," Lorena countered. "Please believe me. My family has lived here for centuries. What I'm telling you is based upon my own fund of knowledge concerning vampirism, but it has been fortified by wisdom that has been passed down to me from generation to generation for the past four hundred years."

Bemused, Lynne said, "That was some fairy tale that you just told us. It was an entertaining story, but a fairy tale nonetheless. If these vampiros do exist, what exactly can you tell us about them from a biological standpoint?"

"I've only encountered three of these creatures in my entire life," Lorena replied, "and it was back in 1979. They were indeed frightening to behold. They're extraordinarily strong and extremely swift. Generally, they'll dine almost exclusively on blood or iron-rich tissues like the heart, the liver, and the kidneys. It's just a myth that they'll exclusively seek out human blood. They've clearly been known to kill livestock in the past. It would appear, however, that they favor mammalian blood over the blood of birds or other lesser creatures."

"Maybe we should just leave some raw liver on the front porch and they'll leave us alone," Blake said with a smile.

"It should be noted that they must frequently feed." Lorena added. "If they don't, they'll literally starve to death within a matter of just a few days. The color of their eyes is yellow, as is their skin. In the old monster movies, vampires have been portrayed as creatures that are immolated by flames if they're exposed to natural sunlight. Frankly, that's just nonsense. However, even brief exposure to direct sunlight will definitely cause extensive damage to their skin, as their tissues can become readily blistered and burned."

"How can you possibly explain that?" Lynne asked.

"I can't," Lorena confessed. "I just don't know. I have no personal knowledge about a vampiro's alleged regenerative abilities. If a vampiro happens to sustain some type of injury, it's not readily known among members of the curandera community if such creatures are actually able to undergo rapid tissue repair. That may or may not be a myth."

"What's their projected life expectancy?" Lynne asked.

"I don't know how long they live. Unlike the movies, it's now generally accepted that a vampiro is a finite and mortal being. They're definitely *not* immortal. I personally witnessed the deaths of the three vampiros that I encountered back in '79."

"Well, if that's indeed the case," Blake asked, "what can actually kill one of these mythical beings?"

"Other than death from a deliberate starvation event, a catastrophic blunt force injury to the brain, or a deep thust with a bladed weapon into a vital internal organ such as the vascular heart or kidneys, neither I nor any of my curandera colleagues have any clear idea as to what diseases or natural illnesses may be responsible for an end-of-life event for a vampiro. There's little else that I can tell you."

Blake Barker became agitated and proceeded to press Lorena for more information. "How could you possibly know about all of this?'

"I just do."

"Tell me now, Lorena; have you ever personally participated in the death of a person or persons in such a fashion?"

"Perhaps I've said enough." Lorena answered. "Perhaps I've said too much."

"All of this reported violence allegedly occurred just because you and your curandera coven thought that you had encountered one or more of these vampiros?" Blake pressed.

Lorena refused to answer any more questions.

"I'm sorry, but that's some sick shit right out of the cat box. You're starting to scare me right about now. Just what exactly are you actually capable of doing?" Blake asked.

"Perhaps Blake and I don't know you as well as we should," Lynne said as she slowly backed away from Lorena.

"Perhaps you do not," Lorena said as she looked away and bit her lower lip. With that foreboding comment, Blake threw the two bright yellow eggs against the floor of the coop and smashed the remnants of the huevos with the heel of his shoe.

"I readily acknowledge that you people don't know what I'm truly capable of doing," Lorena said. "I've done things. Things in the past, that, well—"

The doorbell rang. Lorena and the Barkers left the avian coop and returned to the farmhouse only to discover that three medical specialists from the federal government, in addition to a military contingency from the local National Guard, had just arrived on the doorstep. Alarmingly, the mysterious visitors were all dressed in full hazmat suits. When the feds dropped in for what was essentially a surprise fiesta, the entire house and all its occupants were suddenly placed under medical quarantine.

3

HUEVO LIMPIA

The three men who arrived from the CDC, in addition to the military personnel, rushed into the house without an invitation as if they were an aggressive SWAT commando team raiding a dangerous Calle Vampiro cartel drug house. "Wait just a minute!" Lynne Barker vociferously exclaimed. "Who in hell are you people, and what're you doing in my home?"

The four men ignored the woman's vehement protestations as they barged directly into the living room. One of the invaders asked, "Is Blake Barker in this house?" Before receiving any type of formal reply, the four men instinctively gravitated toward the only other male figure in the room. They proceeded to encircle the stunned individual.

Blake raised his hands as if he were under arrest and said, "I'm the man you're looking for. What on earth have I done? Who are you people? Am I under arrest at this time?"

"My name is Dr. Seth Blanks," one of the CDC officials replied, "and this is my team of investigators from the Centers for Disease Control and Prevention out of Atlanta. The man on my left is Dr. John Henry, and the person on my right is Dr. Ralph Fairbanks. The other men here belong to a contingency from the local National Guard."

A short but stocky National Guardsman armed with an electric stun gun and an M16 assault weapon slung over his shoulder stepped forward and said, "Sorry to startle you folks. I'm Stumpy Wheeler. You people are *not* under arrest. However, everybody in this household is under quarantine for the next seven days. Is there anybody else in this home besides you three people?"

"Well, there's our little boy, Nathan, but he is sick in the back bedroom," Lynne answered. "Please don't disturb him right now. He's not feeling well."

One of the officials anxiously replied, "Oh, sweet Jesus! It looks like we are already too late. It sounds like we might be dealing with a night crawler!" The three CDC officials brushed aside the Barkers and Lorena and proceeded down the hallway to confront and evaluate the ill child.

Lorena tried to dissuade the three unwanted visitors from entering Nathan's bedroom. Lorena reached out and grabbed the arm of Dr. Blanks. "Stop! Are you *el cerebro* of this organization? He only has the chickenpox! He's not infected with anything more serious than that!"

Ignoring Lorena completely, the four men lunged into Nathan's bedroom. Once awakened, poor Nathan, absolutely certain he was about to be kidnapped by hostile aliens from another planet, started to scream at the top of his lungs: "Mommy, Daddy! Save me!"

Alarmed, Blake tried to wrest away one of the men who was tormenting his child. "Now, see here—" It was already too late. Blake was suddenly shot with the stun gun by Stumpy Wheeler. He convulsed as his body fell upon the floor.

Lynne dropped to her knees to assist her fallen husband, but the trigger on the stun gun was still being pulled and Blake's body was electrified. When she touched her husband to render assistance, the powerful electric current passed directly to her, and she also became suddenly incapacitated.

Lorena retreated into the corner of Nathan's bedroom. "Stay away, *pinche cabron*!"

When he realized he had been insulted, Stumpy Wheeler

countered, "Perhaps you want more of the same! I strongly suggest that you sit down and shut up."

Nathan howled in anguish when Dr. Blanks drew blood out of the terrified boy's tiny arm with a purple-top Vacutainer tube. Then Blanks did the same to Lorena against her will. As Lynne and Blake Barker were still in a lethargic fugue state, they were certainly not fully aware of what was going on when they were subjected to similar blood collections.

"Are you people happy now?" Lorena hissed. "Can't you see that the little boy only has the chickenpox? I can assure you, he has not been infected with the disease that you *think* you're looking for."

Dr. Blanks stepped forward to confront the curandera. "What is it exactly that you think we're looking for?"

"You and I both know what's going on here," Lorena answered defiantly.

The team leader turned to one of his partners and said, "Ralph, I'm going to take this lady into the kitchen and interrogate the shit out of her. I want you to stay here until these two other people wake up from getting zapped. For the love of God, try to keep that damned kid from screaming like that! I think he's already blown out both my eardrums."

"What about us?" Dr. Henry asked.

"I want you and Stumpy to make sure nobody else is hiding out in here. And let's document the names of everybody in here who must now undergo quarantine," Dr. Seth Blanks ordered.

Lynne was the first to regain her faculties. When she realized what had happened, she implored her rather rude visitors to spare her family from further harm. "Please, don't hurt us anymore. We'll do anything that you ask of us."

The sound of Lynne's voice finally aroused her husband from his stupor. "Why are we being quarantined?" Blake Barker asked.

"You and your family may have been exposed to a dangerous infectious agent," Dr. Ralph Fairbanks explained.

"What on earth did we get exposed to?" Barker pressed for clarity.

"Something very bad, I'm sorry to report," the CDC official answered.

"Did it have something to do with the dead woman I found in front of my hardware shop?"

"That's exactly the case," Dr. Fairbanks answered. "The woman was infected with the bubonic plague, which is a deadly infectious disease. We had to forcefully draw blood out of everybody in this house. We'll be back in five days, and we'll perform a repeat blood draw at that time. Maybe you people will be ready to cooperate next time. If the samples that will be drawn on the five-day mark turn out to be negative, this quarantine will end on day seven, and you people will be allowed to go about your business at that time."

"I'm not about to be stuck in this house for the next seven days," Blake said. "I'm not sick with anything, and I certainly don't believe a word you're telling me. Where's Lorena? What have you done with her?"

"She's undergoing a private interview at this time," Ralph Fairbanks replied. "Whatever is going on out there is none of your business." Once Nathan calmed down and dozed back off to sleep, the CDC agent said, "Come with me, Mr. Barker. I need to show you and your wife something very important. I want you to take a look out your front door."

Blake and his wife followed the CDC agent into the living room. Dr. Fairbanks opened up the front door to allow Blake and Lynne to peer out. On the front of their property was a stationary military jeep with two additional men fully armed with automatic M16 assault weapons.

"If you, or anybody else in this house for that matter, attempts to leave the confines of this ranch before the quarantine has been lifted, know that the men in that jeep have been authorized to use lethal force to prevent that from happening," Ralph Fairbanks explained. "Don't make me repeat what I just said."

Although frightened, Blake and Lynne sat quietly together on the living room couch and patiently waited while their domestic caretaker was raked over the coals by Dr. Blanks at the kitchen room table. The thorough interview with Lorena lasted over an hour. Then the intruders finally departed without any further explanation.

Blake and Lynne took Lorena aside in order to conduct their own interrogation of the young woman. Upon their departure, the CDC had taped a large poster on the front door of the home that in no uncertain terms indicated that the house and all its occupants were now under a state of quarantine until further notice.

Lynne furrowed her brow and stared at Lorena Pastore. "Those boys from the CDC took you aside for a very long chat. They seemed to be *so* interested in what you had to say, were they not? Is there anything else you need to tell us?"

"Dr. Blanks kept repeating that Blake was exposed to the plague," Lorena replied. "Well, I don't buy it. He claimed that the plague is all that they're concerned about, but it's just a load of nonsense."

"How so?" Lynne asked.

"If these people actually believed that we have been exposed to be the bubonic plague, we would have all been given prescriptions for a simple generic antibiotic called doxycycline. I learned in nursing school that this drug is dirt cheap and is highly effective in treating the plague. All of this business about the bubonic plague must simply be some kind of cover story."

Was that all Lorena had spoken about with the officials from the CDC? No matter what Lorena said at that point, the Barkers were now quite suspicious whether or not their live-in domestic was a person who could be fully trusted.

Lorena paid a visit to Nathan to make sure that he was okay before attending to other household matters. The young boy awakened upon her arrival to his bedside. "Lorena, will you put some more 'ba-po-rub' on me? I like the way it smells." Nathan was referring to the topical liniment Vick's VapoRub, which is a medical necessity that no self-respecting curandera would ever be caught without.

"I'll bring the Vivaporu right away, *mijo.*" As Lorena applied a thick layer of the eucalyptus-impregnated petroleum-based jelly to the young boy's chest and the soles of his feet, she began to sing him a lullaby in an effort to expedite his recovery from the painful and pruritic chickenpox vesicles that peppered his frail frame. A gifted soprano, Lorena softly sang, "*Sana, sana, colita de rana.*" The translation from Spanish to English is "Heal, heal, little frog tail."

When Lorena found that Nathan was still very much awake, she added the oft-neglected second verse, "*Si no sana hoy, sanará mañana,*" which means, "If it doesn't heal today, it'll heal tomorrow." Nathan smiled and reached up to give Lorena a hug and a kiss before he pulled the covers up to his neck and went back to sleep.

After Nathan dozed off, Lorena became acutely aware that Blake and Lynne had been peering at her through a crack in the door the whole time she had been in Nathan's room. She had no doubt that the Barkers were spying on her, and she sadly understood that her employers no longer trusted her. She got up from the side of Nathan's bed, marched briskly over to the bedroom door, and opened it wide to confront the Barkers, who were still standing in the hallway.

"*Qué lástima.* I could feel your eyes on the back of my neck. I can tell that you were trying to give me the *mal de ojo.* I'm not afraid of you giving me the stink eye. You can't put a curse on me no matter how hard you might try!"

Lorena pulled on a chain that was around her neck, and a small gold crucifix popped out from beneath her blouse. "See? Unlike you people, I'm not an atheist. I also have this bracelet of red and blue beads around my left wrist that I have worn since I was a *bambina*. *Mi madre* gave me this in order to keep evil away from me. Evil like you."

"Wait just a moment, Lorena," Blake said. "We weren't spying on you. We just wanted to make sure Nathan was okay."

"*¿Parezco un idiota?* I can obviously tell now that you're not happy with the services I've been providing to you and your family," Lorena said. "If you so desire, all you have to do is simply ask me to leave this place as soon as the quarantine has been lifted from your home. I assure you that I'll disappear and never bother you people ever again."

Caught flat-footed, Lynne blushed when she said, "Now, Lorena, you've completely misunderstood what—"

It was too late. Lorena was furious. As she stormed a path to her own quarters, she brazenly hurled harsh invectives at her employers in her melodic native Spanish tongue.

⊶⊕⊷

Blake and Lynne retired for the night. Lorena was determined that her particular set of skills as a folk healer were not going to be thwarted by the Barkers' narrow-minded superstitions. She was bound and determined to provide the extra medical and spiritual care that she believed young Nathan needed. Not only was it imperative to protect him from what she believed was a possible attack from a vampiro, but also she had to help him recover from the troublesome chickenpox infection.

Although she had already performed a standard huevo limpia ceremony on his behalf over these matters, it was quite apparent to the curandera that she would have to repeat the rote tradition. When she was certain that Nathan's parents were sound asleep, she went out to the coop and recovered a standard, normal white chicken egg and took it back to her room.

She lit a votive candle that had an image of Saint Jude painted on the small glass cup in which the candle was set. After the flame came to life, she gently rolled the egg above the flame while she prayed the Twenty-Third Psalm. Once done, she snuck back into Nathan's bedroom and repeated the huevo limpia ceremony while he slept. While praying, she repeatedly passed the egg over the young child, who was deep in blissful slumber. Once this ceremony drew to a conclusion, she hid the egg underneath his bed.

She recovered the white egg from beneath Nathan's bed the following evening. Again, when she was certain that his parents were fast asleep, she fractured the huevo limpia into an eight-ounce clear drinking glass that contained about four ounces of water. After checking the egg carefully for any impurities that might have been spiritually drawn away from Nathan's body, she took the glass containing the egg into the backyard. After digging a shallow pit in the garden, she dumped the contents of the eight-ounce glass into the hole and quickly buried the material. Hopefully, all that she had done would expedite Nathan's recovery from the chickenpox.

Before returning to the house, Lorena looked over the side yard fence and sadly noted that two military personnel were still entrenched at the front of the property. They continued to keep a sharp-eyed vigil at the entryway of the Barkers' small family farm to ensure that the quarantine order was not breached.

When Lorena reentered the house through the back door, she was startled to encounter an awake and energetic Blake Barker, who was pouring himself a glass of milk from the refrigerator. "Lorena, I looked through the kitchen window and could see that you were outside milling around in the backyard over by the garden area. What on earth were you doing out there at this hour?"

Lorena had to think quickly. "I thought I heard some unusual noises in the backyard, and I decided to go outside and check it out. I wanted to make sure the alpacas were okay."

"Well, was everything okay out there?"

"As best as I could tell," Lorena replied. Fortunately for Lorena, Blake had failed to recognize that his domestic caretaker was still holding an empty water glass that previously cradled the residue of the huevo limpia ceremony. Had he noticed, when she reentered the home, it surely would have been a difficult predicament for her to weasel her way out of.

—◁∭◁∭◁∭▷—

On the evening of third day of the quarantine, Lorena found a clandestine opportunity to repeat the huevo limpia curandera ceremony for Nathan, but she purposefully declined any attempt to include Blake and Lynne Barker in the spiritual cleansing procedure. After all, she fully believed that the Barkers had tried to condemn her with a "mal de ojo" curse. Although nothing could be further from the truth, Lorena was suspicious by nature and obviously believed the Barkers had bad intentions.

If there was a vampiro afoot, Lorena also planned to perform the secret ceremony upon herself. On this occasion, she was able to utilize two new bright yellow chicken eggs that she had harvested earlier that day from the chicken coop.

As this new ritual was performed to protect Lorena and Nathan from a future vampiro attack, Lorena planned to keep the yellow eggs in place underneath the beds for as long as possible. This time around, she did not plan to break the raw eggs into a glass of water and then bury them in the backyard at the end of the ceremony. To be an effective prophylaxis against an attack from a vampiro, the contaminated yellow eggs had to remain intact and close by. Lorena obviously realized that if the Barkers ever discovered these new hidden huevos limpias, she would likely be fired on the spot.

Because she cared for the little boy, this was a risk that was well worth taking.

—————

On the fifth day of the quarantine, the three CDC officials returned to reevaluate the family and get additional blood samples. By that time, Nathan was recovering quite nicely from his chickenpox. The majority of the painful pruritic vesicles on his skin had almost completely regressed. Now that the blood had been collected from all four people in the household, it would only be another forty-eight hours before the quarantine would be lifted if all went well.

During the early morning hours of the seventh day of the quarantine, the Barker family farm was paid an unwelcome visit by the next-door neighbor. The trespasser was a man in his early twenties named Romero Lopes who was actually a resident on the property adjacent to the Barker farm.

Although Romero had a part-time job as a weekend waitperson at a well-known restaurant in La Mesilla named El Chopo, he still lived with his parents, Cappy and Josephina Lopes. Well, to clarify the situation, he had lived with his parents up until the very moment that he murdered them and then sequentially consumed their decaying remains over the course of several days.

Lopes attacked his mother first while she was preparing dinner in the kitchen. She was actually still very much alive and aware of what was going as Romero harvested her internal organs for consumption. His father, Cappy, walked in on the grisly scene and tried to strike his son in the head with a sledge once the carnage was evident. It was all in vain as Romero had become incredibly strong. He was easily able to subdue his aging father and truss him up like an old sow.

In this fashion, Romero was able to keep his father alive so he could be dined upon at Romero's leisure for several days before all the old man's soft, iron-laden viscera were completely consumed. In the end, all of Cappy's vascular plumbing had been drained as dry as the northern Sonoran Desert.

This nocturnal visitation was Romero's second illicit appearance at the Barker family farm in as many weeks. Previously, he had raided the coop and absconded with a turkey hen, three chickens, and a clutch of eggs. Sadly, one of the chickens and more than one of the eggs were contaminated with the night stalker disease. After he had consumed his ill-gotten aggregation of chickens and their by-products, a sudden change overcame the young man. Romero Lopes was now infected. Romero Lopes was now un vampiro.

Romero personally noted a dramatic increase in aggressive behavior and a new unquenchable thirst for blood. Oddly, he found these physical and psychological changes to be exhilarating but not frightening. Several nights before he ate his parents, he exercised his astonishing physical prowess to satisfy his newfound dietary requirements with a young woman named Ruby who had assumed the lotus position in front of Blake Barker's Nuts and Bolts hardware shop.

She was an easy meal, and she didn't even put up a fight. In fact, she never knew what hit her. While Lopes was evacuating the entire blood volume of his chosen victim, the vampiro's reproductive member actually throbbed in his loins as his young victim's life ebbed away.

After his first human meal, Romero found that blood alone was not enough to satisfy him. He started to crave the gustatory consumption of soft, pulsating viable internal organs. This disturbing behavior would have been no surprise to a knowledgeable curandera.

Although the curanderas who lived in New Mexico did not fully know or understand all the facts about the biological circumstances that accounted for human vampirism, they nonetheless had a very good understanding of the expected behavior of somebody who was an infected vampiro, especially if that person had been a particularly evil or aggressive individual to begin with.

Romero easily jumped over the wire fence that separated the Barkers' property from his own family farm. He did it in a single bound. He went straightaway to the shed, where the two breeding alpaca were sleeping. Upon Romero's appearance in the alpaca stall, the two animals happily awoke to see they had a visitor. The alpaca relished human contact, but sadly, Romero Lopes was no longer fully human. The male arose from its bedding of coarse straw and proceeded to amble over toward Romero. When the animal got within just a few inches of the visitor, he lowered his neck and put his head against Romero's chest, erroneously believing that reciprocal affection would be forthcoming.

Romero Lopes gently stroked the alpaca's face and neck. "My, you're a soft, fuzzy, and friendly beast, are you not? Yes indeed. Would you like to become my brand-new hairy friend? I know what you want; you want some lovin', don't you? Don't you worry, I'm going to give it to you. Yes, you are definitely going to get it right now."

With that, Romero Lopes plunged his inch-long incisors into the neck of the startled alpaca and viciously tore away at the creature's long neck muscles until the jugular and carotid vascular complex was readily exposed. The animal tried to escape its assailant, but its efforts were futile. Romero drove the animal over to its left side and then sucked away at the bright red life force of the defenseless creature.

When the female alpaca witnessed that her life mate was being violently murdered by an intruder, the animal ran out of the shed and began to woefully bay an alarm as loud as she could. She charged the back door of the Barkers' house and started to kick and stomp her hooves in an attempt to awaken the family and notify them that something was awry.

It was Blake who was first awakened by the din of the slaughter. "Lynne, wake up! Something's in the alpaca shed!" He threw on a pair of jeans and ran out of the house into the backyard in his bare feet, toting a Winchester pump that he had on hand for the family's protection.

Lynne and Lorena were directly behind him when the three frightened individuals plowed into the entrance of the shed. By scant starlight, the Blake battalion could barely perceive the silhouette of a figure looming over the fallen male alpaca.

"Holy shit!" Blake exclaimed. "A bear!"

Blake leveled the barrel of his shotgun at the intruder and blasted away. He unleashed two twelve-gauge loads of buckshot. Each pull of the trigger resulted in a loud and distressful guttural moan unleashed from the intruder. Surprisingly, Blake was unable to drop the animal that had attacked his alpaca. Instead, after being shot twice, the intruder turned away and crashed through the back wall of the wooden shed. It then simply fled away into the darkness in the blink of an eye.

Lynne returned from the house after she had recovered a flashlight. When the scene of the attack was illuminated, Lorena broke down and began to weep. Not only had the alpaca suffered from having its throat ripped out, but also the unfortunate creature was eviscerated. The predator had purposefully removed the liver, heart, and kidneys from the alpaca with the apparent intent of consuming these organs at its leisure. However, after the assailant had been shot, it left a trail of these vital tissues strewn upon the ground, leading directly toward the broken-down back wall of the shed.

Blake was stunned. "Wow! I knew that bears were powerful creatures, but I just can't believe that I was unable to kill the damned thing. After all, the three of us were only about twenty feet away when I pulled the trigger. I must have at least wounded it, don't you think?"

Black bear are quite common in New Mexico. These omnivores will occasionally wander out of the Black Range Mountains east of Hatch and wreak havoc on the local agrarian community. It was quite natural for Blake to believe that the marauder he encountered in those early morning hours was an aggressive black bear.

"There is no way you could have missed it," Lynne answered. "Surely, you must have at least winged it."

"Look here," Lorena said. "The animal was able to crush two of the shed's vertical-frame beams. It's as if it were a car that plowed through the back end of this shed! I'm amazed."

"It's hard for me to believe that a four-hundred-pound black bear could have done this." Blake surmised, "Could a ten-foot-tall, thousand-pound polar bear cause this kind of damage? No problem. How about a giant, angry grizzly bear? There would be no doubt about it. What about a common New Mexico black bear, which is a much smaller creature? Not likely."

As the house was still officially under quarantine, there were still two military personnel from the National Guard who were staked out at the front of the property to make absolutely certain that the "bubonic plague" isolation protocol was not compromised. When the sound of the two shotgun blasts was noted, the two privates stationed in front immediately opened up a radio channel with their commanding officers to report what was going on.

The two soldiers received instructions to carefully investigate the situation, but they were informed to stay at least twenty feet away from the occupants of the home. When the two National Guard privates reached the backyard through the side gate, one of them shouted out, "What's going on back there? Is everybody okay?"

When it was explained to the two guardsmen that the Barker family had sadly lost an alpaca to what must have been a wild animal attack, this information was immediately transmitted by the military personnel over the Jeep's communication radio to a host of local, state, and federal government officials.

When one of the privates returned to the backyard after having made a brief trip back to the military Jeep, he informed the Barkers and Lorena to go back inside their home and stay there, saying that help was coming from the military, local police, animal control, and even the CDC to secure and sanitize the alpaca shed and surrounding area. How could a sad but simple wild animal attack that resulted in the death of a single domesticated alpaca warrant such attention? As Blake and Lynne pondered out loud about this apparent oddity, Lorena quickly ascertained the nature of what actually had occurred in the darkness. If a black bear was not the culprit responsible for causing such a calamity, there was likely only one other viable suspect to consider...

—◆◆◆—

In the morning, the three officials from the CDC arrived at the Barker family farm. They informed the Barkers and Lorena that the quarantine had been lifted. Except for Nathan's previous outbreak of chickenpox, nothing was reportedly out of the ordinary. The family was now free to go about its business. If that was indeed the case, why were the three men still wearing hazmat suits? This observation just didn't make any sense whatsoever.

Dr. Blanks, the lead investigator from the CDC, was about to perform a song and dance routine that no doubt would go unappreciated by the Barker clan. "I understand that there was a wild animal attack on a domesticated alpaca that lived at this farm. I'm actually going to ask you people to leave the house today and lock it up tight for the next two hours. Please feel free to go into town."

"Are you sure?" Lynne asked.

"Absolutely!" Dr. Blanks cheerfully answered. "You should go out grocery shopping, or maybe go out to a nice restaurant and enjoy yourselves. We have a team of experts coming in. They're going to be cleaning up your backyard area and the alpaca shed."

"Why all the fuss?" Blake asked.

"Don't worry," Dr. Blanks said to offer assurance. "There won't be charge for this valuable service. Just consider that it's a generous gift from your uncle. This is just a complimentary interdiction that the government would like to bestow upon you. It's all for your benefit."

"Really, now?" Lynne querried with considerable skepticism.

"I hope your little boy has recovered from the chickenpox,"

Blanks said as he tried to strong-arm the Barker family out the front door. "Young Nathan will need to leave the house with you,"

"Thanks, but no," Lorena countered. "I don't feel like going out at this time. I'm quite tired. After all, I've been awake most of the night. I hope that you won't mind if I just stay here and watch what you people are doing. I promise to stay inside and just look out the window, if you don't mind."

The CDC official replied, "Actually, I do mind. You're not allowed to stay here for the next two hours. Am I making myself clear?"

Lynne sensed that there was something much more to this alleged "bubonic plague" outbreak than what met the eye. She would make a point of talking to Lorena more about this matter, but she wanted to do it in private. She knew that her husband was quite dull and lacked intuition when it came to human-to-human interactions. He was often unable to discern the nuances of facial expressions or the intonations that occur even when somebody was speaking to him in a frank and direct manner.

Lynne had to put on a good face. She cheerfully replied, "I do believe that this gentleman's suggestion is indeed a capital idea. Let's all go out and have a nice lunch. After being trapped in this house for an entire week, we all deserve a treat. Let's go over to El Chopo. I'll bet our neighbor Romero Lopes is working there today."

"I know Romero Lopes," Lorena said. "Actually, I've known him all my life, and he's—well, we're not exactly friends."

"I wouldn't know why that would be the case," Lynne said. "He's such a sweet young man. You know, we haven't seen Romero's parents for quite a while. Do you think that everything over at their farm's okay?"

"That's certainly a good question

"For some reason, all their sheep are now gone," Lorena observed. "I wonder just what in the heck is going on over there?

The place looks empty. We should find out if Jo and Cappy Lopes have bought the farm."

Blake felt compelled to correct his domestic caretaker. "I believe that you meant to say that you wonder if the Jo and Cappy Lopes have *sold* the farm, not *bought* the farm, as the latter expression has an entirely different meaning."

"I know what I said!" Lorena exclaimed as she glared at Blake Barker. "My original verbiage stands as spoken!'""

"Oh, how silly!" Lynne laughed nervously. "Lorena, I want you to go upstairs and get Nathan ready while Blake brings the car around to the front."

When Lorena entered Nathan's room, she said, "Mijo, let's get you dressed. Mommy and Daddy are going to take you and me out to a restaurant, and we're all going to *try* to have a nice time."

Lorena reached beneath Nathan's bed and grabbed the bright yellow huevo limpia. With great care, she put it safely into a side pocket of her purse. Just like the slogan about the American Express credit card television commercial from a bygone era, she was not about to leave home without it.

4

EL CHOPO

When the Barker family arrived at El Chopo, the restaurant was already moderately crowded with the weekend lunchtime patrons. This particular day happened to be Sopapilla Saturday, as any entrée order came with two complimentary hot *sopapillas*, local wildflower honey, and real butter for dessert. When seated at a table by the window, Blake asked the maître d' if Romero Lopes happened to be working that day. When Blake was given an answer in the affirmative, he proceeded to request if Romero could be their waitperson for their early afternoon lunch.

When Romero arrived to wait on the Barker family, it was quite clear to Lynne and Lorena that his usual cheerful demeanor had changed, and not for the better. He was wearing a red waiter's jacket and had on a pair of white gloves. He seemed to be both tense and surly. It was quite odd that he obviously tried to avoid eye contact with the people who were his immediate neighbors in the township of La Mesilla. It was as if he didn't recognize the Barkers or their live-in domestic. This was most inexplicable, as Lorena Pastore had known Romero Lopes for many years.

"I hope you had an opportunity to review the menu," Romero said in a dull monotone. "Are you folks ready to order?"

Lynne was startled not only by Romero's attitude but also by his general appearance. The young man apparently favored his left arm as if it had been recently injured, and he also looked, well, *different.* "Romero, don't you recognize us?" Lynne asked. "We're your next-door neighbors! We've even eaten here twice before."

Romero Lopes shrugged.

"Are you not feeling well today?" Lynne asked.

"No, I'm fine," Lopes replied. "In fact, I've never felt better."

Lorena intuitively realized that something evil was afoot and standing directly in front of her. *"Hola, El Maguito, largo no tiempo verte."*

"The Little Magician?" he countered with a bilious retort. "We're no longer in grade school, Lorena. I'm now way beyond the realm of being a magician, *tarado.* Nobody would dare consider me to be a mere mago any longer."

"Is that so?" Lorena asked.

"For your own self-preservation, I would strongly suggest that you never refer to me in such an insulting manner ever again. Am I clear, *muchacha?*"

"Crystal."

Romero chuckled as he said, "So, you're now a famous curandera, are you not?" He was probing Lorena for some chink in her armor, as Romero's ego had been seriously bruised by Lorena's insult. The young man needed to bolster his perpetually low self-esteem. "Let me fill you in on something, amiga: *ya no soy un mago. Ahora, yo soy el gran brujo.*" Romero garnished enough hubris and pomposity to refer to himself as a grand warlock just then. He scowled at Lorena and demanded deference. "So, now that you know, I believe a little respect is in order here. Do you not agree?"

After Lorena composed herself, she scoffed at Romero. "You're not a gran brujo. It would seem to me that from any parameter one may employ, the attribute known as maturity is sorely absent in you. You're still a child." Lorena proceeded to cut Romero deeper than any meat cleaver possibly could when she said, *"¡Usted es nada más que un pendejo grande!"*

Romero balled up his fists, but Lorena kept her foot on the proverbial accelerator. "You seem to have a definite pale and yellowish hue to your skin. It seems to me that your left arm is bothering you as you have continued to rub it vigorously as you've stood in front of our table. Did you sustain a recent injury of some sort? Tell me, did it happen last night?"

Realizing what Lorena was doing, Lynne was now suddenly suspicious about her next-door neighbor. Nonetheless, she needed to defuse a situation that was on the threshold of spiraling out of control. "Relax, Lorena. Let Romero do his job. He's obviously a bit under the weather. Maybe he picked up something."

Lorena folded her arms and then leaned back in her chair as she had peered at Romero from over the top of her eyeglasses. She slowly nodded her head and exclaimed, "Yeah, like a load of buckshot!"

With bright yellow jaundiced eyes, Romero Lopes turned to glare malevolently directly at Blake Barker. After what seemed to be an eternity, the vampiro finally confirmed that he was indeed the wicked assailant who killed the Barkers' beloved male alpaca. "Well, you should know. All of you were there!"

It was quite apparent to both Lynne and Lorena that Romero was about to lunge out and strangle everybody who was sitting at that table with his bare hands. Blake, for his part, was totally unaware of the potential danger.

Lorena had to act fast. She reached down to the floor, where she had placed her handbag that contained the prophylactic infected huevo limpia. She pulled up the purse and set it on the edge of the table directly in front of Romero. As soon as she did this, it caused the hostile waiter to back up several steps in what appeared to be a reflexive response of self-preservation.

Just as Lorena previously professed, vampiros rarely tolerated the presence of other vampiros, and the faint odor emanating from the hidden yellow egg in Lorena's purse turned out to be quite an effective deterrent. Romero mistakenly believed that Lorena was one of his own kind. He looked directly at Lorena and noted, "So, it would seem that you and I have something in common, Lorena. I'm sorry. I didn't know ..."

She scowled at Romero. Now it was her turn to demand deference. "So, now that you do know, I believe a little respect is in order here, don't you?" Lopes took a deep breath and softened his aggressive posture.

After Lynne and Blake placed their orders, Lorena told Romero, "As you well know, I can't eat any food of this nature. Be gone with you!"

Before Romero left the table, Lorena stood up and whispered a specific warning into his ear. "If you plan on contaminating any of their food with your blood to turn these people into vampiros, I'll hunt you down and I'll bleed you. The Barkers are mine. Am I clear, muchacho?"

"Crystal."

Romero left the table side to turn the meal order in at the kitchen. Lorena sat back down in her chair, but her legs were shaking in abject terror. Nonetheless, she was quite proud of herself for having the ability to pull off the ruse that she was a vampira with considerable *bravada*.

Blake was totally oblivious to what was going on, but Lynne started to appreciate that there was validity in what Lorena had previously blown a bugle about. "I'm going to the powder room to freshen up. Lorena, you need to come with me. Now!"

Lorena followed Lynne into the women's restroom. No sooner had Lorena opened the door to the restroom, it was time for Lynne to offer a most sincere apology. "I'm sorry I doubted you. It would appear that Romero is now a vampiro."

"I stand vindicated!" Lorena proudly proclaimed.

"Other than that, Lopes doesn't appear to be incapacitated," Lynne observed. "In fact, he looks considerably stronger. He didn't have muscles like that the last time I saw him over the fence back home—and that was only a week ago! I suspect that he is the one who raided the alpaca shed. Why do you think he's wearing white gloves?"

"I have no doubt in my mind that he's protecting himself from direct sunlight," Lorena replied. "I'll bet a box of sopapillas that the tops of his hands have been burned from exposure to *el sol*. I have an idea; it's time for us to provoke him. The smell or sight of fresh blood should be irresistible to him. It will drive him crazy. I wouldn't be surprised if Romero is emotionally fragile. If he hears any criticism that is directed toward him, it may incite a fight-or-flight reaction. I remember from my vampiro encounter in the past that some of these beings have short fuses."

"Don't do anything that would put us in danger," Lynne said.

"Because they have supersensitive hearing and vision, bright lights and loud noises can also occasionally deter them from attacking," Lorena reported. "Do you have a straight pin in your purse?"

"No, but at the front of the restaurant they have a corkboard mounted on the wall where patrons pin their business cards," Lynne replied. "What exactly do you have in mind?" Lorena quickly explained her plan to Lynne. The two women returned to the table to rejoin Blake and young Nathan.

Once the plates of food arrived, in addition to the complimentary sopapillas, Lorena stated, "Romero, I have not seen your parents for a while. I'd like to come by and pay them a visit after we finish our lunch today."

"No! Don't come by," Romero Lopes replied. "My parents have left town for the weekend. I think they went off to Casa Grande, Arizona, to visit Tio Pedro." Romero mumbled when spoke in an effort to prevent the Barker party from noticing the inch-long incisors deeply rooted in the upper maxillary bone of his skull.

It was Lynne's turn to ask a question. "What happened to your livestock? You had a half dozen breeding sheep on your farm, but I have not seen them in a while. Don't tell me Cappy and Jo sold them off. He told me just last week that they were looking forward to getting more sheep. What's going on over at your place?"

When Romero did not reply, Lynne took the straight pin that she had taken from the corkboard at the front of the restaurant and proceeded to poke the tip of the index finger of her left hand. Once this was done, blood dripped on the edge of the table where Romero was standing.

"Lynne, what in hell are you doing?" Blake Barker asked as he looked on in amazement.

"Our neighbor Romero looks hungry," Lynne said. "I thought I would offer him a little afternoon snack."

By this time, Romero became quite agitated and started to shift weight from one foot to the other as his nostrils began to flare.

Lorena added the straw that broke the camel's back. "These sopapillas are cold. Take them back to the kitchen and microwave them. Do it now!"

The vampiro grabbed one of the cold sopapillas and used it to mop up the blood that Lynne had dripped onto the edge of the table. Then he proceeded to ingest the few drops of blood by sucking on the tip of the cold sopapilla.

"Romero, that's disgusting!" Blake exclaimed. "Is everybody in this restaurant crazy? What's going on in here?"

Romero pulled the small pastry pillow out of his mouth, poured honey on it, and slammed it against the window behind the dining room table where the Barker family and Lorena were sitting. "Get out! I'm not going to microwave your goddamned sopapillas! Get out, now!" With that, Romero flipped over the dining room table, sending the plates, glasses, and silverware crashing to the floor. When he proceeded to growl like a predatory wild animal, the restaurant patrons quickly fled in terror.

The maître d' leaned across the podium to see what was causing the commotion. Upon their departure from El Chopo, the Barkers and Lorena ran back to the family sedan. As the family sped back to their homestead, Blake was looking for answers. "Would somebody mind telling me what just happened in there? Lynne, why did you prick your finger?"

"There was a method to my madness," Lynne answered.

"What were you thinking?"

"I simply had to prove to you what exactly is really wrong with Romero Lopes," Lynne explained. "You're just too dense to figure out what's going on."

"Spill it; what's wrong with Romero?" Blake asked. "You really torqued his lug nuts. I actually thought he was going to physically attack us back there!"

"Blake, you're a dumbass," Lynne replied. "Can't you see? It would appear that Lorena was telling us the truth all along. Romero has become a vampire! He likely got infected when stole the contaminated yellow chicken eggs from our coop."

As the family sedan pulled into the entryway of the farm, Blake countered, "What a load of crap! I'll figure out what's going on. Maybe he has hepatitis or something like that. If he does have some kind of infectious disease, he shouldn't be serving food. I wonder why the restaurant manager didn't send him home when he showed up to work looking like that. He's just ill, nothing more, nothing less."

"Well, he is indeed ill," Lorena said, "but I assure you, he's infected with something a whole lot worse than just hepatitis."

"I aim to disprove your superstitious and foolish theories," Blake said. "Once we get settled in, we're going to march right over to the Lopes's farm and have a little chat with Cappy and Jo. Maybe they have some kind of idea as to what in hell is wrong with their son."

"That's the smartest thing you've said all day," Lynne said. "I'll come with you."

"Should we just walk over there?"

"Not so fast," Lynne replied. "What if we need to make a fast getaway? Let's drive." Blake was not about to argue with Lynne over this trivial matter.

Upon their arrival back home, Blake realized that there was

something drastically wrong. Although there was no residual sign of the National Guard or the three men from the CDC, there was an envelope taped to the front door. Inside the envelope was a letter offering an apology. It seemed that the authorities had found it necessary to confiscate the female alpaca and all the chickens in the coop!

Lorena rushed to the backyard. What she saw caused her to bellow out, "No! No! No! No! No!"

Hot on her heels, Blake and Lynne saw the devastation that was left behind in the backyard; the alpaca shed and chicken coop were completely gone, and the ground on which they previously stood upon was smoldering with the stench of burnt petroleum.

Without the forensic evidence of any incinerated plywood or residual 2 × 4 wood framing, it was apparent that the shed and coop had been completely disassembled and carted away in short order. There was no sign of the aforementioned structures. Why would the military find it necessary to torch the ground if the chicken coop and alpaca shed had already been disassembled and hauled away?

The gravity of the situation was not lost upon Lynne or Lorena, but Blake just stewed in anger over what he had believed to be a primary example of the overreaching arc of an intrusive and capricious federal government. Blake Barker looked at his domestic caretaker and said, "I'm not ready to concede anything to you at this time, Lorena, but something is clearly going on around here. And whatever it is, it's far out of the ordinary. The United States White Sands testing facility is not far from here. I wonder if the government has been fooling around with either biological or chemical warfare agents. If that's indeed the case, I'd be willing to venture that something got loose."

Lorena scoffed. "Something got loose, all right. It's called un vampiro."

On the floor behind the bar at El Chopo, the mortally wounded bartender fruitlessly clawed at the salad fork embedded in his left eye. The line cook and weekend manager carefully backed into the kitchen to make a last-ditch defensive stand against their blood-thirsty assailant.

After the chaotic violence the two colleagues had just witnessed, it was implicit that they would have to stand, fight, and likely die together on this particular Saturday afternoon. A raging grease fire in the kitchen blocked the back door egress and thwarted any reasonable chance that either man had to actually escape from what would likely be a brutal and excruciatingly unpleasant demise.

The line cook grabbed the headless torso of the maître d', hoping it would be an effective shield against the attacking vampiro, while the restaurant manager armed himself with a pot of boiling water that he'd just taken off the stove.

"For the love of Jesus, what are you doing, Romero? Stop! Stop, damn you!"

When Romero lunged at the neck of his supervisor, the vampiro was greeted with a shower of boiling water thrown directly into his face. Romero recoiled in agony as the line cook decided to cast aside the lifeless torso he was using as a barrier. While the vampiro was briefly incapacitated, the line cook grabbed a cleaver from the kitchen counter and struck Romero in the chest. Surprisingly, the vampiro recovered from these major injuries almost instantaneously.

The two men were mesmerized. In abject horror they saw Romero flash a malevolent smile that exposed his inch-long canines. The vampiro proceeded to delicately dig the deeply imbedded cleaver out of his own chest cavity, using only the thumb and index finger of his right hand. It was as if Romero was but a mere love-stricken dandy extracting a bloom of delicate wild sage from a roadside pasture to honor his betrothed.

With a backhanded slash, Romero buried the recovered cleaver deep into the supervisor's skull. As the dead man fell away, the line cook, uninjured up until that point, decided to make a desperate break, in an attempt to escape. As he brushed past Romero, he grabbed a filet knife from the kitchen countertop. Hopefully, this particular kitchen implement would prove to be a much more effective deterrent than the cleaver or the pot of scalding water, both of which had proven to be completely useless. Once he was rearmed, the cook sprinted to the restaurant's foyer in an attempt to reach the fire alarm that was mounted on the wall behind the podium of the dead maître d'. He almost made it ...

Romero was on top of the line cook in a flash. He tackled the terrified man. The vampiro said, "Now, now, there's no need to leave the party early, buddy boy! It would be only polite for you to have a nightcap with me before we parted company." Romero dragged the cook back up to his feet and pinned him against the wall before he plunged his fangs into the man's neck.

The cook bravely concluded that if he was going to die, he was at least going to go down swinging at the plate. As he still had the filet knife in his hand, he repeatedly stabbed Romero in his left lateral rib cage multiple times before the vampiro loosened his grasp. As the cook fell away from his assailant, by pure luck, his fingers found the lever on the fire alarm.

To Romero, the painful ninety-decibel cacophony from the alarm felt as if ice picks were being driven through his eardrums. Once he relinquished his death grip on the cook, he could only cover his ears with his hands as he proceeded to crash through the back door fire escape, impervious to the flames from the grease fire that blocked the exit. Once the wounded vampiro was free in the back alleyway, he disappeared like a cheetah on a dead sprint with the filet knife still firmly lodged deep into the recesses of his left lung.

⊷⊶⊷

After putting Nathan in front of a television to watch the

cartoon character Yosemite Sam ride a stubborn camel across the desert in pursuit of Bugs Bunny, the Barkers decided to drive over to the farmhouse of Cappy and Jo Lopes. Lynne had given Lorena strict instructions to call the authorities if she and her husband were not back within a half hour.

Lorena cautioned, "I'm afraid that Cappy and Jo are already dead. If not, they will be soon enough. If nobody answers the door, you need to get back here right away. We'll call the police. Please get back here before the sun goes down. Once it gets dark, el vampiro will definitely have the upper hand."

"Please, I've heard enough talk about vampires," Blake replied. "Obviously, Romero is deranged and likely ill with some sort of serious mental and medical problem, but he's certainly not a vampire. They just don't exist, Lorena. I'm sick and tired of hearing such nonsense."

When the Barkers arrived at Cappy and Jo's small farm, nobody answered the door despite multiple attempts at pressing the doorbell. Blake, ready to give up, said, "There's nobody home. Let's get out of here."

"Not so fast, Blake," Lynn replied. "Take a peek through the living room window." Although it was nearing twilight, Blake and Lynne could both readily see that blood was splattered all over the walls of the Lopes homestead.

Blake was quite alarmed when he said, "Good grief! It looks like a war zone in there. Romero must have gone berserk. He must be a psycho killer! Can you see any dead bodies in there?"

"No," Lynn replied, "but we've to get out of here and call the police right now."

Suddenly, the Barkers heard a low-pitched growl coming from behind them. They both turned and were terrified to see that Romero was standing only ten feet away from them. The enraged vampiro was blocking their path to get back to the safety of their sedan. The vicious ghoul still had a filet knife stuck deep into the lateral aspect of his left hemithorax. "Well, it would appear that I have two lovely and delicious-appearing visitors. Nobody is going to call the police. In fact, nobody will ever be going home after today. After I finish you off, I'm going over to your house to beat Lorena to death. After I punish your curandera for her rather rude manners, I'm going to get your son."

"Leave Nathan alone!"

"I bet I'll find the little bastard hiding underneath his bed," Romero said. "I'll drag him out from there, and then I'll slowly disassemble him, joint by joint and limb by limb. I'll thoroughly enjoy hearing every bloodcurdling scream that your precious little baby boy will utter before he dies."

"Why are threatening my family? What did we ever do to you? I swear, if you lay one finger on me or my family, I'll personally—"

The crushing backhanded slap hit Blake with such force that he crumpled to the ground. His eye socket was fractured.

"Stay down, Blake," the vampiro continued. "I'll come over there and finish you off in a minute. Before I do, I'll answer your question about what you've done to piss me off so badly. You people have ruined everything for me. Life was perfect until you showed up at the restaurant today and started to provoke me. Why did you do that? You should've just minded your own business. I'll have you know that you caused me to lose my temper, and things got a bit out of control after you left the restaurant. In fact, I ended up making one big bloody mess over at El Chopo. After what happened today, nobody will ever be able to tidy up after me with just a broom and a dustpan."

By this time, Lynne rushed over to attend to her stricken husband. This caught Romero's undivided attention. "Oh, how sweet is this? What do we have here? A tasty woman has just arrived on the scene to try to render assistance to her fallen spouse. My, oh my, oh my, oh my; that just warms the cockroaches that dwell in the chambers of my heart. Adios, Lynne. I never did like you very much anyhow. I'm going to bleed you and then save your liver for a snack."

Blake rose up to his hands and knees, but he was totally

incapable of stopping the vampiro from slaughtering his wife. Romero pulled out the filet knife that was embedded in his side and used it to viciously slash away at Lynne Barker. As Lynne whimpered with each thrust of Romero's knife, the vampiro was singing a song made famous by the Walt Disney cartoon *Snow White and the Seven Dwarves*: "Whistle While You Work."

While holding a cold compress against the fang wounds on the right side of his neck, the line cook looked up at Dr. Seth Blanks, who was walking toward him. The team director from the CDC started to circle around the cook in a small arc. The circumference of the circle was becoming ever smaller with each pass, as if Dr. Blanks were a predator moving in for an attack. The cook pleaded, "Look, pal, I'll tell you everything you want to know, but please have one of the EMTs take a look at my neck. I swear to God, it hurts like hell."

"I'm sure it does," replied Dr. Blanks. "I'll make sure your wound gets cleaned and dressed as soon as you've answered just a few questions. Who are you, and what happened in here this afternoon?"

"Why is everybody in this restaurant dressed up in a Halloween outfit like they just stepped off of flying saucer from Venus?"

"Biohazard suits—for our protection," Dr. Blanks answered.

"Protection from what?"

"Quit dicking around!" Blanks demanded. "Answer the damned question. Who are you, and what happened in here this afternoon?"

"As far as who I am, see for yourself," the cook replied. "Here's my wallet. It's just like I told the cop, and it's just like I told the army guy, and it's just like I told some bald dude named Henry from the CDC who must be working for you. I still can't figure out if Henry is the first name or the last name of that big son of a bitch."

"His last name *is* Henry," Seth Blanks replied.

"Well, then, what's his first name?"

"Doctor. You can call him Doctor Henry," Blanks said. "I don't care what you told anybody else. I need you to tell me who you are and what happened in here, and I need you to do it right now."

"Are you also some kind of doctor?"

"I am indeed. I'm Dr. Seth Blanks. I'm also from the CDC."

"Well, hell's bells! If you're indeed a doctor, why don't you do your goddamned job and patch me up?"

"Quid pro quo, son," Blanks said. "You talk first."

"What does that mean?"

"Give-and-take," Blanks said. "You talk first, and then we'll get you patched up. I'm not going to ask you again."

"Fine. Pay attention. You better have a pen and paper to write all of this down because this is the last time I'm going to talk to any of you jokers about this. My daddy named me John Stewart. I'm originally from Lubbock, but my family moved here to New Mexico when I was just a kid. I'm twenty-three years old, and I've worked here since I graduated from high school. As far as what happened in here, just open your eyes and look around. One of the guys who worked in here was a waiter. His name was Lopes. I never did bother to learn his first name, 'cause I always thought that the guy was a major-league pussy."

"Lay it down for me," Dr. Blanks said.

"With what had happened today, I guess I was wrong about the dude. As it turns out, Lopes wasn't a pussy. He was an animal! The son of a bitch went purple monkey shit all over the place, and then he killed three of my coworkers just like that. The bastard would have finished me off too if I hadn't poked him repeatedly with a filet knife."

"Okay. We'll get to that," Dr. Blanks said. "First things first; who are the dead guys on the floor?"

"Well, it would be a bit tough right about now to specifically identify these individuals by just looking at their faces, but based upon how jacked up they got, I can certainly point out who's who. The guy stretched across the bar floor who has the salad fork driven into his brain is David Guard. As for the headless horseman in the kitchen, that guy was named Robert Shane."

"Tell me what happened when Robert Shane got decapitated." Dr. Blanks asked.

"Beats the shit out of me. To be honest, I don't exactly know how Lopes completely whacked off the dude's dome."

"He must have used a knife," Blanks said.

"If I had to swear on a stack of Bibles, I'd say that I just don't know. If he did have a bladed weapon, I never saw it."

"What else?" Dr. Blanks asked.

"Look over by the stove," John Stewart said as he nodded in the direction of the last victim, who was splayed out on his back in the kitchen with a meat cleaver driven into his skull. "That's Nicholas Reynolds. He was our one and only weekend manager. He was a good boss, and I liked him a lot. He was really fair to all of the employees. Of all the guys who got whacked, Nick was the only one who had a wife and kids. Is somebody going to tell his family what in hell happened here?"

"It'll be taken care of in short order," Seth Blanks replied.

"Have I answered enough questions yet?" the line cook asked. "I'm really starting to feel a bit lightheaded right about now."

Dr. Blanks needed one last question answered before he would relinquish John Stewart to the care of the EMTs who were on hand. "I've got just a few more items to ask you about, and then I'll let you get medical attention. This character Lopes, who allegedly did all this damage—what was he like today? Was he acting different on this particular Saturday afternoon?"

"Listen, Doc, there's nothing 'alleged' about any of this. It was Lopes. I saw him do it with my own eyes."

"Fair enough," Blanks conceded. "I need to know if something set him off before he launched into this rampage to account for his violent and aggressive behavior."

"Well, come to think of it, he did appear to be ill today," John Stewart noted. "He looked sort of yellow, and even the whites of his eyeballs were nasty, almost like the color of piss. I remember another odd thing about his appearance; his forearms were quite blistered." When Nick Reynolds noted how Lopes looked, the boss man told Lopes to go back home and get well before he came back to work. Lopes refused, so Reynolds backed down."

"How did this waiter talk the restaurant manager into staying at work?" Dr. Blanks asked. "That just doesn't make any sense."

"Beats the hell out of me," John Stewart replied. "Lopes just looked into the manager's eyes and told the boss to buzz off. Mr. Reynolds let Lopes have his way, but boss man at least made sure that Lopes wore white gloves to cover the sores and blisters. As far as if anything happened that may have set Lopes into some kind of violent rampage, I have no idea. I was working in the back kitchen area."

"When did you finally figure out something bad was going down?" Dr. Blanks asked.

"I heard a loud crash in the dining area. When I stuck my head out from behind the kitchen grill to see what in the heck was happening, Lopes had just flipped over a table and started to scream for everybody to get out of the restaurant. He was pissed off about something, that's for sure."

"Which of your colleagues was taken out first?"

"That would be the maître d'," Stewart explained. "Dude left the podium to confront this Lopes character and find out what in hell was going on. The next thing I saw was Bob's head rolling across the floor. After that, Lopes bounced across the room and took out the barkeep with a salad fork. I'd never seen anything like that before, not in my entire life!"

"Did the bartender struggle in his own defense?"

"Poor bastard never knew what hit him. Nick and I were in the crosshairs for what happened next. Seeing that we were going to get whacked for no apparent reason, we backed up into the kitchen and both decided that we were going to go down like Davy Crockett at the Battle of the Alamo. You're not going to believe this, but I hit Lopes square in the chest with a meat cleaver after Nick splashed a pot of boiling water in his face. Maybe Lopes was on angel dust or something, because nothing seemed to faze him."

"How long did it take for Lopes to recover from the injuries that you and Nick inflicted upon him?"

"Seconds."

"God almighty," Blanks said in awe.

"No, Doc," John Stewart said wistfully. "In light of what went down here today, I can assure you that God was nowhere in the vicinity. Lopes pulled out the business end of the cleaver from his chest and then split open the manager's skull with it. That's when I made a mad dash to the emergency alarm switch in the front. I was somehow able to trigger the bell, but not before that psycho bastard bit me in the neck."

"Did he draw blood?"

"What do you think?" Stewart answered. "All the while, I was running a filet knife into his side. Barely slowed him down. The crazy son of a bitch must have thought that he was some kind of self-ordained vampiro or maybe some other type of a bloodsucking night crawler."

"What makes you say that?"

"Can you explain what happened here?" Stewart asked.

"Did it hurt?"

"What, the bite? Check this out: at the time he buried his teeth into my neck, it kind of gave me a rush. It actually felt *good*. How can you explain that, Doc? In any event, it hurts like hell right about now."

"How did you escape?" the physician from the CDC asked.

"Our fire alarm bell is really loud. Lopes put his hands over his ears and started screaming. He blasted out the back door that leads into the alleyway and disappeared like a puff of bong smoke. Poof!"

"Anything else?"

"As a matter of fact, there is," John Stewart said. "You need to find this crazy fucker and then put a round of hot smoking lead into his brain."

"That might be a bit harsh."

"Listen to me; there are some things in this world that are just so evil and foul that no attempt should ever be made to address such crimes through the criminal justice system. If and when Lopes is found, he needs to be exterminated on the spot, no questions asked. Do not pass go. Do not collect two hundred dollars."

Dr. Seth Blanks laughed nervously as he briefly considered his own opinions regarding such dire, weighty matters. "Well, perhaps we should take your recommendations under consideration." With that, Dr. Blanks motioned over to the emergency medical technicians to finally attend to the wound on the line cook's neck and also to obtain a series of blood draws from the injured man.

John Stewart asked, to no one in particular, "Will somebody please tell me what in hell is going on around here?"

A burly captain from the National Guard stepped forward and said, "You're certainly a man who deserves some answers. I heard that you were the only person to survive the mayhem that occurred in here today. I'm truly sorry for the trauma that you experienced, and I'll venture that you have a ton of questions about what's going on. I want you to come with me to the restroom, as there is something in there that I need you to see."

"Wait just a moment, Morales," Dr. Blanks said suspiciously. "What do you think you're doing?"

The officer dismissively waved off the physician, moving his hand up and down, suggesting that he wanted the doctor to take a seat. Morales reached under the line cook's arms to pull him up to a standing position and said, "Okay, John, I want you to take a little stroll with me."

When the two men reached the restroom door, the military captain pushed it open and politely motioned to John to move forward.

He said, "After you, my good man." As John entered the restroom, the military officer unholstered his service weapon and leveled the barrel of his .45-caliber pistol at the back of his neck.

The military personnel had draped out all the walls and the floor of the restroom with heavy plastic vinyl sheets. Realizing that he was about to be executed, John kept his back toward Captain Morales and exclaimed, "Please, Captain Morales, you don't have to do this! I can keep my mouth shut if that is what you want me to do. I can keep a secret. For the love of God, I'm only twenty-three years old. I've not been anywhere! I haven't even seen a redwood tree! Don't you think that a man should at least behold the glory of a redwood tree before he dies?"

"If you would just shut up, this will all go down a lot easier for both of us," Morales said. "I'm truly sorry, but I have my orders."

"I've never even been in love! I haven't done anything in my life. Please spare me. Just give me a chance. I'll do anything you say."

Assuming the universally accepted posture of a man in the process of surrendering, the line cook thrust his hands into the air and then slowly turned around. John Stewart was simply compelled to personally confront the army captain who was apparently willing to put a bullet into an innocent man's brain in the alleged name of national security.

Before the entire contents of John Stewart's skull were deposited upon the thick vinyl sheets taped over the contrasting pink and brown tile floor, the door to the restroom burst open. Dr. Blanks briskly entered to disrupt the pending festivities. "Not on my watch. Don't even think about it!"

"Look, asshole, I'm in charge of the military aspects of the Night Crawler Protocol, and you're in charge of the scientific arm of this investigation. Never the twain shall meet, if you ask me," Captain Morales said. "Don't interfere in what needs to be done! This is my call, and I suggest you vanish. Get out of here! I'm dead serious, Blanks. Don't get dragged into all of this."

Seth Blanks bravely maneuvered himself to stand right in front of the barrel of the gun. "Go ahead and do it." Dr. Blanks reached out and slightly adjusted the muzzle of the automatic held in the right hand of the captain from the National Guard.

"I think you're going to have a hard time trying to explain why you had to terminate the life of the lead CDC investigator on the Night Crawler Protocol. Look, Morales, we need to learn as much as we possibly can about what's going to happen from a medical standpoint now that John Stewart has had a close encounter with a bona fide vampiro. That bloodsucking bastard actually took a bite out of his neck. Can't you see? We know absolutely nothing about the natural history of human vampirism. If you don't get that, then you're an absolute idiot."

A deeply rational thinker, Seth Blanks had to help the volatile Captain Morales sharply focus on what would be the next best course of action. "I suggest we quit dicking around. Mr. Stewart has now identified a man named Lopes who may very well be the point of origin for this outbreak. We need to smoke this guy out and put him down before we have an epidemic on our hands. I suggest you round up your posse. Then we should all get the hell out of here."

Captain Morales pushed his service weapon back into its holster before he called in the military police to disrobe John Stewart and burn his clothing. Forced to dress up in full hazmat protection gear, John Stewart was handcuffed and taken into protective custody. Stewart realized that only moments before he had been standing on the edge of an abyss. The line cook was wise enough to accept the fact that the next best course of action would be for him to keep his mouth shut and not cause any trouble whatsoever when he was hauled away.

The military police on hand were able to locate the owner of the restaurant, who was quickly able to provide the complete duty roster of the employees who worked at El Chopo. Once the address of Romero Lopes was found, it was time for Uncle Sam to hunt him down and figuratively and literally light him up. It was only a matter of minutes before a platoon of heavily armed men, armored personnel vehicles, and an attack helicopter were on their way to pay the vampiro named Romero Lopes an unwelcomed surprise visit.

5

IMMOLATION

After Romero thrust the filet knife into Lynne's torso more than a dozen times, she was no longer making any sounds. In fact, she was no longer moving at all. Blake pulled himself up to his feet with the door handle of the car and charged at Romero one last time to try to spare his wife from the grisly assault, but it was an act of utter futility. Romero, sensing that Lynne's husband was fast approaching from behind, wheeled around and backhanded him, causing him to collapse to the ground yet again. On this occasion, Blake sustained a fractured left clavicle. Blake Barker was crushed from the force—two strikes and two broken bones.

Romero loomed over Blake and said, "It must be frustrating to you that I just butchered your wife and you couldn't do shit about it. I'm going to take your wife inside and have my way with her. By now, I don't suspect she'll put up much of a fight, do you? I'll come back out and get you after I lay the wood to her. Now don't run off; I'll be back soon."

With that, Romero Lopes leaned over and began to lick Blake's face, much like an ecstatic canine would greet his master after the latter had made a trip to the pet store to obtain a big leather chew toy for the beloved pet. Then Romero returned to the more pressing task at hand. He reached down and grabbed the dead woman by the wrist and began to drag her toward the front door of the Lopes family farmhouse. Blake realized it was too late to try to save his wife. He knew the vicious assailant would be coming for him next.

As his defensive measures had failed, Blake quickly came to the tactical realization that it was time to go on offense. The seriously injured man, however, needed some kind of a weapon, and he needed it fast.

—◦◦◦—

As the heavily armed unit from the National Guard rumbled down the dirt roads just west of the township of Mesilla, Dr. Blanks was sitting beside Captain Morales in the lead vehicle. Upon the government's activation of the Night Crawler Protocol, Dr. Seth Blanks considered Captain Morales to be a strong ally and an integral component of the plan to protect society at large. Now, after the captain appeared to have been completely willing to murder the line cook at El Chopo restaurant, Dr. Blanks was quite certain that there were deep elements of the federal government, and perhaps even some citizens in society, who erroneously viewed the Constitution of the United States as a fluid and mutable document.

Dr. Blanks shook his head and wondered when matters of good and evil had suddenly become fluid and mutable. He was deeply aggrieved to accept the idea that many people likely held the conviction that there were no longer any absolutes in the universe. In light of these revelations, maybe Captain Morales was no longer a man whom Dr. Blanks could fully trust.

"Your team worked up the last night crawler outbreak almost a decade ago," Morales said. "If my men and I are going into harm's way, I need you to fill in the blanks, Dr. Blanks."

"During the last outbreak that occurred back in 1979, there were a total of six specimens that were harvested, but three of the creatures were viciously put down by a coven of local curanderas," Blanks said.

"What happened?"

"It was a slice and dice extravaganza—nastiest thing I ever saw! The mess that those old ladies left for cleanup on isle six would've made Jack the Ripper gag. There was no way in hell that the curanderas took a chance of leaving anything left behind to crawl around. It's as if those poor vampiros were run over by a riding lawn mower while they were still very much alive! Perhaps they were..." Blanks explained with a pang of regret. "In spite of all that, we did have closure. I'll be honest with you; we all just looked the other way.

"I would have done the same," Morales said.

"I have no doubt about that," Blanks replied as he glared at Captain Morales. "In any event, the curanderas were never prosecuted or even reprimanded for what they did. The other three infected specimens were in our custody, and at that time, we had no idea what their dietary requirements were. It appeared that these creatures needed to feed at least at forty-eight- to seventy-two-hour intervals."

"Only blood meals?" Morales asked.

"Mostly, but the infected individuals also relished raw internal organs," Dr. Blanks explained. "Because of our ignorance of human vampirism, the three infected specimens we imprisoned in a maximum security environment quickly expired. To be honest with you, seven years later, we don't know much more from a physiological standpoint about what makes a human vampire tick. We're uncertain as to the vector of this disease process, although we think it's a virus. If that's the case, there must be some type of reservoir in nature that we just don't understand because the outbreaks happen every twenty years, or so."

"Reservoir?"

"Dr. John Henry thinks that the reservoir may be among native birds and waterfowl. That's just pure speculation on his part thus far. I just don't know about this particular outbreak, however. This one showed up at the seven-year mark from the last cycle. I wonder if the natural history of this disease process is starting to change."

"Let's just hope that's not the case."

Seth Blanks noted that the convoy had just passed the intersection of Calle Murciélago and Avenida Chupadores de Sangre, the same agricultural district where the Barkers and Lorena Pastore resided. It appeared that the target residence, which was the home of the alleged assailant named Romero Lopes, was the small farm immediately north of where the Barkers lived. This could *not* be a coincidence! Even though the Barker household had the quarantine lifted earlier that morning, there had to be some kind of occult connection to the very nidus of the night crawler outbreak.

With the palm of his hand, Dr. Blanks started to bang the top of the helmet of the lead convoy driver. He said, "Stop! Stop! Stop! Before we go any further, I have to check on the welfare of this family."

Captain Morales was unaware of the circumstances and didn't know how the current night crawler outbreak was linked to this agricultural district of the township of Mesilla, so Dr. Blanks had to explain to him that it was Blake Barker who had found the first victim of the vampiro attack under the portico of the nearby Las Cruces Nuts and Bolts hardware shop.

Morales quickly agreed with Dr. Seth Blank's logical conclusion. "Take two armed men with you just in case you stumble into trouble. Be quick about it."

When Dr. Seth Blanks banged on the door of the Barker home, it was answered by a very nervous Lorena Pastore. Nathan was clinging to her left leg. "I'm glad that you're here," Lorena said. "I didn't know who to call or what to do. We went out to have a nice lunch at El Chopo. Our waiter was Romero Lopes. You must believe me: *Romero no es un hombre. Romero no es un ser humano. Escucha a mí; ¡Romero ahora es un vampiro!*"

Seth Blanks replied, "Okay, Lorena, you have to calm down. Where are Blake and Lynne now?"

"Blake and Lynne went over to the Lopes's farmhouse to check on Cappy and Jo," Lorena answered. "They've been gone for a long time. I'm worried about them."

Without saying another word, one of the soldiers turned toward the parked row of military vehicles and made a circular horizontal motion with his left arm to fire up the convoy. As the three men sprinted back to the lead vehicle, Lorena was left wondering about the ultimate fate of Blake and Lynne Barker. She closed and bolted shut the front door of the home. Then she went out to the backyard patio to behold the pending fireworks display.

⟞⟝⟞⟝⟞

Well, of course Blake had a powerful weapon at his disposal. It happened to be the two-ton 1985 four-door Crown Victoria sedan powered by a five-liter V-8 engine that was immediately adjacent to him. As Romero dragged Lynne's dead body toward the front door of the Lopes's farmhouse, Blake was able to muster up enough energy to crawl into the front seat of the car, slip the key into the ignition, and fire up the gas-guzzling behemoth. After putting the transmission into drive, Blake floored the accelerator, plowing straight into Romero and driving him through the front wall of the farmhouse.

Blake crawled out of the car and went over to Lynne's body. He felt for pulse, but she had none. Stifling a sob, he pinched her nose, put his lips to hers, and exhaled with as much force as he could muster. His dimly remembered CPR training would not be enough to save her.

Is it true that there are no atheists in foxholes? Perhaps that is the case. Certainly, for Blake Barker, from that point on it would prove difficult for him to adhere to his nondeist assumption that the vast universe simply created itself out of nothing. "Dear God, help me! Help Lynne, please!"

While Blake implored for Divine intervention, he was absolutely stunned to see that the big sedan was being easily pushed out of the hole that it had made in the front wall of the farmhouse. It would seem that Blake had not heard the last from Romero Lopes. As soon as the big sedan's front fenders cleared the big hole in the wall, Blake realized that Romero Lopes was standing in front of the car, fit as a proverbial fiddle and apparently without a scratch on his body. Blake screamed out, "How could this be? Die, you nasty bastard! Just die!"

"Hello, Blake. Did you miss me? I would like you to take a moment and explain to me in detail just what in hell you were thinking."

"I'm going to kill you!"

"That's a pretty bold statement there, Blake," Lopes responded. "Tell me, who is going to clean up this mess? I would be most appreciative if you would at least consider covering the insurance deductible. If you did that, I would be willing to consider us all squared up. No, come to think of it, we'll never be square. Bend over and drop your drawers, city boy. It's time for you to get a spanking! It's often been said that one can't get blood out of a stone. Although that may be true, I'll venture that I'll be able to get blood out of Blake Barker. What do you think?"

Blake couldn't bring himself to accept the fact that Romero Lopes was indeed a vampire. For a brief moment, he wondered if Romero was on PCP. Allegedly, this substance could give temporary superhuman strength to many who abused it. In addition, angel dust reportedly could induce paranoid ideation in conjunction with extraordinarily violent behavior. *That's the ticket. That has to be it.* Blake had very little time to contemplate in detail the pathology that he'd just witnessed as he had scrambled to get back into the car, lock the doors, and attempt to beat a hasty retreat.

Blake put the car in reverse and floored it, but Romero Lopes sprinted after him. The vampire was gaining ground! Blake believed that he had one last chance to try to escape the psychotic murderer, and that chance was to try to run Romero over one more time. Maybe Blake would be lucky enough to crush Romero's skull under the front wheels of the big sedan.

Blake was enraged with such fury after he'd witnessed his wife being slaughtered that if he were indeed to succeed in running Romero over, he would then roll the big sedan back and forth over the assailant's body as many times as necessary to flatten his corpse to the thickness of a manhole cover. He had to make sure that the son of a bitch was finally dead.

Blake Barker slammed on his brakes and came to a dead stop. Romero Lopes had not anticipated this strategic maneuver. The vampiro hit the front bumper of the car and flew across the hood, his head blasting through the windshield. Romero's body was trapped in the hole in the windshield, and his face was just inches away from Blake Barker!

"You know, Blake, I think your Crown Victoria could benefit from a nice detail job at the car wash," Lopes said. "There are pellets of broken safety glass all over your dashboard. I must say, it's all rather untidy in here. Can't you see it? Here, take a better look!" Romero wedged his right arm through the hole in the windshield and grabbed Blake by the throat. It appeared that Romero had enough brute strength to actually attempt to pull Blake through the gaping hole in the windshield.

Blake put the transmission back in drive and floored the accelerator, propelling the car back toward the farmhouse. Within a few feet of hitting the farmhouse, Blake slammed on the brakes. The momentum threw Romero free of the windshield, causing the vampiro to hurl back through the existing hole in the living room wall.

This time, Blake did not stick around to see what would happen next. As he was able to negotiate a 180° turn and speed away, he heard Romero Lopes call out to him. "If you're going home, Blake, I'll be over directly to pay you and what's left of your family a little visit."

Suddenly facing an unexpected avalanche of headlamps of vehicles coming down the driveway and heading toward the Lopes's ranch house, Blake had to pull to the side to allow the military convoy to complete its mission of encircling the house. All the while, a Cobra attack helicopter weaved menacingly overhead. Captain Morales and the cavalry had just arrived, and not a moment too soon.

⚓

Two soldiers who had been trained as emergency medical technicians were fully garbed in hazmat suits. They quickly approached the front of the Lopes's farmhouse. They had been given the grim and unenviable task of recovering the dead body of Lynne Barker, placing the corpse on a canvas litter, and then hauling her earthly remains out of what would become a direct line of fire from automatic weapons. Captain Morales assessed the perilous situation before he turned to Dr. Seth Blanks and said, "I'm guessing that you expect us to try to take this nasty beast alive."

"Well, it would be a bonus, that's for sure," Blanks replied.

"I'll try to reel this guy in, Doc," Captain Morales said, "but I can't make any guarantees."

The captain of the National Guard finally acquiesced to the request of Dr. Blanks, but with one caveat; the safety of the men under his command was a paramount consideration. "Okay, Seth, here's the setup. The farmhouse has already been breached courtesy of Blake Barker's sedan. I will send in half a dozen men along with your right-hand man, Dr. Henry. We'll confront Romero Lopes and demand that he surrender to us. If he does, all's well that ends well. However, I need to make something perfectly clear: if any of my boys are injured or killed, we'll immediately raze the house to the ground. I assume that you can live within these parameters."

"Wait just a moment," Dr. Blanks countered. "What if Romero's parents, Cappy and Jo Lopes, are still alive in there and are being held captive?"

Captain Morales let out a big sigh through pursed lips and reiterated his previous policy without seeking any further opinion from Dr. Blanks. "If any of my boys are injured or killed, we'll immediately raze the house to the ground."

Morales turned to his platoon and said, "Okay, boys, you know what to do. Let's get to work. Somebody get me the bullhorn. Mr. Barker, you need to stand over here by me. If there will be retribution tonight, you should have the honors of being an eyewitness who will be able to give testimony of what happened here. What I'm offering you is outside the realm of standard military rules and regulations, but if it were my wife who'd been brutally butchered by a bloodthirsty bastard, I would take great satisfaction in seeing a swift and ruthless dispensation of justice."

The emotionally traumatized Blake Barker moved forward to stand beside Captain Morales, but Blake was too distraught at the time to say anything. After all, at that point he didn't have the opportunity to grieve.

Captain Morales took the bullhorn, placed it to his lips, and made an announcement. "Look, Romero Lopes, come on out with your hands in the air, and then get on your knees and interlock your fingers behind your head and stay completely still. Nobody else has to get hurt tonight."

The vampiro shouted out a reply from the big hole punctured into the living room wall of the farmhouse. "Don't shoot! I'm injured! I don't think I can move my legs. My back must be broken, and I'm paralyzed. I surrender! Please send help."

⸻

Sometimes, old lessons learned in warfare are sadly forgotten much too quickly. During World War II in the Pacific theater, the Japanese Imperial soldiers would come out of their caves and pillboxes waving white towels, ostensibly giving up the fight. Oftentimes these combatants would still be armed with explosives strapped to their bodies. Acting as suicide bombers, these Japanese soldiers wiped out scores of unwitting American servicemen. Sadly, these events are well-documented historical facts.

Was it possible that the evil vampiro Romero Lopes was disingenuous when he proclaimed that he had been injured and even paralyzed? Dr. Henry and several men from the National Guard were about to learn the painful lesson that history often repeats itself.

—◦◦◦—

"Okay, Lopes," Captain Morales bellowed through the bullhorn, "I'm sending in six military personnel and a medical scientist from the CDC named Dr. John Henry. I promise that we won't hurt you if you don't put up a fight."

"Sergeant Frey, pick five men to go with you," Captain Morales ordered. "John Henry, as you are a civilized man of letters, I want you to take point on this mission. You need to try to calmly persuade this individual to surrender without further incident."

John Henry turned to address Sergeant Frey and the other soldiers who were about to follow him into the breach. "Listen to me, men; if things go south and I'm taken down, fire at will."

"You have my word, Doc," Sergeant Frey promised. "We'll have you covered."

The interior of the farmhouse was as black as tar. It appeared that the main electrical circuit breaker had been disengaged. The men, armed with powerful flashlights, systematically swept through the house. The remains of Cappy and Jo Lopes were found in the kitchen. It was clear they were victims of predation. Dr. John Henry looked over his shoulder to again address the six military personnel who accompanied him. "Good God in heaven, I hope this guy doesn't go down swinging..."

Just then, the voice of Romero Lopes called out from a bedroom down the hallway. "Help! I'm in the back room!" The soldiers

reached the closed bedroom door where Romero Lopes was calling for help. "Come in, boys. I have been waiting for you. What
took you so long to get here?"

As Dr. John Henry was point on the probe, he cautiously opened
the bedroom door and walked into the room first. "Romero Lopes,
I'm an epidemiologist and infectious disease specialist from the
CDC. My name is—"

Dr. John Henry never completed the sentence. His body was
still standing upright when his severed head bounced across the
floor. The maniacal voice of Romero Lopes called out, "Is anybody
up for a game of soccer? Well, our Mexican friends call it *fútbol*!"

Romero kicked Dr. Henry's lifeless head with such force that
it lodged into the Sheetrock of the bedroom wall. As if he were a
play-by-play television sports announcer who was reporting on a
Mexican League soccer match on the Telemundo network, Romero
raised both of his arms toward the ceiling and cried out, "Goooooal!
Goal, goal, goal, goal, goooooal!"

"Fall back! Covering fire!" Sergeant Frey ordered. His five remaining compatriots leveled the barrels of their M16 automatic
weapons in the direction of the vampiro and began to hose down
the interior of the farmhouse with a deadly shower of lead. The
brave men, in great haste, retreated to escape the menacing, blood-
thirsty ghoul. However, trying to shoot Romero Lopes was an act of
futility, akin to trying to put a bullet into a moth that was fluttering
about the room. The vampiro was just that fast, and his gyrations
were just that erratic!

Once Sergeant Frey and his commandos exited the farmhouse
through the gaping hole in the living room wall and retreated to
safety, Captain Morales gave the order, "Fire at will! Fire away now,
goddamnit. Fire away!"

While keeping his head down, Dr. Blanks crawled up to Sergeant
Frey and asked, "What in the hell happened in there? Where's Dr.
Henry?"

Sergeant Frey started to scream. "Lopes ain't human! Do you

hear me? He's in there right now playing volleyball with the head of John Henry! I'm sorry, Doc, but your friend didn't make it!"

In a five-second debriefing, Captain Morales was informed that the bodies of two elderly decaying people were seen in the kitchen, presumably the corpses of Romero Lopes's parents. No other living beings were seen in the farmhouse besides the vampiro. Captain Morales got back on the bullhorn and instructed, "Nothing gets out of there alive!"

As the Lopes family farmhouse began to disintegrate, Captain Morales issued a radio communication to the circling Cobra assault chopper. "Cut loose with the snakes! Expend all of your ordnance on that farmhouse. Am I clear?"

In accordance to the original tactical plan of Captain Morales, the Lopes family farmhouse was burned to the ground. By the time that the home was reduced to red glowing cinders, the vampiro must have been long dead, right? Move along, folks. There's nothing to see here, so just move along …

The following morning, a forensic team arrived and carefully sifted through the burned rubble. The charred remains of Dr. John Henry, along with the partial skeletal debris from two other individuals who would soon be confirmed to be the late parents of Romero Lopes, were quickly recovered. The remains of these unfortunate souls were zipped up into heavy plastic body bags and then taken to the county morgue.

Dr. Blanks immediately petitioned that the bodies should be extradited to Atlanta, or at least to the Armed Forces Institute of Pathology (AFIP), in an effort to make absolutely certain that no stone was left unturned during a thorough postmortem evaluation. As an executive decision had been made that no biological material, infected or otherwise, would be allowed to leave the state of New

Mexico, all forensic evaluations would have to take place at an in-state location.

Captain Morales attempted to assuage the anxiety that Dr. Blanks had about the whole matter. "You need to cool your tool, Doc. This decision is out of your hands, and frankly, it's also out of my hands. Fear not; I've worked with our regional forensic pathologist, Dr. Evelyn Stern, and her diener, Miguel Pastore, during the last outbreak here back in '79."

"What of it?" Blanks prostested. "I don't care. These remains need to be taken to the CDC."

"Stern and her diener are real pros. They're both as informed about human vampirism as anybody else on the planet. I assure you, they'll knock any post out of the park. You'll be happy with the work Dr. Stern will do." This was all quite true. The only caveat was that Dr. Stern and Miguel Pastore would have to stay alive long enough to give the night crawler task force any answers ...

There was only one residual burning question to be answered: where in hell was the corpse of Romero Lopes? There was no possibility that the evil son of a bitch escaped. His body must have still been buried somewhere under the smoldering debris.

To even a casual observer, it would appear that Captain Morales enjoyed using a bullhorn to communicate to those under his charge. Having a booming, electronically amplified voice made the military officer feel, well, more *important* somehow. "Okay, people, help me out here. Somebody needs to get their sorry ass back in there and find the body of Romero Lopes. He didn't escape, and he certainly didn't disappear into thin air."

Captain Morales was suddenly transformed into his alter ego Captain Ahab, who in another place and in another era pursued a particularly angry, toothed, cetaceous albino with similar manic resolve.

When the military officer slipped his right hand deep into the pocket of his trousers, he offered an additional incentive to the search team. "I fondle now a gold doubloon that shall be cheerfully rendered upon any fair lad who is the first one fortunate enough to spy the burned bat!"

Sadly, if truth be told, the only thing that Captain Morales fondled in his pocket was a brick of Bazooka Joe bubble gum.

⚊⚊⚊

At the break of dawn, after being attended to by the medical personnel who were present at the vampiro's farmhouse, Blake Barker refused to take an ambulance to the hospital. Instead, he retreated to his home. As he was in a near fugue state, he slowly walked back to his residence, having abandoned his battered sedan on the dirt driveway of the estate of the dearly departed Cappy and Jo Lopes. As for Lorena, she witnessed the entire violent military assault on Romero Lopes from the back porch of the Barker farmhouse, and she knew that there had been casualties. Upon Blake's return, she was already well aware that Lynne Barker had fallen in the melee.

Lorena lamented, "*Lo siento, Señor Barker. Sé que su esposa, Lynne, está muerta ahora. Que horrible. Que terrible. ¡Lo siento! ¡Lo siento! ¡Lo siento!*"

Lorena reached out to embrace her forlorn employer, but he would have none of it. "Please, not now, Lorena." Barker gently pushed her away and slowly sat down at the kitchen table. He added, "Given the way I feel right now, I don't think I could ever allow anybody to touch me again. My wife is gone. Just like that! I watched Romero butcher her right before my own eyes, and I was powerless to stop it."

Lorena inquired, "Blake, I need you to tell me something. Did Dr. Blanks and his army friends ever find the dead body of Romero Lopes?"

"Well, if they did," Blake responded, "it wasn't prior to my return trip home. The nasty bastard has to be buried in the rubble somewhere over there. The house was surrounded all night long, and there is no way in hell he could have ever escaped that firefight."

Lorena, visibly upset by what Barker had just said, noted, "I hope you're correct. If not, I expect Romero will someday show up on our front porch and knock on your door to seek revenge."

"Not bloody likely," Blake countered. "I need you to sit down and talk to me. Look, Lorena, you say you have known Romero Lopes all your life. You need to fill in the details about him right this minute. What happened between you two at the El Chopo restaurant yesterday? I have a feeling that there had been bad blood between you two that was on a slow simmer for many years. I don't understand what that was all about. Up until yesterday, Lynne and I both believed that Romero was a pleasant, polite, and decent young man."

As Lorena sat down, she shook her head to indicate that she certainly had a different opinion about Romero Lopes. "I'll be frank with you, Mr. Barker. You must be a very bad judge of character if you thought for even one moment that Romero was a pleasant, polite, and decent young man. Nothing is further from the truth. Let me set the record straight about your next-door neighbor: he was always a social outcast."

"What do you mean?"

"His bizarre attraction to the occult and to demonic forces made him a pariah in this community," Lorena explained. "Romero Lopes was a loser. Even as an adult, he was an underachiever with absolutely no ambition in life. That's why he still lived at home with his mother and father. That is, of course, until he decided to murder his parents and then eat them. Are you familiar with a rough-and-tumble schoolyard game called *chinchi al agua*? It's a playground favoroite that both boys and girls can play."

"I think I'm somewhat familiar with the game," Blake replied. "It's like a team sport version of the game that we gringos call leap frog. As challengers successfully jump upon the backs of their adversaries, they yell out something that sounds something like 'cheen-chee-la-wa,' if I'm not mistaken."

Lorena smiled. She reached over and patted Blake on the top of his hand. She said, "Yes, you know the game! When my class-mates played this at school, Romero Lopes was always picked last as a teammate because he was such an odd person. In fact, I was always chosen ahead of him, and he hated me for that. That was always such a serious affront to his fragile ego."

"Just because you were a girl?"

"Mira, he believed he could cast magic spells. Lopes would screw around with Ouija boards and tarot cards. That's how he was given the nickname El Maguito."

"The Little Magician," Blake said. "An insult, no doubt."

"It seemed as if he was always attracted to dark, evil forces. You won't believe this, but at one time he actually declared that he wanted to be in league with demonic beings."

"Is that why you think Romero Lopes believed that he had become a vampiro?" Blake Barker asked.

Lorena waved off his hypothesis. "No, you don't understand. Romero Lopes didn't just *think* that he was a vampiro; he *was* a vampiro! He got infected with an illness. When he got infected, this illness just amplified his underlying dark and evil nature."

"So, Lopes was already primed to commit acts of evil?"

"Although I didn't witness this event with my own eyes," Lorena elaborated, "my friend, Sissy, claims that she actually saw him walking in a perfect circle on his family's farm with the bloody torso of a dead goat perched upon his head. The entrails of the unfortunate animal were draped around his neck as if the intestines were a scarf!"

"What a ridiculous story," Blake scoffed.

"Like me," Lorena said, "Sissy is a curandera. I believe what she said was indeed the truth."

"Well, what does all of this nonsense mean to me?" Blake asked. "I told you that I don't believe in vampiros. I'm certain now, more than ever, that Romero was strung out on amphetamines or angel dust. Nothing more and nothing less."

"I know that you are looking for answers," Lorena said. "Mira, mira, Señor Barker; there are two separate but equally important factors to explain why Romero Lopes went off the deep end and fell into a moral vacuum. The first factor, in my opinion, is as follows: Romero Lopes was no longer a human being. He became un vampiro.

The second matter would seem to be even more important than the first: Romero Lopes was pure evil, something he has always been. If he's still alive, it is something that he'll always be."

"Can people not change over time?" Blake asked. Although his question was not rhetorical, no answer was forthcoming...

<hr>

After a brief respite and bodily replenishment with ice-cold carbonated beverages, the forensic investigators resumed their search for the missing body of Romero Lopes. By midmorning, a singed mattress was discovered amid the rubble. Once the drywall debris had been cleared away, the mattress was flipped over and the burned body of the vampiro was discovered by the National Guard private named Stumpy Wheeler. "Hey, guys, I found the son of a bitch! Somebody bring a pitchfork back over here so I can scrape this shit up and stuff it into a sandwich bag."

"Hey, Stump," Sergeant Frey said, "before you bag the beast and it gets hauled out of here in a meat wagon, are you absolutely certain that this bloodsucking bastard has kicked the bucket?"

Stumpy Wheeler replied, "Well, the damned thing certainly looks dead to me."

It would have been most appropriate at that moment if historians had been present to duly record Private Stumpy Wheeler's flippant last comments in the burgeoning *Annals of Famous Last Words* for posterity.

6

RESURRECTION

With the arduous task of performing no fewer than seven postmortem evaluations on a Monday morning, the coroner Dr. Evelyn Stern was definitely going to require manpower support from the Department of Anatomical Pathology at the New Mexico State University College of Medicine in Las Cruces. In addition, any assistance that could be rendered by Dr. Ralph Fairbanks from the CDC would be most appreciated. Although Fairbanks was now working as an epidemiologist for the federal government, he was board certified in both forensic and clinical pathology.

Dr. Stern and Miguel Pastore were already quarantined to the morgue, and they'd been ordered by the CDC to wear hazmat suits for several more days. Although under quarantine, they were still allowed to proceed with postmortem evaluations. New Mexico State University (NMSU) had loaned the associate professor of medicine Dr. D. Clayton Thomas and his pathology resident, Lucretia McWeevil, to help ramrod through the autopsies. When the outside assistance arrived at the morgue, Dr. Fairbanks, Thomas, and the resident physician all quickly climbed into their hazmat gear before joining Miguel Pastore and Dr. Stern and getting down to business.

"How are things at the zoo?" Miguel asked Dr. Thomas.

"Your alma mater is thriving, Miguel," Dr. Thomas answered.

"My offer stands if you ever want to jump ship and come home someday."

"Thanks, Doc," Miguel replied, "but I'm happy here. Besides, there's a good reason that NMSU has the specific nickname, the zoo. If I ever came back to the university, maybe I'd just be another animal on display!"

"Maybe so, Miguel," Dr. Thomas mused, "but just like at any zoo, the preditors are always destined to get more attention than the herbevores. At least give it some thought."

"Are you saying I'm destined to become a preditor, Doc?" Miguel asked.

"If the shoe fits, son!" Dr. Thomas answered with a grin.

"Quit trying to steal away my diener, Clayton!" Dr. Sren warned. "We have to examine the logistics as to how we are going to tackle this workload. In the three separate lockers on the left side of the morgue, we have the stiffs that were collected after the El Chopo restaurant massacre. On the right side of the refrigerated vaults, we have the bodies that were recovered after the firefight at the Lopes family farm."

Dr. Ralph Fairbanks counted the corpses lined up in the vaults from left to right with his index finger and interjected, "Hang on, here. Where is the body of Lynne Barker? Don't tell me that she's been resurrected and is now una vampira mexicana at large?"

Dr. Evelyn Stern waved off his concern and said, "Relax, Ralph. As a consideration to her surviving husband, Miguel Pastore and I knocked out the gross on this case prior to your arrival. As there were no bite marks on her, it was imminently clear that her cause of death on the post was massive blood loss and internal organ damage after she was stabbed more than two dozen times during the brutal assault. It appeared to be a crime of passion actually, as if the alleged murderer Romero Lopes had a primal and, if I may dare say so, evil hatred for this unfortunate victim."

"What then?" Dr. Fairbanks inquired.

"The body was released to Hillman's Mortuary Service in a

biohazard bag for direct and immediate cremation. This will take place this morning. If anybody is interested in paying their last respects, her interment ceremony is slated for this Thursday. As far as the rest of the corpses in here, I'm hoping that the crew from New Mexico State can readily manage the dead bodies listed on the 'El Chopo Restaurant Massacre' side of the autopsy ledger."

"Can do," Dr. Thomas replied. "If we get the gross done on this end, would you like us to move over to your neck of the woods?"

"Absolutely. It would be most appreciated," Dr. Stern replied. "The middle vault holds the corpse of Dr. John Henry. He was murdered at the farmhouse. I've known John since the last night crawler outbreak back in 1979, and I considered him to be a good friend of mine. In fact, he was much more than just a friend. I just don't have the stomach right now to even slide out the body tray from the fridge and cast my eyes upon his remains. There was a time when John Henry and I became—well, I guess you could say that he and I were close. I remember when we even talked about the prospects of us someday getting—" Tears welled in the eyes of Dr. Stern. Her throat tightened, and she was not able to complete her sentence.

"For the love of Jesus," Evelyn Stern pleaded, "I just can't do it. What's wrong with me? Please, forgive me."

"Stay frosty, Dr. Stern. The Aggies will handle it," the pathology resident bravely interjected. Unfortunately, Lucretia McWeevil was socially awkward and was totally unaware that she was making a pun, a very sick joke, and an embarrassing double entendre all at the same time when she said, "We've got it covered, Doc; it's in the bag!" Her declaration was met with a howl of anguish from Evelyn Stern.

Dr. Ralph Fairbanks stepped forward and looked at Dr. McWeevil with astonishment. The other members of the autopsy team cast their eyes away at that awkward moment. Ralph narrowed his eyes and studied the resident physician with disdain before he raised his hand in front of her face as if he were a traffic cop at a busy intersection. "No, don't bother. I'll do the gross on the late Dr. Henry myself. Although we weren't exactly friends, this man was my colleague at the CDC. At least I'll treat him with the respect that his earthly remains deserve. Perhaps that's more than I can say about you, Dr. McWeevil."

Dr. Fairbanks turned toward Dr. D. Clayton Thomas from NMSU and said, "I suggest you keep your resident physician on a short leash, D!"

"Sorry about that," Dr. Thomas replied.

"You should be," Fairbanks added. "I'll tell everybody right here and right now that I'll also be doing the microscopic assay on all these subjects, and I'll be doing that work back in Atlanta, not here in New Mexico. The executive order that we all received stated that the gross will be done here in New Mexico, but it didn't say a damned thing that would prohibit the microscopics to be analyzed at the CDC. Does anybody have a problem with that?"

As there was no obvious voice of dissent, Dr. Fairbanks stepped away from the dim-witted resident physician. Lucretia McWeevil remained totally oblivious of the enormous and callous faux pas that she'd just committed.

"Well, I guess that leaves the other remains from the farmhouse to me," Dr. Stern concluded after she composed herself. "My diener and I will tackle the vampiro and the presumed remains of his dead parents as soon as we jump into some fresh hazmats."

Dr. Stern slowly looked over her professional colleagues in the morgue to ascertain if they were actually up to the task at hand. As she slowly nodded her head in grim determination, she barked out an order: "Miguel Pastore, front and center! It's time for us to yet again climb into the saddle. Let's get back to work, mi amigo."

Before the autopsy procedures even commenced, the pneumatic doors to the morgue slid open. Captain Morales, Sergeant Frey, and Private Stumpy Wheeler all entered the room. "I hate to pull rank on you people, but you'd better keep Romero Lopes on ice for now," Captain Morales said. "We're no longer authorized to do the post on this vampiro."

"Bullshit!" Dr. Stern exclaimed. "This is our case. The vampiro is specifically *my* case. With what happened to John Henry and these other unfortunate souls, I'm actually looking forward to slicing up this night crawler bit by bit."

"We're professionals here," Dr. Fairbanks said as he pulled Evelyn Stern away by the elbow. "Try to remember that."

"When I do it, my only regret will be that he's still not alive to enjoy the experience," Dr. Stern said as she pulled away from her colleague. "Somebody must have the balls of a brass monkey to pull the rug out from under my feet like this!"

"The brass balls of which you speak sadly belong to the Department of Defense and the US Army Department of Biological Warfare," Morales said as he moved forward to confront the angry pathologist. "They just sent me a new direct order. The corpse of Romero Lopes will be sent to the AFIP for an evaluation. Before anyone says another word, don't start a fight with me, okay? It's not my call, so don't even think about coming over here and trying to pull a ham sandwich out of my ass."

"This is in direct contradiction to the previous orders," Dr. Stern said.

"This isn't right," Fairbanks said. "As far as I know, the CDC has the ultimate jurisdiction over the medical and scientific matters according to the established guidelines and the Night Crawler Protocol."

"Sadly," Morales added as he raised his index finger, "it now seems that some administrative peon at the Department of Defense has a concrete cinder block shoved up his rear sideways about this matter. Personally, I don't believe any of this material should ever leave this morgue, but as I said, it's not my call."

"What about the other dead bodies in here? We have a traffic jam in this morgue!" Dr. Thomas said.

"The standard autopsy procedures that you've planned out for the other six subjects will be allowed to be performed here in New Mexico," Captain Morales answered with confidence, "but any material harvested for microscopic analytics will *not* be going to the CDC after all."

"What are you talking about?" Dr. Fairbanks asked. "The CDC facility is the best in the world to assess the microscopics. Who's going to be commissioned to do that extra work? I can tell you right now, Morales, I'm the one who needs to do this job!"

"Sorry, but no dice," Morales explained. "There's also been a change in venue for the future microscopic postmortem work. As of now it will all be done at the AFIP. The meat wagon will be coming here directly, and the vampiro carcass will be hauled off to Albuquerque to be processed at Kirkland Air Force Base. From there, it will be out of our jurisdiction." Dr. Morales handed the confirmatory memo to Dr. Ralph Fairbanks for his personal review.

Ralph Fairbanks scowled as he shrugged his shoulders. As he passed the memo to his other colleagues, he asked, "Is Seth Blanks on board with all of this?"

"Your boss is not on board with *any* of this," Captain Morales replied, "and neither am I for that matter. If these matters were up to me, I would exterminate anybody infected with this night crawler disease as a matter of public safety. I would personally have absolutely no qualms about committing the act of executing an infected individual on sight. Come to think of it, this situation is *way* beyond a matter of public safety. This is actually a matter of national security, in my opinion. I don't believe any of these dead bodies or any of this other material should ever leave the state of New Mexico, I tell you."

"What does the state of New Mexico have to do with any of this?" McWeevil asked.

"Well, you're in it now up to your neck," Morales explained, "so I guess it is time for me to take out a crayon and color between the lines. From time to time, we've had reports of this disease occurring only in our neck of the woods along the Rio Grande Valley north of El Paso, and these outbreaks date back many years. In this country, this disease has only been recognized in this state. We need to keep it that way. It would seem to me that the army and the DOD are making a big mistake."

"How so?" Lucretia asked.

"New World vampirism has never been recognized outside of Latin America or past our state borders. To my knowledge, the nidus has always been right here in the Land of Enchantment. As far as I'm concerned, if we allow any of this material or any of these dead bodies to leave the confines of this territory, we'll just be putting civilians at risk of a national epidemic, if not a worldwide pandemic. However, what do I know? I'm just a *loco moco* with the National Guard. I'm lower than whale shit on the food chain, boys and girls, and those who are standing higher up on the pyramid don't want to hear my opinion—or anybody else's opinion for that matter."

Ralph Fairbanks raised his hand as if he needed permission from the teacher to ask a question. "Speaking of which, where in hell is Dr. Blanks? If I were a betting man, I would wager that he would go down the warpath over all of this. After all, he's the damned government's point man for this disease, and he's served in this capacity since the last outbreak back in 1979. I'm surprised that he's gone AWOL at this crucial time. I'll venture that he blew a gasket once he learned that the AFIP is going to have a crack at not only the gross but also the microscopics. He fully anticipated the CDC was going to handle all of this."

"Well, you're right about Seth Blanks, I must say. Prior to this juncture, I thought that Dr. Blanks was little more than a weak-in-the-knees, by-the-book bureaucrat. As for now, I can assure you that he is in the process of drilling a new asshole into some new asshole who's working over at the Department of Defense," explained Captain Morales. "The only problem as far as I can see is that I don't know how successful he'll be with our collective formal or informal complaints."

"How on earth could the Department of Defense think that

the AFIP could possibly be any better equipped than the CDC?" Dr. Evelyn Stern asked Captain Morales.

Morales looked back at Dr. Stern, obviously filled with angst. "Wake up, Evelyn! If the Armed Forces Institute of Pathology is getting involved with this case, that could mean one thing and one thing only: the *military* is eventually going to take over the direct management of the state of New Mexico's Night Crawler Protocol. I can tell you right now that the project will eventually be federalized and then subsequently weaponized. It would seem, through no fault of our own, that Uncle Sam has a much grander, global vision of the work that we've done here thus far."

"Good grief," Dr. Fairbanks said. "What on earth are you referring to?"

"I'll tell you what I am talking about: the US Army Department of Biological Warfare in San Antonio, Texas. Think about it; the feds must be planning on taking whatever discoveries we stumble upon to the next level. However, what that next level could possibly be is anybody's guess. I have my own opinions about this situation that I would be willing to share if anybody is interested in listening to my rant. Perhaps the federal government is no longer particularly concerned about the overall welfare of the American people."

"Have they ever been?" Miguel asked. "The only thing the federal government is interested in is the federal government. Can't you see that?"

"Well, there you have it," Morales said. "There are now bigger fish to fry. After all, it was only a matter of time before human vampirism would eventually be looked upon as a new potential tactical and strategic tool in the shed of the United States' weapon systems."

The resident pathologist Dr. McWeevil certainly appeared to have more misplaced trust in the virtues of the federal government than anybody else in the autopsy suite on that particular Monday morning. She openly rejected the pessimistic prognostications that Captain Morales had uttered. "I'm sorry, *el capitán*, but that just sounds like a load of crapola to me."

"Oh, really?" the captain replied. "What do you know about biological warfare research that has been performed in the recent past? I'm not talking about germ warfare; I am talking about utilizing higher life-forms that have been weaponized. This is not a new concept."

"If it's not a new concept," McWeevil said, "then why haven't I heard about it?"

"I suspect it's because you've had your face stuck in front of a textbook for far too long," Morales replied. "I'm fully aware of the fact that back in the summer of 1981, the Colombian army contracted the primatology kennel at the Gulf Coast College of Medicine in Houston, Texas, to try to train the great apes to heave monkey shit on command. If that relatively simple task could have been accomplished with any degree of regularity, the prospects of having a chimp pitch a hand grenade would then not be a far-fetched idea. See?"

"I never heard of such a thing," Miguel said. "What happened to that particular project?"

"The plan failed, largely as a consequence of the mysterious disappearance of the lead research investigator in the spring of 1982," Dr. Morales explained. "The lead primatologist who oversaw the project, Professor Denny Sassman, was doing follow-up research on the original HAM project."

"What was HAM?" Lucretia McWeevil asked.

"Does anybody remember HAM?" Dr. Morales asked. "That is the acronym for the Holloman Air Force Monkey. If there's a stiff breeze outside, the Hollman base is within spitting distance from this point where we're all standing right now. Well, in any event, a monkey from the HAM project happened to be the first primate that the United States launched into space on a Nike booster."

"That was a long time ago," Ralph Fairbanks noted. "You're now dialing Mr. Peabody's Way-Back Machine to the late 1950s."

"You don't really think that we quit monkeying around after we beat the damned Ruskies to the moon, now, do you?" Morales asked as a rhetorical question. "In any event, Dr. Sassman personally told me that he was onto something before he mysteriously vanished from the Gulf Coast College of Medicine."

"He said he was involved with higher life-form biological warfare?" Dr. Stern asked.

"Sassman's entire experiment involved training chimps to heave solid objects on command. It was undertaken to try to combat the vicious crimes that the Calle Vampiro drug cartel, among others, were committing across the border."

"What you're saying sounds batshit crazy," Dr. Stern said.

"Not batshit crazy, Doc. I'm talking purple monkey shit crazy! If the great ape project had turned out to be successful, our federal government was in the queue to take it way beyond benchwork research. Can you believe that? We're talking about a simian weapon system, of all things. That gives you a rough idea of how devious our very own Uncle Sam can truly be at times."

"How on earth do you know about all of this?" Dr. Thomas asked.

"Simple," Captain Morales replied. "Sassman went to the osteopathic school of medicine in El Paso, Texas, straight down I-25. I previously was the head of campus security at that facility, and Sassman and I had become friends. That's how I eventually met his sister, Alba, one day. Denny played matchmaker, and Alba and I started dating. It all turned out well, as we eventually got married. I was happily hitched to Alba for several years before she sadly died from complications of metastatic melanoma a while back."

"My condolences regarding your loss, but it sounds to me that Dr. Sassman was telling you information that should have remained classified," Dr. Thomas added.

"Well, what do you expect? After all, the dude was my brother-in-law," Morales said. "When he was on the faculty at the Gulf Coast College of Medicine in Houston, he told me about events that occurred that made the hair stand up on the back of my neck! Check this out; it appears that this particular facility had its own entrenched 'clinical justice system.' Prisoners incarcerated within the penal system who were subsequently transferred to that hospital for advanced medical care were subjected to all kinds of terrible things."

"Well, I personally have no problem with any of that," Miguel Pastore chimed in, "but how is this relevant to any biological warfare project that the United States government may or may not be participating in now?"

"Think about it. It has everything to do with it," Captain Morales continued. "Dark things happen in the shadows all the time, and there were certainly very dark things that going on at the Gulf Coast College of Medicine a few years ago. Before Dr. Sassman simply disappeared into thin air, he was doing contract work for the secret US Army Biological Warfare Research Facility in San Antonio, Texas, where they're currently investigating some really wicked shit. I'm privy to the fact that Uncle Sam was slipping a few extra shekels under the table for Professor Sassman to keep his research findings on the q.t. I suspect the university had suspicions about what he was up to, but Denny never got fingered for his nefarious clandestine research at the time."

"Well, what do you think happened to your brother-in-law?" Dr. Stern asked.

"Beats the hell out of me," Morales answered, "but he was likely the victim of foul play for one reason or another."

"What was the purpose of selecting San Antonio as the site of the US Army Biological Warfare Research Facility?" Fairbanks asked.

"In my opinion, it would appear that the federal government has a genuine hatred for the state of Texas," Morales opined. "If there would ever be any kind of biological warfare catastrophe, or if a weaponized higher life-form containment breakdown would ever occur, the federal government would be more than happy to see the citizens of the Lone Star State get shit upon first."

"You can't be serious," Miguel Pastore said.

"Morales might be right about that," Dr. Thomas agreed. "In light of the animosity and contempt that the Northeastern Corridor of the United States has for the South, and especially for the state of Texas, that certainly seems plausible."

"Look, everything in the universe is connected somehow," Morales opined. "I have no doubt that Uncle Sam would relish the prospect of dropping a nuke on the state of Texas with little, if any, provocation. In any event, I do know about several examples of higher life-form biological warfare activities that are well documented."

"Look, I was in the military during the height of the Southeast Asian war games," Dr. Fairbanks said, "and I have no earthly idea what in hell you are talking about."

"You might not; however, your boss, Dr. Seth Blanks, certainly does. Just hear me out," Captain Morales explained. "Utilizing the historical vignettes that are wedged within my own brain, I know details that go as far back as World War II, and even before that time. During the Great Patriotic War, as it is now referred to by the current Soviet Union, Soviet troops were able to successfully train canines armed with explosives to run underneath the Nazi tanks and armored personnel carriers. Boom!"

"I didn't know that," Fairbanks said. "Anything else?"

"Prior to that," Morales added, "in the 1930s, some crazy evil Russian son of a bitch named Josef Stalin actually funded experimental studies that tried to create 'supersoldiers' through the forced mating of chimpanzees and human beings. Nice. As a prospective consideration, how would the concept of a weaponized vampiro be any different from what I have just told you?"

The members of the autopsy team could only look at Captain Morales with their mouths agape. As the officer turned to leave the morgue, he stated, "I'm going to wander off, cop a whiz, and then find out what kind of progress Seth Blanks has made with the Department of Defense, but don't get your hopes up. In the meantime, I'm going to leave Sergeant Frey and Private Wheeler to stand guard in here just to make absolutely certain that everything goes according to Hoyle. Before I leave, would you boys and girls like me to sing a personal rendition of 'America the Beautiful'?"

"Maybe I'll take you up on that offer if you know all the lyrics, but I just don't think that we need to have any armed military personnel in here at this time. In the end, what could possibly go wrong? After all, we'll just be working with a bunch of stiffs."

—⊸⊷—

Blake's younger sister, Elizabeth, was able to fly into El Paso from Lubbock on a Southwest flight as a standby. She was able to depart the same Monday morning when she learned that her sister-in-law, Lynne, had been brutally murdered. Renting a car at the airport in El Paso, she made it up north to Mesilla in just a few hours after the jet's wheels touched down on the runway.

For Blake, it was good to have his sister come for a visit at this difficult time, especially since he had always been close to her. As Blake was the older brother, he'd always looked out for his baby sister. In a clandestine fashion, Blake was able to chase away more than one aggressively amorous interloper during Elizabeth's high school years in a chivalrous effort to ensure that his sibling remained chaste. Blake did not want his sister to become a "soiled dove" at the hands of a male suitor who was nothing more than a horny teenager whose libido was amped to the gills with endogenous adolescent testosterone.

After everybody had turned in for the night after his sister's arrival from Texas, Blake suddenly awoke in the wee hours of the morning. Even after a successful micturition allowed him to evacuate his strained bladder, he found that he was unable to return to the realm of slumber. He dragged himself back out of bed in an effort to try to find some overt meaning to his own continued miserable existence.

From the top drawer of his dresser where he stored his socks and jockey briefs, he pulled out the mysterious razor-sharp obsidian knife that he'd previously reclaimed from the right hand of the dead cosmic hippie named Ruby. "What in hell are you? What purpose do you serve?"

The blade of the obsidian knife was sharpened to an extraordinarily thin sharp edge only a few molecules in width. Blake unwittingly laid the business end of the weapon across the palm of his left hand. The simple gravitational force that the planet exerted upon the sharp edge of the dark milky-green glass-like matrix of volcanic origin was enough to render an open laceration. "Shit. Oh dear, what have I done?"

Blake proceeded to rinse the blood off the knife and then dry the weapon very gently. All the while, he made absolutely certain that he did not injure himself with the sharp weapon yet again. Blake proceeded to place the knife back into the top drawer of his bedroom dresser. As Lorena was a professed curandera, Blake would have to make a point of asking her if she had any specific knowledge about the peculiar weapon.

After attending to the open wound on the palm of his left hand with the application of a thick layer of triple antibiotic ointment and a fresh gauze wrap, Blake retreated to the living room, where he reclined on the sofa. Finding nothing to do that would constructively occupy his time, he proceeded to turn on the television.

After 1:00 in the morning, commercial television stations would discontinue broadcasting until 5:00 in the morning. During that void, television stations would fill the blank screen with what was known as a test pattern. Usually the static image of the US flag, a bald eagle, or a Native American warrior would fill the television screen for several hours before the resumption of regularly scheduled broadcasting. Blake was instantaneously mesmerized by the static image of a chief from an unspecified tribe of Native Americans, resplendent with a full-feathered warbonnet.

Oddly, the television test pattern that warranted Blake's undivided and prolonged attention suggested that the head of the Native

American chief was actually lined up in the proverbial crosshairs. Blake laughed to himself and paid sarcastic homage to the doctrine of manifest destiny. "I guess some things never change!"

The soft yet high-pitched whine of the television woke Nathan, who climbed out of bed only to find that his father was staring at the television test pattern without apparently blinking. "Daddy, are you okay?" Blake failed to answer his son's question. The forlorn man was actually unaware that he was not alone in the room. When Blake failed to answer Nathan's question a second time, the young child crawled onto the sofa and proceeded to place his small head upon his father's lap.

Nathan softly whimpered, "I miss Mommy. I miss her so much." Nathan took the palm of his hand and began to sweep it across his frail chest and abdomen. "Daddy, what's wrong with me? I hurt here. I hurt all over!" Nathan repeated his heartbroken lament. "I hurt here. I hurt all over!"

Suddenly aware that his son was present, Blake clutched the young child and held him close. "There is only one thing that you can do: be brave, Nathan, be brave …"

As Nathan reached out to grab his father's right hand, Blake responded, "I hurt too, Nathan. I feel like I have a hole in my heart." Blake rubbed his recently lacerated left hand over his chest and abdomen as he confessed to Nathan in the darkness, "I hurt here. I hurt all over!"

As Blake's tears dripped down upon Nathan's face in a steady stream, the young boy asked, "When will the pain stop?"

Blake finally mustered an answer that was as honest as it was painful—as painful as the hole that was rendered in his own beating heart and the beating heart of his young son. "No, my son, it will *never* go away."

This brutal truth caused Nathan to cry out, "What can I do if I can't ever see Mommy again?"

As Blake continued to openly weep, he stammered, "There's only one thing that you can do: be brave, Nathan, be brave."

In Blake's kitchen on the following morning, Elizabeth asked, "Blake, is there anything I can help you with? When Mom passed away, I helped Daddy pack up all her clothing, and then I sent it to the Salvation Army."

"I don't remember that," Blake said as he poured a cup of coffee. "I never really knew what happened to all of Mom's old stuff."

"It was a great relief for him that I was able to help him in that way. I'll tell you what; why don't you just kick back and relax? I just talked to Cletus on the telephone. He can't get a flight out of Houston until tomorrow. When he gets here, he said, he'll have a nice spread catered for us at the wake."

"I can *always* rely on Cletus to do the right thing," Blake said as he tugged at the sleeveless T-shirt that he'd worn to bed the night before.

"I'm going to dig a bit more into the phone book and find out what local restaurant might be able to pull that off for us. I heard there is a decent place called El Chopo. Maybe that would do the trick."

"That would be nice," Blake replied, "but I'm certain that El Chopo will be closed for quite some time while it undergoes an industrial-strength steam cleaning. Nonetheless, I am sure that Cletus will be able to pick up the tab for whatever caterer you decide to use."

Blake and Cletus became estranged after their father passed away, likely as a consequence of the fact that in the last will and testament, dear old Dad consigned his gold pocket watch to Blake. Cletus was two years older than Blake, and it was inexplicable why the eldest offspring was abruptly passed over during the dispensation of the old man's earthly possessions. To make things right, Blake considered giving the gold watch to Cletus as a gift upon his arrival. After all, doesn't the oldest son deserve his father's gold watch?

"In the meantime, I think I will go out for a nice jog in the neighborhood," Blake said. "A little exercise might help clear my mind. By the time I get back, you and Lorena should have the job of packing up Lynne's stuff finished."

Elizabeth had a look of concern on her face when she said, "Are you sure that exercising right now is a good idea? You still have your left arm in a sling, and your face is all swollen up like a stomped-on horny toad. Why don't you just mellow out and rest here for a while?"

Blake, waving off his sister's well-intentioned concerns, replied, "Well, it might be a stupid idea, but I want to give it a try nonetheless."

"Once we start to get everything all packed up," Elizabeth said, "do you want us to leave out a nice dress for Lynne to be buried in?"

"No, Liz, I forgot to tell you that Lynne's body was sent to the Hillman Mortuary Service for a planned cremation after the coroner's office finishes up with the autopsy," Blake replied. "We'll have a memorial service for her on Thursday, and then I'd like you and Cletus to help me think of a nice natural setting to disperse her ashes. Be that as it may, if you're really willing to pack up Lynne's stuff, that would be a big help. I want you to keep all of Lynne's jewelry as she had no living relatives. The only thing that I want to keep as a memento is the engagement and wedding ring set that I gave her."

Elizabeth was pleasantly surprised by Blake's generous offer. She leaned over to kiss him on the cheek. "I would be honored to have her jewelry collection. Thank you very much."

"I remember that Dad lived only another year or so after Mom passed away," Blake continued. "I swear, he must have died from a broken heart. Well, Liz, I wonder if the same thing's going to happen to me."

"That's morbid!" Liz exclaimed. "Stop it! Don't talk like that, Blake. I'll bet a box of jelly doughnuts right here and right now that Blake Barker is the kind of guy who could theoretically live forever."

It had been a long time since Blake Barker had done any exercise, but now that his wife was gone, perhaps it was time for him to turn over a new leaf. He now wanted to try to do a better job of taking care of himself for the sake of his young son. After all, for the longest time, Lynne had been harping on him to lose the extra weight that he accumulated in the time since their marriage ceremony. He always made promises in the past to start an exercise program, but he made as many lame excuses to justify his chronic procrastination.

Now, he felt that it was mandatory to honor his wife in some way, shape, or form, and the best tribute that he could possibly offer, he believed, would be for him to try to get into some semblance of improved physical condition.

Blake decided to jog down to the intersection of Calle Murciélago and Avenida Chupadores de Sangre, but he found that he was far too ambitious in his attempt at physical exertion. After only one hundred yards of jogging, Blake's legs cramped up and he felt a painful throbbing sensation in his face and left clavicle from the injuries that he had sustained from his encounter with the vampiro Romero Lopes.

Blake quickly realized that it would be the better part of valor to start out at a slow and steady pace. He decided to make the near one-mile round-trip by executing a brisk walk, but this also proved to be a rather daunting challenge as frequent rests were mandatory. It took Blake thirty-five minutes to walk the circuit. His heart was still pounding when he entered the front door.

"Señor Barker," Lorena said, "you should rest a bit. The next time you go out to exercise, you need to remember that la tortuga is the animal that won the race!"

"I swear, Lorena, la tortuga would have kicked my ass today!" Blake replied after catching his breath.

"Your sister, Elizabeth, and I have finished packing up all of

Lynne's clothing. Would you like to take one last look at any-thing before we tape the boxes closed and haul them over to the Salvation Army?" Lorena asked.

Blake was silent for but a moment. He finally concluded, "No, I don't suppose that would be a good idea. That would just be too painful, and I would start up bawling like a baby once again."

Blake helped Lorena and Elizabeth load the few boxes of Lynne's clothes into the trunk of the sedan. If truth be told, Blake's wife did not possess much in the way of anything at the time of her demise. Most of what she had in life was the simple collection of colorful work scrubs that she had worn at the doctor's office where she was employed.

After Elizabeth and Lorena departed to the Salvation Army store where Lynne's clothing would be donated, Blake received a stream of visitors. The doctor's office where Lynne worked had been gracious enough to send over a catered meal that included a whole roasted duck, potatoes au gratin, broccoli with cheese sauce, fresh flour tortillas, and a box of candied pinion nuts. Blake offered Lynne's coworkers an opportunity to stay and visit, but needless to say, visiting a bereaved family member is often a very awkward situation. As these visitors departed, they promised they would all be there for the memorial service that was slated to occur in the next two days.

No sooner had Lynne's coworkers returned to their place of employment at the doctor's office than the doorbell rang yet again. This time, the visitor was decidedly *not* a well-wisher. The person at the door this time was none other than the franchise owner of the Las Cruces Nuts and Bolts hardware shop. Blake assumed that his boss, Mr. I. B. Terdly, had come by to pay his respects. However, this was not the case.

Blake attempted to politely address his catastrophically obese and malodorous employer. "Hello, Irwin, I'm pleased to see you. Would you like to come in?"

"Please refer to me from now on as Mr. Terdly," the franchise owner replied. "I'm not comfortable with any of my employees addressing me by my first name. No, I'm here strictly on business. Look, Mr. Barker, it's come to my attention that you have had a bit of a tough spell lately. You were in some kind of a medical quarantine last week, and now your wife has kicked the bucket."

"Well, that is all very true," Blake said. "In fact, I would have to say this is the worst time I have ever experienced in my entire life."

"None of these issues are my problems, do you understand?" Terdly asked. "I'm wondering now if I perhaps hired the wrong person to be the new manager for my store. As you're currently under probation as an employee, I can terminate you at any time without cause. I understand that your wife's funeral service will be on Thursday. Fine. I expect you back to work bright and early on Monday morning."

"I'll be there bright and early. I promise."

"If you need bereavement time," the shop owner said, "I suggest that you figure out some way to do it on your own accord. By the way, I've suspended any salary for the time that you have been absent without my permission, and I will also be docking your future pay for the inconvenience that you subjected me to during your absence. If you want to keep your job, you need to get off your ass and get back to work by the beginning of next week."

Blake looked on in stunned silence as his corpulent employer left the premises. Immediately after his employer's departure, Blake thought to himself that he should have murdered this nasty, heartless fat bastard on the doorstep. Fortunately, for the time being, rational thoughts ultimately stayed Blake Barker's hand of retribution. As for Mr. I. B. Terdly, this sorry excuse of a human being would certainly not be as fortunate the next time he went out of his way to piss somebody off.

The doorbell rang a third time, and on this occasion it happened to be the tax assessor. "Mr. Barker, allow me to introduce myself. My name is Mateo Levi, and I'm from the assessor's office. It has come to my attention that you no longer are raising alpacas on your farm and that your chicken coop is now gone. You're hereby in violation of the agricultural land use regulations as established by the local municipality. From here on out, you are duly notified that you will be fined one hundred dollars per day until this situation is rectified. I cast shame upon both you and your foolish wife for trying to hoodwink the Land of Enchantment out of property taxes that are owed!"

"Listen to me, you useless tool. My wife just died this weekend, and the federal government disassembled both my alpaca barn and my chicken coop before they put a torch to the ground site. By the way, I have two dozen pecan trees planted out back. They are, as best I can tell, alive and in good shape," Barker responded harshly. "To be honest with you, I don't know shit about trees, but I can still tell you face-to-face that what I planted out there are all still viable and healthy. Am I clear? That alone should confirm to you that my property is still a functional farm."

"Let me be frank with you: I don't care about your petty, silly-ass problems, do you understand?" the tax assessor said. "At this time, your trees are too young to be productive. However, just to show you that the public servants who work for this government are also actually working for the little man, you included, I am going to let you off the hook for just a few days with a warning. The next time I come by for a visit, however, there has to be some evidence of active, immediate commercial agrarian activity. Have a good day, sir."

For Blake, the taxman was just another asshole who had to be added to the growing ledger of names on the official asshole list.

⸺⧫⸺

Because the Department of Defense and the US Department of Biological Warfare had both claimed an active interest in assuming responsibility for performing the official postmortem evaluation on Romero Lopes at the AFIP, the biohazard bag that containing the corpse of the vampiro had been set aside on a gurney awaiting to be transferred by a refrigerated mortuary vehicle to Kirkland Air

Force Base in Albuquerque. Dr. Stern and her diener were, pardon the pun, engrossed in their work, while the CDC physician Dr. Ralph Fairbanks had the unenviable task of evaluating the earthly remains of his former colleague Dr. John Henry. In addition, the forensic pathology team from New Mexico State University College of Medicine toiled away on the multiple autopsies that had to be performed.

Nobody was aware of what was going on when the biohazard bag containing Romero Lopes was slowly and quietly ripped open from the inside. As the vampiro stepped out of his containment bag and placed his feet on the floor, he said, "Hello? I hate to interrupt you nice people at this somewhat awkward moment, as I can readily tell that you are all quite busy."

Romero drew himself up to his full menacing measure and continued. "I really don't mean to be much of a bother; however, as I'm actually quite thirsty, I was wondering if somebody would be so kind as to give me a drink."

Romero proceeded to recite a Latin *ante cibum* which was a culinary challenge that perhaps one chef might post to another: "*Entre tu arte y mi arte, prefiero mi arte.*" The English translation would come across as, "Between your art and my art, I prefer my art." To the members of the autopsy team, this statement was quite alarming, as it readily indicated that the resurrected vampiro Romero Lopes was intent on consuming a robust and satiating meal.

"Although I truly prefer type O positive, I surmise that even type AB negative would do rather well for me. Indeed, I now find myself in bit of a nutritional pinch," Lopes noted. "I would like to thank you all in advance. Your prompt attention to my specific dietary requirements would be most appreciated!"

7

INFECTION

"For the love of Pete, listen to me, Dr. Blanks. For the last time, I did *not* see a knife, a sword, or any other type of a bladed weapon. The son of a bitch made a karate chop, and the next thing I knew was that Roberto's head was rolling across the floor," explained John Stewart.

"No blade of any sort?"

"Not that I could tell," Stewart confirmed. "Besides, who gives two hoots in hell as to how Bob lost his head? When your team came into El Chopo that night, you saw the poor bastard's dome on the floor just like I did."

Dr. Blanks unknowingly released too much information to the line cook when he replied, "Well, I have an unsubstantiated theory about Romero Lopes. I truly believe his behavior is a throwback to an older time and an older place."

John Stewart threw his head back, laughed out loud, and then exclaimed, "Quit jerking my chain, Doc. You can stop right now with this line of nonsense about bubonic plague or some other type of conventional disease bullshit. What a load! Look, I might not have had enough money to go off to get a fancy college education once I graduated from high school, but that sure as shit doesn't mean I'm stupid."

"Nobody said that you were stupid."

"Fine. Tell me the truth, then: Romero has been transformed

into a vampiro!" John Stewart exclaimed. "I've lived in the Rio Grande Valley for years. I've heard the stories. Fess up."

Dr. Blanks shrugged his shoulders as he cast his eyes toward the floor. "Is there anything else you can possibly enlighten me about regarding this whole matter, Mr. Stewart?"

The line cook raised his left index finger into the air as if he were about to say something quite profound. "Yes, come to think about it, there's a very important thing I learned from all of this."

Dr. Blanks slowly nodded as he carefully studied John Stewart's tense facial expression. "Well, son, stand up and testify. What great epiphany have you had about the massacre that occurred at El Chopo?"

"The next time there are some customers who complain that their sopapillas are too cold," Stewart replied, "I'm going to reheat the goddamned things in the microwave for them. In fact, I'll not only do it with a smile, but also I'll give them extra pats of real butter and a half gallon of clover honey to choke it all down with!"

"Yes, in retrospect, that might be a very good idea," Dr. Blanks said with a smile. "In the meantime, I'm sorry to tell you that you're going to be our guest here in isolation for the next five days. Just try to make yourself comfortable."

"So, is 'isolation' a new, sophisticated way to say 'prison'?" Stewart protested.

The scientist from the CDC answered, "You need to relax. Don't make this situation harder than it has to be."

John Stewart was naturally a bit more than curious about his predicament. "Well, what happens after that? Just suppose during my quarantine period that I become transformed into a vampiro. Is Captain Morales going to come back here and put a hole in my head, or would he just starve me to death? If I have any choice in the matter, I'd personally select option number one."

"I promise you, John, I won't allow either of those two terminal events to happen to you," the research scientist from the CDC replied.

Stewart pursed his lips and then replied, "To be honest with you, Dr. Blanks, you might not have too much say-so in the entire matter. I tell you what: if I transform, I insist that your team undertake the task of studying me so that medical science may finally get a handle on this weird shit."

No sooner had John Stewart uttered this rather altruistic proclamation than Captain Morales entered the room. The line cook at that time felt bold enough to tempt fate. He proceeded to openly insult the military officer who, no fewer than two days before, overtly contemplated Stewart's homicide. "Well, look who's come to pay me a visit. The angel of death incarnate has apparently dropped by to finish off what he started in the restroom at El Chopo! You seem disappointed, Captain Morales, that I've not turned into a night crawler as of yet. After all, isn't this why you are here?"

Captain Morales glared at Dr. Blanks intently as he wondered what conversation the two men had engaged in. Blanks raised both his arms in a defensive gesture and said, "Don't look at me, Morales. I had nothing to do with this. Stewart was smart enough to figure this out all on his own accord."

The captain paced back and forth in front of the holding cell that incarcerated John Stewart before he spoke. "Shut up, asshole. You should count your lucky stars that you're still breathing. Mind your p's and q's, buddy boy, as I still might get a crack at you before the end of the week. Dr. Blanks, step out with me and fill me in on where things stand with the Department of Defense and what the boys from the biological warfare division might be up to."

Before Dr. Blanks left the holding cell, he turned to John Stewart and said, "It would seem to me that you have a pretty good idea of what is going on around here. To be frank, we'll likely need your help even if you don't transform into a vampire. I'll come back in a little while and talk to you about some ideas I have."

John Stewart shrugged his shoulders and said, "Well, I certainly fit the description of being a captive audience. You'll know exactly where to find me."

After leaving the holding cell, Captain Morales peered at Dr. Blanks and asked, "Okay, Doc, what's the skinny?"

"An apparent compromise has been hammered out between the Department of Defense and the United States Army Department of Biological Warfare," Dr. Blanks answered. "This is how it will all go down. We have no further authority to perform any postmortem evaluations on the corpse of Romero Lopes. Essentially, I've been instructed to stuff the bastard into an icebox and have him hauled off to Kirkland. The AFIP will grab the ball and run with it from there. Unfortunately, as things usually go, we'll never know the ultimate outcome of what they might discover. Now, nobody is absolutely certain if this current outbreak is on the threshold of winding down or not. The boys in San Antonio have now decided that they only have a desire to evaluate a living specimen, and they'll be giving you a call with a new specific protocol you should follow if you actually are able to harvest a vampiro in the field."

"I can tell you right now, I'm not comfortable allowing *any* infected specimen to leave the damned state," the military captain replied. "What do these geniuses want us to do with our friend John Stewart? I'm certain that 'Uncle Spam' will have specific plans for the future 'bat boy' we have locked up next door in an isolation holding cell."

"How thoughtless of me." Dr. Blanks gave a sly smile when he answered. "It would appear that with all of the stress I've been under since the implementation of the Night Crawler Protocol, I simply forgot to tell either the DOD or the biological warfare research boys in San Antonio about this peculiar predicament. Tell me, Morales, should I call them back and let them know about my silly oversight?"

"Doc, you're one sneaky son of a bitch," Captain Morales said as he chuckled to himself. "Dig this: I strongly suggest at this point that we just let sleeping dogs lie. Are you downstream from me?"

"I am indeed," Dr. Blanks replied, "although I have one simple and humble request: please refrain from pulling out your pecker and copping a whiz in the Rio Bravo if you're indeed upstream from where I'm standing right now."

Momentarily, another soldier arrived. He reported, "You have an emergency phone call from Stumpy Wheeler, Captain Morales. There must be a lot of chaos going on right now down at the morgue. It sounds like you'd better take this call right now."

———

Upon Lopes's unexpected resurrection and subsequent self-liberation from the biohazard body bag, the visage of the vampiro was indeed shocking to behold. As the members of the autopsy team recoiled defensively, various medical implements were reflexively grabbed by the medical personnel to be used as weapons.

When Stumpy Wheeler previously loaded the seared body of Lopes into a sealed vinyl bag at the farmhouse to transport him to the morgue, the ghoul had nearly 100 percent third-degree burns over nearly 100 percent of his body. Now, after only a thirty-six-hour recuperative period, Romero had already autoregenerated nearly 30 percent of his integument. Although there was still a considerable amount of charred and nonviable flesh that hung from his extremities as if they were mere flimsy window drapes, Romero Lopes was now reanimated and was ready to tango. All he needed was a dance partner, willing or otherwise!

Stumpy Wheeler and Sergeant Frey immediately drew their sidearms and ordered Romero Lopes to raise his hands into the air and then drop to his knees. Perhaps Romero Lopes had developed diminished auditory acuity during the time of his incarceration in what was essentially a giant ziplock sandwich bag. Perhaps Romero Lopes acquired an expressive aphasia and could not verbally respond to the orders that were given to him. Perhaps Romero Lopes was simply an obstinate and evil son of a bitch who had difficulty accepting social hierarchy simply because he no longer needed to defer or show any respect to authoritarian figures. For whatever reason, Romero Lopes held the order to obey that the military personnel had given in utter disregard.

Like the curandera Lorena, Romero Lopes had known Miguel Pastore all his life. Sadly, that did little to spare Miguel from being the first victim in the bloody tidal wave that was about to crash down upon the members of the autopsy team. Lopes swooped in like a peregrine to take a quick bite from Miguel's neck. Miguel attempted to slash away at his assailant with a short bone saw, and although he scored several strikes on the side of Romero's face with the stainless steel orthopedic surgical tool, it had no bearing on the fact that the morgue diener had been bitten by the vampiro and was possibly infected.

Once he had tasted the diener's essence, Romero Lopes spit Miguel's blood out of his mouth and onto the floor in disgust while saying, "Miguel, you taste like shit! You're pretty pathetic if you are only eating *arroz y frijoles*! You need to hang out with the gringos a bit more often."

The diener raised the saw blade to make another strike on the vampiro, but Lopes made a fist with his right hand and popped the diener in the face with enough force to knock him to the ground. From his own experience from the last night crawler outbreak that occurred back in 1979, Miguel realized that he was now powerless to try to help his colleagues who were in the autopsy room. He only had one chance to save a single person, and that person was himself.

While Frey and Wheeler discharged their weapons in the direction of Romero, Miguel crawled on his hands and knees to try to escape the gunfire. Lightheaded and unable to make it to the exit, Miguel decided that the next best course of action was simply to hide. He found refuge in the sixteen-square-foot electrical utility room where the control panel that managed the temperature of each individual vault in the morgue was located. He locked the door from the inside and was able to peer through the ventilation grate at the bottom of the door, giving him a front-row view of the carnage that was unfolding.

Dr. Stern was valiantly waving about an electric oscillating cranial saw that was running at high speed when a stray round from Wheeler's pistol inadvertently struck the resident physician Lucretia McWeevil in her upper-midsternal region. She slowly slumped over one of the autopsy tables. Dr. Thomas instinctively attempted to resuscitate her as Stumpy Wheeler received a vicious head butt from the vampiro that had left him unconscious. Dr. Thomas applied direct pressure to the open chest wound of his young colleague, not knowing she was already dead.

The resuscitative efforts that Dr. Thomas initiated made him an easy target for Romero Lopes, who moved in for the kill. Dr. Thomas was briefly mesmerized when he looked Romero Lopes right into his jaundiced eyes. He was able to fend off the vampiro as the ghoul verbally tormented his next meal. "Look, Doc, I don't mean to be rude, but you should have brought your own dance partner. This woman is *mine!*"

Lopes pushed Dr. Thomas aside and grabbed the corpse of Dr. McWeevil. "When I was a little boy, I watched my mother and father dancing a tango on the kitchen floor," Lopes whispered into the ear of the dead pathology resident. "Please give me the honor of the next dance." The vampiro started to dance with the dead body, all the while singing the Cole Porter lyrics to Leroy Anderson 1952 hit song called "Blue Tango": "Here am I with you in a world of blue, and we're dancing to the tango when we first met. While the music plays, we recall the days when our love was a tune that we couldn't soon forget. As I kiss your cheek, we don't have to speak. The violins, like a choir, expressed the desire we used to know not long ago. So just hold me tight in your arms tonight."

With the dead body of Dr. Lucretia McWeevil draped over his shoulders, Lopes made high-speed passing attacks on the now doomed Dr. Thomas. The professor of pathology was about to die, but he didn't know it yet. Even if he had, there was, sadly, nothing he could do about it. Initially when Dr. Thomas was strafed by the claws and teeth of his assailant, Romero tore way at the hazmat suit the pathologist was wearing. Finally, after the extremities and the head and neck region of Dr. Thomas were finally and fatally exposed, it was time for the vampiro to partake of this delectable tasty snack at the buffet table.

Armed with a scalpel, Dr. Thomas flailed away in futility at each of Romero's swooping strikes. It was as if Romero was a bipedal piranha! The pathologist's flesh was slowly stripped away, and his blood was ingested. Each lightning-fast offensive parry that Romero employed against the scalpel vainly wielded by Dr. Thomas as a defensive foil only ensured that the pathologist's strength would quickly falter. Nonetheless, Dr. Thomas remained defiant to the very end. He cried out, "Stay still, goddamn you! I'm going to cut your heart out!"

Romero, continuing to torment the dying man, said, "No you won't, but you have certainly given me a great idea. Come to think of it, a beating heart would be a pretty tasty treat right about now!"

Out of bullets, Sergeant Frey charged the vampiro with a Ka-Bar. Lopes was briefly distracted as he continued to enthusiastically dine on Dr. Thomas, who at that time was struggling for his last breath.

The sergeant's knife was plunged deep into the flank of Romero Lopes, missing the vampiro's kidney by a mere centimeter. If Romero's renal artery had been severed by a knife wound, the blood-thirsty ghoul would have bled to death internally in mere moments, as there would have been no way for the vampiro's body to have enough time to recuperate from such an injury. Sadly, such was not the case.

While Romero fell to his knees and cried out in anguish, Dr. Stern and Ralph Fairbanks found this to be the perfect opportunity to try to finish off the vampiro with the oscillating blade of the electric cranial saw. As the two pathologists charged the vampiro,

Romero Lopes reached out and grabbed Dr. Fairbanks around the neck and ripped his throat out, and he did it straight through the doctor's hazmat suit. The CDC physician was dead before he hit the floor. Upon witnessing her colleague's grisly demise, Dr. Stern momentarily hesitated. Although she quickly gathered her wits and finally pressed the oscillating electric saw against the skull of the vampiro, it was too late. Romero regained the upper hand before the powerful blade penetrated his braincase.

The vampiro pushed Dr. Stern away while he pulled the knife out of his flank and dropped it to the floor. Then he slammed Sergeant Frey's head on the top of autopsy table to crush his skull. Once this surprisingly formidable adversary was neutralized, Romero turned his attention to Dr. Stern, who at that time was paralyzed with fear. "Why don't you just be a good girl and hand me the saw. I promise if you cooperate that I'll be gentle with you."

Although still somewhat dazed from the concussion that he suffered, Private Wheeler had the wherewithal to cry out from his recumbent position. "Run, Dr. Stern, run!"

Romero Lopes turned to Wheeler and said, "I should eat you too, but I need to keep you alive. I want you to be able to stand up and testify about what I'm truly capable of doing. Would you be a good boy and afford me this simple courtesy?"

Wheeler jumped to his feet and took a swing at Romero with the butt end of his depleted sidearm, but the vampiro simply caught Wheeler's right fist with his left hand as if he were an outfielder catching a line drive. After he peeled the pistol out of the private's grip, the vampiro ripped away the glove on Wheeler's hazmat suit and slowly extended each finger of the soldier's right hand. One by one, Romero proceeded to daintily bite off Wheeler's fingers as if biting into a chocolate bar.

It was as if the ghoul had been reared in the Old World etiquette of gentile table manners. After each bite, Romero made certain to gently dab at his fangs with a torn scrap of cloth from Stumpy's hazmat suit. The soon-to-be mutilated National Guard private was rather pleased that the vampiro was indeed polite and gracious when each digit was sheared off at an interphalangeal joint.

Each severed finger was then forced into Wheeler's mouth before Romero issued a new set of instructions to the private. "I want you to suck on your own fingers and stay quiet. If you try to cause a fuss one more time, I will come over there and finish you off. Am I making myself clear?"

Stumpy nodded his head in affirmation as he collapsed against the back wall and looked on in horror. Ironically, he came to the conclusion that his lifelong nickname, Stumpy, was now at last well deserved.

Dr. Stern should have listened to Wheeler's sound advice. She should have run for her life. If she had only tried, maybe she would have made it out of the autopsy room. Even if she had only pulled the fire alarm, she would have been saved. Sadly, that was not to be.

Romero was not through dining. He turned his attention to Dr. Stern and he spoke to her with a very soft and soothing voice. He addressed the doomed woman much in the same fashion that he had used to address Blake Barker's ill-fated alpaca.

"Okay, what I would like you to do now is to remove your clothes, and then I would like to lie facedown on the table in front of me. Will you promise me that you'll stay as still as you possibly can throughout this whole process?"

Like a lamb being led to the slaughter, the victim was unable to disobey Romero's orders. There was something irresistible about him that forced Dr. Stern to complicitly contribute to her own pending demise. "I will do everything that you ask me to do." With that, the final item on the dessert menu disrobed and assumed the prone position on the table. The vampiro began to lick away at his new victim vigorously.

Dr. Stern, keeping her word, remained completely still when the vampiro turned on the electric oscillating cranial saw and plunged the gyrating blade into her spine between the C7 and T1 vertebral body, which instantly rendered acute quadriplegia. Once this was done, the vampiro rolled Dr. Stern over onto her back to allow her to face the ceiling.

She was fully conscious and able to speak, but she found that the act of breathing had become a modestly taxing experience. Having no volition of her own at that point, she tried to maintain a cheerful disposition. To placate the vampire, she said, "Well, I guess all in all, that didn't hurt too bad. It's interesting that I now find that I can barely move my fingers! You will be happy to know, however, that I'm not particularly uncomfortable at this time."

"Well, that's just dandy," Romero Lopes replied.

Dr. Stern felt some pressure sensations but no major pain when the vampiro again turned on the oscillating blade of the cranial saw and cut away at her breastplate to expose *el corazón*, the pinnacle pulsating muscular organ of the vascular system. The size of a human fist, the heart is located in the mediastinum, which is anatomically found beneath the sternum and between the two lungs. Once the pathologist's pleural cavity was surgically violated, her symptom of shortness of breath, which was mild at first, dramatically worsened.

Miguel Pastore, still hidden in the locked electronic control room, had to avert his eyes from what was about to happen. Although the diener's blood, for whatever reason, had left a bad taste in the mouth of the vampiro, lethal danger was just a few feet away. Miguel could end up back upon the menu before the day was over.

Dr. Stern batted her eyelids and gave Romero a "come hither" grin when he pulled up within an inch of her and said, "I am going to give you a special treat since you have been so cooperative with me today. How would you like to see your beating heart when I rip it out of your chest? Boy, that would be a hoot, would it not?"

Although the vampiro lacked an accordion or a brass section to accompany his musical rendition, Lopes began to sing a verse from the old Latin song "Cielito Lindo" made popular by Los Panchos in the 1950s: "*Ay, ay, ay ay, canta y no lorres, porque cantando se alegran, cielito lindo los corazones."* How lovely! The precise meaning of these romantic lyrics, when translated into *el lenguaje de los gringosas,* is "Sing and don't cry, sing and be happy, my darling beloved heart!" As it turned out, it was actually an appropriate tune that Romero Lopes sang in a captivating baritone voice.

By design, he made this selection to seduce his next meal. For her part, Dr. Stern could only stare at the ceiling with her eyes wide open and with an alluring smile of anticipated romantic fulfillment. After the vampiro peeled away the tough, naturally protective fibrous pericardial sack that protected her heart throughout her life (much like a biological shock absorber), he extracted the pulsating organ forcefully.

The heart contracts on its own accord through the electrochemical impulses generated by its internal pacemaker located in the superior portion of the heart that medically is known as the A-V node. Even when a heart is surgically extracted from the human body, the muscular tissue will, at least for a short while, continue to carry out its assigned biological duty to perform as an efficient vascular pump.

The pheromone-induced spell that the vampiro had cast over Dr. Stern was abruptly broken. Once Romero presented Dr. Stern with her own beating heart, she was still conscious! Dr. Stern was forced to consider her dire circumstances in the last eight seconds that her cerebral cortex continued to function. Although she was overcome by the compulsion to say a prayer, it was sadly far too late for that. Mercifully, her life would be over in but another moment.

⸻

After enjoying the heart and liver of Dr. Stern, Romero picked up the corpse of Lucretia McWeevil and began to dance. This time, the evil ghoul elected to hum the song "An der schönen blauen

Donau," which is German for "By the Beautiful Blue Danube." This is of course the famous waltz by the Austrian composer Johann Strauss II, originally composed in 1866. After taking several well-choreographed spins around the autopsy room, Romero Lopes suddenly came to a dead stop. He violently tossed the dead body of his dance partner aside when he ascertained that something was awry.

At first, Romero took his index finger and carefully counted the number of dead bodies in the room. When he finally came to the realization that somehow the body of the diener was missing, he flittered about the room in a delicate and almost feminine manner to investigate if Miguel Pastore was still alive and hiding some-where. Perhaps the diener had simply crawled off to find a quiet place where he could die in peace. At least this was Romero's hope.

When the search failed to yield any evidence of Miguel Pastore, either dead or alive, Romero looked up to the ceiling and bellowed out in anger. He rushed toward Stumpy Wheeler, pulled the severed fingers from the injured man's mouth, and asked, "Tell me now, what happened to the man named Miguel? He was the first person I bit, but he doesn't seem to be around here anywhere. Be truthful with me, or I will put your head in a sack and keep it as a souvenir."

In the melee, Wheeler had actually lost track of what happened to Miguel Pastore, but this particular predicament presented him with an opportunity to deceive the vampiro into thinking that perhaps the diener somehow escaped the slaughterhouse. "Well, he booked toward the door and bolted out of here the second after you bit him in the neck!"

Romero Lopes, furious, asked, "Why didn't you tell me this information earlier?"

"Well, you didn't ask me, asshole," Stumpy Wheeler replied. "Besides, I'm quite certain that everybody else witnessed him fleeing the autopsy room. Just ask anybody in here. Oh, my mis-take; everybody in here is already dead except for me. Before

Pastore split, I heard him tell Sergeant Frey that he was going to bring back help. A *lot* of help. Frankly, I'm quite surprised that George Armstrong Custer and the Seventh Cavalry aren't here yet. Maybe they're just going to nuke us from orbit. What do you think?"

"What would I care?" Romero Lopes asked. "After all, *yo soy un gran brujo.*"

"It would seem to me that you heal up pretty quick, but I'm not certain if you'll be able to haul off and get any meaningful chassis work done once you're reduced to subatomic particles from the blast of a kiloton-range tactical nuclear warhead. I'd guess your core body temp would reach, oh, I don't know, maybe a million degrees Celsius or so if it's a ground-zero surface burst."

"You're full of it."

"Oh, am I now?" Stumpy asked. "I suspect you've heard of the Night Crawler Protocol. What in hell do you think that's all about? You don't think for a minute that Uncle Sam is going to let your nasty-ass disease spread outside the confines of New Mexico, now, do you? If I were in your shoes, I would strongly consider the prospects of getting the hell out of Dodge."

"Maybe I should haul you out to the front parking lot, and we can get vaporized together," Romero said. "That would be romantic!"

"It's your call," Stumpy said. "In any event, I'm quite surprised that you didn't see Miguel Pastore bail out of here. He ran away from the autopsy room like he was a scalded cat. He did it right in front of your face! You're an idiot. You weren't paying attention when he said adios. You probably had your head up your ass, like you this very moment."

"If I were you, I'd be very careful about what words you choose to say to me right about now."

"Now that it is all said and done, I should have unloaded my entire magazine into your skull before I scraped you up and put you into the body bag when I found your body at the burned-out ranch house. You are, without a doubt, the lowest and nastiest form of life that's walking about on the face of this planet," Stumpy said. "Hell's bells, boy, you're a pussy. I'm not afraid of you. Besides killing me, what else could you possibly do to me to make things any worse than they are right now? What are you going to do to me now; bite my dick head off, you dickhead?"

Romero scoffed at Stumpy Wheeler. "Tell me the truth. The military isn't going to nuke us, now are they?"

"Do you have any idea why I'm here?" Stumpy asked. "Do you have any idea about the nature of the military team that burned down your farmhouse during the wee hours of Sunday morning?"

"No," Lopes answered. "Who in hell are you people?"

"We're the military contingency for the Night Crawler Protocol, which was just initiated after this most recent outbreak of human vampirism," Wheeler honestly answered. "If a containment breakdown were to occur, the federal government would indeed utilize low-yield tactical nukes if necessary. Make no mistake about it. Go ahead and stick around if you want to find out. I'll see you in hell when it is all over, and I promise that I'll kick your sorry ass for all eternity, you sad-sack bloodsucking tick."

With that, Romero Lopes dropped to his knees and repeatedly, yet gently, licked the face of Stumpy Wheeler. When the vampiro reached his hand down the pants of the soldier to manipulate the private's privates, Stumpy summarily rejected the amorous advances.

Perhaps it had something to do with the fact that every finger of Wheeler's right hand had been violently severed. Stumpy also likely had a residual amount of emotional agitation, in addition to being afflicted with at least a modest amount of lingering discomfort that throbbed in his now fingerless mitt. For what ever reason, the soldier was now resistant to the vampiro's intoxicating pheromones. As Stumpy Wheeler was actually disgusted and horrified, the injured soldier was unable to achieve an erection despite

Romero's most vigorous efforts at flogging the poor soul's reproductive member.

In fact, Stumpy was more than a bit perturbed that he was now,
well, "stumpy." Because he was afflicted with acute erectile dysfunction, this displeased Romero Lopes immensely.

Wheeler's rather inconsiderate rejection of the vampiro's amorous intentions left his assailant embarrassed and in a rather foul
disposition. Sexually frustrated, Romero gently nuzzled into the
loins of Stumpy Wheeler and bit off the soldier's penis at the curly
cues before fleeing the morgue without saying another word.

Unbeknownst to Stumpy Wheeler, his bold proclamation that
the federal government would consider utilizing low-yield tactical
nuclear weapons in a situation where there was a vampiro containment breakdown turned out to be no idle threat. What Wheeler
unwittingly boasted about was indeed the secret last-ditch contingency plan that was buried deep within the top-secret documents
that outlined the final chapter of the Night Crawler Protocol.

———

Upon Romero Lopes's hasty departure, Stumpy Wheeler
crawled over to the telephone that was sitting on the pathologist's
desk in the autopsy room. He was able to place a phone call to
Captain Morales, who was still at the detention center where John
Stewart was being held in isolation. Fortunately, Wheeler was able
to explain to his commanding officer the gravity of the situation:
all the members of the autopsy team were dead, and there was now
a vampire containment breach! Before Wheeler collapsed, he made
one request: "Send help, Captain. I'm hurt. Hurt bad ..."

Miguel Pastore remained securely hidden within the confines of
the locked electrical control closet while he awaited the cavalry to
arrive and save the day. He felt compelled to render aid and provide
comfort to the critically injured private, but as the diener had been
bitten, he had no idea how he might be treated by Captain Morales

or Dr. Blanks from the CDC upon their arrival. The better part of valor would be to see how the military would respond to one of their very own who had been attacked and bitten.

If it turned out that Stumpy Wheeler was going to get appropriate medical care, then Miguel would avail himself to the authorities. However, if it appeared that the injured Stumpy Wheeler would be treated like an enemy combatant, Miguel Pastore would be ready to go underground and on the lam. Time would soon tell what Miguel's best course of action would be.

Dr. Blanks turned to Morales and asked, "What was that important phone call you received from Stumpy Wheeler? Did they find any important information during the autopsy procedures?"

"No, I don't think so," Morales lied. "Stumpy called to tell me that the boys from Kirkland are on their way over and that I have to go over to the morgue and do some paperwork before those fatheads at the DOD take over the management of this investigation. I'll give you a call as soon as I get over there, and then I'll give you an update."

⚜

Captain Morales quickly donned a fresh hazmat suit before he entered the autopsy suite. Stumpy Wheeler, weak from the attack, could barely speak. He looked up in surprise at Morales and asked, "Where are the rest of the troops? For the love of my penis, please don't tell me you came in here alone!"

Morales brushed aside the concerns of his private and asked, "Where's the vampiro? Is he hiding out in here somewhere?"

"No, Elvis has left the building," Stumpy answered, "but it doesn't mean he won't come back. Captain, you're not going to believe this, but we threw everything we had at that son of a bitch, and we couldn't stop him. He just kept coming! He just kept coming! He just kept coming! Frey unloaded an entire clip of nine millimeters into him. It barely slowed Lopes down. Then the sergeant lunged forward to pig-stick the bloodsucker with his Ka-Bar. Sarge rammed it home right to the hilt! Listen, Cap, I was hoping you were going to bring an entire deployment. We have to get the hell out of here! I need to get to the hospital as soon as possible. If not, I'm going to bleed to death!"

Morales pressed for more details to piece together what went down. "What exactly happened when the vampiro got stabbed?"

"That bastard Lopes howled at first when he took the blade, but he just pulled that seven-inch Ka-Bar out of his back with a smile on his face!" Wheeler added. "Then he bit off all the fingers on my right hand as if enjoying a gourmet snack. I must admit, he was at least polite about the whole matter. In any event, there was nothing I could do to stop him. After he jammed my severed fingers into my mouth, I thought he was going to give me a deluxe hum job, but that was not the case; he proceeded to bite off my pecker at the base."

"Your pecker?" Morales asked. "Well, where is the damned thing?"

"Can't rightly say. I think he ate it. I shit you not!" Stumpy exclaimed. "No bun, no mustard, no relish, no onions, no chili, no grated cheese, and none of any of the other bullshit condiments that one would likely throw on a wiener."

Stumpy Wheeler was becoming delirious as a consequence of his blood loss, and he began to spew a semicoherent rant. "I recently learned that you can get tossed in the hoosegow in some precincts if you try to apply ketchup to a wiener. Or is it catsup? Well, I'm not readily certain if there is any real difference between those two tasty tomato-based culinary condiments. If the truth be told, the Department of Education considers ketchup, or perhaps catsup if indeed that's what it's called, to be a vegetable if served as part of a government-sponsored school lunch. I shit you not."

"Take it easy, son. Save your breath," Morales said. "You are not making any sense."

"Do you know what the mandatory items are that constitute a bona fide Chicago dog?"

"No, I don't."

"Well, let me give you the lowdown: take a red hot, slap it in a poppy seed bun, and add mustard, (or is it 'muff turds'?), fluorescent green sweet relish, chopped onions, a dill wedge, tomato slices, and sport peppers. Now, I need to be honest with you about something: sometimes I put a little bit of mayonnaise on one side of the bun. It adds a little bit of a greasy texture to a Chicago dog. Helps it slide right down the ol' gullet. At this point in my life, I don't think I'm going to be worrying about fat or cholesterol. It might be sacrilegious, but I exchange the sport peppers for jalapeños. After all, I'm from Texas!"

"I know you are, Stumpy."

"I think those assholes who bitch and moan about sport peppers being too spicy are just a bunch of wimps. They should try jalapeños; now that's something that'll wake 'em up."

"You are absolutely right, Stumpy," Morales said as he cautiously surveyed the room to make certain that everybody else was already dead.

"Jalapeños are far superior to sport peppers," Stumpy professed. "There's one last point that I'm compelled to emphasize, Captain."

"Lay it down, son."

"For God's sake, don't ever put ketchup on a hot dog!" Stumpy proclaimed. "That'll just fuck up everything all the way to last Friday, and then some."

"I'm down stream to you on that matter, Stumpy. No ketchup, no catsup, or anything in between—got it." Morales said. "I can't figure out why Lopes left you alive. Perhaps he just wanted to infect you."

"Maybe so. I'm starting to ramble a bit," Stumpy realized. "Frankly, Cap, I've had a rather unpleasant day. In the end, I think Romero didn't kill me outright because he wanted me to be a witness to what he had done. I also think you're correct: he was planning on turning me into a vampiro. I tell you right now, Captain

Morales, I'm not about to put up with that vampire horseshit. No, sir! Not one bit. No how, no way. Do you think I might have been infected? I don't want to turn into a vampire."

The officer replied, "Take it easy, son. Help is on the way. Don't worry; I'm not about to allow you to turn into a vampire. It's not going to happen on my watch. I promise, I'm going to take care of you."

"You're a good man, Cap."

"Before I do, tell me something. I see a knife on the floor by the autopsy table. Is that the Ka-Bar that Sergeant Frey used? If so, that is an important piece of scientific evidence. If we can harvest the vampire's blood off the blade, then perhaps we can figure out what we're dealing with here."

Stumpy Wheeler pointed to the bloody knife using the index finger of his left hand to confirm that Morales was indeed looking at the right weapon. As was the case, Stumpy only had a left index finger, the only index finger that Stumpy had left. "It is right there, Captain. You got it."

Morales used a pair of forceps to pick up the bloody knife, and then he deposited the weapon into a plastic specimen bag. Then he set the kit on the edge of the middle autopsy table. He took a piece of paper and a ballpoint pen and wrote the following words on the bag in large block letters: KNIFE WITH VAMPIRO BLOOD COLLECTED BY SGT. FREY.

Once done, the National Guard Captain put the ballpoint pen in the hand of the corpse of Dr. Thomas. Morales then turned to his critically wounded soldier and said, "It's time, Stumpy. I need to take care of you now."

The officer found the spent sidearm that belonged to the late Sergeant Frey. He pulled out the empty magazine and inserted one live round from his own weapon into the clip.

Although his sensorium was clouded, Stumpy Wheeler was starting to become quite alarmed as he realized what was about to go down. "Captain, what in hell do you think—"

The question was never finished, as the weapon was discharged straight into the heart of Stumpy Wheeler. Once Morales confirmed that the soldier was dead, he placed the weapon back into the right hand of the dead body of Sergeant Frey to make it appear that Wheeler had been accidentally shot by friendly fire during the bloody, chaotic melee.

Of course, there would be no fingerprints to contend with, as Captain Morales was wearing a full hazmat suit that included protective gloves when he murdered poor Stumpy. Although Morales was simply following orders from D.C., he nonetheless did what he believed had to be done. There was no way in hell that the captain was going to allow one of his beloved soldiers to transform into *un vampiro malo*.

Miguel Pastore witnessed the murder of Stumpy Wheeler in stunned silence. There was no way that he would now come out of hiding and show up in front of the authorities. It was clear at the time that if Captain Morales realized that Miguel had been bitten, the misfortunate diener would meet the exact same fate that had befallen the dearly departed Stumpy Wheeler. After all, Miguel Pastore probably also had the infection after being bitten in the neck, although the vampiro had found the taste of the diener's blood to be unpalatable for whatever reason.

Once Captain Morales stepped out into the hallway, where he stripped off his hazmat suit, he wandered off to find a telephone to call Dr. Blanks and inform him of the catastrophe he had just discovered. Now that this one loose end concerning Stumpy Wheeler was successfully tied up, it was time for Captain Morales to order a full deployment of the night crawler emergency task force to arrive at the morgue and take care of the business at hand.

Captain Morales would of course have to claim that he hadn't stepped inside the autopsy room before anybody else arrived. The story he would profess during the upcoming mandatory debriefing would be that he simply peered through the door's window into the autopsy suite and saw absolute mayhem and then turned away to call for backup. In fact, the officer would soon profess that he had concerns that Romero Lopes may have still been on the premises, and perhaps he was even still hiding out in the autopsy suite, although Morales secretly knew that such was not the case. If he were able to sling this platter of corned beef hash with emotional conviction, he was certain he would be able to skate away from the heinous crime he had just committed.

As soon as Captain Morales slipped down the hallway that led away from the autopsy suite in an effort to find a different telephone with an alternative extension number, Miguel Pastore abandoned his hiding post in the electrical control closet of the morgue and he quickly and quietly disappeared into the twilight.

8

SIBLINGS

The transmitter for the WOAI radio station was not located in San Antonio but was actually in the small township of Marion, Texas. Long ago, this fifty-thousand-watt blowtorch was bestowed a specific and highly coveted Clear Channel designation by the FCC. If anybody in the Lone Star State was looking for a stimulating talk/news radio format, it could be readily found at the 1200 mark on the amplitude-modulated (AM) dial. The station's electromagnetic transmissions could always be easily received throughout South Texas, and sometimes, just sometimes, the transmission could actually be heard all over North America, especially on cold, clear nights when the signal would bounce off the ionosphere. Who knows? Perhaps the radio signal could be heard as far as away as the planet Mars. Although it had abandoned its musical format years ago, people still tuned into WOAI to find out what was going on in the world.

It was a sibling tradition for Miguel and his sister, Lorena, to try to find the WOAI signal on the simple transistor radio they shared. Late at night when the children were scared, lonely, or perhaps spiritually lost, they would crawl into bed together with a flashlight and scan the dial on the radio to try to capture a communication signal from some other wild and untamed civilization from some other wild and untamed town called San Antonio. Incidentally, the

Alamo City was six hundred miles away on the nose from where the children were reared.

Whenever they were able to tune in to the signal from WOAI, they would squeal with delight. They would often listen together until the wee hours of the morning, until one of two things would occur: either they would fall asleep while they were holding each other's hand, or else they would be busted by *su madre y su padre*, who would lovingly turn off the radio and then gently tuck their beloved children into their own separate beds, after a soft and angelic kiss had been rendered upon their foreheads. It was a beautiful kinship that the siblings shared. It was a beautiful family that the siblings shared. In the end, it would be a beautiful memory that they would cherish until their final days.

⸻⚬⸻

It was now late winter, but it would be still be many weeks before the New Mexico State University Aggies would begin their clandestine spring training for the upcoming 1986 college football season. Between the hash marks on the practice field, it was clear that the grass turf had sustained serious, but certainly not life-threatening, injuries. As Miguel Pastore stood in the middle of the practice field waiting for his sister to arrive, it was already approaching the midnight hour. Miguel brought along a small transistor radio, and he tried in vain to find a long-distance electromagnetic umbilical tether with the state of Texas, or any other civilization for that matter.

If he had only found a signal, any signal, perhaps he could have been reconnected to a universe that seemingly was no longer controlled by the laws of Newtonian physics. Miguel felt as if he were hurtling away from the life he had known at the speed of light, and soon he would be cast into a dark and dangerous place where even the energetic photons generally found within what is known as the visible spectrum of light would be unable to penetrate.

Miguel Pastore had time to deeply contemplate the circle of life as he looked upon the dry brown leaves that the wind had blown across the dry brown winter turf. It was his conviction that intelligent design was self-evident. Within a mere few weeks, the landscape would yet again start to dramatically change. As the days would begin to lengthen, there would be a regeneration of life-sustaining chlorophyll, and soon the world would return to the lovely color of green.

It was this very world of budding new life that Miguel would soon no longer be connected with. He had come to believe that if the bite that he'd received from Romero Lopes would actually lead to an acute transformation into vampirism, his remaining existence would be a perpetual winter of dry brown leaves being blown across a seemingly lifeless turf of dry brown grass. He would soon be consigned to a dark and cold void lacking not only color but also what was left of his human essence.

Painfully aware, one way or another, that his projected life expectancy could be radically different from the biblically projected three score and ten years, Miguel became tearfully reminiscent of his lost youth and the life that he had so enjoyed with his sister and parents so many years ago. That was all gone now. Sadly, for all living persons, the past can never be the present, and when it's all said and done, what will any of us have left but memories?

⎯⎯⎯⎯⎯⎯

"I don't know for certain, but I don't think the wound in your neck looks too bad right now," Lorena hopefully said to her younger brother as she dabbed away at the bite marks on his neck with a handkerchief.

"Easy now!" Miguel protested as he pushed his sister's hand away.

Lorena noted that there was very little redness around the puncture marks. She didn't detect any swelling that would suggest there was pus accumulating in the soft tissues adjacent to the injuries. "I hope that you're up to date on your tetanus booster shot," Lorena said with cautious optimism to her younger brother.

"Tetanus?!" Miguel exclaimed. "Lorena, are you kidding me? What in hell are you talking about? At this time, why would I ever give two shits, or even a flying fuck, about tetanus?"

"I'm just trying to help," Lorena said as she defensively stepped back from her brother, who'd become unexpectedly agitated.

"Well, if that's the case, you're not trying very damned hard. As best as I can tell," Miguel surmised, "contracting a terminal case of tetanus would be a blessing. As for now, all that I care about is whether or not I've been infected with whatever causes human vampirism!"

"Maybe you didn't get infected," Lorena bravely added.

"Oh, yeah?" Miguel said. "Maybe I did. That's the *only* damned thing that I'll ever worry about for the rest of my miserable life. After all, if I somehow get through this, the rest of my existence on this planet will be gravy. Pure gravy. *¿Entiendes usted?* What else could possibly matter?"

"You better calm down right now and lower your voice, Miguel," Lorena replied. "You know I don't like it when you use foul language."

Miguel put his right thumb up to his mouth and began to nervously drag his thumbnail across his front teeth. It created a clicking sound reminiscent to the noise that his old bicycle used to make after he had affixed a playing card to the front suspension forks with a clothespin. In his youth, it was great fun to have a playing card protruding into the bicycle spokes as he cruised about the neighborhood.

"Tell me something, Lorena, what percentage of patients who get bit by un vampiro will actually turn into un vampiro?" Miguel asked. "Is it 20 percent?"

"*No se,*" Lorena answered.

"Is it 50 percent?"

"No se," Lorena answered.

"Is it 90 percent?"

"No se."

"Tell me something, Lorena: what is the projected natural life expectancy of a patient who actually gets attacked by one of these ghouls and then turns into un vampiro?" Miguel asked. "Is it fifty years?"

"No se."

"Is it one hundred fifty years?"

"No se."

"Is it five hundred years?"

"No se."

"You were only twenty-six years old when the last outbreak occurred. I distinctly recall the time when *la vieja bruja del mar* told you that these outbreaks would only occur about every two decades, but this one has appeared after only a seven-year hiatus. Do you believe that the cyclical nature of this disease is now going to be occurring more frequently?"

"No se."

"If so, is it a consequence of the fact that human beings are destroying our own planet, or is it from sunspots, or is El Diablo on the loose, or is it because the Democrats are controlling the House and the Republicans have the Senate?"

"No se. Please, *Hermano*, there's nothing I can tell you that you do not already know," Lorena said.

Frustrated, Miguel continued interrogating his younger sister. "Although you may be una curandera with a respectable reputation in this community, it sounds like to me that you don't know shit about shit! If somebody is going to transform into un vampiro, how long does it generally take?"

"When I was held under quarantine with the Barker family, the government officials from the CDC and the military from the National Guard kept us locked up for an entire week," Lorena explained. "Based upon that observation alone, I suspect that the authorities believe that if somebody does not undergo a transformation by the one-week mark postexposure, then a transformation is not likely to happen. Personally, I believe that whatever microbiological entity, if such a thing is indeed responsible for human vampirism, must have a very short incubation period when the infection is horizontally transmitted from one human being to another."

Miguel's angst certainly could not be relieved by his sister's theory. "That's not good enough, Lorena. I need a solid and definite answer." Miguel's prognosis of dedifferentiation into a bloodthirsty and murderous predator certainly could not be projected by what was merely an imposed contingent quarantine that was based upon an unsubstantiated postulate at best.

"So, can you guarantee me that if I make it out to the one-week mark from the time that I was bitten and I do not undergo a transformation by then, I will definitely be in the clear? Is that what you are saying?" Miguel asked.

Lorena threw up her hands in disgust and answered one last time. "Goddamn it, Miguel, can't you see? I just don't know for certain!"

"You better calm down right now and lower your voice, Lorena," Miguel replied. "You know I don't like it when you use foul language."

Lorena tried to embrace her older sibling, who also happened to be the very best friend that she had ever had, but Miguel held her at arm's length. Perhaps it was time for Miguel to withdraw into physical and emotional isolation. After all, if a canid or other social creature is facing a terminal illness, it may wander away from its pack to die alone. Could it be that the dying animal behaves in this fashion because it has empathy for its pack mates and it hopes to spare its extended family members the grief and heartache that will invariably occur when the life of the doomed creature has finally drawn to a conclusion?

Maybe that theory is just a load of anthropomorphic hogwash. It could be that the terminally ill animal simply wanders away from its pack mates because it instinctively knows it will likely be eaten by its extended family members even before it's able to draw its last breath. Perhaps human beings are not much different. In any event, Lorena was intuitively aware that her beloved brother was now embracing a strategic emotional retreat. She began to weep.

—◦◦◦◦◦◦—

Dr. Ron Shiftless and his team from the United States Army Department of Biological Warfare had just flown in from San Antonio. In addition to the boys from the Lone Star State, a full-bird colonel named Augustus Placard dropped in from Fort Huachuca on a special assignment to help mold some solid form from the chaotic void left behind as a consequence of the bloody battle at the county morgue. Augustus Placard was present to greet Dr. Shiftless and his minions from Texas upon their arrival.

Although they were definitely not on friendly terms by any stretch of the imagination, Ron Shiftless and Colonel Placard had served together as snipers during the Southeast Asian war games just prior to the time that the United States' interdiction in the Vietnam conflict turned to shit in a handbasket during the 1968 Tet Offensive.

After the war, Placard remained with the military snd his twenty-year stint was soon drawing to a conclusion. Before he was put out to pasture, however, he was definitely looking for an opportunity to leave some kind of noteworthy legacy.

The fact that the United States of America had lost the Vietnam War as a consequence of feckless politicians had left a perpetual bitter taste in Colonel Placard's mouth. Placard was bound and determined to end his military career with a win for the home team. Standing at 5'11" with salt-and-pepper hair, he was as fit and trim as on the very day that he first joined the army almost two decades before.

The military career of Dr. Ron Shiftless came to a much more abrupt conclusion when he contracted a severe case of malaria while he was out in the bush trying to assassinate "Victor Charles" and any of his colleagues who came walking through the jungle wearing black pajamas and a pith helmet while toting an AK-47 assault rifle. Following a prolonged convalescence after the war, Ron Shiftless took advantage of the G.I. Bill and got a bachelor's degree in biology before getting a PhD in physiology from the Dick Dowling University in East Texas.

With his military background, Ron Shiftless was the natural choice to become the scientific director of the United States Army Department of Biological Warfare in San Antonio, Texas. Also standing at 5'11", Ron Shiftless still had a shock of jet-black curly hair, but as he now eschewed physical activity, he was a stout thirty pounds overweight since the time he had fought in Vietnam nearly two decades earlier.

In what would be forever known as the "massacre at the morgue," the forensic investigators were just starting to piece together the violent bloodbath that had just occurred. Straight out of the poop chute, Colonel Placard quickly noted that the biological weaponeer from San Antonio was little more than the callous and insensitive juvenile delinquent he remembered from the war. Colonel Placard realized that Ron Shiftless had probably never achieved complete maturation of the frontal lobes of his brain. If a man fails to have complete maturation of his frontal lobes by the age of twenty-five, he may very well turn out to be a perpetual frat boy—Peter Pan incarnate!

Such individuals are easily recognized, as they remain "party hearty" guys throughout their entire lives. Being a rowdy frat boy in one's early twenties will make a man nothing but a delightful individual to be around. Conversely, being a rowdy frat boy in one's early forties will make a man nothing but an annoying individual to be around.

"You've not changed at all, Colonel," Shiftless said. "That was meant to be a compliment!"

"You've not changed at all, Shiftless," Placard said. "That was meant to be an insult!"

With that, Dr. Ron Shiftless picked up the bullhorn from the counter. "That bullhorn belongs to me," Captain Morales cautioned. "If something needs to be addressed to the group, that's my responsibility."

"Relax, Captain," Shiftless said. "I've got this." It was clear from the very moment when Shiftless and his team from the Department of Biological Warfare entered the autopsy suite that toes were about to be stepped on and egos were about to be bruised.

A bizarre spectacle was about to unfold as Dr. Shiftless embarked on his one-man stand-up comedy club routine. "Holy smokes, Batman, we need a major-league cleanup on aisle six! It looks like the fat lady who's wearing the bird-of-paradise floral print muumuu has just accidently knocked over the salsa fresca display near the chitlins. Stop her at the cash register!"

"What in hell are you doing now?" Placard asked.

For his part, Ron Shiftless completely ignored the colonel's protestations. "Get the janitor over here, and make sure he brings a big-ass mop and a box of kitty litter to clean this shit up!"

Colonel Placard's jaw dropped in astonishment as Dr. Shiftless continued to grandstand. "Attention, Kmart shoppers, we have a blue light special on aisle six! Watch your step, ladies and germs; I suspect the floor might still be a little bit slippery when you get over there! Now please be polite, my fellow shoppers. No pushing or shoving."

Not only was his sophomoric humor inflammatory by its very nature, but also Dr. Shiftless appeared to totally blasé about the unspeakable gore that figuratively buried the research scientist up to his elbows. As if he had just heard the greatest joke ever told, Shiftless laughed out loud while he repeatedly slapped his knee with great enthusiasm.

Colonel Placard turned to an associate of Dr. Shiftless named

Dr. Hoefferle and asked a pertinent question to the younger scientist, "What in hell is wrong with your boss? Is he like this all the time?"

The associate research investigator turned toward the military officer, shrugged his shoulders, and replied, "Look, Colonel, you remember this guy, don't you? I was under the impression that you and Dr. Shiftless were—how should I say—'siblings' in the art of warfare back in the Nam. Ron boasted that you boys were sappers together south of the DMZ back in '68. I swear to God, don't get me started. Some guy at the DOD must have had his head up his ass when Shiftless was put on point for our vampiro bioweapon team." Dr. Hoefferle shook his head in disgust. "I'm the one who should be calling the shots for this operation."

"What puts you on top of the pyramid?" Placard asked.

"We have an opportunity to collaborate with the Leben Kur AG pharmaceutical firm out of West Germany on this project. They could make all of us filthy rich as private consultants, but Shiftless has other ideas."

"Like what?"

"He's not a team player," Dr. Hoefferle said as he glared at Dr. Shiftless, who was now standing on a chair and spewing off-color jokes through the megaphone. "It's self-evident that somehow and someway he plans to line his own pockets on the research that we're doing on human vampirism."

Placard calmly informed Dr. Hoefferle, "Well, maybe a man like you should indeed be in charge. Step back, son. I'm going over there right now to stomp the dog shit out of that son of a bitch."

Colonel Placard pulled the megaphone from the hand of Dr. Shiftless and threw it overhead like a baseball across the room. It smashed against the lateral wall of the autopsy suite. Captain Morales protested, "Just a moment, Colonel Placard, that was my favorite bullhorn. You just broke it!"

Any further protests from Morales were immediately stifled by a hostile glare issued by the colonel. Turning his ire back toward Dr.

Shiftless, Augustus Placard said, "Listen to me, you crazy bastard, we don't need a man like you. Any help that you think you may be able to render will not be welcome here. If you're still standing in front of me by the time I count to three, I'm going to shoot your sorry ass myself. Am I clear?"

Ron Shiftless calmly extricated himself from the angry grasp of the commanding officer and smugly noted, "So, you proclaim that you don't need any of my help. Oh, really? Well, I beg to differ. I'm looking at the center autopsy table, and I see that somebody named Sergeant Fry must have run a blade through the vampire. After that, the good Dr. Thomas must have been thoughtful enough to leave the knife in a plastic specimen bag for our forensic benefit while everybody was dying all around him. Those men were heroes, if you ask me."

"How so?" Placard asked.

"It's amazing to me that this miraculous feat was undertaken before the hungry vampiro finished everybody off. Obviously, Sergeant Fry and Dr. Thomas somehow saw the big picture before they were taken down."

"Perhaps," Placard answered.

"Quite remarkable, wouldn't you say, Morales?" Dr. Shiftless asked as he eyed the National Guard captain with a considerable amount of well-deserved suspicion. Morales failed to answer the direct question from Ron Shiftless, keeping his eyes affixed upon the tile floor.

"In any event," Dr. Shiftless said, "this is the most precious piece of evidence in this room, and it would appear that nobody as of yet has had the wherewithal to ship the goddamned knife off to the AFIP. It should have been done yesterday! Obviously, nobody else in here can see the big picture. You people are pathetic. All of you people need to pull your heads out of your asses and start paying attention to the details. Now, Colonel, what were you saying about not needing a man like me?"

It seemed to Blake Barker that the medium-size bag of clothing and toiletry articles that he pulled off the luggage carousel at the airport in El Paso could have easily fit into the airplane's overhead compartment without difficulty when his brother, Cletus, flew in from Houston. Although Cletus vehemently protested that his luggage should have been able to fit into the above-seat baggage compartment, the airline carrier just didn't see it his way. Ergo, the bag had to be checked whether Cletus liked the idea or not. Assuredly, Cletus did not like the idea, and this only contributed to the expected irritability and fatigue that was caused by a nine-hundred-mile flight.

"God almighty, I just cannot imagine what you are going through right about now, Blake," Cletus said as he tucked in the shirttail of his black T-shirt. "How are you holding up?"

Blake shrugged his shoulders and replied, "Well, as best I can, I suppose. To be honest, I'm still in shock. I'm sorry that you weren't able to bring Fanny. Did she get tied up at work?"

"Not exactly."

"So," Blake asked, "how are you and Fanny getting along? I figured by now that you would have given her a ring."

Cletus didn't answer the question. He simply followed Blake out of the airport lobby. The two brothers walked out to the curb to pick up the shuttle that would ferry them out to a remote airport parking lot. For a brief moment, Blake was distracted by his own misfortunes and initially failed to realize that Cletus and Fanny had gone their separate ways. Nonetheless, Blake would have the opportunity later to chastise his older brother for a litany of failed romantic relationships. In retrospect, when it came to matters of the heart, Cletus was his own worst enemy.

Blake finally came to a screeching halt when his brother failed to answer a very pertinent question. "For shit's sake, you blew it, didn't you? To be honest, I don't think you're going to get many more chances at this thing called love. What did you do this time? Don't tell me that you screwed around on her. Lynne thinks—"

Blake caught his own mistake, rewound the audiotape in his cerebral cortex, and again hit the play button in his vocal cords. When the second attempt was made to convey his heartfelt thoughts to his brother, Blake correctly edited his verbiage to accommodate a begrudging, real-time acceptance of his current sorrowful life circumstance. "Let me try that again; from my own perspective. I always thought Fanny was perfect for you. Tell me, what in hell is the matter with you?"

Cletus remained silent until the two of them found Blake's car, which was parked near a utility pole with a large metal sign affixed to it with the designation, Row J. Before Cletus climbed into the passenger seat of Blake's car, he spit a wad of chewing gum out of his mouth in disgust. "I'll tell you what's wrong with me; I'm an asshole," Cletus readily admitted.

As Blake laughed, he turned his head toward his sibling and said, "Maybe so, but at least you're an honest asshole. Man, oh man, I'm so glad you're here. Cletus, I brought you something that I believe should be rightfully yours. I want you to have it this very minute. I'm not even going to crank over the engine until I get squared up with you. I've needed to patch things up with you for a long time, and I'm sorry that it took me until now to fix this problem between us."

"What is it?"

"I loved Pops as much as you did, but you were his oldest son, and he should have given this to you when he died." Blake reached into the pocket of his sports jacket, pulled out the gold watch he had inherited from his father, and handed it to Cletus. For his part, Cletus choked up and couldn't speak.

"Let's go to the farm. Baby Sis and my caretaker, Lorena, are waiting for us," Blake said. As the two men left the airport in El Paso, they both had a myriad of reasons of their own for quietly shedding tears as they drove north to the township of Mesilla, New Mexico.

9

TRANSFORMATION

When Blake and his brother arrived at the farmhouse, it was early in the afternoon. Lorena and Elizabeth were waiting for the boys on the driveway. By the look on Lorena's face, Blake knew something was awry when he and his brother stepped out of the vehicle. While Elizabeth gave Cletus a hug, Blake asked, "Where's Nathan? Is everything okay?"

"Nathan's fine; he's inside drawing with his crayons," Lorena answered.

Blake turned to introduce his loyal domestic to his brother. "Lorena, I want you to meet my brother, Cletus." Lorena shook the older man's hand and said, *"Con gusto mucho,"* as she batted her eyes at him.

"Okay, fill me in. What's going on around here?" Blake asked.

"I have bad news. I've spoken to my brother, Miguel. It's hard to believe, but Romero Lopes is still alive! To be honest, Elizabeth and I actually saw Romero Lopes with our own eyes just a short while before your arrival," Lorena said. "He turned up at the morgue and butchered everybody there. My brother was injured, but I hope he'll be okay in the end. He's gone into hiding because he's in fear for his own life!"

"Now, Lopes is the psychopath who murdered Lynne, is that right?" Cletus asked. "How could he be still alive? Blake told me he died in a house fire."

"Lorena, you must be mistaken," Blake added. "I had a front-row seat to everything that went down. There is no way in hell that Lopes could have survived that inferno."

"Listen to what Lorena is saying," Elizabeth said. "Before you boys got here, a person whom Lorena identified as Romero Lopes showed back up at the scene of the crime. We each watched him through a pair of binoculars. He was sifting through the charred rubble as if looking for something of value."

Blake was still incredulous when he asked, "Well, what happened? Did you call the authorities?"

"Of course we did!" Elizabeth answered. "Before the grunts got back up there, Lorena sprinted right up to the burned-out farmhouse. When Lopes took one look at her, he ran away. It was almost as if he was afraid of her for some reason. The National Guard came back out, and they're still over there now as far as I can tell. The authorities are going over the entire area with a fine-toothed comb as we speak, but I have a sneaking suspicion that Lopes got away yet again."

"Lorena, what were you thinking?" Blake asked. "Romero Lopes could have attacked you."

Lorena shrugged her shoulders and answered, "If you must know, I was thinking that I was going to kill the son of a bitch with my bare hands. That's what I was thinking. It would seem to me that he must have been searching for something quite important to him. Why else would he expose himself out in the open and in broad daylight that way? It just doesn't make sense to me. I wonder, what was he looking for over there? If the National Guard comes up empty and they book out before it gets dark, maybe we should go back up there and see what's going on."

"That's a good idea," Blake said. "I'll pull out a metal rake and a shovel from the toolshed before we head over there. Cletus, I have an over and under in a camo bag in the front closet, along with my twelve-gauge pump with a new box of slugs. On the top shelf, you'll also find a box or two of Magnum buck. You might as well grab those while you're at it. After you get your suitcase and belongings squared away in the spare bedroom, come back out to the living room and get the safari kit loaded up. I think it's time we all go on a little scavenger hunt."

As Dr. Blanks extended both hands horizontally, his palms faced the ceiling in an act of apparent submission. "Well, on your behalf I butted heads with Uncle Sam. You'll be happy to learn that I was able to render a substantial compensatory increase on the most recent document that you now have in your hot little hands. I think what we're now proposing is a rather generous offer, but what do you think?"

For his part, John Stewart only stared at Dr. Blanks with disdain. Initially, Stewart didn't even lift one finger to examine the new employment offer.

"Let me review with you the specifics of this revised contract," Blanks said. "We'll pay you three thousand dollars per month with a full medical and dental package in addition to a retirement plan. How about that? Life is about to get pretty good for you."

Like a caged fox, John Stewart arose from his chair and paced back and forth within the confines of his maximum-security isolation cell. He finally grabbed the contract from the table to contemplate what overtly seemed to be a highly incendiary contract offer that was rife with problematic legal terminology. John Stewart finally conjured a definite decision regarding Uncle Sam's compensatory offer.

"No dice. This contract offer will definitely need to be modified," Stewart said. "First off, there is no way in hell that I am going to agree to this particular section in the contract that says, and I quote, 'The federal government reserves the right to terminate the employee at any time without cause.' Are you shitting me? I insist that this specific language get rectified *immediately*."

"Well, what's the problem with the wording of the contract offer, if I might ask?"

"I'm perfectly okay with the prospect that you may terminate my *employment* without cause; however, I am not particularly keen on the idea that someday you might decide to terminate *me* without cause."

"No, that' just a matter of legal mumbo-jumbo," Dr. Banks said. "Of course it means termination of your employment and not termination of your life. This is not an execution clause. How could you think otherwise?"

John Stewart began to jump back and forth between his right foot and his left foot. He asked, "How could I think otherwise? Is that what you just asked me? Because your best buddy, Captain Morales, seriously contemplated an act of cold-blooded homicide by subjecting me to a lethal case of lead poisoning."

"That's a bit harsh," Blanks said.

"You think so?" Stewart asked. "Before you walked in on us at El Chopo, Morales was about to introduce a significant mass of elemental lead into my brain with a handheld high-velocity heavy metal injector, specifically known as a Model 1911, .45-caliber automatic pistol!"

"Well, it didn't happen," Dr. Blanks said.

"Fine. I don't want to be rude, but if you don't change that specific language per my request, we don't have a deal, and you can take that contract and shove it up your ass!" John Stewart defiantly folded his arms and stared at Dr. Blanks.

Dr. Blanks slowly nodded his head and said, "I'll see what I can do, but I can't make any guarantees. Do you have any other special requests, such as specific modifications, addendums, or deletions regarding this contract offer?"

The now retired line cook from El Chopo had one additional demand. "There's one last thing that I'd like to have added to my compensation package. For what you have asked of me as per my job description, it must be codified that I will never pay any federal taxes ever again for the rest of my miserable life. That includes income tax, minimum alternative tax, Social Security tax, masturbation tax, urination tax, defecation tax, life tax, death tax, flatulence tax, earth tax, wind tax, water tax, fire tax, and any other type of bullshit tax that Uncle Sam can and will think of in the immediate or distant future."

"You must be joking."

"If Uncle Sam plans to levy a tax someday to fund research on the projected natural life expectancy of the emerging population of albino pygmy owls in Siberia, and whether or not such birds, if they do indeed exist, actually get near-equivalent salary compensation compared to their closest mammalian competitors who are toiling away amongst other day laborers found within the workforce of a temperate conifer forest, then you may rest assured that I'm not going to pay for that bullshit either," Stewart answered.

"It doesn't seem that you have a realistic concept of how pedantic Uncle Sam can be over such matters," Blanks said.

"Also, I don't give two shits if the black boys who are walking around on this planet are packing puny peckers compared to their white male counterparts in American society. Does our culture now burden me with the guilt of having the privilege of being born a white male? Fuck that noise! If that's indeed the case, I'm certainly not going to pay any taxes for a federal research project to study that kind of horse shit, chicken shit either. No, sir! I'm not going to do it. This last request to you is actually quite simple, see? If you make it happen, Doc, I'll do the deal."

Dr. Blanks set his elbows on the small wooden table in front of him. "Now, that's one tall order. Although we have a very decent conservative in the White House and the Republicans, at least for the time being, hold the Senate, the House is controlled by liberal Democrats. Keeping a boot on the back of the neck of Mr. Joe Blow American citizen with crushing federal taxes is actually a religious doctrine for liberals. I can tell you right now, your request for a personal lifetime exemption from the federal tax code is a pipe dream."

With that rebuke, John Stewart stretched out on the mattress in his isolation cell. As he rolled over to face the back wall of his cuboid enclosure, he said, "Well, Dr. Blanks, I guess we don't have anything else to talk about. When my quarantine is up at the end of this week, I'll just plan on saying adios to all of you dirtbags one last time. After that, I'll just disappear, and you'll never see me again."

"Now, wait a minute," Blanks pleaded. "Let's be reasonable here."

"I *am* being reasonable," John Stewart countered. "If you'd be so kind, please kill the overhead fluorescent lights in here. They're giving me a pounding headache. Incidentally, the on–off switch is by the exit."

"I'm not done yet," Blanks said. "Let's work this out."

"I'm done with you," Stewart said, "but please send the security guard back in here. I'll have him tell me a bedtime story because, in my humble opinion, his ideas about life, liberty, and the pursuit of the elusive American dream make a shitload more sense than anything that spews out of your boca."

"Don't throw away a life-changing opportunity here, John."

"Enough!" Stewart exclaimed. "Don't let the screen door slam you in the ass on your way out of here."

—⊶⊷—

"How do you possibly think you can manage using either a rake or a shovel with your left arm still in a sling?" Cletus asked.

"Don't you worry about a thing," Blake responded. "I can still use my right arm. We need to get over there and take a look around before the sun goes down. I don't know if we will find anything, but it's worth a stab. Liz, are you coming with?"

"No. Why don't I stay here with Nathan?" Elizabeth replied. "Besides, there's no question in my mind that Romero Lopes is deathly afraid of Lorena. He booked out the minute he saw her. I think it would be a much smarter idea if she went along with you two boys instead of me."

Lorena agreed. "Give me one of the shotguns. Before we head up there, I need to get something out of my bedroom. This will only take a second." Lorena made a beeline to her quarters, reached under her bed, and pulled out the bright yellow ritualistic huevo limpia that she had hidden there. Once the egg was safely secured in her fanny pack, she called out, "¡Vamos, muchachos! ¡Ahora!"

Hidden at the tree line, Romero Lopes watched in fascination as his three adversaries trespassed upon what once was his homestead. Although he was certainly not fearful of the shotguns, he was certainly wary of Lorena, whom he erroneously believed was a powerful vampira. He was mortified when he suddenly realized that they were sifting through the charred rubble of the old farmhouse. What if these unwelcome interlopers were to find his powerful obsidian knife?

Although Lopes fully realized that the misplaced opaque black blade that was crafted from volcanic lava was not directly the etiology of his particular vampiric curse, he nonetheless believed the superstitious lore that this particular weapon was the very tool that elevated him from the lowly and oft-ridiculed El Maguito to what he now considered himself to be: un gran brujo.

If the truth be told, the obsidian knife was actually been more than a psychological crutch to quell the dangerous creature's loathing that he had for the human being he once was. Oddly enough, the bloodthirsty beast still had considerably low self-esteem. Before he lost the knife, the ghoul could, at least temporarily, elevate himself to new stratospheric heights in the darkness whenever he fondled the blade gently with his left hand, while he ferociously masturbated away at the other effete blade that could be found among his emasculated loins with his right hand.

—⸗⸗⸗—

After Cletus carefully dusted away the ash from the peculiar object that he had found among the rubble, he handed it to Blake. "Wow, look at this; it's really quite odd. If I'm not mistaken, Blake, this looks similar to the old obsidian tool you found near Kilbourne's Hole years ago, although the one I just found here appears to be much darker in color."

"Well, this is really weird," Blake said. "Maybe it was damaged in the house fire and it's covered with soot, but I'm not certain. Maybe this is somehow an important memento to Romero Lopes. What do you make of this, Lorena?"

"This must have been what he was looking for when we saw him sifting through all this debris earlier today," Lorena said. "At El Chopo, Lopes claimed that he was a grand warlock. Well, an obsidian knife is believed by many to intrinsically hold magical powers. Blake, as you already own one of these things, I ask you now to please keep it in a protected place."

"Well, I certainly do," Blake replied. "I keep mine in my top dresser drawer, wrapped up in a hand towel."

"Good! As for this one that Cletus found, I'm afraid it could draw Romero Lopes back to our house," Lorena opined. "Are you sure you want a vampiro to come by and pay us a visit?"

"Enough of this vampire nonsense," Blake said. "Look, Lopes is just a psychotic killer, nothing more and nothing less. Now don't get me wrong, he's dangerous, but he is not a vampire! He was probably just all juiced up on angel dust or some other shit when he butchered Lynne. If the authorities don't find him, I will. When I do, I'll personally rip him apart."

"I wish I could make you see the truth about what we are dealing with here," Lorena said.

"Here, Cletus, I want you to have this black knife. I sure as hell don't need two of these damned things," Blake said. "Do me a solid favor, however; if you run into Romero Lopes before I do, kill him."

"I don't want the damned knife, Blake," Cletus said. "If Lorena is correct and this Romero Lopes character is going to come back someday just to find it, he just might decide to cut my head off and leave it on your front porch as a trophy. However, this is without doubt the sharpest knife I've ever seen. I bet it could split a hair. I'll tell you what, Lorena: why don't you keep it?"

"I would be honored to do so," Lorena said.

"If Romero Lopes ever does come back around to pay you a visit, I know that you're the type of woman who could really give it to him—and then some!" Cletus professed.

"I promise you, I would do just that," Lorena proclaimed.

"Good. Then it's settled. Lorena, the knife now belongs to you," Cletus said with a smile as he softly rubbed the top of Lorena's hand.

As an afterthought, Cletus turned to Blake said, "If it is okay with you, Liz and I plan to stay one more week."

"I'd be happy to have the company."

"We promise not to wear out our welcome," Cletus said. "By the way, it's still quail season here in New Mexico, is it not?"

"They won't pull the plug on quail season until later this February," Blake answered. "If I'm not mistaken, it'll all be ending the following weekend."

"After Lynne's memorial service, let's hike into the Big Sacramento uplands, or even further into the San Andres range east of I-25. I'll bet you a box of jelly doughnuts that we'll be able to bag a few Mearns, just like old times. What do you think?"

"Now, Cletus, there you go again," Blake said. "You don't even own a New Mexico hunting license. It would cost you a boatload of money to buy one now since you're a resident of another state. As you're from Texas, they'll probably charge you twice as much than if you were a resident of the state of New Mexico. It appears that New Mexicans actually hate people from Texas."

"Oh yeah? Well, so does everybody else," Cletus said with a laugh. "I'm used to it by now. Look, if next weekend is indeed the end of quail season, there's no way that 'Ranger Rick' will be out stomping around. In fact, I always go out on the very last day of hunting season without a license regardless of what the game may be or what state I might find myself in. As of yet, I've never been caught," Cletus said.

"Cletus, you're incorrigible," Blake said.

"I hope I resemble that remark."

Hidden within just a few feet of the tree line, Romero Lopes was carefully listening to the uninvited visitors to his burned-out farmhouse. The vampiro was quick to note that Lorena was now in possession of the mystical object of his desires. Somehow, he would have to hatch some kind of a plan to retrieve the weapon from an individual whom he deeply feared, as he continued to erroneously believe that she was una vampira.

——

The night before Lynne's funeral service, Blake, against his better judgment, agreed to go out to a local bar called Cueva del Chupacabra in nearby Las Cruces with his brother to have a cold beer. Cletus held the conviction that it would be a fitting way to close what had turned out to be a painful chapter in the life of his younger brother. The ideas that Cletus had about these matters were, at the very least, well-intentioned. Of course, the road to hell is thus paved …

As an establishment, Cueva del Chupacabra was just as seedy, uninviting, and inhospitable from the inside as it was from the outside. It was the kind of place where if one was drinking a cold beer, it would be wise to put the beverage back into the refrigerator in between each sip to restrict the number of six-legged alcoholic cucarachas from diving in and swimming the backstroke in the foamy head.

Cletus turned to Blake and said, "Keep my beer cold while I pick up an Andrew Jackson from the big hairy monster juggling with the cue over by the tables." Within no more than a few moments after the break shot, the looming competitor crowed, "Well, dude, it looks like you're stuck behind the eight ball. That sucks for you."

"Unless you are referring to one of the documented positions noted in the Kama Sutra, which incidentally would happen to be well beyond your realm of heterosexual encounters, you should know that I've never been stuck behind the eight ball in my entire life, pal," Cletus chirped.

"Now, wait just one minute," the hirsute beast replied in anger. "Did you just insult me? If I'm not mistaken, you just accused me of being one of them there 'homo-satchels'!"

After the giant reared back and popped the man who'd just offended him in the mouth with a clenched fist, Cletus stumbled to the floor. In defense of his older brother, Blake jumped up from his chair and threw himself upon the back of the behemoth. The pool player proceeded to peel Blake off his back as if merely pulling off a dirty T-shirt. He then pitched the much smaller man out through the saloon door.

Momentarily, Cletus also flew out of the exit as if he were a graceful swimmer performing a swan dive off a high board at the municipal swimming pool. To add insult to injury, Cletus proceeded to rudely crash on top of his younger brother.

Once Cletus arose from his embarrassing predicament, he proceeded to dust himself off. He laughed out loud when he said, "It's been a long time since I've been tossed from a bar. I swear to God, that was real a hoot and a half!"

Blake Barker, for his part, was in a much more somber mood. "As soon as my arm heals up a bit, I'm going to come back here some night to kick that man's ass! Mark my words."

"Miguel, where have you been hiding? You've not answered your telephone for the last several days. Are you feeling all right? I have bad news to tell you: Romero Lopes has returned to my neighborhood. I'm quite certain that we've not seen the last of that vicious animal."

With the toe of his right shoe, Miguel dug away at the dry winter turf on the New Mexico State University football practice field. The curandera looked directly at her brother, but she had a great deal of difficulty discerning his features in the darkness.

"Lorena, I'm going through the transformation," Miguel confessed.

"What do you mean?"

"My eyes and skin are yellow now. Today, I ran down a jackrabbit out in the desert on a dead sprint. I found that I was as fast as a speeding car, and I could change directions on a peso."

"Did you, well—"

"After I drank the poor creature's blood," Miguel continued, "I proceeded to devour its internal organs. It was as if I had never seen food before! God forgive me, but I ate the rabbit raw."

"Hermano!"

"Listen to me, Lorena, I brought Pappasito's gun with me tonight," Miguel confessed. "I'm simply not brave enough to do this to myself, so I need your help. I am going to get down onto my hands and knees, and I want you to stand behind me and unload this gun into the back of my head. I hope and pray that as my sister, you love me enough that you are able to do this for me. I'll forgive you if you do this. I know that God will forgive you if you do this."

Lorena burst into tears and cried out, "No, Miguel! No, no, no! Don't ask me to murder you! I won't do it. Don't despair. Maybe you can find treatment somewhere. Do you remember Dr. Cloud? He's an attending physician now and an assistant professor of medicine at the Saint Francis College of Medicine in Santa Fe."

"How could I forget?" Miguel replied. "He is that nice-looking Indio from the Zuni tribe. Nice guy ..."

Lorena corrected her brother. "No, he's Navajo, not Zuni. If you ever make a mistake and accidentally call him out to be a member of the Zuni tribe to his face, he will kick your balls up to your neck!"

Miguel nodded and said, "Oh, that's right; he's Navajo." For a brief moment, Miguel was distracted from his own plight. He took the opportunity to chastise his sister, citing a litany of her failed romantic relationships. When it came to matters of the heart, Lorena was her own worst enemy.

"For shit's sake, why did you blow up that relationship? I don't think you're going to get many more chances at this thing called love. How can you screw up something like this time after time? Tell me, what in hell is the matter with you?" Miguel asked.

Lorena shrugged her shoulders. "I'll tell you what's wrong with me: I'm an asshole."

As Miguel laughed, he turned his head toward his sibling and said, "Maybe so, but at least you're an honest asshole. So, how do you think Dr. Cloud will be able to help me?"

"They have a top-shelf hematology–oncology program in Santa Fe," Lorena said. "Dr. Turk Masters is the head of the experimental cancer and blood disease projects up there, and apparently he has a crackerjack fellow who works for him now with the name Dr. J. D. Brewster. He's from the Gulf Coast College of Medicine in Houston."

"I have a hell of a lot more than just a problem with my blood," Miguel said.

"The infectious diseases department at the Saint Francis College of Medicine is also first-rate," Lorena said. "You need to get up there and get admitted for an evaluation before the military police hunt you down and kill you like a rabid dog. Promise me that you'll do this for me."

Miguel pulled out the pistol and held it in the air. "I promise. Here, Lorena, I want you to keep Pappasito's gun. Take it now before I change my mind and I put a bullet through my own head."

When Miguel tossed the gun onto the ground in front of Lorena, she returned the favor, concurrently tossing a small gold ring looped with a silver chain onto the ground in front of him.

"What's this?" Miguel asked.

"My class ring," Lorena replied. "Keep it as a memento so you won't ever forget the precious time when we were, well..."

When Miguel picked up the silver chain with the small gold class ring attached, he quickly draped it over his neck. Just then, the newly commissioned vampiro felt a few pangs of hunger. With good reason at that very moment, Lorena's brother suddenly feared for his beloved sister's safety and well-being. When Miguel turned away from Lorena, he simply vanished. In the blink of an eye, he fled into the enveloping darkness without even saying so much as a goodbye. Despite the deep, lifelong, and heartfelt love that the two siblings had shared, they would be destined never to see each other again.

10

NIGHT CRAWLER

D r. Blanks banged on the door of the locked-down isolation unit with his fist. The National Guardsman on the other side of the door responded by looking through the peephole to see who had come for visit. The scientist from the CDC held up his credentials and identification badge to the peephole. Once he was recognized, the door creaked open.

"Well, I guess unless he changes his mind once and for all, we'll have to release our friend Mr. Stewart here into the wilderness of the Land of Enchantment. Is that not so?" Surmised the MP.

Dr. Blanks smiled and winked at the military personnel who had held John Stewart captive for an entire week and said, "Well, the quarantine is now over. If he was going to transform into a vampiro, he would have done so by now. That's a fact. We'll need to do just one more blood test for confirmation. If his blood is clean, we'll have to put him on the launchpad and send him out of here. However, I have in my hot little hands an offer from Uncle Sam that just might be good enough to entice our guest to say adios to New Mexico once and for all. If so, we'll be heading out to Atlanta later today!"

"Well, Doc, I mean no disrespect, but unless the federal government is willing to deed the Big Bend National Park to Mr. Stewart, he may very well tell you to go pound sand, if you catch my meaning," the military guard said.

Dr. Blanks laughed out loud and said, "I believe this compensatory package will be much more valuable to John Stewart than any national park in this country, or even a free lifetime sideline pass to every home game the Dallas Cowboys will ever play from now until when hell finally freezes over. If you would be so kind as to bring him out of his holding cell, I would like to talk with him in private in the conference room."

"You seem pretty sure of yourself, Doc," the guard said. "Do you really think that he'll jump on board with all of this? I would be willing to bet a box of jelly doughnuts to the contrary. Now jelly doughnuts are near and dear to my heart, and I don't go about betting them in a random or willy-nilly fashion."

"You're on, son," Blanks said, "but when I win this bet, I get to pick what doughnuts get put in the box!"

—⁓⁓—

"How does it feel to be a free man?" Blanks asked.

John Stewart interlaced his fingers behind his head, leaned back in his chair, and answered the question with a smile. "I tell you what, Dr. Blanks, it feels pretty darn good. To be honest with you, except for an unpleasant meeting or two I had with Captain Morales, you folks have treated me quite nicely. My only complaint, I suppose, is that life is short and I just burned up a whole week. I might as well have put a match to it. I have nothing to show for it. Well, if that's all, I wish you gentlemen the best of luck in hunting down Romero Lopes. Call me up when you finally put the son of a bitch down. I want to be the one to run him through the wood chipper."

Dr. Blanks extended his hand to gently slow John Stewart from making his planned departure. "John, before you leave, your uncle would like to make you one more offer. I would ask you to please take a look at this revised compensation package. I believe it will readily address all of the issues and concerns you expressed at the time of our last meeting."

Stewart thumbed through the document. When he saw that he

was granted dispensation from having to pay federal income tax in any way, shape, or form for the rest of his life, he threw his hands into the air as if he had scored a touchdown and said, "You've got yourself a deal, Dr. Blanks. Give me a pen and show me where I need to sign! For the love of God, please tell me why I am so valuable to you, Doc?"

Dr. Blanks smiled as he shrugged his shoulders and offered a simple reply. "Because, my friend, you are the one who is immune."

—∘∘∘∘∘—

The ER attending, Dr. Dove, at the Saint Francis College of Medicine emergency room looked at the blood work of Miguel Pastore and was literally stunned to see the results. Whether it was the peripheral blood cell count results or the bizarre chemistry panel findings, all the laboratory parameters indicated that the patient who was occupying the gurney in stall number four was on the threshold of death. As Dr. Dove was a member of the Zuni tribe, he had to swallow his pride when he picked up the telephone to call Dr. Cloud, a member of the adversarial Navajo tribe, to come down for an urgent consultation.

"For heaven's sake, Cloud, must you be an absolute dick every single day of your life?" Dove asked over the telephone. "Just come down and see for yourself. The dude is hemolyzing like mad, and he's spilling out blasts, a shitload of them. He has the lowest hemoglobin and hematocrit of any human being I have ever seen who's still breathing." Dr. Dove scribbled an order and passed it over to a nearby nurse as he continued to speak on the telephone.

"How low?" Cloud asked.

"I'll tell you how far off the bell curve this poor dumb bastard is right about now; his hemoglobin is only 1.6, and his hematocrit is 4.8," Dove answered.

"Impossible," Cloud said.

"I shit you not!" Dove exclaimed. "As we speak, he's going into high-output failure. His heart is taching along at 155, and his BP is circling the tubes. I have four units of packed cells lined up for him, but they are only type-specific. None of the blood has been cross-matched."

"What do you want me to do?" Cloud asked.

"Come on, man, get down here and help me pull this patient's chestnuts out of the proverbial fire! I'm going to need a crab picker on this case. See if you can scrape up the fellow, Dr. J. D. Brewster, and drag his ass down here to help us out. I don't know where he is, but you need to find him and do it pronto."

"I'll venture that if he's not in the doctors' lounge watching the televangelist Rectal Roberts dancing around on television and waving a bunch of snakes over his holy hillbilly head," Cloud postulated, "then he's probably jerking off in the broom closet over by the gynecology clinic."

—————

Ostensibly the two physicians should have at least considered each other to be mutual colleagues in the art of healing. However, the animosity that Dr. Cloud and Dr. Dove held for each other was so great that they didn't even have enough civility to shake each other's hand upon Cloud's arrival to the emergency room suite. Ancient territorial disputes within the Land of Disenchantment had left bad blood between the Navajo tribe and the Zuni people that in all likelihood would never be completely resolved within the lifetime of the two medical professionals who stood and stared at each other from a distance of only a few paces.

Dove passed over a ream of stat blood work results to the internal medicine assistant professor. "Your opinion, please."

Dr. Dove had highlighted the peculiarities of the laboratory parameters with a yellow marker and reviewed the findings with Cloud. "I don't know about you, but I have never seen an indirect bilirubin at 35. In addition, his LDH is to the moon. He must be trying to hemolyze every single red cell in his body."

Cloud furrowed his brow and asked a very complex question by uttering just one word, and one word only: "Coombs?"

"That's just it," Dove said. "Both direct and indirect are negative, so this doesn't seem to be some type of autoimmune hemolytic process. I asked the hematology section to do a reticulocyte count, and it's zero!"

"Dead marrow?" Cloud asked.

"If his bone marrow isn't dead yet, it's awfully sick if it's incapable of creating any new red cells on its own accord. Maybe the marrow is packed up with blasts. In addition, his urine is as black as a cup of coffee. Where in hell is J. D. Brewster?"

"I gave the Turk a call, and he's relinquishing his fellow to us as we speak," Dr. Cloud answered.

"I need to get him to take a look at this patient's peripheral in blood and sort out what kind of weird shit is going on in this dude's circulation. Have you ever seen anything like this before?" Dr. Dove asked.

"Well," Cloud answered, "maybe, but I'm not sure."

"To be honest," Dove said, "I'm actually feeling quite nervous about this entire situation."

"Before I submit an opinion," Cloud said, "let's take a good look at the patient. What's his name?"

"Miguel Pastore."

"Damnation!" Cloud said. "I know this guy."

Cloud pulled back and drew curtain to the emergency room stall to visit the critically ill individual. "Hello, Miguel. I'm sorry to see you again under these circumstances. How's your sister?"

"Hard to say," Miguel answered. "It's good to see you again, Cloud, but Lorena and I have parted company."

"I'm sorry to hear that," Cloud said. "In any event, I'm now the head of one of the internal medicine teams at this facility. In your own words, can you tell me what happened to you and what brought you here to our facility? You're here from Mesilla, and that's not exactly spitting distance, as you very well know. What have you been up to?"

"I finally graduated from New Mexico State with twin master degreees. I'm proud to say that I'm now a morgue diener down south."

"Good for you."

"Perhaps that's not quite the right thing for me to say." Miguel stopped to correct himself. "I should repeat what I just said utilizing past-tense verbiage or some linguistic facsimile thereof. I *used* to be a morgue diener. That's certainly a more accurate description of my peculiar situation. I should apply for workmen's compensation and eventually request long-term Social Security disability."

"Why not?" Cloud asked. "After all, if the feds are willing to squander billions of dollars in foreign aid on countries that absolutely hate the United States, perhaps it would be appropriate for our government to actually care about its own citizens from time to time."

"Precisely."

"Maybe we'll be able to sort this out on your behalf," Cloud said optimistically. "Nonetheless, I need you to tell me, in as succinct terms as possible, what in the blue blazes happened to you."

"Okay, Doc, pay attention. Are you ready to hear some wicked shit? Here's the pitch: I was attacked by a vampiro in the morgue, and I was bitten in the neck. The only reason I'm still alive is that the evil beast didn't like the taste of my blood. I should have died back there with the rest of my colleagues."

"That's morbid," Cloud said. "Don't talk like that."

"I admit to you that I'm pissed off! What was wrong with the taste of my blood? Not a damn thing, I tell you. After all, the vampiro who attacked me *is*, or at least *was*, Hispanic. Although I have gone through a transformation, I'm still very much Hispanic.

And I'm very proud of my blood and also of my bloodline, I'll have you know!"

"I'm sure you are."

"My people came to America less than a century after Christopher Columbus set sail from Europe and stumbled upon the New World on behalf of the crown of Spain. I don't know about now, as I've now gone through the transformation and become a vampiro myself, but at the time I was bitten, I would be willing to attest to you that my blood was perfect in every way. Why did the vampiro dislike my blood?"

"Maybe we can give you some answers," Dr. Cloud replied.

"I wish he'd just finished me off then and there," Miguel wistfully remarked. "In any event, I have again apparently digressed. The vampiro became reanimated while he was still zipped up in a body bag, but he popped out like a goddamned jack-in-the-box and proceeded to kill everybody in the autopsy suite except for one person. That one person happens to be me. I'm the only survivor."

"How can this be?" Dr. Cloud asked. "I haven't heard anything about such an event on the television news, nor did I see anything about this type of catastrophe in the local newspaper."

"There's a news blackout over the whole ordeal," Miguel answered. "The government doesn't want the citizens of the fair state of New Mexico to know what's going on. Mark my words: a sham cover story will eventually be released by the press. The truth of this matter, after all, will have to be deeply buried. The major news outlets will probably report that several medical professionals were killed in a gas leak at the morgue or some such nonsense."

Dr. Cloud was surprised at what he had heard. "Now, I really don't think the government would lie to us about something like that."

"Doc, did you even hear what you just said?" Miguel scoffed. "You are, after all, a Native American, and you have the audacity to ask whether or not the federal government can tell a lie? For the love of Jesus, are you serious? How many binding treaties that the feds signed with Native Americans were irrevocably fractured? Don't be naïve!"

"Now hold on," Dr. Cloud said, "that's all *ancient* history."

"It's all *current* history, Doc," Miguel Pastore countered. "To be frank, perhaps the main reason why I dragged my lame ass up here is not because I thought so much that you would be able to help me, but maybe, just maybe, because I needed a place to hide out. When the military finds me, they'll either kill me on the spot or else l ship me off to San Antonio to turn me into some type of biological weapon."

"If you promise not to bite me and infect me with whatever nasty shit that's swimming around in your bloodstream, I'd like to take a look at you." Dr. Cloud put on a face mask and donned a pair of rubber gloves. With only an initial cursory evaluation, the attending physician confirmed that Miguel Pastore's skin was extremely jaundiced and his eyes were markedly icteric. When Cloud looked inside the patient's mouth, he was stunned to see the prominent sharp incisors in his upper maxilla. Dr. Cloud also noted that Miguel's skin was raw and blistered. "Were you out in the sun too long?"

"No, I was just outside for a few minutes, and this is what happened to me," Miguel replied.

"So, perhaps what you are afflicted with is a subset of porphyria superimposed upon bone marrow failure and a leukemia state," Dr. Cloud surmised.

"No, you're not listening to me," Miguel answered. "I don't have porphyria. I don't have leukemia. I don't have ingrown toenails. I don't have male pattern baldness. I don't have liver disease. I don't have heart disease. I don't have an autoimmune hemolytic anemia. Pay attention now, Dr. Cloud. Here's the skinny once and for all: Yo soy un vampiro."

The clinical picture was finally starting to sink into the psyche of Dr. Cloud. "If that is indeed the case, exactly when did you get infected?"

"It was just a week ago," Miguel Pastore answered. "I guess my life's over. In retrospect, I should have known that it was a mistake for me to come up here looking for help. It would have been far better if I'd just killed myself."

Without saying another word to the patient, Dr. Cloud stepped out of the emergency room stall. It was finally time to answer Dr. Dove's pertinent questions. Cloud looked at Dr. Dove and said, "Maybe I do have an idea what this is all about. Look, we've got the first unit hanging up, and it's dripping in just fine. Step over with me to the conference room. I need to talk to you in private about some serious shit."

As the two jousting partners entered the conference room, Dr. Dove professed, "We have to get this guy to the ICU as soon as possible. I don't want him to circle the drain while he's down here."

"Putting this patient into the ICU may very well be the worst thing we could possibly do," Cloud replied. "We need to protect the staff at this facility and our very own population at large. We need to put this patient in a guarded isolation room. I want you to understand that I believe this man is afflicted with some type of as of yet unidentified infectious disease. He's been transformed into a night crawler. I've seen a case like this in the past. It was over seven years ago."

"Well, I was afraid that was what you were going to say," Dr. Dove said.

———

After evaluating the patient and making a round trip visit to the laboratory, the hematology–oncology fellow returned to the emergency room to further discuss the case of Miguel Pastore with Dr. Dove and the internal medicine attending physician. "I took a look at this fellow's peripheral blood underneath the microscope. He's clearly spilling blasts into his bloodstream, but fortunately the blast cells only constitute about 15 percent to 18 percent of the WBCs in circulation. I'm going to do a diagnostic bone marrow aspiration and biopsy on him this afternoon, check a serum haptoglobin level, and also grab a urine hemosiderin assay to confirm what appears to be a comorbid gross idiopathic hemolysis."

"Well, Tex, you must have some ideas here," Dr. Dove said.

"If you have any ideas, spill it now. I know you too well, Brewster," Dr. Cloud added. "A ratchet jaw like you is always scheming up something. Are you going to get a blessing from the Turk on all of this before you pull out your six-shooter and spew out a zillion dollars' worth of lab orders?"

"I already have a green light from Dr. Masters."

As Brewster was just a first-year fellow, he was still wearing his "training pants" as far as the university was concerned. "In any event, there's something weird with this Miguel Pastore patient. I'm going to have to present this case to the tumor board ASAP, but I can't officially call this a case of acute leukemia at this time. Mr. Pastore's disease process would appear to be some type of smoldering or subacute leukemia, but frankly it looks like his blast counts are on the threshold of being launched off into outer space."

"What about the hemolysis?" Dr. Dove asked. "You must have some kind of plausible explanation for this phenomenon."

"Beats the hell out of me," the fellow replied. "I truly don't understand how this primary bone marrow problem can be tied to such a severe hemolysis if his direct and indirect Coomb's tests are both negative. I saw a brisk hemolysis like this in the past when I was at Houston. Some boat people made it to our shores and their RBC hemolysis was a consequence of intraerythrocytic protozoan parasites commonly known as malaria. If this is a hemolysis that's caused by an infection, it would have to be from a submicroscopic viral entity, but honest to God, I can't think of any infectious process that could act this way."

"What does the Turk say about all of this?" Dr. Dove asked.

"He hasn't had an opportunity to look at the peripheral smear under the scope with his own eye as of yet," Brewster answered. "I hope you don't mind, but I was thinking about dragging in a few other braniacs to take a look at this situation, including Parker Coxswain and Booker Marshall. Frankly, they're both a shitload smarter than me."

Unlike Brewster, both Coxswain and Marshall were dual-trained, both with MD and PhD degrees from the Gulf Coast College of Medicine. As for Brewster, he graduated with just an MD degree and he lacked the research experience of his two colleagues.

"That's all okay with me, but I thought Booker was recently sidelined with an acute sickle cell crisis flare-up," Dr. Cloud said.

"You might consider him now to be one of the walking wounded," Brewster replied.

"Well, in any event, I knew it would be only a matter of time before you three musketeers would collaborate on something," Cloud noted. "I swear to God, you Texans are as thick as thieves, aren't you?"

"That's why they derisively call this place the University of Texas at Santa Fe!" Dr. Dove wryly agreed. "I'll have you know that editorial comment was an indictment. It was certainly not meant to be a compliment to you or your colleagues in any way, shape, or form."

"You guys need to know one other thing," Brewster added. "I saw the dude's black urine, and I suddenly had a crazy idea. I asked the chemistry lab to run an iron level on the specimen. You're not going to believe this, but the analysis on his urine revealed an astounding iron level of 332 micrograms per deciliter."

"That can't be," Dr. Cloud said as he scoffed at the data Brewster just presented. "The normal *serum* iron only goes from 30 to 160 micrograms per deciliter, and you're telling me that what you noted was the amount of iron in his *urine*."

"Are you insane?" Dr. Dove asked. "If that's indeed the case, then he has more iron in his urine than he does in his bloodstream. Physiologically, that just can't happen unless somebody has a traumatic kidney or bladder injury and is passing pure blood in the urine. In fact, the human body has absolutely no excretory mechanism for iron outside of blood loss or the shedding of a small amount of iron in the biological turnover of normal tissues."

"So I've been told," the hematology–oncology fellow agreed, "but the numbers don't lie, gentlemen."

"Let me see that lab report," Dr. Dove insisted.

"Take a look," Brewster said as he passed over the lab report. "It's right here in black and white."

"The urinalysis that was obtained upon the patient's admission to the emergency room was negative for the presence of any blood by microscopic review," Dr. Cloud said. "Ergo, the test report that you just informed us of must have been an error. Otherwise, what you reported is not humanly possible."

"I thought the same thing," Brewster said. "That's why I had them run a serial analysis no fewer than three different times. Listen to me very carefully: all the results came out essentially the same. They were all within the margin of acceptable laboratory analytical variance from test to test to test. Are you boys ready for this? I have an idea. I've certainly been reluctant to utter this hypothesis up until this very moment. Maybe when you hear what I have to say, you guys are going to laugh me right out of this medical college. Well, here it goes: maybe Miguel Pastore is no longer human."

⚜

Somehow, Romero Lopes would have to recover the obsidian knife that Cletus Barker found amid the rubble at the site of the burned-out farmhouse. However, as he was frightened of Lorena, he would have to be very careful in how he would execute his ultimate plan to have a spiritual reunion with the precious ancient weapon.

When the brothers were engaged in a night of debauchery at Cueva del Chupacabra, Romero Lopes decided to cautiously pay a visit to the homestead of Blake Barker. Maybe, just maybe, Lorena had also left the premises in Blake's car and it would then be safe for Romero to ransack the home and recover the missing obsidian knife. If by chance Blake's younger sister, Elizabeth, or the child, Nathan, were still at home, it would afford Romero a tasty nocturnal snack before he retired.

The vampiro, able to peer through Nathan's bedroom window, saw that the little boy was tucked in for the night. He gently tapped on the window to awaken the child, and when he had, Nathan opened his eyes to see that his next-door neighbor had come over for a surprise visit. As Blake's only child was lonely, the boy had become very fond of the young man named Romero, whom he considered to be not only a neighbor but also a friend. Young Nathan, sadly, was totally unaware of the trauma and all the drama that had occurred the previous week. All he knew was that his mother was now gone and that he would never see her again.

Nathan threw open the window sash and squealed with excitement. "Romero, I haven't seen you in forever! Come in! I want you to play with me like we used to do. I want you to blow bubbles against my tummy and then give me a big kiss on my neck!"

Fortunately for Nathan, the yellow huevo limpia was still safely nestled beneath his bed.

"No, Nathan," Romero answered, "although I would very much like to crawl through this window and have my way with you, I can't come in for a visit. Nathan, I want to ask you a question. Earlier today, Cletus found a special knife up on my farm, and he gave it to Lorena. Well, that knife belongs to me, and I would like to have it back. Do you know if Lorena still has the special knife?"

"Yes, I know she does," Nathan answered. "She showed it to me. She said it had special powers. Lorena and Aunt Liz are watching TV in the living room! I'll go get Lorena if you'd like. She's been talking about you a lot. She told me that she just can't wait to run into you again sometime. When she does, she said that she wants to 'give it to you.' I don't know what *it* is, but I bet she wants to give you a big present. Let me just go get her. It will only take a second. I bet she'll give it to you right now, and then some!"

"No! No! No! Don't do that!" Romero said. "I have to run off and go out to get a bite to eat now. Listen, Nathan, don't tell your father, Lorena, or anybody else that your 'uncle Romero' came over for a visit. Let's keep this visit our little secret. Can you promise?"

Nathan vigorously shook his head to affirm his promise. "Yes, I can keep a secret. Bye-bye, Romero! Bye-bye!"

Romero would now have to exercise plan B in an effort to recover his obsidian knife. Perhaps he would have the opportunity to return and find the knife after Blake and Cletus left town to go on the quail hunting trip they both planned for the following weekend.

Long after the vampiro disappeared into the darkness, Liz went into the young boy's room to ascertain if everything was okay. Inexplicably, the young boy's portal sash had been released and the bedroom window was wide open. Alarmed, Liz quickly reclosed and locked the window.

"I have to be more careful from now on," Liz explained to Lorena. "An open window tempts flies, mosquitoes, and ticks to just march right in and set up shop!"

Yes, indeed. After all, it was as if Nathan had offered these bloodsucking critters an open invitation to enter his bedroom...

Although he was feeling exhausted, Romero Lopes had to feed. He came to realize that he needed a meal of either blood or iron-rich viscera every few days or else he would likely starve to death. There would be no coming back from that kind of a predicament. Consuming blood at two-day intervals would be most ideal. However, in a pinch, a vampiro could stretch out a feeding cycle to, at most, maybe seventy-six hours. After that amount of time, the vampiro would have hemolyzed essentially every single red cell in his body and would succumb to a clinical state of high-output congestive heart failure.

Romero Lopes was not about to let that happen. His best feeding opportunities would be a bit further south in El Paso, where he could easily prey upon the migrant workers who were trying to find a better life on the other side of the Rio Bravo. There was no time, however, to get down to El Paso. He was running out of options. It was incumbent upon him to find a meal in the Las Cruces area.

Technically, the vampiro could be sustained by any blood source, not necessarily human blood. In fact, the blood from any vertebrate would do just fine. The only criterion was that the vampiro needed hemoglobin. His body could not produce red cells at all unless he was absorbing an adequate supply of the iron-rich heme molecules directly across the lining of the digestive tract.

It was the exogenous heme ingested from a blood meal that would be directly incorporated into new red cell production. Without exogenous foreign hemoglobin, a vampiro would not be able to engender any new reticulocytes. In layperson's terms, without hemoglobin from a meal of blood or iron-rich viscera, the vampiro was not capable of creating any new red cells on its own accord at all. Once a vampiro was nutritionally bankrupt, the reticulocyte count, which reflects the production of new red blood cells, would drop essentially to zero and the organism would soon die.

Complicating matters was the fact that the life span of the red cells that a vampiro would be able to produce after a blood meal was only on the order of about three days. If one were to contrast the life span of a red cell produced by a vampiro directly with the life span of a red cell produced by a noninfected human being, the differences would be striking. After all, the average red blood cell in a noninfected human being has a life span of about ninety days.

If a red cell dies as a consequence of reaching its ninety-day projected life expectancy within the confines of a noninfected human being, the iron is quickly recycled in the production of new reticulocytes, so there is always a steady supply of a new red blood cells to replace the red blood cells that have expired as a consequence of natural senescence. This is, after all, a perfect example of biological conservation. This normal physiological condition is not found among any human beings afflicted with vampirism, though.

There is a peculiar and self-destructive iron-loss gradient occurring at the renal level in the vampiro ensuring that all available free iron is eventually excreted directly as waste.

In light of this situation, a vampiro is *always* in search of an iron-rich or blood-rich meal. That being the case, why was Romero Lopes compelled to viciously attack fellow human beings instead of lesser animals farther down the food chain that *Homo sapiens* have generally considered to be conventional and relatively noncontroversial food sources for eons, such as cows, pigs, and chickens? The answer to that question was readily apparent: Romero Lopes was, well—*evil*.

An opportunity for a blood meal inadvertently presented itself to Romero Lopes in downtown Las Cruces near the Nuts and Bolts hardware store that particular evening. A young pilgrim, Lucy, had just arrived from San Francisco. As she was a member of the Jody Is Alive! religious cult, she had assumed the lotus position in front of the shop in anticipation of a spiritual convergence with the prophet Jody on Halley's Comet. Well, in light of what was about to happen to young Lucy, maybe it was actually going to be a ride on "Halley's vomit."

"Excuse me, young lady, but are you looking for something?" Romero asked.

"I most certainly am!" Lucy replied. "I was hoping I would encounter a night crawler that might be able to fine-tune my chakra to a deeper level of awareness."

For Romero, this was just too easy. "Little sister, I am El Gran Brujo that you've been waiting for. Let's get to work!"

The young woman put up her hand and said, "Now, wait just a minute. Before I allow you to eat me, I must insist that you allow me to eat you. I'm obligated to give you a hum job. Those are the rules."

"Fine by me," Romero said, "but make it snappy. I have a 'rumbly in my tumbly,' and I need to chow down pretty soon."

When they entered the back alley, Lucy attempted to sexually service Romero Lopes with a vigorous act of fellatio, but the young woman was visibly disappointed that the night crawler had an atrophic penis, in addition to testicles that were so small that one would need two hands and a flashlight to find them on a sunny day. As it turned out, the evil predator was incapable of achieving an erection.

The young woman began to laugh at Romero Lopes and said, "You sure have a puny pecker for a night crawler! If I didn't know any better, I would guess that I was trying to gum down a salty Slim Jim, and a soft and soggy one at that! Is that the best you can do? You're pathetic ..."

Lucy should not have provoked Romero Lopes by debasing him with such a scalding critique of his masculinity or lack thereof. When the night crawler finished his assault and subsequent consumption of Lucy, there would simply be no residual forensic evidence that she had ever even existed.

<hr />

Señora Zuleta from the Nuts and Bolts hardware shop volunteered to watch Nathan during the scheduled chapel service at the mortuary to allow Lorena to attend Lynne's memorial service. Lorena was compelled to be present when the earthly remains of Lynne Barker were presented to Blake in an ornate funerary urn. It was quite a surprise to both Liz and Cletus that Blake had actually asked a Presbyterian minister to render prayers at the ceremony.

After the recitation of the Twenty-Third Psalm, Liz took her brother aside and asked, "Blake, have you had a spiritual reawakening? I am happy to see that you brought a minister out here for today's funeral services. I'm quite pleased. To be honest, it would not have seemed right to me otherwise."

Gently embracing the vessel that contained the carbonized

remains of his dearly departed wife, Blake replied, "Well, perhaps I'm not ready yet to go over and pay a visit to the Big Man at his house on every Sunday, especially in light of the upcoming football season this fall. However, I'm at least starting to have brief conversations with Him from time to time. As it turns out, Liz, I've had a lot to talk to Him about lately."

Cletus had been eavesdropping on the conversation. "I'm glad to hear this, Blake. I know that when you and Lynne lost your first child, you both blamed God for the accident. It was blasphemous for you to curse at God that way."

Blake replied, "I realize that. I even realized that very fact at the time when we lost baby Elizabeth. I had to blame somebody, and frankly, God was the only one who came to mind at the time. In retrospect, I suppose he was the only one big enough to handle the hatred I spewed out against the universe and everything in it. Lynne blamed not only God but also yours truly for the accident."

"Yeah, I know that," Cletus said.

"Sadly, Lynne never made peace with God or even me while she was still alive, and now—well, now ... well, you know ..." Blake felt a compulsion to talk to God yet again, but sadly at that very moment, he did not know exactly what to say. Perhaps under such circumstances, few of us mere mortals would.

"You know, Blake," Liz interjected, "I don't know if I ever told you how honored I was when you and Lynne named your first baby after me. I should have told you that a long time ago. Now I don't know why I failed to do so ..."

As it turned out, Liz realized that there were a lot of things she should have said to her family members but never shared. Perhaps this reluctance to fully embrace the love that should be fostered among members of one's family is simply an underlying character flaw that is deeply imbedded in human beings and part of the human condition. After all, is it not commonplace that many take their own family members for granted?

Cletus and Liz had pulled off a masterful feat, making certain that the reception at Blake's house after the funeral was well orchestrated. The guests mingled, and humorous anecdotes about Lynne's full, albeit brief, life were retold time and again.

Unexpectedly, Nathan appeared from his bedroom holding two bright yellow eggs. He had discovered the huevos limpias hidden beneath both his bed and Lorena's bed. He presented the two eggs to his father and said, "Daddy, it looks like the Easter Bunny came earlier this year!"

Blake remained calm when he took the two eggs from his son's hand and said, "Lorena, may I see you in the kitchen for moment?"

While Lorena looked on in horror, Blake broke both eggs into a ceramic dish greased with a thin layer of vegetable oil. He scrambled up the eggs, and before he put the dish in the microwave oven, he sprinkled a bit of graded *queso fresco* on top.

"Mr. Barker, please don't do this," Lorena pleaded. "You don't know what you're doing! Those yellow eggs are contaminated with the vampiro infection!"

Once the timer bell on the microwave oven went off, Blake Barker took the ceramic dish out and gobbled down his tiny omelet in just two bites.

"Listen to me, Lorena, there are no such things as vampires and there are no such things as huevo limpias infected with some kind of vampire germ," Blake Barker professed. "I don't care if you consider yourself to be a curandera either. Can't you see? I've eaten these eggs now, and I feel completely fine. Please, Lorena, I'm not in the mood for any more of your superstitions."

"You're making a horrible mistake!"

"Romero Lopes is not a vampire, warlock, ghoul, or magician," Blake said.

"He's all of that and so much more!"

"Grow up, Lorena. He's just a sadistic evil being who's lost his humanity." Well, at least Blake Barker was correct with that final assessment.

Lorena was beside herself with grief. "Mr. Barker, what have you done? What have you done?"

What Blake Barker had done when he ingested the two huevos limpias was to take the first step on a dark journey from which there would be no return.

11

FUND OF KNOWLEDGE

D r. Parker Coxswain, wearing his trademark black leather motorcycle cap that appeared as if it had been appropriated from a high-ranking officer of the Nazi Schutzstaffel, entered the doctors' lounge in search of his two colleagues. Parker discovered that the hematology–oncology fellow J. D. Brewster was mesmerized by a television broadcast, his face only a few inches away from the TV screen. Brewster appeared enthralled when the neoevangelist Rectal Roberts walked out on stage in front of his television congregation. The reverend was all dressed up in white like Colonel Sanders, complete with perfect snow-white hair that was plastered down in a flawless double jelly roll with either a whole tube of Brylcreem or perhaps a quart of thirty-weight motor oil. Rectal Roberts was about to perform an exorcism on a young man named Joe Cephas Smoot.

Sister Rawleen Smoot claimed that Joe Cephas was now in cahoots with Lucifer after her brother had eaten an evil yellow egg that came out of Aunt Norma's chicken coop. Aunt Norma told Joe Cephas not to do it, but the impetuous young man just couldn't help himself. He devoured the peculiar yellow egg for breakfast after he apparently added a bit of queso and salsa atop the tasty treat.

The minister challenged Joe Cephas and asked, "Why did you eat the evil yellow egg? Did yo' mama drop you on yo' head when you be a youngin? Tell me now, boy, are you in league with the devil?"

"No, I just thought Aunt Norma was being superstitious," the young man replied. "Look at me now: I am all yellowed up, and my teeth grew big! I had to get a job at the poultry processing plant just so I can drink blood. I swear, I never hurt nobody, and I just try to keep to myself. Reverend, I want you to know that I still read the Good Book every now and again, and I still go to church most every Sunday, although I'll confess I may no longer be on the up and up when the football season rolls back around this fall!"

"You're an evil agent of Satan!" Rectal Roberts said. "You're hereby banned from going to church! I command you not to even try to talk to God. He won't listen to you! Get down on your knees in front of me, you demon!"

Once Joe Cephas kneeled in front of the minister, Rectal Roberts grabbed the young man by the back of his head. The frightened man's face was then jammed into the crotch of the televangelist, as Rectal Roberts shouted out, "Hallelujah! In the name of Jah-heeez-us-uh-huh, I cast you out, you evil minion of Beelze-bubba!"

In front of God, his congregation, and a television audience that must have amounted to several dozen or so spiritually deranged individuals across the country, Rectal Roberts extracted a tungsten-handled mattock previously hidden away in his holey (holy?) undershorts and smashed Joe Cephas in the face with a mighty blow. As the unrepentant sinner collapsed to the ground and bounced unconsciously upon the floor, the congregation went wild with a pious and repetitive course of "Hallelujah!" The church members extended their right arms into defiantat fists at a forty-five-degree angle toward Rectal Roberts, while the hands and feet of the unresponsive Joe Cephas Smoot twitched and writhed ever so slightly in a nonpurposeful manner.

The usually cynical hematology–oncology fellow shouted out, "Amen and praise be!" with reverential enthusiasm.

"Turn that shit off or else you'll go blind in your left eye!" Parker harshly ordered Brewster. "If somebody else walks in here right now and sees this crap, you're going to give Christianity a bad name!"

Brewster waved off his fellow colleague from the Lone Star State and said, "Oh, you are wrong, Sansei! This is some good old-time Gospel, I tell you. This show is being broadcast straight out of Hope, Arkansas!"

"Well, in my opinion, nothing good could ever come out of Hope, Arkansas. Besides, asshole, the name Jesus does *not* have five syllables."

"It does if you're from Arkansas."

"By the way," Parker said, "what in hell are you working on over there, Brew? It looks like you are actually trying to get some work done."

"Check this out," Brewster replied. "I'm busting my balls over here on pure, unadulterated, industrial-strength chicken shit."

"Well, spill it, won't you?"

"The Turk told me that the hematology–oncology division is getting into a ringer and experiencing a financial squeeze right about now," Brewster explained. "The bean counters in admin are demanding a 5 percent cut in department expenditure. Now, although I am just a humble first-year fellow, I've been assigned the daunting task of trimming some fat from our departmental budget."

"How do you plan on doing that?"

"One of the things that we do in our department is to send out a sympathy cards to the surviving family members after one of our patients gets eaten alive from a nasty crab and mercifully croaks at the vey end."

"That's a really nice sympathetic gesture," Parker said. "I admire your compassion. I didn't realize you folks in heme–onc did that. Is that a policy that you came up with since you started your fellowship training?"

"It's a simple thing to do," Brewster answered, "but nonetheless, it's certainly the right thing to do. Anyhow, our department spent thirty-eight dollars on sympathy cards this past year, and the bean counters are having a hissy shit-fit about the whole situation."

"You can't be serious!"

"I'm as serious as a case of stage IV metastatic melanoma with multiple brain mets right about now," Brewster said. "That's why I'm working on a new, simplified form letter that we'll use in the future to send out to surviving family members after one of our patients ends up kicking the bucket."

"I assume that the letter you're working on right now is your very first draft," Parker surmised. "Pass over the goods and let me see what you've written down thus far."

"Read it and weep," Brewster said as he handed the draft over to Parker to be critiqued. "Let me know what you think after you take a gander. Now mind you, my objective is to get this entire ridiculous administrative project shitcanned. Without a doubt, what I've just handed you is the *worst* job that I could possibly do under the circumstances, and I'm absolutely certain that the bean counters will rescind their rather draconian budgetary constraints that our department is apparently about to be saddled with."

The letter stated as follows:

> Dear [fill in the blank],
>
> The Department of Hematology–Oncology would like to offer our sincerest condolences on the passing of your [circle one of the following] parent/ spouse / sibling / concubine / illicit homosexual or lesbian lover. This patient, named [fill in the blank], faced [circle one of the following] his / her terminal illness from cancer with [circle one of the following] bravery / ambivalence / dignity / abject terror in conjunction with inconsolable despair. May [circle one of the following] God / Mother Gaia / the universe / Allah / Vishnu / Tezcatlipoca / the ridiculous bullshit pagan entity that you worship provide you with at least some measure of

comfort, no matter that it's self-delusional, during your time of unrelenting sorrow, which will likely be as perpetual as it will be spiritually crushing, without any hope of finding redemption, salvation, or existential meaning in the purpose of life.

Please do not contact us under any circumstances for any reason in the near or distant future unless the health insurance company or the estate of the dearly departed has met all of its financial copay obligations to this institution. Have a nice day.

Sincerely,
The Department of Hematology–Oncology

"You're a fucking genius. Don't change a thing. Have the Turk sign off on this project, and then send it over to administration right away for their immediate approval. If I were you, I'd do it immediately," Parker said after he read the draft. "In case you didn't already know, I'm obligated to inform you at this juncture that you're going straight to hell."

"In a handbasket," Brewster conceded.

Upon the arrival of Dr. Booker Marshall, the three musketeers whom Dr. Dove and Dr. Cloud derisively referred to as the members of the University of Texas at Santa Fe reclined in the doctors' lounge to have a cup coffee and brainstorm over the peculiar case of Mr. Miguel Pastore, who had become transfusion dependent. The patient required no fewer than four units of blood to sustain his life, and he needed this blood product support at approximately forty-eight-hour intervals.

It was the first day back to work for Booker Marshall after having been out of commission since the time he suffered from an exacerbation of sickle cell disease. If a patient has a flare-up of sickle cell disease, the medical emergency is often referred to as a sickle cell crisis. This life-threatening malady is given that particular moniker for a very good reason.

"How do you feel, Book?" Parker asked. "I can tell you haven't bounced back yet."

"Well, how do I look?" the near cachectic-appearing black man responded.

The hematology–oncology fellow J. D. Brewster made no bones about the situation when he added, "Frankly, Book, you look like shit."

Booker smiled and said, "Leave it to you, Brewster, to tell it like it is. If that is indeed the case, I am happy to report to you boys that there is a direct correlation between my overt shabby appearance and my subjective sense of well-being, or lack thereof as the case may be."

"How bad was it this time?" Brewster asked.

Booker Marshall proceeded to run down the laundry list of medical problems that he was now afflicted with. "I had a retinal infarct, and I'm now blind in my left eye."

"Nice," Parker said.

"Do you have any idea what it's like to be blind in your left eye?" Booker Marshall asked as he cast a gaze toward J. D. Brewster. "Well, let me tell you, it sucks major league."

As Brewster circled his head in a slow counterclockwise motion, Booker Marshall continued. "My kidneys appear to be, at best, in a very foul mood. When I left the hospital, my creatinine was up to 3.4. It's certainly not in dialysis range as of yet, but to be frank, I'm frightened about my situation. Check this out: my tallywacker got poned up hard with priapism. The pain was unbearable. I ended up with a nasty infarct in my penis. When I developed gangrene in old Mr. Hoo-Ha, the urologists came out with their long knives."

"That sounds terrible!" Brewster exclaimed, unable to see the big picture. "What did they end up doing to you?"

Parker Coxswain proceeded to give Brewster a vicious slap on the back of the head and said, "For shit's sake, Brewster, do you have to be a dumbass every single day of your life? Wake up! There are just some things that a man can't discuss with another man. I don't know how you've made it this far in life without somebody taking you out into a back alley and bitch-slapping the dog crap out of you!"

Brewster's mouth slowly dropped open in shame when he finally realized that his black colleague from Houston had been, for no better available colloquial terminology, nipped in the bud. Booker Marshall was only thirty-three years old. Sadly, at his current rate of rapid decomposition, it was highly unlikely that he would live long enough to enter his fifth decade.

—⚟—

It's absolutely extraordinary that one single point mutation in the human genome is responsible for so much grief. The inherited sickle cell gene results in a single amino acid substitution of glutamic acid to valine at the number six position on the beta-globin chain. If an individual has inherited one set of this peculiar sickle cell gene from one parent, then such individual is a heterozygous sickle cell genetic Hb AS *carrier*, with the letter *A* representing a normal hemoglobin complement and the *S* representing the sickle cell anomaly.

If an individual is unfortunate enough to inherit two sickle cell genes (one copy of the sickle cell gene from each of the parents who were presumably relatively asymptomatic carriers), then said individual has a homozygous genetic complement. He or she will develop a full-blown case of the genetically inherited Hb SS sickle cell *disease*, manifested once an individual possess two copies of the horrid cursed genome. Sadly, to put it in as succinct terms as possible, a person unfortunate enough to be afflicted with a full-blown case of sickle cell disease is totally screwed, and assuredly it's up one street and down another.

More than four million unfortunate individuals walking around on the planet at any given time are afflicted with a full-blown case of sickle cell disease, and the number of carriers of the trait account for an additional tenfold of the previously stated number. Sadly, more than one hundred thousand people die every year from sickle cell disease. African Americans are sadly underrepresented in the national bone marrow registry program and this is rather problematic, as bone marrow (stem cell) transplantation is the only current treatment known to be curative.

Generally, in an unstressed clinical state, the red cells of a patient with sickle cell disease function quite normally. However, under situations where regional or systemic hypoxia occurs, the abnormal hemoglobin found in patients afflicted with sickle cell disease will begin to crystallize and bridge abnormally to elongate the affected red cell into a rigid C-shaped erythrocyte that can easily cause thrombosis of the body's microcirculation.

The severe circulatory problems that occur in patients afflicted with sickle cell disease will cause an increased lifetime risk of infections, cerebrovascular accidents, renal dysfunction, gallstones as a consequence of the excessive bilirubin waste production from the high red blood cell turnover, blindness, penile infarctions with necrosis as a consequence of priapism from vascular congestion, pulmonary hypertension, and ultimately a short and brutal life of chronic pain. During the 1980s, most patients who were cursed with a diagnosis of sickle cell disease had a life expectancy of only about forty years.

How could such a destructive oddity persist in the human genome? It's interesting to note that as early as the mid-1950s, it was recognized that those who inherited the sickle cell gene had a markedly decreased risk of acquiring malaria, which of course is a tropical infectious disease rampant throughout sub-Saharan Africa. The malarial trypanosome is generally transmitted through the bite of the anopheles mosquito.

It would appear that the single-cell parasite that causes malaria does not particularly enjoy the "taste" of sickled hemoglobin, and that's why individuals who possess the sickle cell gene are relatively resistant to malaria! Is that not odd? Perhaps if one possessed the sickle cell gene, one might be protected not only from infectious diseases transmitted by mosquitoes but also, perhaps, from additional diseases transmitted by other nasty bloodsucking creatures...

Brooker Marshall addressed his two colleagues as if he were preaching to a congregation. Unlike the televangelist from Arkansas, Booker was able to formulate a bona fide insightful spiritual overview of his existential circumstances. "I don't know about this premonition that I've had for a while, but for some reason I think that I am getting closer to the finish line of my life."

"You've had a good run, Book," Parker said.

"Maybe so," Booker said. "My only regret is that I missed a chance to be loved. If that had happened, even for a fleeting moment, I think I would truly feel that my life was complete. I guess it just wasn't meant to happen for me. It's the awareness of our mortality that gives our lives any meaning at all."

"What do any of us have?" Brewster asked. "If a person is lucky, maybe he or she will have four score or so spins around the sun. That's it. That's all we get."

"That's the whole point," Booker said. "I can't help but be philosophical about all of this. I believe that we're all called to find some tangible mission that's righteous and good. That's why we're here. That's my conviction. At the end of the day, we should always try to find the right thing to do. That's all that matters."

"At the end of the day, we should always try to find a cold beer," Brewster said. "That's all that matters."

Booker's insightful revelations regarding a more harmonious and fulfilling pathway through the briars and brambles of life had apparently been cast before swine.

Parker Coxswain broke the tension by busting Booker Marshall's chops. After all, the three men were from Texas. That's what Texans do best to each other. "Look, Booker, if you plan on kicking the bucket anytime soon, I've got the dibs on your Otis Redding collection. You better take care of it, because I don't want it all scratched up and shit upon by the time I get my hands on it. I don't care about any of that disco crap you have. You can give all that urban bullshit to Brewster."

"Enough, gentlemen. It's time to get back on track here. I took a look at all of Miguel Pastore's charts and labs. I didn't see the results of the diagnostic bone marrow aspiration and biopsy, however. What's the deal on that, Brewster? Did you look at the dude's marrow with your own eye under the scope?"

"I looked at it, and I did my own five hundred cell count," the hematology–oncology fellow replied. "The pathologist hasn't signed off on it yet because he doesn't know what to make of the situation."

"Who's the pathologist on the case?" Parker asked.

"Dr. Wanker."

"He's a tool," Parker said. "I wouldn't be surprised if he dropped this load of work on somebody else to finish up."

"Be that as it may," Brewster said, "I saw that the marrow was comprised of a uniform-appearing population of blasts not otherwise specified, accounting for about 17 percent of the bone marrow population. What's odd is that these blast cells were extraordinarily huge. They appeared to be twice the size of your average marrow progenitor. It looks, as best as I can tell, like a refractory anemia with an excess of blasts in transformation. It's not full-blown leukemia, but in my opinion Mr. Pastore's peculiar disease is standing on the edge of a cliff."

"Well, why has it not been signed out yet?" Booker asked. "What's holding up the official report? Tell me about the blasts; are they myeloblasts or are they lymphoblasts? Parker, you supervised the flow study. Cough it up, son! What did it show?"

"Jack and diddly," Parker Coxswain said, "and in whatever combination you want to use those two words."

"I don't understand," Brewster said. "What in hell were the surface markers?"

"It showed nothing!" Parker answered. "The flow didn't mark out anything at all. The cells look like blasts, but this disease, whatever it is, looks like it's comprised of a population of cells that have dedifferentiated into an extremely immature state. They behave as if they're nuclear-powered pluripotent embryonic stem cells."

"Bullshit," Booker interjected. "That makes absolutely no sense."

"Check this out; I'm going to tell you something very disturbing," Parker continued. "Until I can confirm the validity of what I am about to tell you, this should stay between us. I took a sample of the marrow aspirate in culture medium and brought it down to Lee Chilton in the animal lab. I had a hunch, so I asked Lee to subject some of the immunologically nude mice to the cells that I'd harvested from the marrow aspirate."

"Well, don't leave us out here flapping in the breeze," Booker said. "What happened?"

"All the mice developed teratocarcinomas representing all biological cell lines, including endoderm, mesoderm, and ectodermal tissues. One of the tumors even grew out teeth! I shit you not!" Parker explained. "Others started to produce tissues that were indistinguishable from mature visceral organs. All of the nude mice died from cancer within seventy-two hours of inoculation. I've never heard of or seen any cell line growing that fast."

"Brewster, is there any kind of human analog that has such a rapid rate of replication?"

"The fastest-growing human tumor cell lines are found in small-cell bronchogenic carcinomas and also in the high-grade B-cell Burkitt's Lymphoma malignancies," Brewster answered. "These cancer cell lines have a tumor doubling time on the order of thirty days or so. Well, given what Parker just said, and according to my calculations, the stem cells that were transferred into the nude mice had a tumor doubling time of hours!"

"That is indeed terrifying," Booker Marshall said.

"Look, I can't explain it," Parker said. "I can only tell you what I witnessed. So tell, me ladies and germs; if what I've witnessed is not an example of pluripotent stem cell proliferation on high octane, then I just don't know what in hell we are dealing with here."

Booker Marshall held his index finger up in the air to draw the attention of his two colleagues. "So, the records indicate that this Miguel Pastore individual claimed that he was bitten by a 'night stalker,' if such a thing exists. If that's indeed the case, we must be dealing with some type of horizontally transmissible agent. The only thing that it could possibly be is some type of virus. Tell me, Brewster, do you still know how to operate an electron microscope?"

"In my sleep," Brewster answered. "What do you have in mind?"

"They still have a fair amount of the marrow aspirate that you collected in the incubator down in the laboratory, do they not?" Booker asked. "Brewster, I strongly suggest you refrain from presenting this case at the tumor board until we have all these unanswered questions buttoned up. Let's reconvene in another forty-eight hours. By then, we'll know a lot more. In the meantime, I propose to my fellow members of the University of Texas at Santa Fe that we all go on a fishing trip and see if we can confirm any viral budding in any of these peculiar marrow stem cells."

"How is that going to help us out in understanding what's going on?" Parker asked.

"I see where Booker is going with this line of reasoning," Brewster said. "You might be blind in one eye and have puny kidneys, Booker, but you're still a pretty smart guy. If we find viral budding, we will be able to explain the hemolytic events in this disease process."

In light of his physically frail condition, Booker Marshall looked to his colleagues and pleaded for help. "I am going to extend my arms now, and I want you boys to gently pull me up and out of this chair so I can get upright and get back to the research lab. If we are able to pull this off, I believe that the forthcoming Nobel Prize in Medicine that will be bestowed upon us would be a pretty good way for me to buff up my resume before I kick the bucket!"

As a man who appeared to have made peace with what would soon turn out to be his premature demise, Booker Marshall added, "I feel compelled to try to leave behind some sort of scientific or medical legacy before I have to take my own personal permanent big dirt nap in the not too distant future!"

———

When Blake Barker awoke the morning after Lynne's funeral, he felt terrible. Abdominal bloating, diarrhea, and a low-grade fever had left him with a very poor appetite. Although at that point no overt changes in the hue of his integument could be readily appreciated, Blake was mildly alarmed when the color of his urine appeared to be quite dark when he evacuated the contents of his bladder into the toilet during his first morning micturition event.

Although Sister Liz had prepared pancakes and sausage patties for the entire family, Blake initially had none of it. Fortunately, by midmorning, his symptoms of nausea definitely started to subside and he felt well enough to try to tackle some of the leftover pancakes. Although they were already cold, Blake peeled one of the pancakes out of the plastic wrap, poured some honey on it, and tried to eat it. Sadly, his attempt to ingest the carbohydrate-rich meal turned out to be an unmitigated disaster. Immediately after swallowing the bite of sweetened pancake, Blake vomited into the kitchen sink.

Lorena, having witnessed the entire event, approached her employer to determine the gravity of the situation. "You don't look so well, Señor Barker. Maybe you've caught an infection. Perhaps you should lie down for a while. Go ahead and rest. You can trust me to keep an eye on things for a while."

"Thanks, Lorena, that's a really good idea." What Blake did not realize was that Lorena was going to keep an eye on *him*. For the time being, that was the only thing that really mattered to the curandera.

From the cover of a nearby creosote bush, Romero Lopes watched with great interest as a young, thin Hispanic male successfully squeezed through a rent in the corrugated steel panel that served as a makeshift barrier between Los Estados Unidos de America y Los Estados Unidos de Mexico. Located due west of the city limits of El Paso, La Frontera, as it was called, was near the tristate intersection of Texas, the Badlands of New Mexico, y el Estado de Chihuahua. At best, it was a sketchy neighborhood in the mid-1980s where bad hombres and bad gringos would frequently lock horns over illegal *drogas, mujeres, y armas de fuego.* Sadly, some things never change.

"Señor, *¿adónde vas?*" Romero Lopes, emerging from the desert brush, asked the transient.

The engaging and polite young man reached out and proceeded to vigorously shake the hand of Romero Lopes. "*Mi nombre es Trinidad. Mucho gusto.*"

Romero Lopes identified himself and replied, "Don't be silly. I assure you, in just a few moments, the honor will be all mine."

Trinidad had explained that he was trying to get to Casa Grande, Arizona, where a vast stretch of farmland had been carved out of the hostile Sonoran Desert as a consequence of the engineering marvel of irrigation. The young man had extensive experience with the physically demanding work of agricultural labor in the past, having toiled in the cotton fields of both Texas and Arizona.

As it turned out, el hermano was already there in Arizona, and he was scratching out a successful, albeit modest, living. Most of the money that the older brother Timoteo earned in the United States was wired back to Mexico to try to support his elderly parents and various frail and ill relatives among his extended family. Timoteo extended an invitation to Trinidad to come north and lend a hand with the abundant work that would available in the cotton fields in the coming spring, which was only a few weeks away.

"I'm taking I-25 north, and then I am going to turn west on Interstate 10," Romero Lopes said. "I'm on my way to Phoenix, and that nasty little shitbird of a town called Casa Grande is on the way. I plan on pulling in to fuel up at the Stuckey's truck stop near the Florence Boulevard and I-10 intersection, so I'll at least get you that far. I would very much enjoy your company for that leg of my trip. Perhaps you could feed me—uh, tell me some stories along the way!"

Trinidad suddenly became suspicious of the motives of this odd hombre. Something was not quite right about the appearance and mannerisms of this stranger who offered him a lift all the way to Casa Grande.

The young migrant pressed Romero for clarity about the peculiar circumstances in which he now found himself. "You and I are about two hundred meters west of I-25 in the desert. If you have a big truck, why are you out here in the middle of nowhere? Surely you didn't need to come out this far just to relieve your bladder. The story you just told me doesn't make any sense."

"Yes, I guess that by now you've figured me out," Lopes replied. "I have no intention of giving you a ride anywhere. My real objectives are to suck the blood out of you and then consume your vital internal organs while you are still very much alive. Boy oh boy, is this going to be fun or what?" When Romero Lopes opened his mouth wide, he flashed the enormous fangs embedded in his upper jaw. "Go ahead and scream! Nobody's going to hear you!"

"¡Un vampiro!" The young migrant tried to sprint toward the relative safety of the interstate, but he couldn't match the speed of Romero Lopes. Once the vampiro overtook Trinidad, the young man who only moments before was seeking a better life was sadly reduced to mere bones and scraps of lacerated bloodless flesh. Satisfied with his vicious handiwork, Romero abandoned the leftovers in the desert as a gift to the roaming packs of wild canids commonly known as coyotes and to the voracious porcine omnivores commonly known as javelinas.

On Sunday morning, Blake Barker was feeling considerably better. In fact, he had never felt as physically fit as at that particular moment in his life, and that included all the days he could recall when he was in college more than a decade and a half earlier. Although it had only been a week since he fractured his collarbone, the previous irregular swelling over the clavicle was completely resolved.

In addition, Blake was curious to note that the contusions and discomfort that accompanied his fractured eye socket also had disappeared completely. How could this be? Not about to look a gift horse in the mouth, Blake decided to go out for a jog.

He explained to Liz and Cletus that he was going out to get some exercise, and then he took off on the one-mile round-trip journey to the intersection of Calle Murciélago and Avenida Chupadores de Sangre. This time, the round trip didn't present any type of physical challenge to Blake. He completed his workout in three minutes and four seconds. It was astonishing that Blake Barker had quarter-mile interval splits of about forty-six seconds. At that speed, he instantaneously became a world-class 400 meter, 800 meter, and 1,600 meter runner. In fact, he had set several world records while he out on his casual jog, although he didn't understand or appreciate what he had just accomplished.

When he reentered his farmhouse, Lorena said, "I thought you were going out for a jog. Back so soon?"

"Well, I put in a mile, and I feel fine," Blake said. Liz and Cletus looked at each other in stunned silence. "I'm not even short of breath right now. Wow, how about that?"

Blake suddenly became aware that Cletus, Liz, and Lorena were slowly backing away from him. He raised his voice and asked, "Why are you people looking at me like that? What in hell is the matter with you all? Knock it off, damn it!"

Lorena was already formulating a plan to try to keep the other family members safe from what her employer was about to transform into. Of all the people she was concerned about, young Nathan was at the top of the list. Blake Barker was already undergoing frightening physiological and aggressive psychological changes, and everybody could see it. Everybody, that is, but Blake Barker.

The following morning, Lorena was surprised to find a rather disturbing drawing that Nathan had put up on the refrigerator door. Affixed by a magnet, the crude work of art had been rendered courtesy of the child's liberal employment of a variety of brightly colored crayons. At the top of the drawing, Nathan had written "To Uncle Romero." Underneath the lettered heading was a drawing of the family alpaca that was brutally murdered by the vicious vampiro. Nathan had taken a red crayon and colored in the blood that was dripping to the ground from the animal's neck. On the torso of the alpaca, Nathan had written "Shark Face."

Alarmed, Lorena pulled the drawing off the refrigerator door and went directly to Nathan's room. "Mijo, *¿qué es esto?* Why did you draw something like this?"

Nathan refused to answer Lorena's questions. In reply he said, "I can't tell you. Uncle Romero made me promise to keep it a secret."

Lorena raised her voice at that point. "Romero?! You wrote the words *Shark Face*. What does that mean?"

The answer that Nathan gave made Lorena nauseous. "That's because Uncle Romero let me touch his top teeth. His teeth are *really* sharp! I have to be careful when I touch his teeth. Otherwise I could cut myself."

"You touched his teeth?!"

"He told me that if I cut myself accidentally when I let him suck on my fingers, he would just suck and suck on my blood until I quit bleeding."

"What are you saying?"

"Romero said that all bleeding eventually stops," Nathan added.

"Oh my God!" Lorena exclaimed. "When did you see him?"

"He's really smart," Nathan continued. "Lorena, tell me something: does all bleeding eventually stop?"

Lorena began to tremble. "Has Romero Lopes been coming by at night to pay you a visit? Why would you call him 'Uncle Romero'? He is definitely not your uncle!"

"I'll tell you," Nathan answered, "but Lorena, you have to keep it a secret. He comes by to visit me every night. I call him 'Uncle Romero' because he said that when the rest of my family leaves me behind like Mommy did, he'll take me with him and he'll make me grow up to be just like him."

"You're not allowed to talk to him anymore!"

"Why not?" Nathan asked. "I can work for him someday. He said that we can even go out hunting at night together! I've wanted him to come into my room to play with me, but lately he says that our house has a bad stink. Last night when he came by for a visit, he said that our house smelled a lot better, and he promised that tonight that he would come inside and go room to room to visit everybody while they're sleeping!"

Realizing the family had lost the prophylactic protection of the odor emanating from the huevos limpias that Blake Barker had consumed in anger, the curandera quickly came to the conclusion that there was little she could do to keep the family from being viciously slaughtered. After the federal government disassembled the chicken coop, Lorena no longer had access to the special eggs utilized in the huevo limpia ceremony. Perhaps she could set a trap to ambush the son of a bitch. All she needed was a weapon—a very *powerful* weapon.

The caretaker softly said to herself, "Well, Lorena, you're in quite a pickle. If you're going to give Romero Lopes a big surprise tonight, it better be a good one. What should I do? Let me see. Let me see ..."

Liz made lovely vegetable lasagna for dinner that evening for the entire family. This particular Italian dish used to be a favorite of Blake when he was a younger man, but oddly he turned up his nose at it. "I can't eat this crap."

Blake went to the freezer, pulled out a twelve-ounce venison steak, and rejoined his family at the dinner table with the rock-hard frozen flesh. His family members stared at him with awe as he proceeded to bite into the frozen piece of deer meat and voraciously consume it. Blake was totally oblivious that his behavior was becoming more erratic.

"After dinner, I want to go back to Cueva del Chupacabra. Liz, I want you and Cletus to come with me."

"Not tonight," Liz said. "Why don't we just have a quiet evening together?"

"I won't take no for an answer," Blake said. "Lorena, I'm going to request that you stay here and keep an eye on Nathan."

"Now, wait just one moment," Lorena said. "This was the night we promised Nathan that he could have that birthday party sleepover at Polo Zuleta's house. I'm supposed to have Nathan dropped off over there by five o'clock this evening."

"Shit, I forgot," Blake said. "Take care of it, Lorena. Make sure that you buy the little bastard Polo some kind of birthday present, but I don't want you to spend too much money on the kid."

"You know, Blake, going back out to that bar might not be a good idea right now," Cletus said. "You don't seem to be acting like yourself. You're behaving like you have a big chip on your shoulder. Liz and I will be going at the end of next week. We should just stay home and enjoy each other's company tonight."

Liz and Lorena fully concurred with Cletus's recommendation, but Blake would have none of it. He stood and loomed over his brother and sister and issued an order that was quite menacing in its tone: "We're going to that pool hall tonight whether you like it or not. I demand that you two come with me!"

—⟞⟞⟞⟞⟞⟞—

With hypervigilant acuity, Liz and Cletus sat down at the bar, with their brother Blake perched between them. With somber trepidation, neither Cletus nor his younger sister felt any compulsion to hoist on high any alcohol-infused libations. Given that such was the case, Liz and Cletus simply ordered club soda with a wedge of lime.

"What in hell is the matter with you two?" Blake asked. "Have you both become a couple of lightweights or something?"

No sooner had those words parted company with Blake's vocal cords than the large, angry pool player who had previously given Blake and Cletus the bum's rush approached the trio. The giant said in a calm but firm monotone, "I told you boys to stay the hell out of here. It would seem to me that you didn't learn your lesson."

He turned to Elizabeth and said, "I beg your pardon, ma'am, but these boys are a couple of smart-ass scoundrels. If they know what is good for them, they'll—"

Blake made certain that the surly giant never finished his sentence. A lightning-fast jab to the left eye socket left the big man dazed. While the big man was reeling, Blake jumped off his barstool and proceeded to drive the man's head all the way through the drywall at the back of the pool room lounge. Once this was done, the head of the giant protruded above the urinal in the men's room as if it were a full-rack bull elk trophy on display in the man cave of a testosterone-endowed Neanderthal.

Blake returned to his siblings, sat back down at the bar, and calmly asked, "Well now, where were we? Cletus, I believe you were just about to tell me about your business trip to Tulsa coming up this March."

As Romero Lopes enticed Nathan to solemnly promise the night before, the boy had left the window to his bedroom unlocked. After the ghoul opened the window, he inhaled deeply through his nostrils to make absolutely certain there wasn't una vampira on the premises. As the prophylactic huevos limpias had long since passed through the digestive system of Blake Barker, Romero did not detect any of the odors that on previous occasions he erroneously assumed had emanated from Lorena.

Because the vampiro's exquisitely sensitive olfactory nerves detected no suspicious fumes, Lopes carefully crawled into Nathan's room, making an effort not to jostle the boy's bed. The specific mission was to murder everybody in the house, find the missing obsidian knife that was recovered from the burned-out farmhouse, and abscond with Nathan. Once successfully accomplished, he would turn the small child into a bloodsucking love slave.

The vampiro was obviously unaware that Nathan was at a birthday party sleepover. The entire house was now vacant except for the curandera. Romero Lopes, in a hushed tone, spoke out, "All right, Lorena, you deluxe bitch, that obsidian knife must be in this house somewhere, and I'm going to get it."

From out of the darkness, the vampiro heard the voice of Lorena Pastore declare, "Hey, *pendejo*; you're going to get it all right. I believe this is what you're looking for!"

Romero Lopes instinctively retreated as Lorena lunged at him with the obsidian knife. She tried to drive the blade into his heart, but she missed the mark. The vampiro fell backward and landed on the floor. The blade was driven deep into the anterior aspect of the right thigh of the evil ghoul. As Lopes scrambled to get to his feet, Lorena held fast to the obsidian knife. The razor-sharp weapon left a gash all the way from the top of his thigh to his kneecap. Romero was finally able to escape through the bedroom window.

Although seriously wounded, he cried out, "You're here?! How could that be when I couldn't smell you? You tricked me, you filthy whore!"

Lorena ridiculed the vampiro as he hobbled away into the darkness. *"¡Sí! Yo engañó usted, porque yo soy una gran bruja!"*

12

A Man of Righteous Convictions

After taking a week off from his job for unpaid, but begrudgingly authorized, bereavement leave, it was now time for Blake Barker to return to work at the Nuts and Bolts hardware shop in Las Cruces. As Blake was still in his employment probationary period as the hardware store manager, he needed to make certain that he didn't further aggravate the store owner, Mr. I. B. Terdly. Blake could ill-afford to have his name placed upon what the other hardware shop employees sardonically referred to as Mr. Terdly's "Pond Scum" list.

Señora Zuleta handed Blake a cup of freshly brewed coffee. She was the first to greet the shop manager that cold Monday morning. "Mr. Barker, I'm so sorry for your loss. Welcome back to work. Are you feeling okay? Your skin is starting to look a little bit pale. I hope you are not coming down with something."

"No, Sophie," Barker replied as he politely turned down her offer of a cup of hot joe. "I might look a little frayed around the edges, but for some reason, I'm actually feeling pretty strong right now." Blake felt compelled to modify his previous statement. "Well, let me clarify that: my *physical* constitution is pretty good, but my *emotional* constitution is pretty messed up. Except for my son, I don't seem to care about much of anything right about now. I want to thank you for keeping an eye on Nathan during

Lynne's memorial service. I just didn't think it would be right to take a five year-old child to his own mother's funeral. Somehow I think that would have been too emotionally traumatic for him. Nathan is just now coming to grips with the fact that he'll never see his mother again."

"Are your brother and sister still in town?" Mrs. Zuleta asked.

"They'll be here until the end of the week," Barker replied. "Before my brother leaves town, he wants to take me out quail hunting like we did years ago."

"You should go," Señora Zuleta said. "It would be good for you."

"To be honest," Blake said, "I'm not much in the mood for doing anything. I'll probably go out on the hunting trip, but I'll just be going through the motions. It would seem that my brother and sister are starting to become a bit overbearing."

"I'm sure they are just trying to be helpful."

"I suppose so," Blake said. "I'm going to put on a good face for their behalf. It will be just a few more days before they leave town. You know, I should not have said that. What's wrong with me?"

"Mr. Barker, you just lost your wife," Sophie Zuleta said. "That's what's wrong with you."

"I find that I am becoming short-tempered with Cletus, Liz, and even Lorena. I really love my family, and I'm glad they are here for me at this dreadful time, but lately I seem to be flying off the handle with very little, if any, provocation," Blake explained.

"Don't be so hard on yourself, Mr. Barker," Sophie said. "It's all quite understandable with what you have been through."

"Perhaps you're right," Blake agreed. "Complicating matters is the fact that there is something wrong with my digestive system. Of late, the only thing I seem able to tolerate is meat in my diet. It is really strange, but sweet or starchy stuff makes me vomit almost immediately. If this persists, I'm obviously going to have to get it checked out. Did you know that Lynne used to work at a doctor's office? Maybe I should give Doc a call sooner rather than later. In any event, from a spiritual standpoint, I'm in disarray. Perhaps I just need to retreat into emotional solitude for a while."

Just then, the front door alarm began to screech out a high-decibel howl as a young tough guy bolted out of the hardware shop with a stolen item. The delinquent adolescent tried to abscond with an expensive Maglite, but he would not get far from the scene of the crime. The loud alarm enraged Blake Barker. He cupped his hands over his ears in an effort to escape the dreadful sound. He sprinted out of the store in hot pursuit of the shoplifter. The would-be thief was dragged down in only a few seconds. Blake Barker managed to pull the heavy-duty metal flashlight out of the young man's hand. Blake repeatedly bludgeoned the miscreant over the head with the big Maglite until the teenager was spread-eagle on the parking lot asphalt, critically injured and in a comatose state.

When Blake returned to the store, he waved about the bloody flashlight triumphantly while he issued a most cruel and barbaric order to the store's numerous employees. "Leave that kid's body out there on the parking lot to rot. Let that be a lesson to any son of a bitch who tries to shoplift from our Nuts and Bolts hardware store. I swear to God, somebody better turn off that goddamned alarm right now or I'm going to kill somebody!"

———

By the time the police arrived at the hardware shop, an ambulance had already taken the shoplifter to the hospital, where he would be admitted to the intensive care unit with a closed head injury. The unfortunate teenager would end up being in the hospital for over two weeks before he was well enough to be discharged to home.

The police officer who interviewed Blake Barker gently tapped a ballpoint pen on his left earlobe while he offered a scathing editorial assessment of the situation. "So, Mr. Barker, it would seem to me that your actions to stop the shoplifter were a bit excessive.

I'm telling you right now, this might end up before a grand jury to consider whether or not what you did constitutes assault with a deadly weapon. For your sake, I hope the teenager on the receiving end of that Maglite has a full recovery."

"Let justice be served," Blake responded. "I swear to you right here and right now, I'll be vindicated!"

The police officer shrugged his shoulders. "We shall see."

—⟨⟩—

Dr. Ron Shiftless and Colonel Augustus Placard approached the gray clapboard house in Hope, Arkansas, with considerable apprehension. When Shiftless knocked upon the front door, Placard immediately placed his right hand on the butt end of his sidearm as a precautionary measure. Fortunately, the colonel's fears were unfounded. It was immediately clear when Joe Cephas Smoot answered the door that he would behave as nothing but a gracious and courteous host.

Smoot went as far as to offer his guests a nice tall glass of iced tea with a wedge of lemon. "Gentlemen, I hope you like sun tea," Joe said. "I have discovered through a simple trial and error process that it takes about eight bags to make a half gallon of tasty tea. Sister Rawleen says that I make it too strong. To my way of thinking, a guest can always water it down just a tad if he or she finds it too strong. Forgive my manners; I forgot to ask either of you gentlemen if you'd like to add any sugar or artificial sweetener to your tea."

"Unsweetened iced tea is fine with us," Colonel Placard said.

"You know, it's very strange," Joe Cephas lamented. "I used to like sugar in my tea, but I have found that anything that tastes sweet, and even simple things like bread and corn, make me sick to my stomach now. It's kind of sad when I think about all that has happened to me. My family used to say that I had a sweet tooth. Not anymore. Now I just have fangs. It seems like the only thing I can tolerate in my diet now is raw red organ meat and animal blood."

"Deal with it," Ron Shiftless said in a somewhat callous manner.

"My boss down at the poultry processing plant is a very good man," Smoot explained. "He's a Christian, and he goes to my church. We've become really good friends, I tell you. He lets me have as much chicken blood as I need. He doesn't treat me like I'm some kind of evil freak like some other people in this town do when they're around me. That is why I just try to keep to myself now. I can't help what I am. As Popeye once said, 'I yam what I yam.'" Joe Cephas tried to laugh, but it was a laughter layered with a thick veneer of personal sorrow.

Dr. Ron Shiftless sat across the coffee table from Joe Cephas Smoot and said, "Do you know how lucky we are to be able to find you, Mr. Smoot? You're the first reported case of human vampirism to our knowledge within the continental United States, outside the borders of the state of New Mexico. I'm sorry to report that the authorities were forced to confiscate and destroy all your Aunt Norma's poultry. Don't worry about Norma; she's safely nestled away in quarantine for a week. In any event, if you hadn't appeared on the *Rectal Roberts Ministry Hour*, we would have never known you were out here."

Joe Cephas asked, "Will my aunt Norma receive some kind of monetary compensation for her financial loss? Her chicken farm, to my knowledge, is her only means that she has to sustain herself. To be honest with you, I'm quite worried about her current circumstances."

"Not a dog's chance in hell," Placard said. "Sorry about that."

"I must say that I find your hometown of Hope, Arkansas, to be a foul admixture of toothless inbred yahoos who surely are afflicted with a variety of nasty, incurable infectious diseases involving their various and sundry reproductive genitalia," Shiftless said as he cast aspersions upon not only his host, but the state of Arkansans in general. "Sadly, with the abundance of microcephalic cretins I see walking about in this neighborhood, I would suspect that this tidal wave of sexually transmitted diseases of which I have spoken ad nauseam are likely to be vertically transmitted to the unfortunate offspring who are now condemned to live in this backwater shit hole."

Although Joe Cephas Smoot was a bit slow on the uptake, he was a righteous God-fearing man who had been reared in the Bible Belt. He had never before heard anybody levy such loquacious insults upon him. He misinterpreted what Dr. Ron Shiftless had said to him as nothing less than a generous compliment. "Well, thank you! We do have a lot of pretty smart little critters running around here. Personally, I would not be surprised if somebody from here became the president of the United States one day!"

"I'd take it up the ass before I would allow myself to live long enough to see that happen!" Shiftless said. Colonel Placard and Dr. Shiftless looked at each other in astonishment before they broke out in ribald laughter.

"Well, Mr. Smoot, that political prognostication could only ever occur if the voting population of the United States someday went totally bonkers with unbridled insanity!" the military officer countered. "Be that as it may, let me get right down to the brass bolts with you. Dr. Shiftless and I are here to talk about a business proposition. How would you like to come down to San Antonio, Texas, and become an employee of the federal government?"

"You boys expectin' me to up and quit my job at the poultry processing plant?" Smoot asked. "I like my job! They treat me real good there."

"We'll set you up at the US Army Department of Biological Warfare," Placard explained. "While you're there, we'll train you to become an undercover operative, and you could eventually be farmed out to other federal agencies to conduct important missions on behalf of the United States of America. If you ever went out on a mission, I would be there with you at all times to oversee the operation. If you're willing to sign on with us, we would happily give you as much blood as you could ever possibly need to keep you alive. I want you to be truthful with me now, Mr. Smoot. I understand that since you have become a vampire, you've not killed anybody. Is that correct?"

"Perish the thought!"

"Well, if that is indeed the case, would you have any qualms about possibly killing an enemy combatant on behalf of your country if such an opportunity were to arise at some time in the near or distant future?"

Smoot was obviously deeply offended. "What do you think I am? I'm a damned vampire, not an evil ghoul! I'll have you know that it's a mortal sin to kill another human being. After all, it's a commandment in the Bible. 'Thou shalt not kill.' Ever heard it?"

"Hang on," Shiftless said. "You're a patriot, aren't you?"

"Now, I got no problem with greasin' some godless heathen gook hidin' in the bush if it's my duty, but we ain't in a war right now," Smoot explained. "I don't trust Uncle Sam."

"Why not?" Placard asked.

"Simple," Smoot answered. "The government sticks its damned nose in places where it shouldn't be. So, you want me to kill folks that our country's got no official quarrel with? Won't do it. How could you ask me such a question? Both of you should be askin' for grace right about now. Shame on y'all!"

Dr. Shiftless threw up his arms in frustration and interrupted Joe Cephas Smoot. "Hang on just a second there, country mouse. I'm going to have to confer with Colonel Placard for a moment in private. Augustus, if you don't mind, would you be so kind to step outside with me to discuss a few matters?"

The colonel left the living room and followed the bioweaponeer from San Antonio out to the front porch of the modest suburban home to have a brief powwow. As anxiety rapidly escalated among all concerned parties, it became necessary to reset the course of their mission which was suddenly careening off the rails.

Dr. Shiftless held an index finger in the air and proceeded to sharply rebuke Augustus Placard's mission parameters. "This is on your head, Colonel! This is just not going to work out for us. You need to go in there and put a bullet or two into that pathetic creature's head, and then we need to get the hell out of here."

"What?!"

"I got an idea—let's go out for lunch after you put this animal down. My treat. After all, I believe it's time that we try to bury the hatchet between us, so I'm buying. Do you like barbecue? When we picked up the rental car this morning, I heard about a place out here called Smokie Sam's. Their hickory rib-rack platter with home-made tater salad and ranch beans is allegedly a kick-ass epicurean extravaganza not to be missed."

"Shut up, Ron!" Placard demanded. "I completely understand where Smoot's coming from. He happens to be a holy man."

"If that's indeed the case, I stand vindicated," Shiftless said. "I told you from the get-go that you were backing the wrong vampire. I just can't see how we're going to be able to turn this man into a cold-blooded killer. After all, Joe Cephas Smoot has just rendered a spiritual testimony that he is, in no uncertain terms, a man of righteous convictions. He may very well be a vampire, but he is certainly not the type of vampire we're looking for."

"To be honest with you, I didn't want to leave Fort Huachuca," Colonel Placard replied. "My life was going along just fine and dandy, thank you very much. I didn't ask to be reassigned to the Department of Biological Warfare, and I certainly didn't have any desire to work with your sorry ass. I did so because I wanted to make a positive difference before I retired. Frankly, you're one slimy son of a bitch."

"Am I now?" Shiftless asked. "If you hold me in such high esteem, I formally withdraw my rather generous offer to buy you lunch."

"If the truth be told," Placard added, "I've hated your guts from the very moment I set eyes on you back in the 'Nam."

"Wow, I can really feel the love!" Shiftless said.

"If I may be so bold as to offer a succinct response to your culinary suggestion," Placard continued, "I will *not* have lunch with you. In fact, as far as barbecue goes, I would like to find a full rack of pork ribs and shove it up your ass. Still, I have an important job to do, and I plan on executing this assignment to the very best of my abilities."

"You can't fix this with two aspirin and a call in the morning, Colonel."

"Look here, Dr. Dickless," Placard countered, "I'm absolutely certain that Smoot is going to be the right man for the job. He's *exactly* what we are looking for, irrespective of your idiotic opinions. I'm going to prove it to you."

"How do you plan on doin' that?"

"Watch and learn, you impudent tool!" Placard answered. "Now, if you don't mind, I'm going to go back in there and close the deal with this Holy Joe. All you need to do is to stand aside and keep your damned mouth shut. I swear to Jesus, if you don't do as I say, I'll shit on you with a ton of bricks from outer space."

"Don't threaten me, Placard," Shiftless cautioned. "You have *no* idea what I'm truly capable of doing. Besides, your new friend, Mr. Smoot, is most assuredly *not* a Holy Joe—he's a Joe Schmo."

"Maybe I should place a call to San Antonio," Placard said. "I'll bet the administrative head of the Department of Biological Warfare would *love* to have a formal debriefing with you when we get back to Texas about why things got sideways out here in in Butt-fuck, Arkansas."

"Stop right there," Shiftless pleaded. "Don't do anything rash."

"You're contracted labor, Ron," Placard said. "If you're not smart enough to buff a turd without getting shit smeared all over yourself, you'll likly get the big pink slip. That'll shut your mouth up, once and for all."

"Okay. Fine. Hand me a tin of shoe polish and a terry cloth rag and I'll start buffin' like nobody's business," Dr. Shiftless said with obvious resignation.

"Glad you see it my way for once."

"It's your show," Shiftless admiited as he retreated from the porch. "It'll also be a long walk off a short pier for you if this doesn't pan out."

Upon reentering the living room, Colonel Placard noted a black, leather bound text of the Holy Scripture resting reverently on top of the coffee table. "Joe Cephas, could this old Bible possibly be a family heirloom?"

Smoot proudly replied, "Aunt Norma gave it to me when I came down with this infection. It's been in our family since before the time of the Great War against Yankee Aggression. It's part of my proud Southern heritage that many of my relatives fought for the 'Lost Cause.' None of my family members were ever slavers, but we never did cotton up to the notion that the Yankees were coming around and pissin' upstream from us. I'm proud to convey to you that my great-great-grandpappy plugged a bunch of those blue bellies at Malvern Hill."

"Joe Cephas, would you mind terribly if I took a look at your family Bible?" Placard asked.

Smoot required no explanation as to why the military officer had made the request. Joe Cephas was simply happy to fulfill what he believed to be an evangelical obligation. "It would be my honor, Colonel."

As Smoot handed the Bible to Augustus Placard, the officer furrowed his brow and said, "Now, Joe Cephas, you professed mere moments ago an alleged adherence to a righteous and noble path of pacifism, and you said you wouldn't take up arms unless our country were at war."

"You got it," Smoot said.

"I certainly respect that, but I tell you right now that our country *is* at war. Illegal drugs are pouring across our border with Mexico. These drugs are killing our young people by the score."

"I don't think it's a war we can win," Smoot said.

"You're wrong, Joe Cephas," Placard said. "Our country *can* win this war. You expressed admiration for your remote ancestors who fought in the War Between the States. By your own account, at least one of them actually killed one or more enemy combatants on the battlefield. Tell me, Joe Cephas, how do you really feel? Are you a pacifist or a warrior? You can't have it both ways."

"I don't suppose so," Smoot said.

"Or perhaps you can!" Placard exclaimed.

"What do you mean?" Smoot asked.

"Maybe under heaven, everything is possible," the military officer surmised, "and maybe even killing is appropriate from time to time. Is this a King James Version that I am holding?"

"I believe so," Joe Cephas answered.

"Let me read you the passage Ecclesiastes 3:1–3: 'To everything there is a season, and a time to every purpose under Heaven; a time to be born, a time to die, a time to plant, and the time to reap,'" Colonel Placard recited from the Old Testament. "This is the most important passage I'm about to read to you. Listen carefully: 'A time to *kill* and a time to *heal* ...' As the Good Book says, 'To everything there is a season.' Mr. Smoot, if that is indeed the case, it's time for you to do the right thing."

"Do you think so?"

"Come join us," Placard offered. "I promise you, you'll be doing something for both God and country."

Joe Cephas pursed his lips as he had nodded his head in acceptance of his fate. "Okay, but you boys have to give me a chance to visit the Alamo before you turn me into some kind of bloodsucking bioweapon."

On Thursday, Señora Sophie Zuleta made a point of slipping away from the Nuts and Bolts hardware shop at lunchtime to conduct her planned clandestine meeting with Lorena, Cletus, and Elizabeth across the street at the doughnut shop. "Tell me, please; you must have noticed the frightening physical and behavioral changes that Blake is going through right now. He has a very short fuse, and I am afraid that during one of his frequent tirades he is going to unload on one of the other employees and somebody is going to get hurt. To be frank, I'm concerned about the health and welfare of little Nathan."

Elizabeth was the first to confirm what Sophie had witnessed. "I don't know who that person is that goes to work in the morning and comes back in the afternoon, but I can tell you right now that it's not my brother Blake. I'm afraid not only for the health and welfare of Nathan but also for this entire family! I have thoughts about taking Nathan and running away with him, but Blake would only hunt me down. I'm not sure what to do."

"Lorena is standing right here," Mrs. Zuleta said as she turned her face toward the young curandera. "I'll tell you, Elizabeth, she knows a lot more about this particular situation than you can possibly imagine."

"Whatever is said among the four of us must remain a secret," Elizabeth said. "I'm quite certain Blake would kill me for such a transgression."

Sophie looked to Lorena and wanted to hear her opinion of the matter. "I know that you are a well-respected curandera in Las Cruces and Mesilla. Be honest with me; do you believe that Blake Barker is infected and is transforming into un vampiro?"

"I know he is," Lorena replied. "We only have a few more days before the transformation is complete. I've seen this all before, Elizabeth. Blake will inflict his wrath upon you before anybody else. I know you're planning on staying until Sunday, but I strongly suggest that you find an excuse to leave here no later than tomorrow."

"Now wait just one moment," Cletus interjected. "I know that Blake's behavior has become a bit erratic, but I think that this is just a consequence of the fact that his wife was brutally murdered and he witnessed it. To make matters worse, Romero Lopes is still at large. It's fine by me if you want to leave for Lubbock tomorrow, Liz, as you have your own rental car and you can leave anytime you like, but I'm going to stay until Sunday. Blake and I are going out quail hunting on Saturday.'

"Do you think tha's a good idea?" Liz asked.

"I'll watch him carefully for any signs suggesting that he would be some kind of danger to anybody else," Cletus said, "including potential danger to your's truly!"

"I assure you," Lorena added, "if you are with your brother on a hunting trip, you'll eventually recognize irrefutable evidence that he's undergoing a transition into un vampiro. You will obviously be armed and will be able to protect yourself on Saturday, but I know on Sunday that Blake is planning to drive you down to the airport in El Paso. Listen to me carefully, Cletus: it would appear that Blake has been getting into verbal arguments quite frequently with you lately. On more than one occasion I was absolutely certain that Blake was about to strike you."

"I felt that way, also."

"If you two end up in any kind of argument during that trip to the airport," Lorena warned, "you'll have no way to defend yourself. Blake seems to be starting fights with *everybody* over any little thing. I have a plan for how we can get out of this mess, but you have to be absolutely certain that what I've told you about Blake is the truth and nothing but the truth."

"What do you have in mind?" Liz asked.

"I'll tell you my plan on Saturday afternoon when you come back from your hunting trip with the person who used to be Blake Barker," Lorena explained.

—◆◆◆—

"Okay, ladies, it is time for show-and-tell," pronounced Dr. Booker Marshall in the doctors' lounge. "Parker, you're up to bat. Please enlighten us."

Parker turned his black leather motorcycle cap backwards and said, "Listen up, class; I'm about to blow your minds. The last time we convened, we didn't have a clear handle on what was going on with Miguel Pastore's hematological parameters. We couldn't even say for certain if the poor bastard was able to produce any new red cells anymore or not. I've not figured it all out yet, but what I'm about to tell you certainly defies logic."

"Well," Brewster asked, "is he able to make new red cells or not?"

"I subjected bovine and porcine red cells to a radioactive isotope. It was a Technetium-99 radio-label to be specific, and it was all through the courtesy of the Nuclear Medicine Department." Parker said.

"I'm surprised those boys were willing to help us out on this project," Booker said with a grin.

"They weren't!" Parker complained. "Bunch of lazy sons of bitches if you ask me. There was no demonstrable enthusiasm on their part to be willing to screw around with pork or beef blood."

"What convinced them otherwise?" Booker asked.

"They were only willing to toss their hat into the ring at the point of a gun!" Parker exclaimed. "That, and a fat lie. I told those jerk-weeds that we'd list the members of their department as coauthors on any peer-reviewed scientific publications that we're able to generate out of ths clinical conundrum."

"Which is why, now and forevermore, the Nuclear Medicine Department shall be officially referred to as the 'Unclear' Medicine Department!" Booker exclaimed.

"I have no idea where Nuke Med gets their radioactive shit," Parker wondered, "but I suspect they just scrape it out of the back of the fridge from the Palo Verde atomic power plant!"

"Quit dicking around. What did you find out?" Brewster asked.

"Patience, grasshopper. Once the red cells were radio-labeled, I offered the animal blood to Miguel Pastore as an oral blood meal," Parker explained. "After that, we ran him under the counter at four-hour intervals in an effort to track the course of the radioactive erythrocytes. Now, pay attention, ladies; this is where things get creepy."

"What happened?" Booker asked.

"The radioactive meal was absorbed through the gastrointestinal tract, and it was then concentrated in the hematopoietic factory of the axial skeleton including the vertebral columns, ribs, and pelvic region," Parker explained. "Soon after, the radiation load was cleared out of the marrow, and it ended up in the patient's peripheral circulation!"

"Don't tell us that the hemoglobin derived from this blood meal was directly incorporated into new RBC production," Brewster said. "That's crazy!"

"That's exactly what happened!" Parker explained. "At that time, there was a *huge* spike in the reticulocyte count, but it was only a transient event. It didn't hold. As the patient experienced brisk hemolysis, the waste products were excreted in the urine. It appears that Pastore is totally incapable of conserving any iron after these apparent cyclic hemolytic events that seem to occur at two or maybe three-day intervals. There must be some type of renal gradient, as *none* of the iron can be recycled."

"I guess that I'm simply unable to see the big picture to all of this, Dr. Coxswain," Booker Marshall said. "Spell it out for me."

"Holy guano, Batman! Let me break this down for everybody. The only conclusion I can draw from these findings is that Mr. Miguel Pastore is unable to construct hemoglobin on his own accord. He needs an exogenous source of red blood cells that's absorbed either through the enteral track or in a parenteral fashion whenever we give him a packed red cell transfusion. When, and only when, the patient has an exogenous intact hemoglobin source, he's briefly, but nonetheless effectively, able to crank out red cells from his marrow like a wild man!"

"If so," Brewster concluded, "he's indeed able to manufacture new retics, but only when there's an exogenous hemoglobin reserve. That means he has functional erythroblasts but they're by and large dormant most of the time in-between blood meals."

"You got it!"

"That sounds like a pretty inefficient way to conduct business," Brewster opined.

"So it would seem," Parker agreed. "When the patient ingested the radio-labled blood meal, it appeared that his erythroblasts that were aggregated within his bone marrow factory rapidly made new red cells, but the rate limitation was strictly the exogenous hemoglobin supply."

"That's all fine and dandy," Brewster said, "but it becomes problematic when you lyse all of these newly produced red cells at intervals of forty-eight to seventy-two hours!"

"Ergo, the need to continuously ingest exogenous hemoglobin if the body is no longer able to perform this task on its own accord!" Parker Coxswain explained.

"How is that possible?" Booker asked. Even a vampire bat is not able to digest intact hemoglobin across its gastrointestinal tract. Hemoglobin, after all, is a big molecule, and it's broken down enzymatically before it's absorbed across the mucosal layer of the gut."

"How else can you explain the big spike in his reticulocyte count when the radioactive material cleared out of the marrow and ended up in his bloodstream, presumably within the new batch of red cells that Miguel's marrow had just produced?" Parker countered. "Now, how can it be that he has a red cell life span of only a few days, compared to a normal red cell life span of ninety days? As I said, I don't have all of the details figured out in my head as of yet. In any event, something triggers a massive coordinated hemolysis, and then the patient will need to either refeed with an additional blood meal or get another packed red cell transfusion for sustenance."

"Nice job. Once I have had a chance to reveal to you all the data I have analyzed, I think I will have a few more answers to the litany of residual mysteries concerning this peculiar case," Brewster said.

"Before you step up to the plate and give us the dope, Brewster, I believe that after the profound revelations I've just imparted to you boys, which incidentally have expanded your fund of knowledge exponentially, I deserve substantial compensation for my industrious endeavors through a transient, nonbinding sexual act resulting in instantaneous orgasmic gratification," Parker said.

"What did you have in mind?" Booker Marshall asked.

"Preferably, such an interlude should be orchestrated by some large-breasted nubile female endowed with an enormous industrial-strength ass," Parker revealed. "In light of these desired parameters, and with serious consideration given to the sad fact that I have never enjoyed the company of a black girl, I'm going to rely on my good buddy Booker Marshall to make that score on my humble behalf. Hey, Book, don't you have a sis?"

"Back off, smart ass!" Booker warned.

"Now, as I know you ladies in here are on a tight budget, I wouldn't expect y'all to spend any more than fifteen or twenty bucks on me for this most deserved romantic interlude that I'm now very much looking forward to. As we speak, faint pheromone-impregnated beads of perspiration are now accumulating on my broad, yet nonetheless acne-free forehead," Parker concluded.

"Yes, I do have a sister," Booker replied, "but she doesn't like white boys. She thinks you guys are uncouth as well generally untidy. In other words, you guys stink with some serious P-funk!"

"Wait!" Parker protested. "I actually have been known to bathe on various occasions."

"Not good enough. You need to become more proficient with the appropriate use of soap and water, and maybe things will work out better for you down the road," Booker said.

"Throw this man a bone, Book!" Parker pleaded. "I'm dyin' here."

"In the meantime," Booker said, "I suggest you talk to J. D. Brewster. If you whisper sweet nothings in his ear, he may be willing to disclose to you his private clandestine retreat in the broom closet near the ob-gyn department."

"What good would that do me?" Parker asked.

"Numerous rumors are circulating around here that the broom closet is the location where Brewster can generally be found jerking off during a full moon. I'm not able to readily ascertain why he likes to use the utility room down by the ob-gyn department. However, I have an unsubstantiated theory that it has something to do with the pervasive and inescapable *odeur d'anchois* in the vicinity," Booker said, ribbing his fellow Texan.

"Damnation, gentleman!" Brewster explained. "I think I'll set up a toll both at the utility room so I can cheerfully stuff a few extra Hamiltons into my pockets as my new side gig!"

"Speaking of J. D. Brewster, let's see if you can knock one out of the park. You're up to bat. Talk to me, boy!"

"Let me show you my cards, gentlemen," Brewster said. "Read 'em and weep! I captured the money shot, ladies!" Brewster passed out a handful of electron micrographs clearly showing viral particles directly infecting marrow red cell precursors. It was all captured on electron micrographic film in black, white, and shades of grey.

"What am I looking at?" Booker asked.

"I reviewed these findings with the virologist Sister Joyce Lipton, who has just returned from a sabbatical at the convent. She confirmed that the small structures affixed to the cellular membrane of the erythroblast marrow stem cells are previously unrecognized and uncategorized viral entities!"

"Touchdown!" Parker proclaimed.

"I don't know what the damned thing looks like inside its external protein coat, but externally, theses nasty buggers look similar to what architecturally would be referred to as Bucky Fuller's geodesic domes," Brewster explained. "The first three pictures show indisputable evidence of the marrow stem cells getting infected. What I can't answer you are the questions regarding the mechanics involved. Specifically, I don't know how some of these cells will dedifferentiate into pluripotent stem cells that then enter the circulation. Although it seems that only some of the infected stem cells dedifferentiate into a multilineage blasts, some stem cells appear to still function in a normal fashion. Odd, no?"

"Congrats, ladies!" Booker said. "It looks like we found the culprit."

"These additional pictures clearly demonstrate an example of infected erythroblasts that are generating new red cells," Brewster added. "Sadly, it appears that these red cells that finally enter circulation as reticulocytes are *heavily* infected with a lethal viral burden destined to eventually murder the infected red cells in question. Booker, I want you to look at the last set of pictures. This answers your question as to why the red cells only have a life span of about three days at most."

"My vision isn't so good anymore," Booker said. "Lay it out for me."

"These last electron micrographs provide indisputable evidence that the causative factor resulting in a coordinated hemolysis among the infected red cells is a rupture that occurs and the subsequent release of zillions more of these viral particles into the blood stream. Can you boys see the direct parallel to malaria?" Brewster asked.

"What do you mean?" Parker asked.

"The exact same thing happens in that parasitic disease process, except we're talking about an infectious prokaryotic *trypanosome* when it comes to malaria, and we are talking about an unidentified *virus* for this damned new disease of human vampirism!"

"We don't even have an official name for this new virus yet," Booker said.

"You want to leave a legacy before you shuck this mortal coil, Book?" Brewster asked. "You got it! Why don't we name this evil little fucker the 'BM1986' virus? There you have it; instant legacy, my man!"

"Bowel Movement 1986?" Parker asked.

"No, you idiot!" Brewster answered. "The Booker Marshall 1986 Virus!"

"Thanks, boys, but it won't be our call. I think the big boys at the WHO or CDC will have a hand in the final moniker that this pathogen is ultimately labled. You know, people who have the sickle cell gene like me are relatively resistant to being infected with malaria. Since I have sickle cell disease," Booker mused, "I'm just wondering if—"

"About what?" Parker asked.

"Oh, never mind," Booker concluded. "Maybe it will be something I can check out on my own accord. I'm going to think about a little side experiment with Mr. Pastore. I'll let you boys know how it works out. Nice work, J. D."

"Not so fast!" Brewster laughed. "I need to ask you boys a question. When I accept the Nobel Prize in Medicine for this discovery, can I wear a tuxedo for the ceremony? I hope so. I look good in a tux. After all, fat middle-aged hippie chicks dig a man in a tux."

"I know that you dig chunky monkeys, but stay focused, Brew," Parker said. "Do you have any possible explanations for the apparent fang-like incisors that Miguel Pastore now sports?"

"I'm sorry to tell you boys that I don't know shit about teeth," Brewster said. "I do a pretty good job with brushing, and if I'm sufficiently motivated, I might work my gums over with some dental floss from time to time. Otherwise, I don't know diddly-squat about dentition. If we go any further with this, we might have to get a DDS involved."

"My turn. There's no way in hell that I'll let you boys outshine me," Booker said. "No, sir! It's not going to happen. I talked to Salamonica Vespucci down in IR, and she was kind enough to get an image-guided biopsy of Mr. Pastore's left kidney."

"Any revelations to share?" Brewster asked.

"Here, I want you boys to take a look at the histopathology from the H and E stains. What do you think of these nephrons?" Booker Marshall asked as he passed around a solitary color photomicrograph. The obvious pathology jumped out and smacked J. D. Brewster and Parker Coxswain in the head as if it were a lead pipe.

"The loop of Henle looks all jacked up," Parker replied. "It's much thicker than normal, and there's dramatically increased peritubular vascularity. This is clearly not an example of glomerulonephritis, but I don't know what in hell we're looking at here. We now know that this virus is marrow-tropic, but tell me, Book; do you have reason to believe that this virus is also nephrotropic?"

"That, my young grasshopper, is an excellent question," Booker answered. "I had part of the biopsy specimen frozen on Brewster's behalf. I think it would be a *great* idea, J. D., if you were to take the opportunity to run the kidney specimen through the electron microscope and see if we can find the same viral elements you found in the cells harvested from the bone marrow."

"Piece of cake. I can do it," Brewster answered, "but it won't get knocked out until after next week."

"Problems?" Booker asked.

"The vacuum chamber on the scope has sprung a leak," Brewster explained. "The much-needed replacement gasket to fix the damned thing won't be available until a week from Wednesday at the earliest."

"Why so long to get the replacement part?" Parker asked. "Is it getting shipped to us from the planet Mars?"

"Might as well be. The replacement part is going to be sent to us from the UNM in Albuquerque. We just won't know any more about this case until then," Brewster explained.

"As I mentioned, I have one more idea about something that we can investigate between now and when the electron microscope is again operational. Once I get it all figured out as to how I want to do this one additional study with Miguel Pastore that I'm kicking around in my mind, I'll fill you boys in on it," Booker said. "I would like you both to be there and help me with this. If I pull this off, however, it will be off the books. *¿Entiendes ustedes?*"

"Sounds scary!" Brewster said. "I'm in."

"Me too," Parker Coxswain added, "as long as you line me up on a date with your sister. I promise you, I'll work on my personal hygiene."

"I'm proud and honored to consider both of you to be my friends and colleagues," Booker said with a smile. "However, I'm still not going to let Parker have my sister's phone number. Just the thought of my baby sister running off to doink some goofy white guy someday, and then perhaps even actually enjoying it, is enough to make me go blind in my other eye!"

***

The pain in Romero Lopes's thigh was absolutely excruciating. He was baffled why the wound showed no sign of spontaneous healing. Since the time that he had become un vampiro, every other injury that he sustained had healed.

Lopes had been doused with a pot of boiling water, cracked in the chest with a meat cleaver, shot on numerous occasions, stabbed in the lung with a filet knife wielded by the line cook at El Chopo, incinerated to the point of being a deep-fried unidentifiable crispy critter in a house fire, and pig-poked in the flank with a Ka-Bar during the massacre at the morgue.

All these previous injuries were potentially life-threatening, but somehow he always survived and healed up quite nicely. Somehow, the insult that he suffered at the hands of the curandera was devastating. Romero Lopes had come to believe that not only was Lorena una vampira, but also that she must indeed be una gran bruja as she had proclaimed on the fateful night when he was critically injured by his own obsidian knife that was still in Lorena's possession.

Although still ambulatory, he found that his lightning speed was now gone. In order for him to kill and consume other human beings, he would have to become an ambush predator, but he simply did not have the patience it took to hunt in such a capacity. At this point, he was reduced to preying upon domesticated livestock. Little did he know, the trouble he was having with his right leg was about to dramatically worsen.

The relationship between Blake and his sister, Elizabeth, had become so strained that on the Friday morning of her departure, she could not even bring herself to say goodbye to him. She kissed Nathan goodbye and took Lorena aside for a private conversation. "You know what to do. Once this is all over, let me know where you are. I'll send you money when I can. I know that you love Nathan as much as Cletus and I do, and I just know that you'll always try to do the right thing."

"Well, I'm not so sure about all of that. I just hope I can live up to your expectations," Lorena said.

"I was once told that a man of righteous convictions is one who is looked upon with favor by the Lord. Lorena, you are indeed a woman of righteous convictions," Elizabeth said with heartfelt pride.

"Now," Lorena said, "don't go around and proclaim attributes that might not actually be in my armamentarium."

"I would like to think that I'm a pretty good judge of character. I've only known you for a very short time, but I believe that you're a sister to me." Elizabeth kissed Lorena on the cheek and then quietly slipped away in her rental car to head down south toward the airport in El Paso.

In their younger days, Cletus and Blake were hunter-gatherers. The primordial hunting lessons that their father taught them created a lasting bond between the brothers, but that sadly was coming apart at the seams. Memories of hunting with their late father were indelibly etched upon their hearts and permanently imprinted upon their souls. Years ago after Cletus had moved east to Texas, Blake gave up hunting altogether. As a hunting trip with his sibling had been a long time coming, Cletus jumped at the chance to spend some time outdoors with Blake once again, despite the fact that his younger brother was becoming quite combative and uncharacteristically irascible.

The ride out to the dirt road known as NM-26 was a trip down memory lane for both of them. Cletus readily recalled the glorious times that he and his brother had spent together with their father hunting dove in the late fall season at the clandestine water tank in the Portrillos, not far from Kilbourne's Hole. That spot was a family secret. Hunters who pursue game fowl are a peculiar breed in and of themselves. Special hunting spots where birds may be consistently bagged are rarely divulged without "the stick" of water boarding or "the carrot" of a bottle of Southern Comfort.

Most longtime residents of southern New Mexico will hunt for fowl en masse at the sod farm or at the old dairy. In doing so, hunters are likely to miss out on the solitude and beauty of the spectacular crimson and turquoise sunsets widely renowned in the Land of Enchantment. In times past, at the end of a day of hunting, there would be a cold Bud for Dad and real Coca-Cola for the boys, to be guzzled down with a satisfying explosion of carbonated bubbles in their mouths.

While the birds that were harvested from the wild were being field-dressed, the sun would be slowly retreating upon the western horizon. Although now only relegated to the memory of Cletus and Blake, these recollections remained a small slice of heaven for the Barker brothers.

In high school, Blake had been the proverbial class clown and an all-around mischievous ne'er-do-well. The only brother Cletus had ever had was always only one step removed from the swift dispensation of justice. Administered through either his father or perhaps the vice principal who was, of course, the school's designated disciplinarian, corporal punishment was often employed upon Blake's backside to keep the demons of his lesser nature at bay.

Although underage, Blake had at one time managed to throw a bona fide kegger at one of the Barker family hunting spots, and it created quite a domestic ruckus. Cletus chuckled to himself. He'd always wondered if Blake had ever taken any of his hoodlum classmates back out into the wilderness, perhaps having sold out the other secret Barker hunting spots.

As the old brown Harvester Scout rumbled down a dirt road and hit a pothole, Cletus was quickly able to compartmentalize his fond recollections, sending them back to the deep recesses of his memory bank. On this particular hunting excursion, the brothers were driving out to the Uvas. This was their special place for quail. Unlike the slow and relaxed pace of an evening dove hunt, a 4:00 a.m. muster for quail was something their dad had always insisted upon.

This special spot was unique for game fowl, as a population of the relayively rare Mearns quail resided in the vicinity. Also commonly known as the Montezuma quail, these particular game birds were considerably bigger, faster, and stronger than the lesser scallies or Gambel's. As quail go, these are the ultimate sporting challenge. On this occasion, the hunting excursion would no doubt be more difficult because the brothers no longer had trusty Bailey to point and "hunt dead." Bailey, a Braque du Bourbonnais, was the best bird dog Dad had ever owned.

Blake had a very close bond with this particular hound when he was but a child. The Braque was unique in that it had the hunting intensity and instincts of a Brittany, but it possessed the temperament and cheerful disposition of any family's loyal Labrador retriever. Dad always kenneled the Brittany spaniels at night, but Bailey would sleep on Blake's bed with her head perched on his leg. It was as if the loyal dog were watching over the young boy. After all, is that not what dogs are supposed to do? Humans and canines have long been part of the same pack. Sadly, there was no loyal dog now to watch over Blake as he began a downward spiral into a black well of inescapable darkness.

They pulled off the road. As the dust from the Scout blew past them, they walked to the rear of the truck and began to stage for the hunt. Blake pulled out his camo bag with the boxes of twelve-gauge eight-shot. This time it was Remington. Dad insisted on *only* Winchester or Remington high brass. He said that a conscientious sportsperson would always pick up his or her brass after the ejection of the spent shell. If a hunter was going to go through the trouble of picking up spent casings, he or she may as well go through the additional trouble to reload the shell! Sadly, shot shell reloading was another bygone family tradition...

Blake pumped the old 870 to make sure it was not loaded and then handed the weapon to Cletus. Instantly, Cletus pumped the shotgun and did the same safety check. That was the very first lesson for Cletus the day that Dad had brought the 870 home from Kmart and subsequently presented it to the lad for his thirteenth birthday present. Dad had taught the boys well. Every gun should be considered a loaded weapon until personally confirmed otherwise.

Had their father been blessed to live long enough to see the political winds in the country blow in a more conservative direction, Cletus had no doubt whatsoever that Dad would have become a proud and staunch Reaganite. "Trust but verify!" Dad always said, and he uttered this mantra long before Ronald Reagan ever rolled up his sleeves to challenge what was then referred to as the "Evil Empire."

Blake unzipped the short green case and produced the barrel and action that was Dad's old over-and-under Browning Pigeon Grade Superposed. It was his father's prized possession, and to this day it is a very sought-after collectible weapon.

As Blake removed the fore-end and attached the barrels to the action, he said to Cletus, "When you flew out here for Lynne's funeral, I was going to give you either Dad's gold watch or the Browning. As you were always such a crappy shot, I figured the best thing I could possibly give you would be something relieving you of your perpetual need to conjure up some lame-ass excuse for showing up late to every damned thing you do. If the shoe fits, wear it; that's why Dad's watch should rightly belong to you."

"I'm honored," Cletus said. "It means a lot to me."

"I remember Mom always said that the king's only responsi-bility is to show up on time," Blake said.

"Dad always told Mom that if he had to be at some import-ant business meeting or social function, he would make a point of showing up either drunk or late, but never both at the same time!" Cletus added. They both chuckled at the recollection. Somehow, it all worked out for Mom and Dad for well over fifty years.

Blake was transforming into some other being, and he was finally coming to terms with the sad reality that his life from that point forward would never be the same. At first, he tried to deny what was happening, but he had to finally accept that he was go-ing through profound physiological and psychological changes. He had demonstrated aggressive tendencies in the past, but now he felt angry all the time and had to suppress urges to hurt some-body. He had to suppress his urges now to hurt *everybody*.

"Cletus, if anything happens to me, I want you to have the Browning. In fact, if anything happens to me, I want you to have Nathan. Keep him safe," Blake insisted. "It will be up to you to pass along some of Dad's wisdom and sportsmanship to Nathan for me. Before we go any further, I want you to make that promise to me."

Without saying words, Cletus reached out and shook Blake's hand, but it was a promise that he would not be able to keep. In fact, very soon, Cletus would be a coconspirator in a plot hatched to ensure that Nathan would be forever sequestered from the only father he had ever known.

The two brothers proceeded to fill their vests with ammo, and then they ambled off for a pleasant walk in the early morning sun.

The Sierra de las Uvas are a beautiful part of the Organ mountain range. The roughest terrain is where one will find the Montezuma quail. Their distinct eerie cries can be heard through the box can-yons. The two brothers spread out and began their march, stopping every few yards and quietly listening for the call of quail. Blake startled a large covey of Gambel's, and most of them flew off. The brothers instinctively charged into the brush from where the quail had taken flight. Their assertive actions led three more quail to break hold and take wing.

Blake quickly swung the Browning and discharged the top barrel, but he overshot the mark. The wad appeared one foot in front of the target. "Very strange," Blake said to his brother. "I'm usually blasting behind them at this point in the season. Well, I guess it really has been a long time since I've gone out hunting with you. It's been a very long time indeed."

The 870 was an old friend or, perhaps better yet, an old defiant warrior who possessed a wooden stock festooned with the scars of many battles. Even now, it was peppered with several bruises and contusions. In addition, the senescent bluing on the barrel was worn a bit thin. In fact, it was this very patina that gave the weapon a special grace and gravitas as Cletus took it to shoulder. "I love this stick," Cletus said as he dropped his first Gambel. It was as if he had been hunting every day, and had been doing so in perpetuity. "Just like riding a bike, little brother," he proclaimed as he stroked the beautiful bird and placed it in his vest pocket.

With that, Cletus waved the rally sign, and the brothers quickly began to charge after the rest of the covey. With no dog to force the birds to cover and hold, it was a race. Cletus could see the distinctive black topknot of the birds as they ran along the ground. They began making calls to regroup the covey. The birds started to ascend a steep cactus-studded rocky canyon wall. Blake was instantly ahead of Cletus and was somehow halfway up the arroyo before his older brother could even exhale one breath of spent air.

"Slow down, you damned jackrabbit!" Cletus broke silence and ordered Blake to keep the skirmish line intact. "Hold fast, Blake. I mean it! We'll do better if we work as a team." Blake had no idea that he had moved so quickly. In a bloodlust trance, he had lost track of his surroundings. As a teenager, Blake always enjoyed the thrill of the hunt, but this was something entirely different.

Cletus tried to make a joke to defuse a potential unpleasant confrontation with his younger brother. "It must be the Hatch green chilies you've been pounding down at El Chopo that made you stronger!"

Blake sneered at his older brother with a malevolent gaze. "Oh, yeah? Perhaps I'm not getting faster. Maybe you're just getting slower. That's what you get for eating fast-food at Taco Hell, Cletus. You know, the reason why they have the Dollar Menu special going on right now?"

"Why?"

"It's to give every gringo the opportunity to get an acute case of Montezuma's revenge!"

"I don't care what you say, Blake," Cletus said in defense of his favorite fast-food restaurant. "If I had the chance, I'd hit up Taco Hell every day of the week and twice on Sunday!"

With Blake's sarcastic comment, and as if on cue, an elusive Montezuma took to wing. Blake took aim and dropped the bird literally ten feet in front of himself. With the top barrel's improved cylinder, the bird had disintegrated into a bloody mess after it received the full force of the shotgun blast from such a short range.

His older brother was awestruck. "Holy shit, Batman, that was truly amazing! In fact, that was gunslinger fast. Tell me, though: how are you planning on eating that pile of bloody feathers?"

Then it happened! Blake was on the bird as soon as it hit the ground. He picked it up and was suddenly overcome with a brutal predatory compulsion. He licked the blood from his hands as Cletus looked on in horror. Blake voraciously ripped open the belly of the bird and popped the heart, lungs, liver, and intestines into his mouth, swallowing the viscera whole without even exerting any effort to chew his barbaric meal.

The manic assault against the dead quail ended only when the bird had completely disappeared into Blake's gastrointestinal tract. Blake's feeding frenzy finally subsided when he recognized that Cletus was yelling at him with uncharacteristic rage, shock, and fury. "We're not going to hit our fifteen-bird limit if you eat them on the spot, you asshole! What in God's name is the matter with you?"

"I'm fine," Blake replied.

"What in hell are you doing?" Cletus asked. "If this is going to be our new family tradition, you can count me out. I'd prefer field-dressing the quail after the hunt on the tailgate of the Scout with a cold Bud."

The rest of the hunt was completed without further bizarre scenes of carnage. As the two brothers marched along and made the considerable trek back to the Scout in silence, Cletus made concerted efforts to sustain a truce with his younger brother. They had taken one quail apiece. In retrospect, this was perhaps a moot point, as Cletus was technically a poacher. After all, he never obtained a New Mexico hunting license before the excursion into the thicket to hunt for game birds.

While cleaning the quail, Cletus noticed that Blake's hands and face were badly blistered with what appeared to be a serious sunburn. When queried about his clinical condition, Blake attributed his acute skin damage to the fact that he had not put on any sunscreen at the onset of the hunt. Blake argued that it was nothing more than a late-winter "farmer's tan."

Cletus thought it was severe enough an injury to warrant a trip to the emergency room, although Blake vehemently resisted the idea. In any event, after the two hunters started back to the township of Mesilla, Cletus noted that the erythematous blisters that had appeared on the dorsal aspect of Blake's hands and face spontaneously waned. The anxiety Cletus had about Blake's dangerous mannerisms, however, did not recede.

As Blake drove the Scout back to the farm, Cletus began to drift off to more pleasurable thoughts. He began thinking about the prospects of fresh quail lightly dusted with salt, pepper, and flour, and then fried brown in real butter. Mom used to sauté the legs separately from the breasts just to make certain each piece was perfectly cooked. Cletus remembered that sometimes Mom would also throw a couple of fried eggs on the side.

"Blake, do you remember how Mom used to serve the birds with biscuits and honey? Damnation! I wish we could go back to that old Formica and metal table just to sit down with Mom and Pop one last time. Those were the days."

For his part, Blake remained silent.

"By the way, I'm happy to hear that you're still in possession of that old obsidian blade we found when we were dove hunting with Dad out by Kilbourne's Hole."

"I used to keep it on display in a glass case at the Woolworth's store in Santa Fe," Blake reported. "I placed that strip of obsidian beside on a chunk of raw silver ore the size of a hand grenade. I also had a piece of raw turquoise among the other items on display."

"I remember."

"As I told you, a stoner hippie chick broke into the display one day and swiped the piece of obsidian. Oddly enough, she left the other items behind. I always thought that it was a very strange event. Yes," Blake admitted, "I recovered the knife and therefore, wouldn't you think that all's well that ends well?"

"Seems to me it should be that way."

"One would surmise," Blake said, "but for some reason, I still have seething hatred for the woman who stole that knife so long ago."

"What's eating you?" Cletus asked. "Is she not dead?"

"That has no bearing on my hatred," Blake said. "Not only for her, but for everything around me."

"Why?" Cletus asked. "If you got the knife back, you should just mellow out. It's all water under the bridge now, right? When it's all said and done, all's well that ends well."

"No it's not!" Blake exclaimed. "I can only tell you that I wish I had caught the woman who stole my artifact in the act. I would have ripped out her throat right then and there! Even though the bitch has kicked the bucket, I'm sorry I wasn't the one who drained her dry!"

"For the love of God," Cletus said with alarm, "what in hell is wrong with you? I just don't know who you are anymore."

At that moment, Blake smiled and proceeded to glare at Cletus. The older brother had the unmistakable sensation that he was simply being sized up to become the next meal. The now completely transformed *nuevo* vampiro flashed the long pair of fangs that currently resided in the maxillary bone where normal human incisors previously dwelled.

Realizing that his own life was likely in peril, Cletus was also suddenly transformed; he was now a man of righteous convictions. At that time, what was even more important than his own life was the safety and well-being of his beloved nephew, Nathan, and his caretaker for whom he now felt a great deal of affection. It had become absolutely imperative to execute Lorena's secret plan no later than the following day.

13

REFUGEE

Once Blake and Cletus had driven away in the old Scout to hunt for quail in the remote Uvas, Lorena took a long fireplace match and started to light votive candles around the home. "Lorena, those candles smell like a pine tree," Nathan said.

"Mijo, do you remember when I taught you how to pray? Every time I light one of these candles in the house, you and I should bow our heads and ask for God to protect our family. These are called Velitas candles, and they are very powerful," explained the curandera.

Nathan was curious why Lorena felt the need to pray for the interdiction of a celestial safety net, as the young boy truly believed he lived in a very safe house on the family's small but isolated farm. He asked, "Why do we need protection, Lorena? Are you afraid of robbers?"

"Listen to me very carefully," Lorena said. "I'm trying to protect us from Romero. I know that you think he is your friend, but I promise you that he's a very bad person. He would like to hurt you and me if he had a chance. Do you remember the yellow egg I hid beneath your bed?"

"The yellow one?" Nathan asked. "It looked like an Easter egg."

"Well, it's no longer there. Your daddy made a *big* mistake: he ate it!" Lorena explained. "That egg was supposed to protect you and me from Romero, but now that it's gone, you must stay inside the house with me until Daddy and Uncle Cletus come back from their hunting trip."

Nathan became visibly upset at the scathing indictment that had just been levied against the vampiro whom he now thought of as an uncle. As he banged his head against the kitchen table, he pointed his finger at Lorena and said, "You're wrong, Lorena! Don't say bad things about Romero. He's not a bad person! He said that he loves me." Nathan broke away from Lorena's protective grasp and sprinted out of the house and onto the front lawn, where he cried out, "Romero, where are you? I need you! Come see me!"

Mortified, Lorena grabbed the obsidian knife from the top drawer of the dresser in her bedroom and proceeded to chase down Nathan in an attempt to secure his safety before the perpetually hungry vampiro had a chance to suddenly reappear. As she tried to put her arms around Nathan, he fought back valiantly against her, trying to extricate himself. The young boy was compelled to run out past the tree line to find the man whom he thought of as a loyal tio and whom he believed had been wrongfully slandered.

Lorena would have none of that! She gave a swift pop to the boy's backside with the palm of her hand in an effort to quell Nathan's acute temper tantrum. Although Lorena's employment of this age-old tactical intervention of corporal interdiction was quite successful in momentarily capturing Nathan's undivided attention, she nonetheless had the inescapable sense that somebody was carefully observing their each and every movement from the shadows emanating from the tree line. As Lorena flashed the obsidian knife above her head, she brazenly challenged Romero Lopes to reveal himself. "¿Por qué no sale, Romero? ¡Yo soy una gran bruja! Esta bastardo. ¡Tengo un regalo especial para usted! Está desgraciado."

Lorena had just declared that she wanted to give Romero Lopes a "special gift," and her meaning was as clear as the bright late winter New Mexico sunshine. In addition, to add insult to his previous injury, the curandera had the shocking bravada to call into question his birthright legitimacy.

For his part, Romero Lopes wanted to engage Lorena at that very moment in a fight to the death. The open wound festering within the anterior aspect of his right leg rendered by the sharp blade of the obsidian knife had, however, crippled him to the point of limited mobility. All he could do was scrutinize Lorena and Nathan from the shade cast by the adjacent tree line with seething hatred. In order for the vampiro to challenge una gran bruja, Lopes would definitely require extensive rehabilitation. Oddly enough, this crippling leg injury that he sustained was destined never to completely heal.

⎯⎯⎯◦⎯⎯⎯

Upon Blake and Cletus's return from their hunting trip, the older brother climbed out of the Scout and approached Lorena, who was waiting on the front porch. "I'm sorry that I doubted you. You were absolutely right." Cletus was quite thrilled when Lorena rose onto the balls of her feet and kissed him on his cheek and then gave him a quick nibble on his left earlobe.

Lorena softly whispered, "Cletus, I'm glad you're back safely. I was so worried about you."

Blake overheard only part of their conversation. The newly transformed vampiro was quite suspicious as to what might be going on. "What are the two of you talking about, Cletus? What is this important matter that Lorena was 'absolutely right' about?"

Cletus was caught flat-footed, but he was able to rebound quickly. "I was confused about the time that I am flying out from the airport tomorrow. Lorena pointed out to me that I'm leaving for Houston much earlier than I at first realized. If I had to rely on my own memory, I'd be late for my flight out of here. I lost my original itinerary. Lorena had to call the airlines on my behalf to find out what time I am heading back to Texas."

"It's just like I told you earlier; you're late for *everything.* You'd better start putting Dad's old gold watch to proper use, or I'll end up taking it back from you." Blake bared his fangs and added, "I would venture that if you somehow manage to mysteriously die this very night, you would even be late for your own funeral!"

Cletus chuckled nervously. He soon retired for the evening.

Lorena said to Blake, "Don't forget, Mr. Barker, you promised me that I would be able to go visit my cousin Maria in El Paso this coming Sunday."

"Of course," Blake replied. "I haven't forgotten that I made that promise. In light of what you did for me and Nathan after Lynne was murdered, I owe you big-time. You deserve to take some time off. Don't worry about Nathan while you're gone. Sophie Zuleta has a teenage niece who'll be able to keep an eye on the boy."

That night, Cletus and the curandera secretly secured Nathan's bedroom door with a makeshift barricade. Their plan was to alternate staying awake throughout the hours of darkness and keep clandestine sentry duty at four-hour intervals until dawn. They both hoped that the shotgun they wielded throughout what seemed to be an interminable, angst-filled vigil would be a strong enough deterrent to ward off any would-be intruders, human or otherwise, until the sun rose in the east.

—⚙—

Dr. Cloud sported thick shiny black hair that was usually pulled back into a tight bun, but on this particular occasion, it was the only time anyone had ever seen him with his hair hanging down at shoulder length. He squinted hard and frowned harshly as he pulled the coffee mug away from his lips. "Brewster, this coffee tastes like shit. Did you make this awful batch?"

Brewster boasted, "Guilty as charged. In deference to the

unparalleled and widely renowned jazz maestro Miles Davis, I call it Bitches Brew. I'm glad you like it!"

Dr. Cloud glared at Brewster while the other attendees filed into the conference room. In what would be an abject repudiation of the hematology–oncology fellow's self-congratulatory skills as an upscale barista, Dr. Cloud added a heaping teaspoon of sarcasm to the unpalatable cup of hot joe. "Personally, I'm quite glad that I've maintained excellent dental hygiene throughout my life. That way, I can strain the coffee grounds through my teeth! Okay, people, let's take a look at the big questions still floating around out there that need to be answered about Miguel Pastore."

Dr. Cloud took an erasable felt-tip marker and approached the whiteboard. He began to write out a number of persistently troublesome unanswered questions about the case of the unfortunate patient with a peculiar hemolytic anemia that was also on the threshold of acute leukemia. In addition to J. D. Brewster, several other specialists and clinicians were invited to the informal presentation to formulate the next best course of action regarding the management of this difficult case.

Parker Coxswain was present, and his reputation as a major-league screwball was further enhanced when he appeared wearing a black Prussian helmet complete with an imposing phallic picklehauben spike extruding from the top. Upon careful inspection of the sharp spike festooning the top of the paleo-Germanic helmet, one would readily note that Parker had a Hatch chili pod, a portobello mushroom, and a wedge of onion impaled on the picklehauben, as if the research scientist were prepping a tasty vegan shish kabob for a Saturday afternoon backyard barbecue.

Parker sat down beside J. D. Brewster. The latter began to nibble away at the array of vegetables as if he were a guest standing at the buffet table at a cocktail party.

When J. D. asked, "You bring any ranch dressing?" Parker proceeded to place his left index finger to the lips of Brewster to petition his colleague to remain silent. Nonetheless, a variety of tasty salad dressings miraculously appeared from the right hip pocket of Parker's full-length white lab coat.

The creamy, tangy condiments, eager to be liberated from a half dozen plastic squirt bottles, would soon dramatically enhance the flavor of Brewster's midafternoon snack. As odd as this behavior was, none of the other members of this assembly of august medical scientists seemed to be particularly surprised or even annoyed. After all, this occurrence was simply a prime example of the standard operating procedures to be expected from the members of the University of Texas at Santa Fe.

Booker Marshall was feeling well enough to attend, in addition to Dr. Turk Masters, who was the current director of the hematology–oncology division. A frustrated clinical investigator, Turk was perpetually at odds with his smart-ass hematology–oncology fellow from the state of Texas who, incidentally, was widely accepted for being the man directly responsible for brewing the world's worst-tasting coffee at any time or anywhere throughout the annals of recorded human history. This infamy easily dated back to the very first time the noble aromatic bean found its way into a pot of boiling water.

Dr. Joyce Lipton, who was not only a virologist but also a practicing Catholic nun, and Andres Reese from Infectious Disease Services rounded out the congregation of adroit scholars to debate the clinical challenges at hand.

Dr. Cloud tried to discreetly spit out the nasty coffee that had befouled his taste buds in an adjacent wastepaper basket before walking up to the whiteboard to brainstorm with his colleagues. "Here's problem number one: the virus. Sister Lipton, do you have any further insight into what kind of animal we might be dealing with?"

"Frankly, I'm stonewalled," the virologist answered as she adjusted the nun's habit upon her head. "From a morphological standpoint, it looks like something that may be related to the feline leukemia virus. From a biological standpoint this would make sense.

However, my lab is not sophisticated enough to do the nucleic acid probes. For further answers, this evidence we have accumulated may need to be shipped out to either the CDC or the Armed Forces Institute of Pathology."

The infectious disease specialist Dr. Reese opined about the current fund of knowledge regarding the viral entity that infected not only the body but also the very life essence of Miguel Pastore. "I wish I could tell you folks something definite about the transmission of this virus. I'm absolutely certain that it is, at a bare minimum, a blood-borne pathogen. As of yet, I've seen no evidence that this is an airborne disease process. However, until we know more, we're still obligated to gown up in full biohazard protective gear whenever we enter the patient's room. I have suspicions that it could also be acquired by an enteral route, but for that to be the case, there has to be some kind of reservoir for this virus in the wild."

"For example?" Cloud asked.

"If you take a look at other viral models, lower forms of mammals or birds are the likely culprit," Dr. Reese postulated. "I hope nobody minds if I put in a call to the CDC and the state health department to talk about this patient."

"I agree, but stand fast on that idea for just another forty-eight hours, Andres," Dr. Lipton countered. "I'll want in on the drafting of this communiqué. If we file a report, we should do it together, as it will add gravitas to what we've collectively garnished to date regarding this clinical oddity. However, let's first make certain we have our ducks in a row. This might be a one-off, and we don't want to get the state or Uncle Sam worked up into a frothy lather if such were indeed the case."

"Here's problem number two: the bone marrow histopathology," Cloud continued. "Excuse my French, Sister Lipton, but the pathology service needs to either shit or get off the pot."

"The Turk and I have been pounding Wanker from the pathology service for an official answer, and he finally decided to get off the pot," J. D. Brewster said while he poured the remainder of the sludge-like coffee into the sink. "Are you boys and girls ready for this? He's officially signing it out as follows: 'refractory anemia-type myelodysplastic syndrome in transformation with undifferentiated blasts.'"

"Well, that's a mouthful," Dr. Cloud noted, "but that moniker is at least something we should be able to hang a hat on for the time being. If that's the case, I want you crab pickers to tell me if we should do a preemptive strike and initiate remission-induction chemotherapy now."

"I don't think so," Dr. Turk Masters replied. "Well, at least not at this juncture. I wouldn't pull the trigger unless the patient progresses to full-blown acute leukemia. It appears that his disease process is already knocking on the door, but it hasn't crossed the threshold as of yet. If and when he really starts to blast off, I'm not even sure what we would use to initiate induction treatment."

"Why not?" Andres asked. "Just pick a protocol and run with it."

"Not so fast," Turk said as he squirmed in his chair from the scrutiny bestowed upon him by his colleagues. "Personally, I would favor the 7 + 3 protocol. However, my numbskull fellow Brewster is making a strong argument to consider a prednisone and vincristine-based treatment."

"Damn right!" Brewster crowed. "If Miguel Pastore's marrow disease evolves into an undeniable acute malignant leukemia, I contend that his disease might respond better to a chemotherapy protocol the likes of which we would employ in a *lymphoblastic* setting. I'm right about this, Turk."

"Leap of faith, son," Turk said.

"Blessed are those who believe yet have never seen," Brewster countered.

"Well, if that's the case, what's on the obverse side of this coin in question for everybody else who's a doubting Thomas in this conference room? Would it be something as severe as damnation or perhaps something as inconsequential as a simple letter of expressed concern from the ethics committee? I disagree with his ideas, but Brewster's opinions are based on the revelation from Sister Lipton that the infectious viral entity found in the electron micrographs may be similar to the feline leukemia virus," Turk explained.

"Miguel's disease is caused by a virus as confirmed by Brewster's recent micrographs," Andres said. "This discovery explains a lot of the patient's situation. We may very well be looking at the first case of a documented premalignant condition induced by an infectious agent."

"As of this current time frame in the mid-1980s, there's been no conclusive evidence that *any* human cancers are actually caused by viral pathogens. If this is indeed the case, I for one am quite glad that we don't have to make any therapeutic decisions yet. If and when we do, I must be honest with all of you," Turk Masters confessed. "I'm just going to grab onto my own ass and jump off a cliff."

"What are you saying?" Booker Marshall asked, hoping for clarity.

"Without abnormal cytogenetics or readily identifiable surface markers by immunohistochemistry, it would boil down to blind guesswork on our part," Turk answered. "I'm afraid that whatever protocol we decide to choose in an acute leukemia setting would likely be the wrong one anyhow."

"Well, I respect an honest stab at the unknown," Cloud said. "Is there anything else from a hematology standpoint?"

"There's one other issue that apparently my hematology–oncology fellow has failed to recognize," Turk said.

"And just what might that be?" Brewster asked defiantly.

"You're getting lazy," Turk Masters said, "and so is everybody else in this room as far as I can tell. Did anybody bother notice the MCHC on the automated CBC readout? Well, the mean corpuscular hemoglobin concentration happens to be over twice the upper limit of the normal range. While this individual might have difficulty constructing native hemoglobin, what he's able to produce from incorporating exogenous hemoglobin into the construction of his new red cells is absolutely extraordinary. The red cell mass that he is able to produce must have a remarkably high oxygen-carrying capacity to help keep him alive. I must say, this patient is a true monster on many levels."

"Perhaps we should refer to his hemoglobin," Parker Coxswain interjected, "as hemo-goblins! Ha! Get it? I made a funny!" Nobody laughed at Parker's lame attempt at levity, but it did result in a swift kick in his shin from Booker Marshall.

"Let's move on to problem number three: renal dysfunction. Booker, where do we stand in terms of finding out if this peculiar virus is nephrotropic?"

"Well, in my opinion it is," Booker said. "However, my opinion is worth diddly-squat unless we find viral budding in the neph-rons. If the technicians who are coming up from UNM can fix the vacuum chamber and get Brewster's electron microscope oper-ational within the next few days, we'll have some solid answers to that question."

Dr. Cloud pointed at Booker Marshall and said, "Strong work, buffalo soldier!" Booker took a slight bow and beamed at the compliment.

"This brings us to the next problem," Dr. Cloud continued. "Miguel Pastore is going through packed red blood cells faster than a humpback camel can suck down *agua fría* at a three-day watering hole. Help me out here, Parker. Oh, by the way, I've got dibs on the Hatch chili skewered on top of your helmet, unless of course Brewster has already drooled upon it."

"Knock yourself out, Dr. Cloud," Parker replied. With that, Dr. Cloud liberated the Hatch pod impaled upon the spike on Parker's helmet, rolled it into a flour tortilla that was liberally sprinkled with grated queso, and popped the treat into the microwave.

Turk Masters followed suit and approached the microwave after Dr. Cloud warmed up the tortilla and Hatch pod. This caused a great deal of consternation among the other members attending the conference. As a case in point, Brewster grabbed the fire extinguisher that was mounted on the wall near the entranceway to the conference room and aggressively pointed the fire-retardant device directly at his mentor. In the meantime, the other members of the conference stood up and instinctively backed away from the microwave in an act of self-preservation. Realizing that his colleagues were rather agitated, Dr. Masters held up his innocuous cold sopapilla for all to see.

"Look, people," Dr. Masters said, "it's just a snack! It's a cold sopapilla! As I promised you before, after my most recent minor mishap, I will *never* stick any other metallic items in the microwave ever again!"

Dr. Masters had type 2 diabetes mellitus and was perpetually harangued by his staff for indulging his sweet tooth. Earlier in the year, Dr. Masters tried to consume a jelly doughnut in a clandestine fashion without any other person knowing about. His plan was to put the jelly doughnut into a surgical mask and then put the mask around his face as if he were about to engage in a diagnostic bone marrow biopsy or some other minor invasive procedure. This rather sneaky endeavor would afford Dr. Masters the opportunity to eat the jelly doughnut as if he were a racehorse with a feedbag strapped around its neck!

Of course, the best-laid plans of mice and men often go awry. As the doughnut was already a week old when Masters decided to try to eat it, the pastry was already as hard as a cinder block. Undeterred, Turk wrapped up the doughnut in the surgical face mask he was planning on wearing and subsequently popped the entire assembly into the microwave to soften up the doughnut. Sadly, Dr. Masters had forgotten that the surgical mask included a flexible metal bar designed to be molded around the bridge of his nose once worn.

When he fired up the microwave, the surgical mask and jelly doughnut burst into flame and the inside of the microwave caught on fire! This potentially catastrophic event set off a smoke alarm, and mayhem ensued. After the hospital initiated the emergency code red protocol, the entire fourth floor of the hospital was evacuated. This snafu was something that Dr. Turk Masters would never live down.

After confirming the benignity of the contents that Dr. Masters planned on zapping in the microwave, Booker Marshall loudly proclaimed, "It's okay, everybody. Relax and take a seat. It doesn't look like that there is any explosive, incendiary, or otherwise flammable material at hand that could put any of us at risk of bodily injury!"

After a collective sigh of relief, everybody in attendance resumed their seats around the conference table.

"Gag me with a spoon, people!" Turk exclaimed. "Did everybody get over their wedgie? Before we get restarted, kudos go out to J. D. Brewster for the very nice form letter he wrote that has turned out to be the functional template letter of sympathy that in the future will be mailed out to the family members of our oncology patients who pass away. The legal department plans on using the letter you crafted without any planned modifications. Nice job, Brew!"

"You're shitting me!" Brewster replied in astonishment. "What I wrote was intended to be a joke!"

"Well, administration simply *loved* it its straightforward honesty and simplicity," Turk said. "As a case in point, the administration has decided to use this draft as the sympathy letter template that *all* the departments at this university will utilize in the future. You will be forever remembered at this college of medicine, Brewster! Congratulations are in order."

"For shit's sake," Brewster replied in disgust. "If that'll be my legacy, I'm going to throw myself under a bus."

"All right, boys and girls, let's get back to work," Turk said.

"In regards to the hemolysis," Parker continued, "it is *not* an autoimmune process. It did *not* respond to a trial of high-dose steroids. The hemolytic event that occurs at two-day or three-day intervals is a direct consequence to the viral infection's induced rupture of the patient's erythrocytes. To be honest, if we don't come up with an efficacious antiviral treatment, I know damned well that we'll never get this hemolytic process under control."

"The blood bank is going purple monkey shit about all of the packed RBCs that this patient's going through at this time," Brewster added.

"Are we at risk of running out of blood products at this institution?" Cloud asked.

"I have a suggestion," Parker interjected.

"Is this anther one of your crackpot ideas?" Andres asked.

"You know it is," Parker replied. "It's high time that we all address the six-hundred-pound Sasquatch that's sitting at the table. What I'm about to say is off the record and must stay within the confines of the four walls of this conference room. Well, here it goes: I believe we should give this patient animal blood to be orally consumed ad lib."

"My word," Sister Lipton said. "I can't believe what you're saying!"

"Hear me out, everybody!" Parker exclaimed. "I believe this will likely resolve a major problem we're confronted with. If it works, we won't have to give him parenteral transfusions anymore. Think about it. We should allow him to consume blood meals. Why not?"

"Medical ethics might come into play," Turk suggested.

"I don't think so," Parker replied. "There's a slaughterhouse north of Albuquerque, and we could place a special requisition to get bovine and porcine blood for this unfortunate individual. I'm certain the slaughterhouse would send us as much animal blood as we would like, because it is all going down the proverbial drain right now as it is."

"What's this going to cost our university?" Turk Masters asked.

"I've already broached the subject with the owner of the slaughterhouse, and he'll do it for us as long as this institution issues him a receipt for the blood products that he gives to our university. He wants to take a big corporate tax deduction at the end of the fiscal year," Parker Coxswain testified.

"Genius idea, Dr. Coxswain!" Booker said.

"The meat processing plant doesn't enjoy paying federal income tax, and the owner of the slaughterhouse would like to reduce this backbreaking burden if he possibly can. I humbly suggest that we do the deal. In an unauthorized trial, I have already proven that this patient can actually sustain himself quite nicely with animal blood meals."

"On behalf of the Saint Francis College of Medicine," Cloud said, "my colleagues and I who are sitting in this room will disavow any knowledge of your actions. If you can work this out with the dietary service, have at it. I just don't want to know anything about it."

"Mum's the word on our part," Brewster said.

"A defensive doctrine of plausible deniability must be preserved at all costs, or else my ass cheeks will be flapping in the breeze," Dr. Cloud cautioned. "By the way, Parker, the Hatch was delish. Thanks for sharing! This brings me to the fifth and final problem I would like us to think about today: pluripotent stem cell dedifferentiation. Can anybody come up with a viable theory?"

When Dr. Cloud's difficult question was answered with deafening silence, the impromptu meeting's moderator instructed his colleagues to ship the medical records and pathology specimens to the AFIP and CDC the following day. Perhaps Uncle Sam should finally have a crack at identifying the mysterious virus that was responsible for this peculiar disease.

The members of the University of Texas at Santa Fe and their colleagues would soon come to the painful realization that the plan to allow the federal government to learn that there was a live, captive vampiro hospitalized at the Saint Francis College of Medicine in Santa Fe was a catastrophic mistake.

Romero Lopes had the inexplicable ability to attract many different types of animals. Various wild and domestic creatures were simply drawn to him for no apparent reason. Romero received sustenance from rodents, rabbits, buzzards, and stray pets that would simply nuzzle up to him, as if these doomed animals were seeking his affection. Although alive and well-fed, Romero Lopes missed the exquisite pleasure of slaughtering other human beings with acts of unspeakable violence and extreme prejudice. There was simply nothing else like the thrill of hearing his unfortunate victims scream in terror at the top of their lungs while they were being devoured.

He was ashamed that the curandera Lorena was in possession of his precious obsidian knife. This person, whom he erroneously believed to be una gran bruja, was the one who had inflicted this nonhealing wound, and he made a vow to the devil that he would track this woman to the ends of the earth to exact his revenge. The first order of business, however, was to address the open wound in his right leg that was now starting to show obvious and unmistakable evidence of gangrene.

An opportunity to surgically remediate the open wound in his right leg presented itself to the vampiro when a friendly stray black cat with pure white socks on its two front paws approached Romero while he was hiding in the shadows. The doomed feline arched its back and extended its tail. It warmly ushered a soft purring sound while it gently rubbed its flank against Romero's right arm. Sadly, that was the very last moment of life for the unsuspecting cat. The lost domesticated feline had simply failed to realize that it was in mortal danger when it inadvertently wandered into the hiding place of the particularly evil bloodthirsty ghoul.

Once the blood of the dead cat had been drained, Romero Lopes found an old blown-out sneaker that still had one intact shoelace. He tied one end of the shoelace to an adjacent tree branch, and then he tied the other end of the shoelace to the tail of the dead cat in order to suspend the misfortune feline in the air. After his usual immediate postprandial defecation, Romero Lopes scooped up his own fly-infested feces with his bare hands and deposited the foul brackish excrement only a few inches below the head of the artfully suspended dead animal.

Within a matter of a few days, the body of the dead cat began to spontaneously writhe about with nonpurposeful choreiform gyrations from an infestation of hungry maggots that were attempting to fulfill their contractual obligation to voraciously consume the dead creature and recycle the putrified organic waste back into the welcoming arms of Mother Gaia.

It was now time for Romero Lopes to engage in a decisive therapeutic intervention. Once the cat was in advanced stages of decomposition, he cut down the foul remnant of maggot-impregnated decaying matter and the vampiro proceeded to layer the semigelatinous mung into the open wound on his right leg with a spatula that he salvaged from his burned-out farmhouse. Romero Lopes took great care to ensure that all of the precious maggots that were gleefully feasting on the corpse of the dead cat were now safely nestled into their new communal residence, found deep within the confines of the linear open wound on Lopes's right thigh.

Once this was done, el gran brujo had made a bandage from a remnant of his T-shirt to bind the decomposed feline and also his new guests, which were the larval stage of airborne coprophagic arthropods, within the confines of the gaping lesion in his thigh, much like one would stuff raw oyster dressing into the ass-end of a turkey for Thanksgiving dinner. Romero Lopes laughed ecstatically as he felt a sexually arousing sensation when the fat white maggots began to devour his black, putrefied necrotic flesh lining the cavity of the leg wound.

At the CDC, Dr. Blanks attempted to create a crude form of immunotherapy by having John Stewart subjected to a plasmapheresis procedure to harvest his immunoglobulins. Hopefully, passive immunotransference would be an efficacious modality to treat the infected poultry that had been confiscated from the farm of Blake Barker. "Okay, John, let me give you an overview of what this procedure is all about and what we're going to try to achieve with the presumed immunoglobulins that we might be able to harvest from your body. We believe that it was your own immune system that made you resistant to the vampiro infection when you were bitten by Romero Lopes."

The former line-cook from El Chopo was quite curious. "Dr. Blanks, did you finally find another living human subject that has been infected with this presumed vampiro virus? I tell you right now that I will *not* be amenable to having my immunoglobulins taken from me and then administered to Romero Lopes if you have him in custody. I won't give a tinker's damn if this is for medical science. Let me make this one point perfectly clear to you: if I discover that Romero Lopes is being held in custody at this facility or at some other location here in Atlanta, I'll rip his head off, and then I'll shit down the stump-hole in his neck. Dig?"

Dr. Blanks replied, "I'll make a solemn oath to you that if Romero Lopes is ever captured alive, you'll have to stand in line behind me to have a crack at the nasty bastard. Don't forget, he took out two of my friends I worked with here at the CDC."

"Sorry about that," John Stewart said. "I remember meeting Dr. John Henry and Dr. Ralph Fairbanks at El Chopo."

"Those two guys were like family to me."

"Well, you just can't use my immunoglobulins on a bunch of infected chickens," John Stewart said. "What's on deck?"

"Just so you know, we don't have any captive living human subjects afflicted with vampirism either here or anywhere else as far as I know," Blanks explained. "I assure you that if we discover some other patient infected with this disease at any hospital or any clinic in this country, the entire power of the federal government will be brought to bear. That particular infected individual would be hog-tied if necessary and then brought here."

"Wait!" John Stewart exclaimed. "I thought we lived in a free country."

"May civil liberties be damned," Dr. Blanks said. "Suspension of habeas corpus. If Lincoln could do it during the War Between the States, it can be done again. If FDR could do it to Japanese Americans during World War II, it can be done again. Don't you see? Desperate times call for desperate measures. It will be done at the point of a gun, or more likely at the points of many guns."

"Doesn't sound like a country I want to live in anymore," John Stewart noted with concern. "I've heard rumors that the boys in San Antonio are looking for a military application with a human vampire."

"I can't lie," Dr. Blanks conceded. ""That's an issue. Of course, we'd need to be spot-on before the bioweapon engineers out of Texas got their hands on some infected poor bastard."

"What would the boys from Texas do if they ever captured such an individual?"

"If that happens, all bets are off as to what would happen next," Blanks answered.

"Where does that leave me in all of this mess?"

"For the time being, the only thing we have to work with be-sides you are the birds that were confiscated from Blake Barker's chicken coop. Several of Barker's domesticated poultry appear to be carriers of the disease. The first stop on what will probably be a very long journey for us is to see if your plasma is able to clear the viral pathogen out of the poultry to the infected eggs. Come with me. It's time for us to get your immunoglobulins harvested again from the pheresis machine."

—◆—

The medical procedure of extracorporeal plasmapheresis

involves the removal of blood from a patient generally through a large, thick-walled, firm vascular access device that is generally inserted into a large-bore vessel in the body, such as the subclavian vein. Approximately 300 cc of blood is removed from the patient at any given time, and then the blood outside the body is temporarily anticoagulated with citrate to prevent blood clotting within the vascular lines and within the machinery used to separate the plasma from other blood products.

Once removed, the blood is subjected to a centrifuge machine that separates the whole blood into its various subcomponents, including white cells, red cells, and of course, the valuable plasma, which is basically the immunoglobulin protein and electrolyte-rich fluid component of whole blood.

Once the immunoglobulins are mechanically extracted from a patient, the rest of the blood, including the red cells, white cells, and platelets, is returned to the patient through the large-bore venous access device on a reinfusion. In a situation where the plasma is removed for therapeutic purposes, the patient will often receive replacement fluids in the form of a combination of albumin-fortified protein and saline, usually in a 70 percent to 30 percent ratio to reconstitute the patient's blood volume in an attempt to stave off the complication of hypotension that is not an infrequent postpheresis phenomenon.

This procedure of plasmapheresis is successively repeated until an adequate amount of the patient's plasma is harvested for its intended therapeutic purposes. In short order, John Stewart was well versed in the science and engineering involved in the quest to harvest his immunoglobulins to create a therapeutic vaccine.

——◆——

After a week of daily plasmapheresis procedures, John Stewart was starting to experience medical complications from repeatedly having his blood washed out. He had troublesome palpitations and

tachycardia with intermittent pounding headaches as a consequence of transient postplasmapheresis episodic hypotension. He
also developed an impressive hematoma below his clavicle where
the large-bore rigid vascular access device was surgically placed by
an interventional radiologist.

By the time the gamma globulins that were harvested from
John Stewart were concentrated down into a single 40-gram vial by
the CDC, it was established that the previously unrecognized and
uncategorized virus that infected the domestic poultry confiscated
from the farm of Blake Barker was indeed a retrovirus. It was quite
disturbing to note that the research scientists found genetic varia-
tions among the viral particles upon analysis. That could only mean
one thing: genetic drift. If that was indeed the case, it would likely
make it nearly impossible to engineer an effective biotherapeutic
vaccine for this malady.

John Stewart was just dying to know if the significant inconve-
niences that he'd experienced over the course of a week—repeated,
arduous plasmapheresis procedures—had resulted in any medical
or scientific breakthroughs that perhaps would eventually contribute to solving the problem of the peculiar viral infection that
seemed to induce vampirism. "Well, Dr. Blanks, are there are any
revelations you would like to share with me?"

"I am happy to report that I think we're making some progress."
The research director had just told John Stewart a big fat lie.

Once John Stewart and the assistant nurse had departed the
examination room, Dr. Blanks was left in a brief state of solitude.
The frustrated physician picked up a wheeled Mayo table and forcefully threw it at an eye chart poster hung by thumbtacks on the wall
opposite him. The collision occurred with such force that the dry
wall behind the eye chart was fractured.

Dr. Blanks and his research team came to the painful realization that they would not likely make any headway in devising a
rational modality to eradicate the yet to be named virus from its
natural avian reservoir. If the virus could not be cleared from its

biological sanctuary within domesticated poultry, then it sure as hell could not be eradicated from infected human beings.

—◁◁◁⎁⏑⏑⏑⎁▷▷▷—

In order for Lorena's plan to actually succeed, the Nuts and Bolts senior employee Sophie Zuleta was recruited as a coconspirator to help hoodwink Blake Barker on the Sunday morning Cletus was scheduled to fly back to Houston. When the telephone rang at the Barker residence, Lorena picked up the receiver.

"¿Bueno? ... Oh, hello, Sophie. How are you doing today? ... Oh no, a fever? I'm so sorry to hear that. ... Let me pass the phone over to Mr. Barker. You can tell him yourself."

The wheels of the deception gristmill were already starting to turn. Blake Barker took the phone. Lorena overheard him tell Sophie Zuleta to take the day off from work and stay home to recuperate from the alleged acute febrile syndrome she suffered from. In order for Blake to allow the store's most valued employee to have the day off, however, he would have to show up at the hardware shop and take over the day shift. Blake was furious because this Sunday was supposed to be his day off from work. He'd planned to either return his brother, Cletus, to the airport in El Paso or drive him out into the nearby desert to suck him dry. As it was quite early in the morning, Blake Barker had not yet come to a conclusive decision on this delicate matter.

"Well, hell's bells. I'm going to have to go into work today. Lorena, I need you to take Cletus to the airport for me so he won't miss his flight. Just take Nathan along with you."

To consummate the charade, Lorena had to initially feign disappointment regarding the circumstances. "Mr. Barker, you gave me several days off so I could go visit my cousin Maria in El Paso. I'll ferry Cletus to the airport, but I'm still going to insist on having this time off. I'll take Cletus in my own car, but you need to give me forty dollars for gas money."

Blake Barker acquiesced. "That will be fine, but you should take Nathan with you for a few days. I'm heading off to work now. Just leave me your cousin's phone number on the refrigerator so I'll know how to get in touch with you." Blake drove off to cover the day shift at the hardware shop. He didn't bother to say good-bye to Cletus or shake his hand before his departure.

After Blake drove off to Las Cruces to go to work, Lorena turned to Cletus and said, "I have all of my personal belongings already packed up and in the trunk of my car. I put all of Nathan's clothes and his toys in a big plastic trash bag and loaded it into the back seat."

"Why on earth would you tell my brother that you would be staying at your cousin's house in El Paso?" Cletus asked. "It's foolish of you to leave your relative's phone number on the refrigerator as Blake asked. My brother will find you, and then he'll kill you. I have no doubt now that he's also fully capable of killing his own son. For the love of Jesus, what were you thinking?"

"Relax, Cletus," Lorena calmly replied. "What I left on the refrigerator for Blake to see is the phone number for a Taco Hell fast-food joint in El Paso. I don't have a cousin named Maria. I'm planning on taking Nathan across the Bravo. I guess that I'm now officially a refugee. I won't ever be coming back."

"You have my phone number, and you have the phone number for my sister, Elizabeth. Let us know when you and Nathan are safe. Then we can wire you money from time to time."

"I've grown a bit fond of you, Cletus," Lorena said. "You're indeed a good man. I consider you to be *un hermano de una madre diferente.*" What Lorena had said was simply not true. She certainly looked upon Cletus as something much more than a brother. She already had a brother, albeit one she would not likely ever see again. The curandera was a lonely woman, and there was something that she'd never truly had: a lover and a partner.

She had come close several times in the past, but for some reason she always found a way to torpedo any fledgling relationship that she had ever been in. She had become a master at constructing emotional barriers.

Lorena developed the unparalleled skill of undermining any potential bond that may have been established with any man she had ever known. She previously broke the heart of Dr. Cloud, who was now living and working in Santa Fe, much as she had broken the hearts of several other men before him. For some reason, she would always make a wrong turn in the course of a relationship, right at the very congested intersection of life known by many as Commitment Road and the Avenue of Retreat.

Lorena was truly afraid that if something were to blossom between her and the ruggedly handsome young man who was gazing upon her, she would go out of her way to fracture the relationship before it even started. She was a deeply flawed person when it came to love and romance. She knew this and accepted the fact because perhaps she was incapable of sustaining a relationship. Lorena tried to pretend that she was a virtuous person guided by ethical standards, but deep down in her soul she felt as if there was something rotten and festering like an abscess. Whatever the nature of this darkness that she felt inside her, it had to be suppressed.

She was but a simple country girl from New Mexico who had harshly castigated herself for being little more than a failure in life. How could she think otherwise? She had not even finished her college education to get a degree as a nurse. Nonetheless, she wore a façade of self-confidence to convince the entire world that she was somehow, well, *normal*.

Lorena brightly blushed when Cletus leaned toward her and proceeded to kiss her with passion. She warmly returned this overt act of affection. Cletus nervously cleared his throat and declared, "Well, to be honest, my feelings for you run much deeper than just being a surrogate brother to you."

When Lorena caught her breath, she said, "Cletus, if you truly feel that way, come with me and Nathan across the border. We can start a new life together, and you and I can start our own family. I know that you don't speak Spanish very well, but it will come to you very quickly. It is a complex and beautiful language that's almost musical to the human ear. Tell me, what's left for you in Houston? The only thing that's holding you there as best as I can tell is your job, and it's a job you profess to hate."

"If I leave with you now," Cletus replied, "Blake will certainly figure out that my sister and I were coconspirators in Nathan's disappearance. We just can't let that happen. It would be best if you just get me to the airport. I promise you that somehow and someway I'll find you when the dust settles. I love you, Lorena."

"I know you do."

Within the confines of her chest, Lorena's corazón pounding like a percussion instrument the likes of which one might readily find amid a marching band during a Memorial Day parade. Once she composed herself, she briskly walked down the hallway, grabbed Nathan by the hand, and exclaimed, "It's not safe here anymore, mijo. We have to go! We have to go now! ¿Estás listo?"

To be continued.

Glossary of Medical Terms

anterolateral: Referring to the position found at the front and to the side of a subject.

blast: An immature cell that is a precursor to a more mature subset.

choreiform gyration: A snakelike, writhing motion.

Coomb's test: A clinical laboratory test to evaluate the presence of pathologic antibodies against circulating erythrocytes. A positive test by either direct or indirect methods confirms an immune hemolytic disease process.

coprophagic arthropod: An insect whose dietary requirements include (either partially or exclusively) the feces of other organisms. Any nasty bug that eats shit.

creatinine: A nitrogenous waste product cleared by the kidneys. A rising creatinine in the serum is consistent with renal dysfunction.

diener: A mortuary assistant.

ectoderm: One of the three primary embryonic tissue planes constituting the outer layer of cells in embryonic development.

endoderm: One of the three primary embryonic tissue planes constituting the inner layer of cells in embryonic development.

enteral: Used in reference to the gastrointestinal system.

erythroblast: An immature bone-marrow-dwelling precursor to a circulating red blood cell.

erythrocyte: A circulating red blood cell.

haptoglobin: An alpha-2 globulin in serum whose concentration is inversely proportional to the severity of active hemolysis.

hematocrit: A measurement in percentage of what component of the blood is actually made up of red blood cells.

hemithorax: One side of the chest cavity.

hemoglobin: The oxygen-carrying molecule found within red blood cells.

hemolysis: The clinical presentation of the pathological rupture of circulating red blood cells by either an immune or nonimmune process.

hemosiderin: A storage form of iron. An increase of this substance in the urine documented by clinical laboratory assay is found during episodes of active hemolysis.

heterozygous: The clinical state of having different genetic alleles within a chromosomal profile.

homozygous: The clinical state of having the same (matched) genetic alleles within a chromosomal profile.

hypoxia: A pathological clinical state where there is a low concentration of tissue oxygen.

icteric sclerae: A visible yellowish discoloration noted in the white part of an eyeball as a consequence of a rising serum bilirubin level.

immunohistochemistry: In reference to a pathology service technique that selectively utilizes various immune markers to help ascertain the nature or characteristics of the tissues being analyzed.

immunologically nude mice: A subset of rodents that lack an intact immune system.

indirect bilirubin: A by-product of hemoglobin degradation that is elevated in the serum in the setting of pathological hemolysis.

inflammatory mitogenic cytokines: A biological or chemical substance that has the ability to induce cellular division, generally in reference to the induction of an immune response.

interphalangeal joint: A joint found between the digits of a finger or toe.

jaundice: A yellowish discoloration of the skin as a consequence of elevated serum bilirubin levels, often noted as a consequence of hepatic dysfunction or extraordinarily severe hemolysis.

LDH: Lactate dehydrogenase. A chemical marker that may be found elevated in the serum during a pathological hemolytic event.

loop of Henle: A nephron component distal to the proximal convoluted tubule.

MCHC: Mean corpuscular hemoglobin concentration, which is an assay to determine the hemoglobin within the confines of circulating erythrocytes.

mediastinum: The center of the thorax where the heart and great vessels dwell.

mesoderm: One of the three primary embryonic tissue planes that constitute the middle layer of cells in embryonic development.

micturition: Urination.

nephron: One of many microscopic filtration units found in the kidney.

parenteral: Beyond the realm of the gastrointestinal tract, usually as a reference to nutritional support administered through an intravenous route.

phlebotomy: The therapeutic removal of a specified amount of circulating blood.

porphyria cutanea tarda: A metabolism disorder of a hemoglobin substructure.

priapism: A pathological unrelenting penile erection often seen as a complication of sickle cell disease.

protozoan parasite: A eukaryotic single-cell infectious organism.

pruritic vesicle: A skin blister with associated itching.

quadriplegia: A paralytic condition that involves both the upper and lower extremities.

reticulocyte: A new red blood cell that just entered circulation from the bone marrow.

sternocleidomastoid: A muscle in the anterolateral position on either side of the neck.

supraclavicular: The region of the body located above the thorax and collarbone.

trypanosome: A eukaryotic single-cell organism that is often parasitic.

Glossary of Spanish Words and Mexican Slang Expressions

acquecia: Aquifer.

adios: Goodbye.

agua fría: Cold water.

amarilla: Yellow.

amiga: A female friend.

amigo: A male friend.

armas de fuego: Firearms

arroz y frijoles: Rice and beans.

Avenida Chupadores de Sangre: Avenue of the Bloodsuckers.

bambina: A little girl.

bastardo: Bastard.

bravada: Feminine bravery.

bruja: Witch.

brujo: Wizard.

bueno: Good. A common way to answer a ringing telephone in a Hispanic household.

cabron: An insult meaning "goat."

Calle Murciélago: Bat Street.

Calle Vampiro: Vampire Street. The name of a Mexican drug cartel.

capitán: Captain.

cerebro: Head, or leader.

chinchilagua: A rough-and-tumble playground sport incorporating facets of the childhood games of leap frog and red rover.

con gusto mucho: With great pleasure.

corazón: Heart. Term of endearment meaning "my love."

cucarachas: Cockroaches.

Cueva del Chupacabra: Cave of the Goat Sucker.

curandera: Folk healer.

desgraciado: An insult meaning "loser."

Dios mío: An expletive meaning "my God."

disculpe: Excuse.

El Diablo: The devil.

el lenguaje de los gringos: The language of the gringos.

entiendes usted: Do you understand.

entre tu arte y mi arte, prefiero mi arte: Between your art and my art, I prefer my art.

esclava: Slave.

España Nueva: New Spain.

Estado de Chihuahua: State of Chihuahua. One of the thirty-one federated states in the country of Mexico.

estás listo: Are you ready.

fiesta: Party.

gringo: Slang word referring to an Anglo male.

hermano: Brother.

hola, El Maguito, largo no tiempo verte: Hello, Little Magician, long time, no see.

huevo limpia: A chicken egg used in a spiritual cleansing ceremony.

La Ciudad Diferente: The City Different. Nickname for the city of Santa Fe, New Mexico.

loco moco: *Loco* means crazy. *Moco* is dried mucus, a booger.

lo siento: I am sorry.

mal de ojo: The evil eye.

mi nombre es Trinidad. Es un honor conocerte: My name is Trinity. It's an honor to meet you.

mijo: Term of endearment. A conjugate word from *mi hijo*, "my son."

mira: Look.

muchacha: Girl.

muchacho: Boy.

mucho gusto: My pleasure.

ninera: Nanny.

no entiende lo que estoy diciendo: You don't understand what I'm saying.

no se: I don't know

Pappasito: Term of endearment; "little father."

parezco una idiota: Do you think I'm an idiot.

pendejo: An insult meaning "loser" or "dumbass."

peso: Mexican penny.

pinche: Meaning, "damned."

por qué no sale: Why don't you come out.

porque yo soy una gran bruja: because I'm a great witch

qué es esto: What is this area.

qué lástima: What a pity.

queso: Cheese.

Romero no es un hombre. Romero no es un ser humano. Escucha a mí; ¡Romero ahora es un vampiro!: Romero isn't a man. Romero isn't human. Listen to me; Romero is now a vampire!

Sangre de Indio: Indian Blood. This is a specific type of obsidian volcanic glass.

Santa Sangre: Sacred Blood.

señor, adónde vas: Sir, where are you going.

sé que su esposa, Lynne, está muerta ahora: Your wife, Lynne, is dead now.

sí: Yes.

silencio: Silence.

sopapilla: Fried bread.

su madre y su padre: Their mother and their father.

tarado: Moron.

tengo un regalo especial para usted: I have a special gift for you.

tio: uncle

tortuga: Turtle.

un hermano de una madre diferente: A brother from a different mother.

un momento, por favor: One moment, please.

usted es nada más que un pendejo grande: You're nothing more than a big dumbass.

vamos, muchachos; Ahora!: Let us go boys! Now!

vampira: Female vampire.

vampiro: Vampire.

Velitas: Tea lights or small votive candles used in spiritual ceremonies.

vieja bruja del mar: old sea witch.

Vivaporu: VapoRub.

y: and

ya no soy un Mago. Ahora, yo soy el gran brujo: I'm not a magician. Now I'm a great wizard.

yo engañó usted, porque yo soy una gran bruja: I deceived you because I'm a great witch.